Quite
THE
Opposite

JADIE BROOKS

Table of Contents

Acknowledgments

I want to thank my betas Florence and Phryne Fisher for their support and excellent editing talent. Their hard work made my story a better one. Also, I wish to thank Faith Moore, my editor.

I am grateful for all of my followers online who have read and reviewed my story. Each one has helped to improve my writing.

I love the Book Cover Design and Interior Formatting by MW Design.

Dedication

I want to dedicate this book to my granddaughter Kalena, who at ten, is already a fan of Jane Austen and likes me to read from my books, and to my friends, Mari and Andrea, who have encouraged (sometimes nagged) me to keep writing.

Prologue

Middle of July 1794

The mid-summer day in Derbyshire was perfect for exploring Pemberley's grounds on horseback. Two boys of about thirteen years hurried along the path from the house toward the stables. One of them used his riding crop to whack at the few weeds missed by the gardeners. Bits of the plants and a few burrs flew into the air and landed back upon him. He brushed the debris from his clothes. Pulling on the burrs, he had an idea. He secreted a few of the larger ones in his gloved hand as he continued on his way.

Inside the large horse barn, he waited until the other boy had made his way into the stall where his horse was stabled and had begun the work of saddling his mount. Quickly he moved to another stall and placed the saddle blanket on that horse and slipped the burrs underneath. After completing that task, he hastened to the next stall and began to saddle his own horse.

The boys were taught early on how to care for their own horses, which included saddling them and caring for them after they were ridden. George Darcy intended that each of the boys learn to do the work, so that they would know both how it was done, and what it took to finish a task well.

Even at age ten, almost eleven, Fitzwilliam Darcy would often remind those around him he had the most tasks to learn as he was the heir of the Pemberley lands and fortunes. Fortunately for him—and his two friends,—this summer was to be a respite from most of their work. They were allowed several hours a day to roam the grounds, swim or fish the streams and ponds, and ride their steeds far from the house.

He ran down the steps of the grand house without looking back. His favourite cousin, Richard Fitzwilliam, and his best friend, George

Wickham, awaited him in the stables. His father had stopped his going with them to ask about his plans for the day. It took all of his patience not to fidget in his eagerness to be gone while he explained the route they had planned to take and about how long they thought they would be gone.

The smile and the wink his father gave him told him that he was being teased, and after receiving a pat on the shoulder, he was released to join the older boys. Upon entering the stable, he was blinded for a minute by the change from the brightness of the sun to the dimness of the interior.

"Hello, William," Richard said as he peered over the side of the stall. "I thought you might not make it."

"Father asked me about our plans." Fitzwilliam sounded a trifle winded. "I shall hurry to saddle Antonio."

As he opened the gate to his horses stall, he was surprised to see George Wickham placing the saddle atop the animal. "I thought I would help, so that we would not waste time."

"Thank you, George, that was kind of you," he said as he moved into the stall. "I will finish. You and Richard can take Pluto and Alexander out to the paddock and give them a warm up. I shall not be long."

"You are welcome." Wickham smiled as he turned and gestured to Richard. "Let us go then."

"You go on ahead, I will not be long." Richard stood, watching the steward's son walk out of the barn as he led his horse.

Lowering his voice and stepping closer to his cousin, Richard whispered, "I do not trust him. He came into this stall first before he saddled Alexander and put a blanket on your horse. I think he put something under it."

Loosening the clinch, Richard felt around under the blanket until he came upon the two burrs and pulled them out. "I was right," he declared triumphantly. "He must have put these there."

Shaking his head, Darcy sighed, "I suppose he meant it as a harmless prank."

His cousin shook his head, but reluctantly said, "You are probably correct. I am only glad that I saw him do it. I would not wish for you or your horse to be injured."

"I appreciate it, Richard. You are a good friend."

1802

Sitting at his desk over a sheet of blank foolscap, Fitzwilliam Darcy began to work on his mathematics assignment. He enjoyed the challenge of solving the complex equations. Even though he would rather have been outside in the sunlight, he was a disciplined student who wished to succeed at Cambridge as his father had before him.

After thirty minutes of work, he was interrupted by a knock at his door. He called out, "Enter."

His cousin Richard swung open the door and closed it behind him. He breathed hard as if he had run some distance.

"Do sit down, cousin," Darcy told him. "Why were you in such a hurry?"

"I have just come from the Crooked Hawk." It was a pub that many of the Cambridge lads enjoyed. They gathered for the fine ale and a chance to play a friendly game of cards now and then. Darcy did not indulge much in such pastimes, as he spent most of his time in his studies.

"It is a bit early in the day for a pint, is it not?" Darcy queried.

"I was searching for Wickham," Richard said with disgust.

"I do not understand."

"A man came to our floor looking for him. He owes the pub for drinks and has several debts of honour," Richard sighed. "I know that it would injure your father if he became aware of Wickham's habits, and I would have paid them myself. However, I do not have enough to cover all of them and the rest of my expenses."

Darcy frowned, but asked, "What is the total? I shall go and settle the accounts this evening after dinner."

Richard gave him the figure before saying, "You do not have to bother. It might cause talk if you are seen there paying his debts. As you have repeatedly told me, I go there rather often. It will not be a strange thing if I go. I shall be circumspect."

Relieved that he did not have to take time from his studies, Darcy gave the money to his cousin and a few pounds extra to tide him over until his next quarterly allowance arrived from his father the earl.

Richard frowned at the amount, and seemed about to protest.

"Take it, Richard, I insist." Darcy slapped him on the shoulder. "Now go, I have studying to do."

1804

Darcy had just readying to leave university when he received word that his father was not well. When he arrived at Pemberley, his father seemed to have rallied although frailer than before. The senior Mr. Darcy began to hand over more of the running of Pemberley to Fitzwilliam so that, unlike others of his class, he did not have the opportunity of leisure.

His cousin Richard came to visit in the autumn of that year. He had recently joined the army after his tour of Europe. Resplendent in his new uniform, he paraded in front of Darcy and his father while boasting of the places he had seen.

Darcy could not help but feel a bit of jealousy, but he tried hard not to show it. He smiled and listened with rapt attention, laughing at his exaggerated descriptions of the people he met.

Noticing that his father seemed to disapprove of some of Richard's tales, Darcy tried to subtly admonish him once they were alone in the library.

However, his cousin did not seem to appreciate this. "At least I do not pretend to be saintly, as Wickham does."

"I thought that he became a deacon somewhere in Guildford."

"That is true, but he is still up to his old tricks," Richard said as he poured himself a large glass of brandy and held up the decanter with a questioning glance at Darcy.

Darcy answered with a negative shake of his head and asked, "How is it that you know this?"

"I have an acquaintance that lives in the parish where Wickham is serving." He took a swallow of the liquor before continuing. "My friend might have been trying to fool me, but he told me that Wickham seems quite popular with the ladies. There have not been any outright scandals there, but I do know of a few women in villages east of Lambton who have been ruined by him."

"How is it that neither I nor my father have heard of this?"

"I am not certain." Richard paused before reluctantly saying, "No, I will not lie. When we both left university two years ago, and visited Pemberley before going our separate ways, the father of one of the girls came to me while I was touring one of the nearby villages. He wished for me to speak to your father about assisting his daughter. I convinced him that it would be better if he did not bother my uncle. I gave him money for his trouble.

"It was the least I could do to keep Uncle George from grief," he added humbly.

1806

Sitting at his father's desk, Fitzwilliam Darcy stared at the papers before him. After his father's death, the funeral, and the reading of the will, he finally had some time to think about what he needed to do next. *I need a list,* he told himself, *of all the people Father's will mentioned.*

Locked away in his safe was the money his solicitor had brought to Pemberley under armed guard as instructed by his late father. George Darcy had wanted all of his monetary gifts to be given as soon as possible after the reading of the will.

George Darcy had been generous to all who had served him so well during his lifetime as well as after his death. Servants and friends alike would benefit from his munificence. William began the task. The first two on his list were his cousin Richard and George Wickham. Neither was surprising, although he did not consider the amounts to be equitable considering what he knew about each one's character.

Richard who, in the army had risen quickly in the ranks, was a captain. They did not see each other as often as they once had because of his service to king and country. Despite that, they remained close friends. His cousin had arrived as soon he could after receiving word of his uncle's death. He had been supportive of both Darcy and his little sister, Georgiana. In fact, George Darcy had named both William and Richard as guardians over his daughter.

It was the amount of the monetary bequest that bothered William. Richard and Wickham were to receive one thousand pounds each. Wickham was to have the living at Kympton when it became vacant, provided he took orders. Darcy was not comfortable with this because of the occasional reports he received of his childhood friend's behaviour. It was probably on account of his father's gratitude toward the older Wickham who had been his steward until he passed two months before, that George Darcy had been so liberal in his gifts to the son. He decided not to worry over it since the vicar at Kympton seemed to be in good health. Many things could happen before that unfortunate event.

The list grew until it was complete. Darcy heaved a large breath in relief. Deciding that he would give the servants their due first, he went to the safe. He counted out the total and brought the coinage and notes to the desk.

After counting out each bequest and wrapping them individually in a folded paper upon which he had written the servants' names, he rang for the butler.

Cramer answered the call so quickly that Darcy knew he must have been waiting nearby.

"Cramer, I want to give you the gift my father wished you to have." Darcy handed the man a packet. "Thank you for your service to the family. You are a valued part of Pemberley."

"Thank you, sir; it is a pleasure to work for the Darcys."

"I would like to have the staff come to my office, one by one, so that I may give them their gifts personally." Darcy cleared his throat. "I would not wish for the servants to compare what they receive with each other. I do not want to have petty jealousies break out amongst them. My father made the choices. I am merely carrying out his wishes."

"I understand, sir," Cramer bowed.

"You may go."

After what seemed like an endless stream of servants marching through the office, Darcy walked to the small cabinet in which his father had kept his brandy and poured himself a small amount. Swirling the liquor to warm it, he remembered the times he had enjoyed brandy with his father. His eyes stung as he recalled the ever-present sadness in his father's eyes since his mother's passing.

Taking a slow sip from his glass, he sat back in the chair. The weight of the responsibility that had been thrust upon him seemed to be unbearable. How he wished that he were a child again when, if he did not know what he should do, his father or mother would help him decide!

As he put the now-empty glass on the desk, the door opened to reveal his cousin.

"Darcy, how are you faring?"

"As well as can be expected," Darcy answered wearily. "Where have you been all day? I thought to see you sooner."

"As you know, I had a few errands to see to in Lambton." Richard walked to the cabinet and poured himself a rather generous amount of brandy into a snifter. "Wickham finally arrived. I met him as I was getting ready to make my way back to Pemberley."

"Did he come back with you?"

"No, he is happily ensconced at the Blue Goose." Richard turned his nose up at the shabby accommodations of that particular inn. "We did have a conversation."

"I wished to give him the legacy left to him by my father." Darcy's tone was one of frustration. "I suppose I shall have to go to him there."

"If you do not wish to go, I would be happy to take it to him."

"I would appreciate it," Darcy said gratefully as he took out some bank notes and counted them out into two piles.

"These are yours. I added five hundred pounds to yours because I do not think my father gave you your due."

Richard scanned the notes, and after a few seconds, he thanked his cousin.

Tucking the money into his breast pocket, he added, "Do you not wish for him to sign a receipt for the funds? I would not want him to claim he did not receive them."

"I am happy you mentioned it," Darcy replied. "My solicitor asked that I get a signature for each gift. There are some Xs from the staff on the list, but most can at least sign their own names."

Darcy pushed a sheet of paper forward, so his cousin could sign next to his name and the amount. Richard affixed his name with an elegant flourish.

"I shall be on my way and will return for dinner."

"That is very good of you, but I think it should be Wickham's responsibility," Darcy protested.

"But you and I both know that he is not a responsible person," Richard said after finishing his drink and pouring another. "Perhaps I should not have told you."

"No, I am glad you did," Darcy replied while telling himself his friendship with the steward's son was finished.

Chapter 1

Late October 1811
On the road toward Netherfield

Fitzwilliam Darcy was in a fury. *What was George Wickham doing in Meryton? How could he smile his greeting in such a friendly manner after all he has done? Truly, I must warn the people of the town about him.* A tumult of thoughts ran through his head as he spurred his mount to go faster toward Netherfield.

"Darcy, please slow down," Bingley called after him.

Taking a deep breath in and out, he reined his horse to a trot. As his friend caught up with him, he apologised, "I beg your pardon, Bingley, but I could not stand to be in company with George Wickham. Surely the people of Meryton know nothing of his wild ways."

"Before I left to follow you, Miss Bennet informed me that he is the new curate in Meryton. I did not find out any particulars since you left in such haste."

How could it be that Wickham was a curate? Darcy knew that he must get to the bottom of this before the man hurt or ruined someone. His mind immediately drifted to the lovely Elizabeth Bennet.

Darcy could clearly remember the missive he received from George Wickham shortly after the incumbent of Kympton had passed away.

Dear Darcy,

It has been a long time since we have been in each other's company or corresponded. I apologise for not at least writing to you. I have been quite busy with my studies. Recently, I heard of the passing of Mr. Stokes. Please know that I was grieved to hear it. He was clearly a man of God who will be sorely missed.

Since I was not at the reading of your father's will as I planned, I do not know whether or not my godfather bequeathed me the living at Kympton. If you have not already given it to another, please know that I am ready and able to take on the task as soon as possible.

Sincerely yours,

George D. Wickham

* * *

Darcy recalled that the outrage had boiled out of him with a curse.

How dare the man expect to be given the living after he had signed away the right for the sum of three thousand pounds?

Striding across the room, he wrenched open the door. Hastening up the stairs, he banged on his cousin's door. Colonel Fitzwilliam often stayed at Darcy House when his duties found him in Town.

Richard's batman opened the door. Upon seeing the expression on the face of the master of the house, he bowed out of the room.

"What has you in such a fuss that you frightened my man away?" Richard teased cheerfully.

"I had a letter from Wickham," he stated flatly.

"What does he want?"

"He wants the living at Kympton."

Richard stood and walked to the window. He was quiet for several moments before he turned to say, "He was given money in lieu of the living. What do you plan to do?"

"Since I have already filled the position, there obviously is no living for him. I plan write him and remind him of the paper he signed relinquishing all rights to it."

"I suppose that would be effective, but I believe it would be best to merely tell him that the position is filled. You owe him no more explanation."

Darcy stared at his cousin for a few seconds, pondering the advice, but since he had always relied on his cousin's counsel, he decided he would not question it now.

"I will do just that," Darcy said with conviction.

"Darcy, will you not answer me?"

Bingley's question brought him back to the present.

"Pardon me, Bingley," he said rather sheepishly, "I was lost in thought. What was it you asked me?"

"I asked if you thought that Miss Bennet looked recovered from her illness." The eldest Miss Bennet had been invited to dine with the Bingley sisters. She had become ill after riding to Netherfield on a horse during a rainstorm. Miss Bennet had spent a week recovering with her sister, Miss Elizabeth, as her nurse.

Forcing his thoughts from George Wickham, Darcy pondered the answer. "I believe that she looked well, and I do not believe Miss Elizabeth would have allowed her to walk so far as Meryton if there was any question of her health."

* * *

After Mr. Bingley rode away, the group left behind could only stand in confused and discomfited silence.

It was Lydia who finally spoke. "Mr. Darcy was quite rude to you, Mr. Wickham."

"Lydia," Jane scolded, "you should not say such things."

"Well, he was," the youngest Bennet girl insisted in a huff. "I shall continue to Aunt Philips's house." She grasped her sister Kitty's hand and pulled her away from the rest.

"I apologise, sirs, for my younger sisters," Jane said, her face pinking with embarrassment.

Next to George Wickham stood Mr. North, the rector of Meryton's church, who said, "You have nothing for which to apologise. Your sisters are high spirited, but they will settle down soon enough, I am sure."

Elizabeth wished to follow Lydia and Kitty to make certain they did not cause more mortification to the family. "I believe our aunt Philips is expecting us. Mr. North, it was good to see you, again. And Mr.

Wickham, it was a pleasure to meet you. I am sure that we will meet again soon now that you are to live in our small town."

"We were also on our way to visit Mrs. Philips. I have been on a mission to introduce as many of my parishioners as possible to my new curate. Your aunt was my next stop. Would you permit us to accompany you there?" Mr. North smiled as he glanced at the remaining Bennet sisters.

"Of course, Mr. North," Jane agreed for them all.

The rector offered his arm to Jane while Mr. Wickham presented an arm first to Elizabeth and then to Mary.

As they continued on their way, Elizabeth could not stifle her curiosity. "Do you know Mr. Darcy and Mr. Bingley?"

"I have only met Mr. Bingley briefly. He came to Cambridge just before I was leaving it, but I was practically raised with Mr. Darcy. My father was the steward at Mr. Darcy's estate, Pemberley. Darcy's father was my godfather. The younger Darcy and I were great friends at one time."

"But . . ." Elizabeth did not know how or if she should ask further, thinking that it would be too much like prying into the private affairs of others.

"You do not understand his manner of greeting? I will not try to explain it either." Wickham grimaced as if remembering something upsetting and shook his head without finishing.

After a few seconds, he smiled and said, "I miss his friendship a great deal."

"I will not say that I am surprised that Mr. Darcy was so cold to you," Elizabeth added without thought.

"Lizzy," Mary admonished.

"I do beg your pardon, sir," Elizabeth said quickly. "My sister is correct to reprimand me. I should not have spoken thus."

"I am not offended, only surprised as Darcy can be quite a sociable man; if a bit shy at first with strangers."

"Mary will likely scold me again, but I must defend myself," Elizabeth said as she smiled at her sister. "He is not well liked in Meryton. Mr. Darcy acts as if he is above his company. He is stern and cross, even to the point of insulting others."

"I am astonished to hear it." Wickham pondered this information for a moment. "I wonder if it is not the influence of his Fitzwilliam relatives.

His uncle is an earl, and his late mother's sister is Lady Catherine de Bourgh. I have not seen him but once in the last five years. I suppose that a person might change a great deal in that amount of time, although I would be surprised if he has truly changed in essentials."

However much she wished to continue speaking on the subject, Elizabeth understood by the tone of the curate's voice that he did not wish to prolong the conversation.

Changing the subject, she asked, "What do you think of our town?"

"It is charming," Wickham answered with relief. "The people have been very welcoming, and I look forward to serving the Lord here. My last assignment was not so pleasant as this one appears to be."

It was Mary who asked, "Where did you serve before, if I may be so bold as to ask?"

"I served in a mission in the Whitechapel district of London. It was not a happy place. There were many disenchanted people living there. Poverty and disease were rampant, but I consider myself blessed to have been given the opportunity to help in anyway I could." His voice took on conviction.

"How is it that you met our rector?" Mary spoke again.

"That is one of the blessings." He paused at the memory. "I was asked by my superior to carry a packet of letters to the overseeing bishop. I had just left them at his assistant's desk, as the bishop was in a meeting, when the inner door opened."

His smile widened as he said, "I will not bore you with all of the details, but because of that encounter, Mr. North asked me to be his curate."

Both sisters offered their congratulations as they arrived at the Phillips's house.

The group looked up at the cheerful greeting from a first floor window.

Their aunt and youngest sister waved, calling for them to come inside for some refreshments. Inside, introductions were made, and tea and cake were served once everyone was seated.

"I plan to have an evening of cards and a bit of hot supper afterwards," Mrs. Phillips declared cheerfully. "Mr. Wickham, please say that you will come with Mr. and Mrs. North."

"That is most kind of you, ma'am." Wickham smiled. "It will be my pleasure to attend."

"Jane, I sent an invitation to the Netherfield party, but it seems that they have other plans for this evening. I was disappointed, but I am sure that we will see them again soon enough," Mrs. Phillips finished with a sly, knowing look at Jane.

"Aunt, have you invited the officers?" Lydia piped up, too loudly for Elizabeth's tastes.

"Your uncle did invite the colonel and his senior officers."

"How wonderful!" Lydia cried, clapping her hands. "I do love a man in a uniform." Leaning closer to Kitty, she whispered, "It is too bad that Mr. Wickham did not join the militia. He would look ever so handsome in a red coat."

The two sisters giggled at Mary's disapproving expression. She had been close enough to hear Lydia's whispered statement.

Mary turned to Jane and said, "Do you think that we should be leaving? We will be coming back this evening, and father's cousin is to arrive soon as well." She had been interested in meeting this as yet unknown relative since Mr. Bennet had read to the family from his letter. It had always been her wish to marry a man of the cloth. If this Collins fellow was suitable, perhaps they might make a match.

Seeing that Jane and Mary were both uncomfortable at Lydia's silly antics, Elizabeth hastened to agree that it was time to leave. She was able to silence the younger girls' protests with a promise that they could borrow ribbons from her for the evening. She was certain to lose one or both in the process, but it was worth it to quiet them for the time being.

* * *

Upon reaching Netherfield, Darcy made his way to his room as quickly as he could extricate himself from the company, much to Miss Bingley's dismay. He paced the chamber as he tried to decide what he should do about Wickham. Perhaps he should speak with the rector about him. How was he to do so without endangering Georgiana's reputation? He wondered if his childhood friend had mended his ways. Could it be possible? Was there a way that he could find out?

Since Darcy did not know how long Wickham had been in the neighbourhood, he decided to wait a while longer. After a week or so he would discreetly enquire of the local merchants as to whether Wickham had any debts with them.

How he wished that Richard were not in the north at a special training camp with the newest recruits. His cousin received his orders at nearly the same time that Darcy had discovered and prevented the elopement of Georgiana and Wickham. He frowned at the memory. The pair had denied any idea of their running away, but Georgiana's companion, Mrs. Younge had confessed that she heard them planning to leave for Gretna Green just the day before.

Darcy had sent Wickham away, paid Mrs. Younge what he owed her before dismissing her from service, and took his sister back to Pemberley with him. She had tried to explain that Wickham was only trying to rescue her from someone else who had been pressuring her to elope with him. However, he would not hear her explanation. It grieved him that his sister would lie to protect Wickham. When they reached his country estate, there was a letter from Colonel Fitzwilliam, relating the news of his new assignment and requesting that his cousins come to London to bid him farewell.

Georgiana refused to accompany Darcy to London, which puzzled and confused him, but he ultimately conceded to her wishes and left her under the care of Mrs. Reynolds until he returned. Richard seemed anxious when he asked about Georgiana's absence. However, once Darcy told him about the failed elopement with Wickham, the colonel, though outraged, relaxed. He agreed that it would not do to expose the plot for Georgiana's sake.

Richard was the only person who knew everything that Wickham had done. Also, he had been the one to previously convince him not to tell the elder Darcy about George's misdeeds at Cambridge since the young Wickham had always been a favourite. After Anne Darcy's death, his father had become depressed. Though he knew his father loved his children, frequently it was George Wickham who had been able to cheer him, especially after he became ill. Darcy heaved a breath in frustration. Since his cousin was unavailable due to the remote location, Darcy would have to do the best he could.

As it was his wont in great times of unrest, Darcy took out a pad of drawing paper and a pencil. Few people knew of his talent, and fewer still knew that he drew to calm himself. He sharpened the point of his pencil before beginning to make seemingly random marks on the page. However soon, a sketch of Pemberley took shape.

Home always soothed him, and this was no exception. As he drew the familiar features of the house in which he had grown up, tension left his body. He would find a solution to this problem as he had with many others in his young life. He smiled as he could almost smell the fragrance of the gardens and the freshly cut lawn. Now that he was composed again, he could face things in a better frame of mind.

* * *

Longbourn buzzed with excited girlish chatter as Lydia and Kitty exclaimed over the prospect of seeing officers. The noise his two youngest and their mother made finally forced Mr. Bennet to his book room as soon after dinner as he could manage. He gave Elizabeth the look that signalled his wish for her to join him.

A few minutes later, she knocked softly and was bid to enter.

"Well Lizzy, I am surprised that you are not more excited about seeing the officers tonight. Are you not ready to make a conquest of a major or even a colonel?" Mr. Bennet's eyes twinkled as he teased her.

"I doubt if anyone will make a conquest, as you call it, tonight," she replied archly. "Although, I suppose Lydia will try."

"Jane mentioned that you have met the new curate," he said as he leaned back in his chair. "What did you think of him?"

"I found him to be an interesting young man. Quite a principled one, I might add."

"Oh? What makes you say that after such a short acquaintance?" Her father was intrigued by this assessment.

"While we were just being introduced to Mr. Wickham by Mr. North, Mr. Darcy and Mr. Bingley came upon us. Mr. Wickham seemed quite happy to see Mr. Darcy and greeted him warmly. However, the ever dour Mr. Darcy frowned ever so crossly before turning his horse around and left."

"What did Mr. Wickham say in explanation?" he asked.

"He told Mary and me that he could not understand it. He was raised at Pemberley because his father was steward there.

"The elder Mr. Darcy was his godfather," she quickly added. "He tried to excuse Mr. Darcy's abrupt and rude behaviour. Mr. Wickham seems to grieve the loss of Mr. Darcy's friendship."

"I am glad to hear that Mr. Wickham is not a gossip. I think there is none worse than a cleric who carries tales or demeans others. If he continues to be this circumspect, we may have ourselves a decent man to take over for Mr. North."

Mr. Bennet pondered the information, before he said in mock seriousness, "He must not be a handsome fellow, or your younger sisters would have told us all at the table."

"Papa," Elizabeth scolded with a grin. "According to Lydia, he wants only a red uniform to make him handsome. Her head is too full of officers to bother over a mere curate."

"And you, my Lizzy?" her father teased.

"I enjoyed his company, but more than that, I cannot say."

* * *

Later a missive arrived by express, which in many words and flowery phrases merely explained that their cousin William Collins would not attend them until the next day. An urgent matter required him to attend his patroness before he could take his leave.

"He takes a great deal of paper to express something so simple," Lizzy commented after her father read the letter to his family.

"I suppose he wished to write enough to make it worth the cost of an express." Mr. Bennet's eyes twinkled as he spoke.

"Well, as for me, I could wish that his patroness would keep him at Rosings for the near future. I cannot abide the thought of this person coming here to look over what is only his by entailment. It is so unfair to the girls and I that we should have to lose our home and make way for him," Mrs. Bennet asserted.

"But remember, Mama, he wishes to extend an olive branch to us," Elizabeth reminded her before she continued. "I do wonder what he could mean by that."

"Ah well, Lizzy, we shall have to wait at least until tomorrow to find out." Mr. Bennet refolded the letter and stood. "I shall be in my book room should I be needed."

Chapter 2

When the Bennets—minus Mr. Bennet who avoided parties hosted by his in-laws—arrived at the Phillips's home, the large parlour was already crowded. Henrietta Phillips was a silly woman like her sister, but her gatherings were always well attended. Colonel Forster and his senior officers stood chatting with Mr. Phillips.

Lydia failed to suppress a squeal when she spied them, but much to the relief of her three elder sisters, the noise of those gathered muffled the sound. As usual the two youngest hurried up to the soldiers with barely a greeting to their aunt. They were followed a bit more sedately by their mother who still enjoyed the sight of a red coat herself.

Sighing in resignation, Elizabeth surveyed the group and observed Mr. Wickham and Mr. North in conversation with Sir William Lucas. She covered her mouth to hide her smile as she thought it likely that the knight was explaining in great detail his presentation at court.

When she spied her good friend Charlotte Lucas walking toward her, Elizabeth moved to meet her.

Charlotte greeted her with a quick kiss on the cheek. "It is good to see you, Eliza. I missed you when you were at Netherfield. Jane looks to have recovered nicely."

"Oh yes, Charlotte," said Elizabeth as she smiled her welcome, "I am very happy to see you and to be away from that place."

"Did you not enjoy your time at Netherfield?" her friend inquired with a raised brow.

"I could not enjoy very much when my sister was ill, and the company there was only tolerable at times." The last word was said with a wink since it was how Mr. Darcy had described Elizabeth at their first contact.

"You do have an intractable resentment, Eliza. Will you never forget his words?" Charlotte mildly scolded her as she was wont to do as her friend.

Sighing dramatically, Elizabeth smiled. "I suppose that I should forgive and forget, but it is so much fun to continue to dislike someone who has injured my pride."

Charlotte looked up to see Mr. Wickham walking their way. "Our new curate told me that you met him this afternoon in High Street."

"Yes, we did," Mary, who had just joined them, stated quietly.

"Ladies, it is a pleasure to see you again." Mr. Wickham bowed and addressed the group.

"I hope you are enjoying yourself, sir," Elizabeth said with a curtsey.

"Indeed, I am. I always enjoy the society of amiable people."

* * *

Earlier the same afternoon, Darcy marked the time and thought that, if he hurried, he would be able to interview several of the shops Wickham was most likely to frequent before they were to leave for their dinner obligation. Deciding not to wait a week to see if the man had started to incur debts, he thought it prudent to know sooner rather than later.

Darcy was pleased to have avoided any of Netherfield's occupants as he exited the house. Before striding to the stables, he left word with the butler that he would return in time for dinner.

It did not take him long to reach the small market town. Darcy had to pause for a group of militiamen who marched down the middle of the street. The parade of uniformed men drew a crowd so that, when he stopped at the tobacconist's, no one was present but the proprietor.

"Good afternoon, sir," the man greeted Darcy with a smile. "How may I help you?"

"Might I see your selection of cigars?" Aloysius Hurst, Bingley's brother-in-law, had a habit of smoking more than his share of Bingley's tobacco. Darcy always found himself with a headache from the foul smelling smoke if he stayed too long with the men after dinner. However, Bingley had mentioned the need to procure more as his supply had run quite low.

"Of course, sir," the man replied as he turned to the shelf behind him. He lifted a silver-clad box from the highest shelf and set it on the table. "These are my finest."

Darcy lifted one to his nose. Since he did not smoke and rarely bought a cigar, he hoped he looked like he knew what he was doing. "Very good, I will take a dozen."

Very pleased, the shop owner retrieved an empty box into which he carefully placed Darcy's order. After he wrapped and tied up the box, he asked, "Is there anything else you might need? Snuff, perhaps?"

"No, but I have what might seem an odd question," Darcy began slowly. "An old acquaintance of mine has recently moved to Meryton. I wonder if he might have an account with you."

"What is the name?" the man asked as he wrote the receipt for the cigars.

"Wickham, George Wickham," Darcy said.

"The new curate?"

"The very one," Darcy affirmed.

The proprietor laughed. "I do not have to look. He has never been in the shop, not even to look around."

Darcy was noticeably shocked at this news. He had paid off Wickham's outstanding account at a tobacconist in London. In fact, his erstwhile friend had left debts at almost every shop in the villages near Lambton after finally quitting his father's home. Shaking his head in confusion, he paid for the cigars and left the building.

In less than an hour, he had visited every establishment that he thought Wickham might frequent with the same results, even stopping at the pubs to see if his father's godson had incurred any debts of honour. If George shopped, he paid for his purchases immediately and cheerfully. In those places, Darcy asked with great subtlety after Wickham's conduct with others, especially with those of the opposite sex. The reports were always the same. The curate is a perfect gentleman, polite and kind.

Bewildered by the result of his investigation, Darcy rode his horse out of town. He was not in the mood to see any of the company at Netherfield while in such a state, so he turned his horse in the other direction. Giving his horse its head, he endeavoured to examine the subject from a different angle. It was a method he had used often at

Cambridge when an equation did not seem to have the answer he expected.

Could it be that his childhood friend had truly become the man that his godfather had wished him to be, or was he hiding his true nature for some unknown but likely nefarious reason? A thought flitted into his mind that Wickham had never been the cad that he had believed, but Darcy did not entertain that idea for long. Of course, he had been. Richard had given him plenty of evidence to attest to it, and he completely trusted his cousin.

* * *

As Charlotte left, at a gesture from her mother, Elizabeth and Mary continued their chat with George Wickham.

"Mr. Wickham, do you still have family in Derbyshire?"

A look of sadness passed briefly over his face, before he replied, "No, my mother died when I was a child of seven. My godfather, Mr. George Darcy, saw to it that I was practically raised with his son, Fitzwilliam. He—that is the elder Darcy—paid for my schooling and later at Cambridge. My own father passed away a few months before Mr. Darcy did. It was a doubly sad time for me."

"I am so sorry, sir," Mary said in deep compassion.

"Thank you, Miss Mary, but I do like to consider Fitzwilliam and his young sister as close as family."

"I do not think that Mr. Darcy would agree," Elizabeth commented bluntly.

"Lizzy!" Mary admonished quietly.

"I cannot but agree that his actions of today might imply as much, but we were very close growing up. I hope to be able to reconcile with him as soon as may be. I miss his friendship greatly."

Mary agreed that it was good to be at peace with as many as it was in one's power to be.

Just as Mr. Wickham was about to respond, Lydia arrived and ordered Mary to play for them. "I wish to dance with the officers, but we need music."

As much as Mary wished to continue her conversation with the charming new curate, she did not wish to argue with her sister in front of him. Willing herself not to sigh in frustration, she stood and excused herself.

Rising, Mr. Wickham said, "May I turn the pages for you, Miss Mary?"

"Will you not wish to join in the dancing?" Mary hoped he was not offering to assist her merely to be polite.

"Perhaps later," he answered. "However, at the moment I am pleased to be of assistance,"

Elizabeth fought a smile as she saw Mary blush with pleasure as she led the curate to the pianoforte at the other end of the room. She hoped that her mother would not tease Mary about having a beau. Her younger sister deserved to enjoy the attention of a gentleman without the interference of her mother.

Soon the furniture and rug had been moved to clear the floor for dancing. Elizabeth stood to the side, watching the young officers choose their partners. She was shocked and dismayed to see Lydia standing up with Colonel Forster. The man was quite tall and handsome, but he was much older than her youngest sister. Shaking her head in confusion, Elizabeth decided that her mother should be made aware. After all, Mrs. Bennet was the only member of the family to whom Lydia seem to listen.

In the crush of the crowd, it took Elizabeth several minutes to locate her mother. Mrs. Fanny Bennet was gossiping with her cronies on the far side of the room. Waiting for her mother to finish speaking took patience, but Lizzy was finally rewarded with her mother's notice.

"Lizzy, why are you not dancing?"

Swallowing back the sarcastic remark that sprang to her lips, Elizabeth spoke softly. "Mama, may I speak to you privately for just a moment? It is important."

Sighing rather dramatically, Mrs. Bennet excused herself from her friends to move to a relatively private area.

She turned and asked impatiently, "What is so important that you took me from my friends?"

"Mama, have you not noticed that Lydia has been spending this whole time with Colonel Forster? He is much too old for her. I think you should warn her."

"Is that all?" Disdain coloured her voice. "He is older, it is true, but your own father is twelve years my senior. I doubt if the colonel is more than thirty years of age. To think! My Lydia, married to an officer at just sixteen! No, I shall do nothing to discourage it."

"But, Mama," Elizabeth started to speak, but her mother merely waved her hand in dismissal and walked away.

Frustrated but determined, Elizabeth decided to speak to her father at the first opportunity. Perhaps he would listen to her objections. She watched the dancing through a full set, happy that no one had asked her to join in. In her current mood, she knew that she would be poor company.

As the final notes of Mary's song were played, Elizabeth thought that her middle sister could use a rest from playing. Hastening to the instrument, she offered to take a turn at the pianoforte.

"There is no need, Lizzy," Mary demurred, "I am willing to continue."

"Miss Mary, I was hoping that someone else would offer to play, so that I might have the chance to dance with you," Wickham said quickly.

"Perfect," Elizabeth exclaimed, as the gentleman stood and offered his hand to Mary.

Blushing prettily, Mary accepted and walked with him to the line that was forming.

Elizabeth heard Lydia's giggling whisper about Mary finally dancing. Gritting her teeth, she wished to scold her unfeeling youngest sister, but she knew that Mary would be even more embarrassed if she did. Instead, Lizzy selected a tune to which she knew all of her sisters could dance well.

* * *

All in all, the Bennet ladies arrived home in happy spirits. Jane, who never seemed to be in any other than a contented mood, smiled as her younger sisters, Lydia and Kitty, compared their winnings at cards and their dance partners. Mary's countenance glowed with the compliment of being the only one of her sisters who danced with the charming new curate. While not pleased with Lydia's situation, Elizabeth could not but be glad that someone had finally taken notice of her middle—often overlooked—sister.

After Mr. Bennet had tired of listening to his wife and younger daughters exclaim over the evening's entertainment, he returned to his book room for his nightly glass of port before he retired.

Once everyone else had gone to their rooms, Elizabeth remained behind and knocked upon his door. At his bid to enter, she smiled as her father greeted her.

"Ah my Lizzy, I thought something was on your mind. Do sit down and tell me what has creased your brow this time?"

"I am concerned over Lydia's behaviour tonight in regard to Colonel Forster. He is much older than she is. Lydia thinks herself so mature, but I am certain that a man of his age and experience cannot have proper intentions toward such a silly flirt as she."

Stroking his chin, Mr. Bennet pondered what she had told him. After a few moments of silence, he said, "I do understand your concern. I suppose that your mother is not worried about the age difference."

At her nod, he continued, "Your mother has told me she is planning large dinner party to which she has invited the senior militia officers, including Colonel Forster. Since they are to dine with us in a couple of days, I will observe them and speak to him if I need to do so."

"Thank you, Papa," she said as she rose and kissed his brow. "I knew you would understand."

"Good night, Lizzy."

"Good night, Papa."

* * *

The following morning found Longbourn a hive of activity. Mrs. Bennet could not seem to settle on a menu for that evening. At first, she had thought to impress their cousin with one of her finest. However, she did not wish to have him want to stay longer than he had originally planned, so she changed her menu and thought a plain dinner would suffice. She decided that the better of the meals would be reserved for the next night when the officers and other guests would come. This better dinner would not be wasted on the man who had the nerve to inherit her home when her husband died.

This distant cousin arrived quite promptly according to his letter of the day before. William Collins was a sturdy kind of man of medium height and rounder at the middle, indicating his tendency to eat more than he should.

As he smiled when introduced to the Bennet sisters, Elizabeth could not help but feel uncomfortable. His manner was too familiar, and he lingered too long on more than their faces. She would have sworn that he licked his lips when his gaze returned to Jane.

He is looking for a bride! The thought came unbidden. *It will not be Jane if I have anything to do about it.* She promised herself. *Jane is for Bingley.*

Finally able to insert a word into Mr. Collins's extensive monologue on the beauty of the countryside, and his cousins, always making sure to mention his patroness, Lady Catherine de Bourgh between compliments, Mr. Bennet insisted that they all enter the house, as it was warmer inside.

This comment brought forth a profound and lengthy apology from Mr. Collins that lasted for several minutes after everyone had gone into the house. That too would have lasted even longer, if Mr. Bennet had not summoned Mr. Hill to escort his cousin to his room to refresh himself.

"I can see that I am going to have to have a talk with him," Mr. Bennet mumbled under his breath, so that only Elizabeth heard him, and she smiled in sympathy.

* * *

Collins insisted upon a tour of his future home after he had freshened up and had tea. As much as he would have wished it otherwise, his cousin, Mr. Bennet, only guided him through the public rooms. The master of Longbourn would not allow the man to see the servants' quarters or any bed chambers other than the guest room. As he did not fully trust this man, there was no need to invade his family's privacy.

At dinner that evening, Collins examined the cutlery and china with greedy eyes. He turned over his plate and knife to read the maker's mark and smiled his approval at what he found.

As the food was served, he did not seem to notice it was simple fare. He ate with relish, often taking large bites and speaking with his mouth full of food. Bits of his meal would fly from his mouth as he tried to speak and chew at the same time.

The family watched in sickened fascination as crumbs began to decorate his serviette, lap, and the table around him. Once, several fragments landed in the gravy boat in front of Collins, Mr. Bennet put down his napkin and stood.

"Mr, Collins, come with me," he ordered.

His cousin stared up at Bennet as if he were speaking a foreign tongue and did not move.

"I mean now!" Mr. Bennet did not shout, but the strength of his words was not to be ignored.

"But, sir, I have not finished my meal," Collins objected after he swallowed.

"The food will still be here when we return."

Mr. Bennet whispered something to the footman who stood near the door before he turned to wait for Collins to walk through it. Once they entered his book room, Bennet walked behind his desk, motioning for Collins to sit in front of him.

"I do not understand what is so important that you would interrupt my meal to bring me . . ."

"Quiet, Collins," Mr. Bennet ordered. "I do not want you to say a word until I ask you a question, or I am finished. Is that understood?"

"Yes, but," Collins began to protest.

"A simple yes or no will do."

Standing and leaning forward with his hands resting on the top of his desk, Bennet began, "I am the master of this house, am I not?"

"Yes."

Bennet nodded. "As the master of this house, I have the right to expect a certain standard of behaviour from my guests, especially ones who came without invitation."

When Collins opened his mouth, Bennet silenced him with a lifted hand. "I am not finished, and that was not a question."

At the click of his cousin's mouth closing, Bennet said, "It is apparent to me that your father did not teach you proper manners, especially those pertaining to meals. One does not speak with one's mouth full of food, and one should only take a bite of food around which one can close one's mouth. You, sir, have spit and dropped food all over yourself and the table. And you ruined a perfectly fine gravy with the food that dropped from your mouth. Is this the way you eat at the table of your patroness?"

"No."

"Why is that?"

"I am rarely asked to dine with Lady Catherine, and I listen to her speeches as she has such wisdom to impart," Collins explained.

"I see," Bennet said, rubbing his chin. "When you do speak, do you have food in your mouth?"

"Occasionally."

"Which is likely why you rarely dine with her," Mr. Bennet said more to himself than to Collins.

"If you wish to eat at my table, you will not talk with food in your mouth. Is that clear?"

"Yes." Collins made to stand, assuming the lecture was over.

"Stay seated, Collins," Mr. Bennet ordered. "I have more to say."

Bennet continued, "I saw you surveying the tableware, especially the silver."

Leaving his desk, Bennet made his way to stand in front of Collins. "All of the tableware that we are using tonight belongs to my wife's dowry. We rarely use those belonging to the Bennet estate, because my wife does not like the pattern. She does occasionally use it, but she will not bring it out during your visit. It is kept in a locked cabinet, and only my wife and I have a key."

Watching the disappointment cross Collins's face, Mr. Bennet smiled. "Let us return to our dinner."

Mr. Hill stood outside the dining room door. Bennet stopped and asked, "Has our food been kept warm?"

"Yes, sir."

"Good, you may open the door."

Chapter 3

There was much chatter at the breakfast table concerning the evening's dinner and expected guests. Lydia and Kitty were the most vocal, speaking of the handsome officers. Mrs. Bennet seemed as excited as her youngest girls as she echoed their comments.

Disapproving of the silly conversation, Mr. Collins glanced around the table. He noticed that Mr. Bennet ate his breakfast with a faint smile on his face. *Why does he not admonish them to be more circumspect?* Collins wondered to himself. The oldest three girls seemed to be embarrassed by their mother and sisters, for they blushed at some of the more absurd statements and did not participate.

Collins was ready to give voice to his concerns when Mrs. Bennet rose and said, "I have decided to go into Meryton. I have heard of a new shipment of goods that is due to arrive at the mercantile today. I would like to see the items before they are picked over. Jane, you must come with me. I rely upon your opinion." Lydia and Kitty quickly clamoured to go along, to which their mother agreed. They were soon off in their carriage.

As the rest of the family continued at the table, Collins remained seated.

He watched as Elizabeth and Mary quietly spoke of seeing the vicar and his wife and curate again. He had thought it would be an easy task to choose a bride from among his cousin's daughters. Although he had narrowed down his choices to Jane, Elizabeth, and Mary, he was not sure whom to pick. Jane was, above all, the most beautiful; Elizabeth was lovely and lively, while Mary had a quiet piety about her, not to mention a desirable figure.

His thoughts were interrupted by his cousin Bennet's removal to his library.

Deciding it was a lucky occurrence that he was now alone with the two targets of his attention, Collins smiled in what he thought was a flirtatious manner. "I would be happy to escort both of you to the drawing room."

Elizabeth hesitated, but when Mary agreed, she did not wish to leave her sister alone with such a man. As she followed Mary and Collins to the drawing room, she saw Mr. Collins seem to trip over his feet. To steady himself, he reached for Mary and held her more closely than was necessary, before he slowly released her, apologizing verbosely for his clumsiness.

Watching Mary quickly take her regular seat by the window, and pick up a book, Elizabeth warily watched Mr. Collins turn and move to meet her. He stepped steadily enough until he had nearly reached her. It was then that he tripped once more with his arms outstretched toward her. She hastened a pace back before grasping his forearms tightly, keeping him in place while he struggled to stay upright.

"Mr. Collins, you should watch your step." Elizabeth stared at him as she released her grip on his arms. "You would not wish to find yourself on the floor, would you?"

He stared at her in shock, as if to say, "you would not dare," while Elizabeth did not break eye contact as if to answer, "I certainly would."

Beginning what would obviously be a long and drawn out apology, Elizabeth interrupted him by speaking to Mary. "Sister, I have something in my room that I would like to show you. I had forgotten it until just this moment."

"But Cousin Elizabeth," Collins protested. "It is not seemly to leave one's guests to themselves."

"I believe, sir, that you are not actually my guest," she stated in reply. "If you cannot entertain yourself for a few minutes, I would suggest that you visit my father in his library. I am certain that he would have a book for you to read."

With these last words, Elizabeth took Mary's hand and led her from the room.

Once they reached her room, Elizabeth closed her door and locked it.

"Why did you lock your door, Lizzy?"

"I do not trust that man not to follow us. He does not seem to have any concept of proper behaviour." Elizabeth dropped upon her bed in an unladylike manner.

Mary joined her with more grace and hugged her sister. "Thank you for thinking of a reason for leaving his presence. I could not believe that he tripped in such a way as to touch me so. I wish I could have been as quick as you to repel him."

"You had no idea that he would trip or grasp you so as to touch you that way," Elizabeth explained. "I saw what he did and expected him to try it with me. He is a repulsive man, but I think that our mother has pointed him in our direction. She still has hopes of Mr. Bingley for Jane."

"I have no wish to be bound to such a man," Mary adamantly declared. "I hope that Papa will not insist that one of us marry him."

"I am quite certain that he will not."

"Did you truly have something for me to see?" Mary asked, changing the subject.

"Actually I did, but I hope will not be offended when I show you," she said sheepishly.

"I do not believe you would offend me on purpose, so please show me."

Elizabeth went to her closet and rummaged through the dresses until she found what she wanted. She pulled out a green frock that she had worn a few years before. It was now a trifle too short, but she thought that it would be perfect for Mary. Her sister and she were of similar colouring and size if not the same height.

"I thought that you could wear this to dinner this evening," Elizabeth explained. "I had grown too tall for it before I had worn it more than twice. I liked it so much that I could not part with it. I had planned to add some trim to the bottom to lengthen it."

"I remember when you wore it last," Mary said as she caressed the fabric. "It is lovely, but you do not have to give it to me. I will help you trim it so that you can wear it again."

"No, Mary, I wish for you to wear this. I think that a certain curate will find you quite captivating in it."

"Lizzy," Mary exclaimed as heat rushed to her cheeks. "Do not speak so. I am sure that Mr. Wickham is only being kind when he speaks to me. I do not want to look as if I am trying to seek his attention."

"Nonsense!" Elizabeth pulled Mary to her feet and made her turn around. She began to undo the buttons of her sister's dress. "We will see how well it fits you. I have some green ribbon for your hair that matches the gown very well."

Mary reluctantly surrendered to Lizzy's ministrations, although she was rather excited about the prospect of a different gown to wear to dinner. Her own closet held only the plain and dull clothing that she thought a pious woman should prefer.

Once Mary slipped into the dress, there was no question as to whether or not she would wear it. The colour was a perfect compliment to her hazel-green eyes. Although the neckline was lower than was her wont, it was still modest. She could not help but hope that a certain curate would indeed be captivated by her appearance.

* * *

As Collins exited his chambers after making himself ready for dinner, he noticed his young cousins leaving their rooms. He bowed deeply, and with the sweep of his hand allowed them to go ahead. Happy to be taller than all but the youngest, he was able to observe their assets as each passed him.

He had first set his mind upon the eldest of his lovely cousins, but after a brief conversation earlier with Mrs. Bennet in which she told him that Jane was soon to become engaged to another, he set his sights upon the next eldest. After all, as the future master of Longbourn, he should have first choice of his beautiful cousins. Armed with this exalted view of himself and his position, he descended the stairs with his head held high.

Guests began to arrive and introductions were made. Collins was unhappy that Elizabeth and Mary immediately joined the curate, Mr. Wickham, and engaged him in a lively conversation. Twice, he tried to break into the exchange, but he was thwarted by another. First Mr. Bennet's neighbour Sir William Lucas wished to speak about his presentation at court, and next Mrs. Bennet wished to introduce him to a latecomer.

When dinner was announced, he tried to reach Elizabeth in order to escort her into the dining room, but she and Mary were led in by

Mr. Wickham before he was halfway across the parlour. Much to his annoyance, he found his two cousins seated with the curate in between them, chatting freely.

As the meal progressed, Collins felt even more frustrated. He sat next to Mrs. North on one side and an elderly lady whose name he did not recall on his other. Watching the smiles that Wickham gave his two cousins, particularly Cousin Mary, caused him to wonder if he had chosen correctly. Although Cousin Elizabeth was beautiful to look at and was fine of figure, when Mary smiled she was nearly as beautiful as her elder sister, but with a quieter manner. The gown she was wearing flattered her larger bosom, causing her to look lovelier than he had previously noticed. He decided that he would not make his mind up so quickly, but he would take his time to weigh the advantages of each.

Collins was finally freed from conversation with his dinner partners and determined to know his opposition. "Mr. Wickham." His voice was loud enough for everyone to hear. "From whence do you come?"

"I am lately from London," Wickham replied politely.

"Did you work there?"

"I did, in a mission in White Chapel."

Collins's lip curled in disgust. In a condescending tone, he said, "I was pleased to have received the notice of Lady Catherine de Bourgh after my ordination this Easter. I have a lovely parsonage and grounds which are just a small distance from Lady Catherine's estate, Rosings Park."

"It was quite to your fortune that she noticed you," Wickham said dryly.

Ignorant of the former's tone, Collins agreed. "Indeed, it is. And it is because of the kindness of my patroness that I have come to visit my cousin and his family. She wishes for me to find a bride here."

The silence in the rest of the room was broken by Mrs. Bennet's eager excitement as she began to extol the virtues of her daughters.

Collins ignored the interruption and smiled what he thought was a flirtatious smile at his two cousins before he changed the subject. "From where did you originate?"

"I was born and raised in Derbyshire."

"Derbyshire!" he exclaimed. "Did you know the Darcys of Pemberley?"

"I was raised at Pemberley." Wickham could not help but smile at the stunned expression on Collins's face.

"How is that possible?" Collins demanded.

"My father was the Darcys' steward. Mr. Darcy was my godfather, and since his son for years was an only child, as was I, I spent a great deal of my time with Fitzwilliam Darcy," Wickham stated without conceit.

"Have you met the current Mr. Darcy's intended?" Collins answered, being certain that this steward's son had never been to Rosings.

"I had not heard that Mr. Darcy was engaged."

Collins answered with a smirk, "He is engaged to Miss Anne de Bourgh, the lovely daughter of my noble patroness, Lady Catherine, and the finest jewel of Kent"

"Not that old tale," Wickham scoffed. "Is Lady Catherine still putting forth that nonsense?"

"How dare you insult such a regal personage as she? I have it on her word that the official engagement will be announced very soon." Collins's face burned with rage at the aspersion to his patroness's word.

By this time, the rest of the table had grown quiet as Collins has raised his voice. They all strained to hear the curate's response.

"She has been badgering Darcy with a fabricated story of his mother and her plans for the two to marry since the children were in their cradles. However, it is a fact that Miss de Bourgh is nearly five years younger than Darcy, and this so-called cradle engagement was never spoken of until his mother died. At that time, she insisted that my godfather sign an engagement contract, even though both were still under age at the time. He refused, saying that his wife had never mentioned such a plan to him. I would have thought that Lady Catherine would have given up on the idea by now, but it would seem with his father gone, Mr. Darcy is once again the target of her machinations."

Mr. Wickham, finally noticing the silence in the room, turned to Mr. Bennet. "Please forgive me sir, for arguing a matter that could have no interest to anyone else. I only wished to defend my old friend."

"No need, Mr. Wickham, but I think that a change of subject would be appropriate." Although Mr. Bennet answered the curate, he glared at Mr. Collins.

Opening his mouth to protest, Mr. Collins seemed to finally understand his host. He picked up his fork and took a small bite, pondering how he could answer this insult to his beloved patroness.

Once the meal was finished, the ladies left for the parlour, while the men enjoyed drinks. They talked of the conflict building with the former colonies and the likelihood that more troops would be sent to defend the British interests.

Collins had little curiosity about the topic, so he attempted to renew his conversation with Mr. Wickham. However, his cousin stopped him by announcing that it was time to rejoin the ladies.

Eager to return to his observation of his two cousins, Collins made for the door but was blocked from leaving by Mr. North, who asked him a question about his parish. He answered as quickly as he was able which meant it took him five minutes, by which time all but Colonel Forster and Mr. Bennet had left the room. He hurried out the door so hastily that he nearly collided with a passing servant.

Smiling at the antics of his clumsy cousin, Mr. Bennet closed the door to his study and poured himself another glass of port. He offered more to the colonel, who accepted.

"Colonel, I thank you for agreeing to stay behind." Bennet took a sip of his drink. "I am concerned about your attention to my youngest daughter. Surely you know that she is not yet sixteen."

Forster met Mr. Bennet's gaze without surprise. "I do, sir."

"Explain to me why you are paying so much attention to a child."

"She is hardly a child, young and a bit flighty perhaps, but not a child." The colonel set down his empty glass. "Miss Lydia intrigues me greatly. She is a lively beauty, and enjoys life. As a soldier, even a militiaman such as myself, I tire of the company of men. I have been looking for a wife for a long time." He paused and took a deep breath, before he continued, "You asked me about my attentions toward Miss Lydia. I wish to inform you that I wish the court her, with the intention of marriage."

Mr. Bennet's mouth dropped open in shock. He tossed back the rest of his port and stared at the younger man. "You wish to court and marry Lydia. Are you out of your mind?"

"I am offended on behalf of your daughter," Forster growled as he moved closer to Mr. Bennet. "I have given much thought to this since she and I met at the Lucases the other night. I know that she is immature, but I can see that she will make me a wonderful wife. All she lacks is guidance. I have helped many a young man improve himself. I know that the love and attention of a gentleman such as myself would be able to channel her enthusiasm into its proper path."

'How will you afford to even keep her in ribbons? I am certain that your colonel's pay is not sufficient." Mr. Bennet astonishment's was still evident in his voice.

"Mr. Bennet, that is a fair question," he responded as he paced to the window and back again. "I must ask for your secrecy in what I am about to tell you. I do not wish to have Miss Lydia to be tempted to accept me because of it."

Mr. Bennet nodded his head in agreement. "You have my word, sir."

"Very well," the colonel sighed. "Few people know this about me. Although I am a second son, my father was a frugal and successful landowner. My elder brother has taken over the family's estate in Sussex, and he does very well. My excellent father wanted me to have a place of my own. I have no sister, and my mother passed away when I was young. So it was that he invested my mother's dowry in another estate in Cheshire. It belonged to a distant relative who wished to travel to a warmer clime.

"Upon my graduation from Oxford, my father told me of his plan. He had hired a steward who is a good and hard-working man. His wish was that I take over the running of the estate upon my twenty-fifth birthday.

"I had always thought I would need to find an occupation, and with that in mind, I joined the militia before I returned home from university. The brother of a fellow student had been conscripted and did not wish to serve. Since my father was a wealthy landowner in the county, I was able to enter as a captain, despite my lack of experience. I was able to rise to colonel after a few years. My father was disappointed in my impetuous action, but he understood my reasoning. I agreed to serve for seven years and to return to my estate soon thereafter."

"I am even more astonished, Colonel," Mr. Bennet stated. "Is your seven-year agreement close to its end?"

"Actually, my father passed away just before its end," he said simply. "I was not ready to become the master of my estate, primarily because I did not have a wife. I stayed in the militia these past three years, earnestly looking for the right woman. I believe I have found her in your daughter."

"I still do not understand why someone with your age and maturity would wish to marry such a young girl. I admit that I am twelve years my wife's senior, but I have learned to regret the impulse that led me to offer for her so quickly. She was quite like Lydia is now." Mr. Bennet rubbed his chin as he awaited the colonel's reply.

"Aside from her beauty and energy, Miss Lydia chose to be with me soon after we were introduced. Of all the officers present that evening with whom she could have decided to spend time, she stayed by my side and listened—truly listened—to what I had to say." The colonel's smile lit his face. "When I was a younger officer, the ladies flirted and danced with me, but even then not one spoke as intelligently about my service and actually listened to my answers."

Mr. Bennet shook his head and smiled ruefully. "I can see that you are smitten. I will agree to a courtship for the time being. If you are still interested in marrying her when you must move to another location, and the two of you have not been involved in any kind of scandal, I shall entertain the idea of the two of you being wed."

The younger man grinned and stuck out his hand.

"There is one more thing, sir," Bennet continued. "Say nothing of our conversation until I have spoken to my daughter. I do not wish to have undue pressure put upon her."

"I understand, Mr. Bennet, and I agree," the colonel said still holding out his hand.

Bennet nodded and shook the colonel's hand. "Shall we join the ladies?"

* * *

While her father spoke to Colonel Forster, Elizabeth sat next to the settee on which Mary and Mr. Wickham sat. He was telling them how much he had enjoyed the meal they had just shared when Mr. Collins moved to stand next to Elizabeth.

Collins did not speak to anyone. He either stared down at Elizabeth or glared at Mr. Wickham. It did not seem that he listened to their conversation although he did harrumph when Wickham spoke of his mission work.

"Mr. Collins, is something the matter with your throat?" Elizabeth asked without looking up.

Collins started and stammered out, "No, my throat is perfectly fine."

"That is good, sir. We would not wish for you to be taken ill." Sarcasm dripped from her voice, but Collins was completely unaware.

"Thank you, my dear cousin," he said with a small nod and an oily smile. "I am of a hardy constitution and am rarely ill. In fact, Lady Catherine herself commented on my good health." Collins went on to catalogue the excellent qualities of his patroness for several minutes, all the while gazing down at Elizabeth.

When Elizabeth happened to glance up, she saw that his eyes were not on her face but lower on her person. A tremor of disgust rolled over her. It was too much, especially after his behaviour that morning. Unable to countenance her cousin's attention any longer, she stood rapidly and excused herself, explaining that she was needed by her mother.

She approached her mother, but Mrs. Bennet was deep in conversation with Lady Lucas. Elizabeth searched the room for her father and found him entering with Colonel Forster. As the colonel walked to where Lydia was standing, Mr. Bennet merely stood in the doorway, surveying the group. He smiled broadly when he spied Lizzy moving in his direction.

"What is it that makes you seek out your old father, Lizzy?"

Heaving a great sigh, Elizabeth answered in a drawn-out, exasperated whisper, "Mr. Collins."

Glancing to where his cousin now stood next to Mary, who was still in deep conversation with Mr. Wickham, he asked, "What has he done now?"

"Most recently, he has been standing next to my chair since the gentlemen returned, saying nothing," she declared with revulsion.

Her father chuckled. "I would think that you would be happy for his silence, Lizzy."

"It is the reason for his silence that brings me to you." Elizabeth paused to calm herself. "He was too busy ogling my person, and since I removed myself, he switched his gaze to Mary. Just look at his expression, Papa."

Mr. Bennet frowned and searched the room for his cousin. When he saw the look of lust on the man's face, he gritted his teeth in anger. "You said, 'most recently.' What other charge have you against him?"

Elizabeth blushed as she explained Collins's failed attempt to grope her and Mary.

"Thank you, my girl, for telling me. Please fetch your sister, Mary. Ask her to play something for us. I shall deal with Collins." Mr. Bennet's anger grew as he pictured his foolish cousin's actions.

Elizabeth did as her father said. Soon Mary was sitting at the pianoforte looking through the sheets for something to play. Bennet heard Collins offer to turn pages, but Wickham was quicker, settling on the bench beside her.

Hastening to intercept Collins before he could join Elizabeth who sat near her sister, Mr. Bennet called out, "Mr. Collins, I would speak to you in my book room."

Collins looked a trifle perturbed to be interrupted in his quest to enjoy the delights of his cousins' bounties and to have time to decide which of the two he would choose for a wife. Giving Elizabeth a low bow, he walked to where Mr. Bennet stood,

"Of what do you wish to speak, Cousin Bennet?" Collins asked crossly.

Grasping his cousin's arm, Mr. Bennet propelled him into the corridor. Once there, Bennet closed the door to the parlour and said, "Please wait here for me. I shall not be long."

Bennet walked swiftly to another door and opened it. Inside the small room, he found his butler giving orders to a footman. Drawing Hill aside, he spoke quietly, explaining what he wished him to do. At the butler's nod, Mr. Bennet returned to Collins, who was now pacing impatiently in front of the book room door.

After unlocking the door, Mr. Bennet bid him enter and gestured for Collins to be seated. "Something has come to my attention which has upset me greatly."

The anger in Bennet's voice caused Collins to hunch in his seat, but he protested, "I do not understand what that has to do with me."

"It has everything to do with you," Bennet replied, his voice low with rage. "I saw with my own eyes how and where you were looking at two of my daughters. I know you have come here with the intention of choosing one of my daughters as a wife, and that my wife has encouraged you in this endeavour. However, I will tell you now, that I shall never agree to you marrying any of my girls. None of them deserves a lecherous cleric for a husband."

"But . . ." Collins began before Mr. Bennet stopped him.

"No excuses, sir," Bennet sternly ordered. "I have asked Hill to have your things packed. You will be leaving first thing in the morning. I do not wish to subject my family to your presence any longer."

There was a knock at the door.

"Come."

Hill stood just inside the doorway. "Might I have a word, sir?"

Mr. Bennet turned to Collins. "Do not move," he ordered threateningly.

Stepping out of his book room, Bennet closed the door and faced the butler. "What is it, Hill?"

Hill handed him several items. "I found these in the bottom of Mr. Collins's trunk. I know they do not belong to him."

Anger building within, Mr. Bennet pondered his choices for a moment. "Do you think your nephew Tobias would wish to make some extra money?" Tobias Hill did the odd jobs in the village that took strength but not too much thinking. Being a large man, he was intimidating to those who did not know him, but he was a gentle giant of a man who did not fight unless it was to protect another.

"I am certain he would, sir."

"Send someone to find him. I wish for him to stand guard above stairs. Who knows what mischief Collins might try to get up to this night?" Mr. Bennet sighed wearily. He did not like taking such action, but he knew it was in his family's best interest.

As Hill turned to his tasks, Mr. Bennet re-entered his study. He found Collins sitting with his arms crossed, obviously unhappy to be detained.

Once he reached his desk, Bennet placed the items on the front edge. "These were found in your trunk. How do you explain their presence there?"

"How dare you invade my privacy?" Collins blustered.

"How dare you steal from my daughters and my wife?" Bennet ground out. "And before you tell me that you were merely taking possession of a few things that will be yours when I pass, I will tell you not one thing you took is part of your inheritance. The pearls belong solely to Jane, as does the necklace you took from Elizabeth's room, and the gold snuff box is my wife's keepsake of her father.

"You, sir, are a thief and a lecher who, besides going into the private chambers of my family, has not so slyly accosted two of my daughters. I will not have such a person in my home. You may turn them out when I am dead but, until such time, you shall not be welcomed in my home again."

By the time Mr. Bennet had finished his speech, Collins seemed to shrink even further into his chair. However, he opened his mouth to protest. He would not endure such insults from his cousin. After all, he had gained the notice of Lady Catherine de Bourgh and would be the means of providing for the whole of the family by marriage to one of the girls.

"Silence," Mr. Bennet ordered, "I do not want to hear any more from you."

Mr. Bennet stood over him, clenching his fists. "Also, I do not want to hear any rumours concerning any member of my family. I have enough evidence that I can send to your bishop. I am sure that he would frown upon your actions. You would be removed from your post. Should any gossip concerning my family come to light, I will press charges against you as well. You will be fortunate if you are allowed to read sermons on a transport ship."

Staring coldly into his cousin's face, Bennet asked, "Have I made myself clear?"

"Yes," Collins assented quietly, fearful that his cousin might hit him. "I shall retire to my chambers."

"You do that, and do not leave your room for any reason. Breakfast will be brought to you early in the morning before my carriage will take you to catch the post."

Bennet followed Collins from the library and locked the door. He saw Tobias standing next to the butler. Walking to them, he whispered, "Thank you for coming, Tobias. Take a chair and sit outside of the guest chamber. Do not allow that man to leave the room until I come for him in the morning."

He jokingly added, "I suppose you can escort him from the room if there is a fire."

The other two men smiled before they went about their tasks.

Chapter 4

Darcy sat in an overly ornate drawing room belonging to some acquaintance of the Hursts who lived a thirty minute ride from Meryton. It was the invitation to dine there that gave Caroline the excuse not to dine with the Bennets.

The Thorndikes were an older couple who had only recently returned from a trip to Bath. The Bingleys' aunt went to school with Mrs. Thorndike and kept her apprised of her family's doings.

Unable to sit still any longer, Darcy moved to the small window and stared out at the darkness. He was still trying to puzzle out the mystery of George Wickham, but his heart kept encouraging him to consider Miss Elizabeth Bennet. She had stolen into his dreams at night and would not be totally banished from his thoughts during his waking hours.

It seemed easier to try to understand how Wickham had made such a drastic change in his life. Darcy remembered when his cousin had come to him with Wickham's demand for money in lieu of the living. Why then was he now a curate here in Meryton when he told Richard he wished to study the law? That his former childhood companion could charm the town's people did not surprise him, but the fact that Darcy had discovered no debts at all in the whole of Meryton did.

One of the other gentlemen, Mr. Arthur Carlson, joined Darcy at his position at the window. "By chance, did you attend Cambridge, Mr. Darcy?"

Darcy gave the man his attention and answered, "I did."

"I wonder if you remember meeting my brother, Matthew. He mentioned meeting a Mr. Darcy once or twice. He said he even won a couple of games of cards with you."

Looking puzzled, Darcy answered, "I am sorry, but I do not recall your brother in any of my courses, and I have never played for money, especially not at university," Darcy answered rather brusquely.

"No, I am sure he did not attend any of the same classes, as he was a few years older than you. Matthew only mentioned your name and his winnings because he does not often win, you see."

"I assure you, I do not gamble, sir," Darcy insisted.

"I beg your pardon, Mr. Darcy," Carlson said, his face flushing in embarrassment. "He must have meant another man named Darcy."

Fully intending to inform the other gentleman that no other Darcy had attended Cambridge except himself and his father before him, he opened his mouth but was interrupted by Bingley.

"Darcy, Carlson, we are going to join the ladies," Charles informed them as they had been playing little attention to the other men in the room.

They nodded and followed the others from the room.

When Darcy arrived back in the drawing room, Miss Bingley was waiting for him. She took his arm to guide him to a settee.

"I thought you gentlemen would never join us," she said as she batted her lashes. "It is cruel of you to stay away so long."

"We were discussing estate matters. Mr. Thorndike has promised to lend me some books on the subject," Charles answered for Darcy.

"How dreadfully boring," Caroline yawned prettily, her hand over her mouth. "I am pleased that it does not fall to my lot to learn management of an estate. You men are to be pitied."

All the men laughed except Darcy who said, "Do not pity me, Miss Bingley. I find every matter pertaining to Pemberley to be rewarding and satisfying."

"Hear, hear," responded Mr. Thorndike with a smile.

"I find it an interesting pursuit, though challenging to a newcomer such as I," Charles stated modestly. "I have much to learn, but I believe I shall one day be nearly as good at it as Darcy here."

"It will be a great feat if you do, as you will never have an estate as grand as Pemberley," Caroline simpered as she flattered Darcy. "Netherfield pales in comparison, and the neighbouring estates, such as Longbourn, are quite insignificant to my brother's leased estate."

"You are correct, Caroline," Charles answered. "However, I do not need such a large estate to prove myself a competent land owner.

Darcy paid little attention to the conversation around him as he pondered his earlier exchange with Carlson. Who could have been using his name? He did not think it was Wickham because, when his cousin had told him about the debts of honour Wickham had acquired, he was certain that Fitzwilliam would have informed him before Darcy came to university.

When Charles asked him a question, Darcy forced his attention back to his present company and off the mystery, resolving to think upon it later.

* * *

That evening back at Netherfield after a miserable carriage ride with Miss Bingley, Darcy bid his hosts goodnight. He could not settle himself to sleep. For that reason, he lit more candles and set them on the small table close to the fireplace and brought out his drawing pad. This time his hands and mind did not cooperate with the idea he had to sketch a portrait of his sister. Instead the dark-eyed beauty of Miss Elizabeth Bennet emerged as the lead of his instrument scratched the surface of the page.

Darcy blushed as he caressed the picture. What was he doing allowing his imagination to flow so freely? It would not do for anyone to see his drawing. It seemed too intimate, too personal. He sighed and put the pad in its place in the trunk. Shaking his head, he blew out the candles and strode to his bed by the firelight.

* * *

Tossing about in his bed, Collins could not find sleep. He was far too angry at his cousin's order for him to leave. What would Lady Catherine say when he arrived so much earlier than he had planned and without a betrothal? It was not to be borne. He would marry one of his cousins. It did not matter particularly whether it was Elizabeth or Mary.

However, his cousin Bennet had been adamant that he would not give permission for a marriage to any of his daughters. Collins tried to think of a solution to the problem. It seemed too late to change Mr. Bennet's mind.

A plan began to form in his feeble mind. Bennet could not refuse if there was a compromise. Collins rubbed his hands together gleefully as he thought of the luscious curves of his cousins. He would simply sneak into the closest room, which he knew belonged to Mary. Even if she screamed when she found him in her bed, there would be no alternative for her or her father but to agree to a marriage.

Slowly opening his chamber door, Collins stepped out in the corridor. There was a candle at the end of the hall, but it did not give much illumination. He tiptoed toward his objective, using his hand to guide him along the wall. After he had gone only a few feet in the near total darkness, he found his way blocked by a solid mass of humanity.

Close to his ear, a quiet but menacing voice said, "You ain't allowed out here." A pair of massive hands lifted him from his feet and turned him around. Tobias then grasped Collins by the nape of his neck and propelled him back into his room and closed the door.

Collins's heart raced as he tried to catch his breath. He had never been so frightened in his life. He was not a small person, and yet that man, whoever he was, had lifted him as easily as one would lift a child.

Collins knew he had failed in his attempt and would not be marrying one of his cousins. Sagging in defeat against the door, fear caused him to shiver. He would need his wits about him to come up with an explanation for his patroness, which meant he needed his sleep. Once he had pulled the blankets up to his chin, he wondered if he could think of a way out of his predicament.

* * *

Just after the sun came up the next morning, Elizabeth dressed warmly and left her room. She smiled and nodded to Tobias who sat in the corridor. He gave a gap-toothed grin and a little wave back.

She slipped down the servants' stairs as was her wont when she planned an early morning stroll. Elizabeth arrived in the kitchen, hoping to find something to take with her.

On the table stood a small basket. Cook greeted her and motioned to the table, speaking in her own lilting way. "There be some fresh buttered bread, fruit, and a wrapped flask of tea and a tin cup. You won't be needing to be back for breakfast, if you don't want to. And you'll be wanting to take that ole rug with you. It's too cold for you to be a sitting on the ground this morning."

Laughing softly, Elizabeth thanked Cook and kissed her on her ruddy cheek before she picked up the basket and the rolled up rug. She donned the thick old coat and woollen bonnet she kept hanging by the back door.

Once outside she hastened down a little-used path that led to another trail that followed the stream to her favourite place in the whole of Longbourn. Elizabeth had discovered the small clearing next to the water when she was about ten years old. Her mother had been particularly critical of something she had done and had sent her outside to consider her behaviour.

At first, Elizabeth had been quite upset at the scolding, since she had only been trying to help the maid with her chores. As a little girl she did not think it was fair that the maid, who was about the same age as she was, had to scrub the floor when Lydia had been the one to spill the milk during a tantrum.

Having run away from the house in her pique, Elizabeth wandered, unaware of her surroundings, until she nearly collided with a tree. She glanced around her and was entranced by the beauty of the quiet place. The shade of the tree let only dappled sunlight onto the forest floor and the stream. The water bubbled cheerfully over the rocks while small fish swam beneath the surface.

Elizabeth had sat under the tree and took in the splendour about her. With her chin resting on her drawn up knees, she smiled and decided that this would be her special place. She began to consider why her mother would scold her merely for being helpful. It must be because she was the daughter of the master and mistress of the house. At her age, she was not certain why that should matter, but it obviously did to her mother. Finally, Lizzy decided she would ask her papa about it. He would explain to her in a way she could understand.

Eventually she did speak to her father, and he explained that while it was very good of her to wish to help the maid, her mama had not had a maid when she was little. She was often the one to mop up spills and do other unpleasant chores. The girls from wealthier families had teased her brutally about her rough, chapped hands and patched clothes. When her own father had finally made enough money to hire household servants, the former Miss Gardiner had promised herself that if she had daughters, they would never have to do maid's work. With a wink, Mr. Bennet had told Elizabeth that it was likely her mother's self-promise that made her cast her eye in his direction, since he was a relatively well-off gentleman's son.

Smiling at the memory of finding her serene retreat, Elizabeth arrived and spread out the rug beneath the shade of her old friend, the willow tree. She sat down and breathed in the crisp, early morning air. It had always calmed her before, but this time her mind would not settle as it usually did.

Happy that her father had dealt with Mr. Collins, and that he would be leaving this very morning, she could be at ease about him. Her father had given her back her garnet cross just before wishing her goodnight, and he asked that she not tell her mother about the theft.

Oddly enough, Lizzy's mind kept going back to a statement that Mr. Collins made during dinner. He had declared that Mr. Darcy was engaged to his cousin, Miss de Bourgh. Mr. Wickham had denied that it was possible and, in her heart, she hoped that he was correct. She nearly laughed at her contrary thoughts. *I do not care for the man, do I? Of course, I do not. He is arrogant, haughty, and . . . handsome.*

Shaking her head, she tried to argue with herself. He had insulted her; surely that was not in his favour. However, could Mr. Wickham be correct, and Mr. Darcy was not comfortable amongst strangers? Mr. Bingley had been badgering him to dance. How she wished she could figure it out.

A rumbling from her stomach reminded her of her hunger and made her giggle. She lifted the cloth that covered her breakfast and took out an apple. As she chewed, her gaze fell on a lone rider in the distance. He was too far away for her to recognize him, and when his horse galloped out of her sight, she figured she would never know who it was.

Elizabeth half filled the tin cup and rewrapped the flask. She was nearly finished with the apple and the tea when she heard a sound downstream from her. Glancing up, she saw the rider coming close to the stream. He paused to allow the horse to drink before fording the brook. Dismounting, he led the animal to a small but lush patch of grass and tied his reins to a limb. The man began to walk her way, and soon she realised that it was Mr. Darcy.

Elizabeth turned her head so that she would not be caught staring at him. She heard rather than saw when he was close enough to notice her and stop.

When he did not move or say anything after a couple of minutes, Elizabeth said, "Will you merely stand there staring, or might you like to join me on my comfortable, if a trifle shabby, rug? It is large enough to accommodate us both with room to spare."

She looked up to see him smile at her impertinence. *He is even more handsome when he smiles.* The thought brought pink to her cheeks. To cover her embarrassment, she moved over to one edge of the rug. "I would be happy to share my breakfast if you do not mind plain fare. I have fresh bread and butter, an apple, and some tea."

Darcy nodded his head and lowered himself to the ground. He accepted a piece of bread thickly spread with butter and took a bite.

As he chewed, Elizabeth poured herself a bit more tea before handing the flask to him. "I did not anticipate having a guest, so I have only one cup. I hope you do not mind."

"Not at all," he murmured before lifting the flask to his lips. He drank thirstily before saying, "I am obliged to you. Miss Bennet. I left Netherfield quite early this morning. I did not expect to see anyone about."

"I am not a lay abed either," she informed him. "In fact, I was the first of my family to arise today. Cook knows my habits, thus this feast."

"Is this still part of the Longbourn estate?" Darcy asked, trying to make conversation.

"It is, sir," she answered and pointed to the stream. "That is Long Bourn Brook after which my home is named. The hedge on the far side is the farthest border between my father's land and Netherfield."

"Then I am trespassing. I should depart," he added hastily, getting to his feet.

"No, sir, please do not go. You have not finished your breakfast," Elizabeth teased lightly.

Easing himself back to the rug, Darcy thanked her for her hospitality and accepted the apple she handed him.

After a moment or two of silence, Darcy spoke. "This is a special place. It is very tranquil. Do you spend much time here?"

"This is my thinking place. I only come here when I am trying to puzzle something out." Elizabeth was not sure why she would tell him this, but she decided she could trust him.

"And may I ask what it is that you are trying to puzzle out?"

"It is not what this time, but who."

"Who, may I ask, is this enigma?"

Elizabeth caught his eye and smiled before she said, "You, sir, are the mystery."

He looked stunned with the apple halfway to his mouth. "Me? What is it about me puzzles you, Miss Bennet?"

"I have heard so many differing reports about you to confuse me greatly. From one person I hear that you are a loyal, kind friend who has had some great hardships in his life. From another, I hear you are a great man of connections and fortune, destined to marry your equally wealthy well-connected cousin. Another says you are a kind, well-meaning man, while I myself heard you insult a young lady while refusing to dance with her when men were scarce and several ladies were in want of a partner."

Hearing his sharp intake of breath, Elizabeth was certain that he would leave for good this time. She felt shame for revealing her thoughts and hoped he would not go, but would explain himself to her.

However, Elizabeth was surprised when he spoke softly. "First of all, I must apologise, for it seems that you heard me make that patently false statement. It is no excuse, but I was in poor temper that night and did not wish to attend. Indeed, I would not have, if I could have been left alone without Miss Bingley. I knew that she did not wish to attend and would have insisted upon staying with me, a fate I am certain you would not wish upon me. However, I was rude and unkind to say such a thing at all, especially within the hearing of a lady. I beg you to forgive me."

Stunned by the speech and the obvious sincerity, Elizabeth could do nothing less than give her pardon. "Of course Mr. Darcy, I forgive you."

"Thank you." He seemed to ponder for a few moments whether to continue, before he said, "I have always tried to be a good friend to Bingley. And he is most amiable to give you such a glowing report of me, but I do not consider my life as one of hardships."

"You mistake me if you believe I was speaking of Mr. Bingley. Although I am certain that he would give you an excellent endorsement, I speak of the testimony of Mr. Wickham."

"Wickham!" There was disgust in Darcy's tone as he stood abruptly, paced a few paces away, before turning to face her again. "I am certain that you misunderstood him. I doubt that he would say anything positive about me."

"Please sit, sir," Elizabeth ordered calmly, surprising herself, but she was determined to find out what Mr. Darcy had against his former friend. "I think that we both would be more comfortable if you were seated."

Darcy seemed to debate whether or not to do her bidding, before he sighed and returned to his place on the rug. He ran his hands through his hair in agitation. Taking a deep breath and letting it out slowly, he began, "I am uncertain as to what Mr. Wickham has told you of our association."

"He told us about growing up at Pemberley, that his father was your late father's steward, and that your father was his godfather. Several times in our short acquaintance, he has spoken of his regret at the loss of your friendship. He would not speculate as to the reason for it, or when it happened."

"Did he tell you that he tried to elope with my sister who was only fifteen at the time?" he asked derisively.

"He did not, and I find it hard to believe that he would do such a thing. Are you certain that he did this?" Her voice was soft but sincere.

"My sister and her companion were in Ramsgate on holiday. I had rented a cottage for their use. After she had been gone for a few weeks, I began to miss her and decided to surprise her with a visit. When I got there, she and Wickham were about to enter a hired carriage with another older woman, a stranger to me. Georgiana seemed happy to see me. She told me that she had not thought her express would have gotten to me soon enough for me to arrive so swiftly."

"How did Mr. Wickham act when you arrived?" Elizabeth asked.

"He seemed relieved to see me. I had just asked them why they were leaving Ramsgate together when her companion ran toward us from up the lane. Mrs. Young was her name. She insisted that she had overheard the two plotting to elope.

"Both Wickham and Georgiana denied such a plan, stating that they were coming to Town to Darcy House to see me. Knowing what I knew about his past, I could not believe him, and it hurt me greatly that my sister would lie to me. She begged me to allow her to explain the reason for their journey, but I would not listen to more lies. I sent Wickham and his hired carriage away, along with the other woman. I dismissed the companion because she had not prevented the elopement attempt or written to inform me of it, after which I took my sister to Pemberley. It was a long silent trip. She refused to admit her folly, saying only that she had good reason, but since I believed her a liar and would not listen, she would not explain." Darcy sighed deeply as he finished his tale.

Elizabeth stared off into the distance, his tale foremost in her mind. She was convinced that Mr. Darcy would not tell something so scandalous about his sister if he did not think it was the truth, but she could not believe that Mr. Wickham was as bad as this.

After several moments of silent pondering, Elizabeth spoke. "You spoke of knowing Mr. Wickham's past as if it were not an exemplary one. What had he done?"

Frowning, Darcy wondered how much he should tell her. He finally decided that if she was to be guarded against the wiles of such a person, he would have to give her some of the details. First, he told her about the debts he had paid for him and the rumours of his seductions of young women. All the while, he gave his cousin as a witness.

"Do I understand you rightly that you did not actually observe any of these things for yourself, that it was your cousin who brought them to your attention?"

"Yes, but I would trust my cousin with my life. He has been a close companion since I was very young, and my father trusted him - so much so that he named him co-guardian to my sister."

"I see," she answered thoughtfully.

"There is one thing I do not understand about Wickham."

"Go on, sir," she encouraged.

"After my father died, he wrote to me, asking for money in lieu of the living at Kympton which my father granted him in his will. I sent him the money, three thousand pounds to be exact. He claimed he would use it in the study of the law. It should have been enough for him to live on for a great deal of time, but a few years later when the incumbent passed, he wrote to ask if the living had been left to him. He claimed to be qualified to take it."

"If all of this is so, and I do believe you, why did he ask for the money in the first place?" Elizabeth asked.

"There lies my confusion. I have no idea, unless he had squandered the money in loose living and was desperate," he said, then added, "If this were so, why would he work at such a desolate mission? Those in charge of the place must not have known what kind of man he is."

Silence reigned again until he pondered out loud, "Perhaps he had repented of his ways and decided to begin anew, but that does not explain his recent, near elopement with my sister."

Seeing his growing frustration, Elizabeth placed her hand lightly upon his arm. "Might I give a suggestion which could possibly lead to the answers you seek?"

Looking down at the dainty hand that rested upon his arm, Darcy marvelled at the warm thrill that the gesture gave him. Lifting his glance to her face, he made himself focus upon her question and replied, "I would be happy to hear your suggestion."

Darcy felt the loss when she placed her hand back in her lap before she spoke. "First, I would suggest that you talk to your sister and listen to what she has to say.

"Also, I believe that it would be a good idea to have Mr. Wickham investigated, beginning with his university years. How did he manage to stay out of debt in the years before you came to school? He told me that he was a few years older than you. Is that true?"

At his nod, she continued, "It would be good for the people of Meryton, be he as bad as you believe, if his past was clearly known to all. If he has been misrepresented to you, would you not wish to know it as well?"

Darcy thought of the good friend Wickham had seemed to be when they grew up. He was kind, thoughtful, and full of wit, bringing joy into Pemberley, especially after Darcy's mother died. George Darcy did not suffer fools either, and yet he trusted Wickham enough to allow him free access to the house and grounds of Pemberley. For his parents' sake, if not for his own peace of mind, he would find out the truth.

The thought came to Darcy that his cousin had not often been at Pemberley once Richard went to university until after the elder Darcy had passed away. He could not help but wonder why that could be.

"I think your suggestion has great merit, Miss Bennet. I will contact my man in London immediately to begin an inquiry."

Her brilliant smile made his breath hitch and his heart race. What was it about this country miss that caught his attention more than any other had ever done? *I must be on my guard* he told himself.

"I must be on my way, Miss Bennet. Thank you for sharing your breakfast and conversation with me." Darcy stood and bowed.

Elizabeth began to get to her feet, and Darcy offered her his hand in aid.

"It has been my pleasure to share my meagre fare with you. I appreciate your candour and your trust. I have one more thing to ask in return, if I may?" Elizabeth could not meet his eye, since what she wished to ask was highly impertinent.

"I believe that you and I are becoming friends. I will answer as truthfully as I can."

Clearing her throat, Elizabeth said, "I wish to know if Mr. Bingley is the kind of man who would toy with a lady's affections. My sister has developed feelings for him, but she is more naïve than I. I do not wish to see her broken-hearted should Mr. Bingley . . ." She could not think of the right words to finish her statement.

"Miss Bennet, I do understand your worry for your sister, having one of my own. I know my friend to be amiable and easy mannered. Many young ladies have found themselves enamoured of him, but he has never trifled with any. I have seen him fancy being in love before, however I have never seem him so besotted as now. I will be truthful. I had not seen any peculiar regard on Miss Bennet's part so I am surprised to hear that her affections have been engaged by my friend."

Forcing back the fierce words of defence of her sister, Elizabeth managed to speak with more composure than she felt. "My sister and I wish to marry for the deepest love. It is a rather lofty idea for gentle-women such as we are, since we have very small dowries.

"As I am certain you have noticed, my mother is quite anxious that her daughters marry. Unfortunately, she does not understand that her boastings and manipulations are so blatant as to frighten away suitors. Jane has endeavoured to hide her feelings so as to avoid the embarrassment that would inevitably fall upon her if the suitor would not be able to withstand the force that is my mother. Jane keeps her emotions under tight regulation."

Darcy rubbed his chin. He felt ashamed for judging a young lady for doing what he had done most of his life to prevent becoming entangled with young ladies of the *ton*.

"Thank you for explaining this to me. I admit my mistake and will encourage my friend should he ask for my advice."

Again the smile Elizabeth bestowed upon him was nearly incandescent. "Thank you, Mr. Darcy. I know that his sisters are not best pleased with his attentions to my sister. I feel that they may try to dissuade him from pursuing her."

"That may be so, but I shall do my best to see that they do not succeed, if my friend wishes to court Miss Bennet."

Darcy bowed once more and left for his horse, while Elizabeth stared after him in wonder. How was it that she could have been so wrong in her assessment of his character? He was indeed a proud man, but he was not overly so. He was truly, as Mr. Wickham said, a loyal, kind friend. She hoped, deep in her heart, that he would one day be more than a friend to her. *Foolish,* she called herself, *how could a gentleman such as he ever be more than a friend?*

Shaking herself from her sentimental thoughts, Elizabeth rolled up the rug and started back to Longbourn.

Chapter 5

As he began his journey back to Hunsford, William Collins still stung from the insult of being forced from Longbourn. To add more offence, his cousin had only been willing to pay for him to ride atop the coach. Afraid that he might fall to his death from such a high perch, Collins had had to pay the difference out of his own pocket in order to ride inside. This left him with little coin with which to purchase food when he arrived at the meal stop in Dinsbury some five miles from Hunsford.

Frustration caused him to nearly collide with a gentleman as he made his way to the cheaper taproom down the street. Collins apologised gruffly before he made to go on his way. A hearty greeting made him pause and look up.

"I did not expect to meet you here, Mr. Collins," the gentleman said, offering his hand. "Your curate told us you would not be returning for at least a fortnight."

"Mr. Langford, I must apologise for my lack of attention. I had planned to stay with my cousins longer, but I found that I was greatly deceived by his letter. He offered me such hope of a reconciliation between our two families. However, he and his family were quite crude and even insulting to a member of the clergy. I could not stay. I am certain that you understand my reluctance to continue in such a situation," Collins finished with a sad sigh.

"Of course, Mr. Collins, of course we do." Mr. Langford turned to the young lady who stood silently next to him. "Do we not, Eleanor?"

"Yes, indeed, Father," his daughter agreed.

"Where were you headed, sir?" Langford asked.

"I was going to take my meal at the Robin's Nest."

"Eleanor and I were intending to return to Wywyn Grove for a bit of refreshment. Why do you not join us?"

Collins's stomach rejoiced at the thought of more than the bread and ale that he could afford at the taproom, but he could not seem too eager. "I could not impose upon your hospitality. Besides I would miss my coach to Hunsford."

Langford slapped him on the back. "Nonsense, my good sir. I will send you home in my carriage. I will hear no more protests, Collins. I insist. My son and his wife have gone to Bath for a holiday. We are quite without company."

Before Collins could say more, the older gentleman had ordered his man to bring the cleric's trunk and load in the back of his vehicle. Langford even made sure that he received a refund for the rest of the ticket cost.

Pocketing the coins, Collins could not but bless his fortune. To arrive in Dinsbury just at the perfect time to meet with the Langfords was a stroke of good luck. Cheered by the knowledge that his belly would soon enjoy good food, he thanked both of them, long and profusely.

The Langfords were not officially members of his Hunsford parish, but they preferred to attend Collins's church instead of their own. There had been some hard feelings when Eleanor's brother, Wilbur Langford, had broken his courtship with the vicar's daughter to marry a young woman with a much larger dowry.

Miss Eleanor Langford sat demurely opposite Collins in her father's coach. At nearly eight and twenty, she kept house for her father, and had done so since her mother took ill and died nine years before. She loved her father and did not mind caring for Wywyn, but he was aging. Both her brother and sister-in-law treated her more like a servant than a sister. Eleanor knew that at her father's passing, things would be even more difficult for her. Her father's disposition had always been optimistic. He thoroughly believed that there was nothing amiss in the household, no matter how she tried to explain. She begged him to provide for her in his will, but he told her that he had Wilbur's promise to take care of her. "You will always have a home at Wywyn," he would assure her. Yes, she would have a place to live in servitude, genteel poverty, and loneliness, but not a home.

Eleanor knew that she was plain, bordering on homely, with her slight overbite, weak chin, and large nose. During her first two seasons, she had garnered no interest since her dowry was too small to tempt a fortune hunter. Her mother's illness had put a stop to her going to London the third year.

Being unused to Town society, she had welcomed the reprieve, thinking that she could go to Bath once her mother recovered. However, her mother never recovered, and now, almost eleven years since her come-out at seventeen, Eleanor was most desperate to find a husband.

It has been rumoured that Mr. Collins had gone to Hertfordshire to find a wife amongst his cousins. Eleanor would try to discern if he had found one in such a short time.

"Mr. Collins, how did you find your young cousins? Are they the beauties they were rumoured to be?" she enquired in a disinterested tone.

Surprised by the questions, Collins sat speechless for a few seconds before he recovered his voice. "I suppose they were pleasant enough, but nothing out of the common way. Their manners were appalling, which is especially unattractive to me."

"I am sorry to hear it," she replied sympathetically, hiding her glee.

"Indeed," Mr. Langford added. "It is difficult when one is disappointed by the behaviour of one's family."

Seeing that they were about to enter the gate at Wywyn, Eleanor smiled and turned to her father. "Papa, do you not think it a good idea, what with Wilbur and Mildred being away, that we invite Mr. Collins to spend the rest of the fortnight with us? He should be allowed to enjoy his holiday, should he not?"

"Excellent plan, my dear!" Mr. Langford beamed at her. "I have felt rather lonely since Wilbur left, without decent company."

Eleanor swallowed the pain her father's comment unintentionally gave her. She had always known that he did not think her intelligent enough for good conversation. Of course, his idea of good conversation consisted of shooting, cards, and horses. At this moment, she was pleased that he had so readily agreed to her scheme, and Mr. Collins seemed to be quite excited at the prospect. Her mind whirled with the plan that was forming, the goal of which was to become betrothed to Mr. William Collins before a fortnight had passed.

* * *

Elizabeth found Longbourn unusually quiet when she returned, until she entered the breakfast room. Her father and sisters sat enjoying their food.

"Ah, Lizzy, you have finally arrived," her father teased. "I had thought to send out a search party."

"I am not so late as that, Papa," she protested lightly as she sat and poured herself some tea.

"Where is Mama this morning?" she asked as she spread jam on a piece of toast.

"Mama is unhappy that Mr. Collins has gone," chimed in Lydia around a mouthful of food.

"So he has truly left?"

"Oh yes, Lizzy," her father's tone was firm. "I would not allow him to stay here any longer."

"And Papa will not tell us why," Lydia complained. "It is not fair."

"I am surprised that you are disappointed that my cousin is gone." Mr. Bennet's expression was serious as he added, "I can always send him a message and tell him that you wish him to call on you."

"No, I do not wish him here," Lydia shrieked. "I only wish to know why he is not."

"We do not always get what we wish for, Lydia," Mary said calmly before she took a sip of her tea.

Lydia huffed, but said no more.

Conversation soon turned to other pleasant topics, including the discussion of the previous night's dinner and company. Lydia was especially animated in her delighted recitations of the charms of Colonel Forster.

Kitty interrupted with a frown, "I found his conversation a trifle boring. However, Mr. Denny's was fascinating. He was quite attentive to me throughout the evening. I was pleased with Mama's seating arrangements."

Ignoring her sister's speech, Lydia made to continue her recitation of Colonel Forster's fine traits when her father put down his fork and stood.

"Lydia, please join me in my study when you are finished with your breakfast."

"What have I done?" she objected. "I am certain I have done nothing wrong."

"I did not say that I wished to scold you," he said with a teasing look. "I merely wish to speak to you in private."

Mr. Bennet winked at Elizabeth before he left the room.

Quite intrigued by her father's request, Lydia hastened to finish her tea and toast before she left the table without excusing herself.

Hurrying across the corridor, Lydia knocked on her father's door and was bid to enter. When he did not speak, she scanned the room as if there was something that would give her a hint as to why her father asked her to come. She had just decided to break the silence when he spoke.

"Please sit down, Lydia."

Smiling at her swift obedience, Mr. Bennet leaned back in his chair. "You behaved very well at last night's gathering. I would have almost thought you were not there if I had not witnessed you several times during the evening. There was no loud laughter or blatant flirting. Can you tell me the cause for such improvement?"

Lydia was taken aback by her father's teasing compliment. It was almost the same way he spoke to Lizzy. So pleased was she that she tried to think of the reason for her actions the previous night. After a few moments of thought, she realised it was all due to the presence of Colonel Forster.

"I am not certain why, but I was so involved with my conversation with the colonel that I did not think to flirt. Papa, he treats me like I am sensible, and that makes me wish to be sensible when I am with him. He is handsome, to be sure. However, it is his manner and conduct that is most attractive. I have overheard his men give him a good name as well."

"So would I be safe in saying that you like the colonel?"

Clasping her hands together over her heart, Lydia sighed, "Oh yes, Papa, very much. He is everything I have ever dreamed of."

"Well, Lydia, it would seem that he feels the same way about you." He paused, almost regretting the loss of his youngest and most lively daughter, as it was almost certain what the outcome of a courtship between the pair would be. "I spoke with the colonel last night, and he wishes to enter into a courtship with you."

Bennet braced himself for the outburst he was convinced would follow his words, but he was surprised by the sudden tears that filled Lydia's eyes.

In a quiet, tear-filled voice, she asked, "So soon?"

Pleased by her subdued tone, he went to sit next to her and took her hand. "I admit that I thought it was quite early in your acquaintance for him to be asking to court you, but he convinced me of his good intentions."

"Did you agree to allow it, Papa?"

Taking his handkerchief out of his pocket, Mr. Bennet wiped her tears. "I did, but we will not announce it until tomorrow when he comes to call. I invited him to come to have tea."

"Oh thank you, Papa!" Lydia threw her arms around his neck and kissed his cheek. "I cannot wait to tell Mama the good news."

When she made to stand, Mr. Bennet restrained her. "No, you must not tell your mother or your sisters either. There will be enough time for her raptures when the announcement is made."

"But Papa, could I not tell Kitty? I am afraid that I might burst if I cannot tell someone."

Patting her hand, her father smiled and answered, "I believe that you may tell Lizzy, but only her. If the news got around to the colonel before your courtship is made official, he might change his mind."

Lydia gasped, "Oh, I would not wish for that. I shall be satisfied with talking to Lizzy about it."

"One more thing before you leave . . ." Mr. Bennet pondered how to express his next thought. He did not wish to shatter the fragile new accord between them.

"What is it, Papa?" Lydia was trying to be patient, but she was anxious to share her wonderful news.

"I think you should ask your sister for advice on how to be a lady." He held up his hand to keep her from arguing. "She is older and has wisdom from which you could benefit. Courtships often end up in marriage. You will want to act as a young woman now, if you are to eventually become an officer's wife. Do you not agree?"

The idea of marrying an officer had always been her dream. However, she had never thought of how an officer's wife might need to behave differently than a young girl such as herself. Colonel Forster did not know her well. He might begin to see her as her father often did. She could be silly, that she knew, and flighty. On the other hand, Lizzy always acted the proper lady, except perhaps her habitual ramblings about the country. Her sister just might be able to show her how to improve, so that she did not lose her chance at the realization of her life-long dream.

"I think you are right. I will ask Lizzy for her help."

"Good girl, Lyddie," Mr. Bennet approved. "You may go now."

* * *

For Darcy, the rest of the morning did not go as well as he would have wished. When he arrived back at Netherfield, he was immediately accosted by Caroline Bingley.

"Mr. Darcy, we had worried that you would never come back," she scolded, while latching onto his arm and batting her eyelashes. "I hope that you are well and that your horse has not come up lame."

"Nothing untoward has happened to me or my horse," Darcy answered while disentangling himself from her clinging hand. "Excuse me, while I change."

Without waiting for her reply, Darcy hastened up the stairs as quickly as he could without running. Inside his chambers, he was helped out of his riding outfit by his man Peters.

"When you are finished with me, I would like to have some tea delivered to my sitting room. I have some correspondence I need to see to before I join the others."

"As you wish, sir," Peters answered quickly.

Soon Darcy was refreshed and seated at the table with his travelling desk in front of him. Ten minutes later, Peters brought in coffee with some fruit and cheese.

As he placed the items on the table, Peters said, "Miss Bingley was insistent that you have more than tea since you did not have breakfast."

Grimacing at his hostess's action, Darcy sighed and lifted the coffee cup to his lips. "I will drink the coffee, though I would have preferred tea. However, I do not want the food. Perhaps there is someone on the staff who might enjoy it more."

Darcy had known the Bingleys for several years. Yet, in all that time, Miss Bingley still had not learned his preferences. He had never cared for cheese, especially not with oranges, but that is exactly what she had sent up to him. He wondered if he were more direct, she might take the hint.

Darcy decided to tell Miss Bingley as politely but firmly as possible that he did not care for cheese and oranges. This might do the trick and not waste food.

"Right away, sir," Peters replied, his lips tight to avoid smiling.

Darcy spent the greater part of an hour outlining in detail what he required from his solicitor. He insisted upon secrecy since he did not wish anyone to be aware of his investigation. On the off chance his cousin had not been completely honest with him, Darcy wanted to have all of the information before he confronted him and acquitted Wickham of wrongdoing. However, Darcy did not expect to find anything but the facts as he now thought them to be.

As he sanded the pages, there was another knock on his door.

"Peters, see who that is." Darcy was not happy at being disturbed once again, until he heard Bingley greet his valet.

"Come in, Bingley, but please close the door," Darcy said.

"I am sorry to bother you since I know you are busy, but I need to talk to you." Charles stood next to Darcy's desk, shuffling from foot to foot nervously.

"Peters, bring that extra chair closer," Darcy said, leaning back in his chair. "Please sit. You are making me nervous, fidgeting like that."

Bingley slumped in the chair and expelled an exasperated breath. "You know that I promised to host a ball as soon as possible after Miss Bennet regained her health."

Nodding, Darcy said, "It should be soon unless you plan a Christmas ball."

"Then you would not object?" Charles sat forward eagerly. "Caroline said that you would not wish to attend a ball in this place."

"As your guest, I am not the one who should make that decision," Darcy paused to gather the proper words. "However, if you wish for my opinion, I think it a fine idea. You have been entertained by many of your neighbours. You have the obligation to return those invitations. A ball would be a good way to do so, and I am certain would meet with a great deal of enthusiasm from the folks in and around Meryton."

"But what of you, Darcy? I know that you did not enjoy the assembly we attended when we first came here." Charles truly did not wish to distress his friend.

"I am not comfortable with people I do not know," Darcy said honestly, "However, I have come to know your neighbours. For the most part, they are kind and friendly, and they do not put on the kind of airs we find in the *ton*. I believe I shall enjoy the ball as much as I have enjoyed any others I have attended."

Charles grinned happily and hopped up from his chair. "Thank you, Darcy. I shall inform Caroline and ask her to begin planning and writing the invitations immediately."

Watching his friend leave the room, Darcy could not help but smile a little. Charles would enjoy his role as host to a private ball and his dances with Miss Bennet while Darcy determined that he would secure a set or two with the lovely Elizabeth Bennet at the first opportunity.

After his impromptu breakfast picnic and conversation with that young lady, and despite her less than lofty connections, he wished to know her better. He would make sure that he met with her before the ball. She should be made aware that he was following her advice. It would also give him a chance to ask for the first set before anyone else did.

Thinking of his conversation with Miss Elizabeth caused him to remember his missive to his solicitor. If he wished to have the investigation done swiftly, he needed to get the letter sealed and delivered. He decided to take extra precautions for the safety of his sister's reputation. He reopened the missive he had just folded and added the specific instruction that any and all correspondence was to be sent express, and to be given directly to Darcy himself and no other. If he was not available the messenger was to wait or to speak to his valet for further instructions. Having done so, he gave Peters orders to send for an express rider.

Chapter 6

After leaving her father's book room, Lydia went to her room to think on the wonderful news. As she sat on her bed, she pondered her future. She was to be courted, and by a colonel. *Perhaps he might propose soon.* It seemed like a dream, or a tease from her papa, but she knew that he was not so cruel. It had to be true. Just the thought of it caused her to feel ready to burst if she did not share it with someone.

Normally, Lydia might ignore her father's order of silence. However, with so much at stake, she did not wish to risk losing her courtship before it began. Papa might just decide she was not ready. She knew he already doubted her. *I shall show him that I can be responsible and mature enough.*

Leaping to her feet, Lydia left her chambers to find Elizabeth. She finally found her in the garden, walking rather absentmindedly along the path through the little wilderness near the house. Lydia liked the untamed look of that part of their garden, especially in the spring when one never knew where a new plant or flower would pop out of the ground as if to say, "Surprise! I wager you did not expect to see me here."

Lydia caught Elizabeth's hand. "Lizzy, I have much to tell and a favour to ask of you."

Although Elizabeth was surprised by her youngest sister's earnest look and gesture, she smiled and asked, "What is it, Lydia?"

Linking arms with Elizabeth, Lydia began, "First of all, you must promise to tell no one, not even Jane. Papa insists that you are the only one who will not gossip."

"If Papa says I should not share it, I shall not disobey him. I will keep your secret as long as is needed," Lizzy agreed with a grin.

"Oh good, thank you Lizzy," Lydia sighed in relief. "Colonel Forster is coming to take tea with us tomorrow. He and Papa will announce that the colonel and I are going to be in a formal courtship."

Lydia squeezed Elizabeth's arm tightly before with a wistful look upon her face, she whispered, "I can hardly deem it to be true. I did not speak with you immediately after Papa told me this morning because I could hardly believe it myself."

"Are you certain that Papa gave his permission? You are quite young." Elizabeth did not understand her father's willingness to agree to such a thing.

"Oh yes, but he did warn me to act more circumspect than I have before. That is why I wish for your help. You are so witty and lively, but you are never silly and loud. Papa thinks you can assist me in being more of a lady."

Giving Elizabeth's arm another squeeze, she begged, "Please say you will, Lizzy, please."

"You have not listened to any of my suggestions in the past."

"You are right, I have not, but I never understood the value in it before. I do not wish to frighten him away with my behaviour. It shall be hard enough for him to withstand Mama's outbursts. I do not wish him to think I am not mature enough to marry."

The earnestness of Lydia's expression was enough to convince Elizabeth to at least try to help her youngest sister. "Very well, Lydia, I will do what I can to help you."

Lydia squealed and threw her arms around her sister. "Thank you Lizzy. Let us go to my room, and you can help me decide upon what I shall wear for the visit."

* * *

Once Peters left to do as ordered, Darcy knew he could not stay in his room all day, as much as he wished it. He stood and straightened his jacket before leaving for the front parlour.

When he arrived, he found Charles and his younger sister in an argument. He turned to leave the room, but Miss Bingley stopped him.

She hurried to his side and touched his arm. "Oh Mr. Darcy, you must help me convince Charles what a dreadful idea it is for him to host a ball here at Netherfield. I know how insupportable it is for you to be in such appalling and uncouth company. Surely it cannot be true that you told him that it was a good idea. I am certain that he must be teasing me for his own amusement."

Upon finishing her diatribe, she glared at her brother who sat with his arms crossed, but said nothing.

"You are mistaken, Miss Bingley," Darcy said as he moved to stand next to his friend as if physically taking Bingley's side in the matter. "He is telling the truth. I think that a ball is something that shall help his standing in the neighbourhood and is what any gentlemen in his situation would do."

Bright red spots flashed upon Miss Bingley's cheeks as she strove to control her temper. She took several deep breaths, which did not seem to calm her. Finally, she croaked out a short, "Very well," and, without excusing herself, she left the room.

"I am sorry that I could not convince her on my own, Darcy." Bingley took a second to consider before he said, "I could ask Louisa to host the ball, but I have a feeling that Caroline will wish to exhibit her skills as a hostess for you once a few pieces of porcelain are broken and her temper cools."

"I am sure you are correct. However, I wish that she would not set her sights on me." Darcy looked his friend in the eye. "I have told you before that your sister is not the right woman for me."

"You have, and I have tried to explain that to her several times, but it is as if she has selective hearing, or she simply refuses to believe me. Either way, I do not think she will stop in her quest to be mistress of Pemberley until you choose and marry another."

* * *

In Lydia's bed chamber, Elizabeth struggled to rein in her youngest sister's enthusiasm, especially when it came to styling her hair. Thinking that maturity meant elaborate, Lydia kept insisting upon piling her hair atop her head and adorning it with her favourite pearl pins as if she was preparing for a ball instead of a morning call.

The more Elizabeth argued, the more stubborn Lydia became until the younger girl was close to tears and the older was ready to give up.

"Lydia," Elizabeth said through gritted teeth, barely containing her frustration, "you asked for my help, did you not? Papa told you I could help, did he not?"

"Yes," Lydia sighed dramatically, "But I am certain that I will look older if I wear my hair this way."

Deciding to take a different approach, Elizabeth said, "How did you style your hair for Aunt Phillips's card party?"

"Much as I always do; with some curls pulled up with a ribbon the same colour as my dress," Lydia answered thoughtfully.

"The colonel has chosen to court you without seeing you with such a sophisticated style. Why would you think that he would wish you to wear one now?" Elizabeth saw the idea finally get through as Lydia's shoulders slumped disappointedly.

"But I so wanted to look my prettiest for him," Lydia protested weakly.

This time, Elizabeth smiled. "And indeed, you will. You wisely chose a colour that flatters you, and yet is modest and mature in tone. All that is needed is the proper trim."

Lydia sighed, "That is one of the reasons I have not worn this particular frock since I received it from Aunt Gardiner. I do not have one ribbon that matches it well enough."

"We shall walk to Meryton, and I will treat you. It is a special occasion." Elizabeth took the dress's matching sash and folded it into her reticule. "We should be able to find the right ribbon if we have this with which to compare it."

Always excited about shopping, Lydia let out a squeak and hugged her sister. "Oh thank you, Lizzy. We shall have so much fun. Kitty shall wish to go as well, but we cannot tell her why we are buying the ribbon."

"Kitty will enjoy the outing, and I may buy her a bit of ribbon so that she does not feel left out."

"Oh yes!" Lydia cried, "I shall find her and tell her." Without another word, she leapt up from the chair and bounced from the room to find Kitty.

* * *

Once Miss Bingley left their presence, Bingley excused himself to see his steward and left Darcy to his own devices. As he decided to return to his own chambers, he realised that he had not received any correspondence from Georgiana. Turning, he located the butler, Fossett and asked, "Have there been any letters for me lately?"

"I could not say, sir," Fossett answered stiffly. "I do not examine the post myself. I have been ordered by Miss Bingley to bring all of the mail to her. She is the one who distributes it at the breakfast table."

"My man did tell you that any express that might come for me is to be given directly to me and no one else?" Darcy watched as the man nodded uncomfortably.

"I wish for you to also deliver any post that is addressed to me directly, not to Miss Bingley first." Darcy commanded.

The butler's face showed his reluctance.

"You seem to have a problem with my request."

"With all due respect," Fossett began, "The mistress gave me strict orders. I will lose my position here if I disobey her."

Darcy stared at the man in disbelief. Miss Bingley would fire a servant for giving Darcy his own correspondence.

With determination, Darcy ordered, "Follow me, Fossett. I believe your master will have something to say about this."

Knocking upon the study door and entering at Bingley's bid of "come in," Darcy stood in front of his friend and the steward who had been studying a piece of paper on the desk.

"Pardon me for interrupting you, but I wish to have a brief moment of your time on an important matter."

"Of course, Darcy," Bingley said as he gestured to a chair. "Do sit down.

Turning to his steward, he added, "Lewis, would you please step outside for a few minutes? Perhaps Fossett might offer you some refreshments."

"Actually, Fossett must stay with us," Darcy stated.

With a nod, the steward left the room and closed the door behind him.

"What might I do for you, Darcy? Has Fossett done something to displease you?"

"No, but when I asked him to give me my post directly instead of to Miss Bingley first as she has ordered, he told me he feared losing his job," Darcy said.

Bingley looked up in shock. "My sister told you that she would fire you if you gave the post to Darcy?"

"Well sir, when you first arrived, she did say that any and all correspondence must be given to her first, no exceptions," Fossett assured him.

"Fossett, I am master of this house, and I alone have the authority to hire or terminate employment. From now on, you will give any post addressed to Darcy or myself directly to us. If my sister questions you about it, you may inform her that I have ordered you to do so."

Fossett's posture straightened. "Yes sir, I will do as you say."

"And unless Darcy has something more about which to speak to me, please leave and ask Mr. Lewis to return."

"Thank you, Bingley," Darcy said before standing. "I will leave you to your business. I have a letter to write."

For the next half hour, Darcy wrote to Georgiana. It proved to be a difficult letter to form since they had barely spoken to one another before he left. Also, after this amount of time apart, he normally would have received at least three letters from her.

He finally decided upon a brief apology for waiting so long to correspond, and asked as kindly as he could why she had not written to him. With that out of the way, he merely told her about Netherfield and the people he had met.

Once he finished the missive, Darcy felt as if a weight had been lifted. He loved his sister very much and missed her more than ever. He pondered as to why, and realised that it was because he had left without reconciling with her. He hoped that she would respond quickly and that she would forgive him.

Sealing the letter, Darcy chose to go to Meryton to post it himself. He wished for it to be on its way as soon as possible. He rang for a servant and ordered that his horse be readied. Within ten minutes he was on his way.

* * *

That same day, the November sun shone on George Wickham's face and woke him. He smiled at the lovely blue sky outside his small window. When he was first led to his room, it had pleased him that it faced east. Although it was not as large as his chambers at Pemberley, it was larger and a great deal more cheerful than the one he had shared at the mission.

Every morning, George blessed Providence for the opportunity to meet and then to work with such a kind and devout man as Mr. North. The parson had not only offered him the position as curate, but he and Mrs. North had welcomed him into to their home. They would not allow him to pay them room and board because they wanted him to save as much of his money as he could toward the purchase of the living at Meryton.

Wickham had invested the thousand pounds from George Darcy's bequest and added to it as often as possible. It had grown over the last few years, but without the generous assistance of the Norths, he did not know when he would have had enough.

Having only two daughters, only one of whom survived to adulthood, Mr. North had no one to whom he could pass the living, which he owned outright. His father, Edwin North, had been a wealthy gentleman with three sons. With only one living to bestow on his younger sons, he had decided to purchase another for his youngest boy.[1] He found out one of his friends was in great need of funds because of his only son's gambling and carousing. Purchasing the living, the senior Mr, North guaranteed that neither of his younger sons would need to join the military. He gave the living to his youngest outright.

Grateful to his father for his generous provision, the youngest Mr. North worked hard and was well loved and respected in his parish. As he was beginning to feel his age, and after searching for several years to find the right candidate, he nearly despaired that he would ever find someone. The chance visit to the mission in London and the glowing report given by the director of the mission convinced him that he had found exactly the right person, especially once they finally met.

---

1 "Legally, advowsons were treated as real property that could be held or conveyed and conversely could be taken or encumbered, in the same way as a parcel of land." See Wikipedia https://en.wikipedia.org/wiki/Advowson

The next summer, the Norths planned to travel to visit their daughter who lived in Durham. After another year, Mr. North was certain that no matter how much or how little Wickham had saved, he would turn over the parish to George's care permanently.

Once George had partaken of breakfast, he decided to make more calls on the parishioners. Mr. North was not feeling well and encouraged Wickham to visit a few of the tenants' homes, beginning with those of Longbourn.

At the mention of Miss Mary Bennet's home, George was eager to make the calls. Having no horse of his own, and not wishing to ask for the parson's carriage on such a fine day, he strolled into town on his way.

Smiling and lifting his hat to those he passed by, George made his way as far as the post office when he saw a horse that looked familiar to him. As he moved closer, he noticed that the horse had a white fetlock on his right front leg.

Smiling, he approached the lad who was holding the reins. "Hello, Ernest, that is a fine animal you have care of. Would it happen to be Apollo, Mr. Darcy's horse?"

"Yes, sir, Mr. Wickham," Ernest grinned proudly. "I am real good with horses, I am."

"That you are, young man." Darcy, who had arrived just at that moment, reached for the reins and tossed the boy a shilling.

"Thank you sir," the boy called out as he ran across High Street toward his father's shop.

"Good day, Darcy," Wickham greeted him genially.

"Wickham," Darcy answered with much less warmth.

George was surprised when the horse moved forward a step to begin nibbling at his coat pocket. Laughing, he rubbed the animal's velvety nose. "I have no treat for you today, but I am pleased that you remembered me after all this time."

Apollo had been a gift to Darcy from his father upon his graduation from university. The senior Darcy had also given a horse to Wickham a few years earlier for the same reason. It had pained George, but he had been forced to sell him when he started working at the mission as there was no place for such a beautiful purebred in the underbelly of London.

"You do not ride Zeus?" Darcy asked in spite of himself.

"I am afraid that I no longer own him," George stated simply.

"I am sorry to hear that. He was a good ride."

Wickham nodded before he changed the subject. "Darcy, I would like to speak to you about what happened at Ramsgate."

Although his first response was to turn his back on his former friend, the sincere look on Wickham's face stopped Darcy. Instead he said with honesty, "I cannot do that at this time, maybe at a later date, but not now."

Melancholy suffused George's face, but he said, "I will be ready when you are, Darcy." He turned and walked down the street and out of Meryton.

Darcy stared after Wickham for several moments. If he had not been present in Ramsgate or heard of the man's deeds at Cambridge, he would have been sure of George's sincerity. The more he saw of his old friend, the more certain he was that opening the investigation had been a good idea.

Wishing that he did not need to return to Netherfield, Darcy began to mount his horse when he heard female voices nearby. He paused and turned to see Elizabeth Bennet with two of her younger sisters. They were exiting a shop, two doors down from where he was standing.

Darcy realised that this might be the opportunity to speak with Miss Elizabeth that he had wished for earlier. Contrary to his usual habit, he called out to her. "Good morning Miss Elizabeth, Miss Kitty, Miss Lydia."

Obviously surprised to see him and to be greeted by him, Elizabeth smiled and said with a small curtsey, "Good morning, sir, I did not expect to see you in Meryton. My sisters and I were just doing a bit of ribbon shopping."

"Are you on your way back to Longbourn, or do you have more shopping to do?"

"I believe that we should be going back to Longbourn. My sisters are eager to show our purchases to my mother."

"Would you allow me to escort you as far as the road that turns toward Netherfield?" Darcy asked as he drew closer to the trio.

"Of course, if you wish," Elizabeth assented on behalf of them all.

As they walked, Lydia and Kitty soon grew bored of the silence and hurried ahead, giggling and chatting about the lovely ribbons they had found.

"I am sorry about my sisters' behaviour," Elizabeth apologised. "I hope they did not offend you."

"On the contrary, Miss Bennet," Darcy reassured her. "I had been hoping for a few minutes of privacy."

"Oh?" Her astonishment was evident in her tone.

"I wanted to tell you that I have taken your excellent advice and started the investigation."

Her pleased smile seemed to wash over him like liquid sunshine. He felt his face heat, but he was quite content.

"I suppose it shall take some time before you know anything," she finally added.

"Yes, I suppose so, but I am relieved to have begun something which may solve the mystery for me."

They walked in quiet contemplation for a few moments before Darcy noticed how close they were to the place where they would part ways. He had one more thing to say, and he hoped that the previous smile was a good sign.

"Bingley is going to host a ball a fortnight from Tuesday next. I would like to secure two sets with you if you would be so kind?"

"As I have just now been made aware of the ball, I find that my dance card is quite empty," she teased with a smile. "Which sets do you wish to secure, sir?" Despite her jovial expression, Elizabeth was stunned and greatly pleased by his asking. Her heart raced as she awaited his answer.

"The first and the supper set, if you have no objection."

They had reached the fork in the road and stopped walking. Elizabeth looked up into his dark expressive eyes and spoke quietly, "I have no objection. In fact, I look forward to the chance to dance with you."

Although he wished to whoop the way he had done as a young boy when he was happy, Darcy merely thanked her, bowed, and mounted his horse. With a tip of his hat, he left in a cloud of dust.

Chapter 7

Deciding to visit Lucas Lodge first, since he would pass it on his way, Wickham was welcomed cordially and invited to take tea. He declined as he told them he had recently had breakfast. Although he did not say it, George was eager to finish at the Lucas's estate, so that he could get to Longbourn.

Finally, despite the long-winded farewells from Sir William and the not-so- subtle hints from Lady Lucas about the eligibility of her eldest daughter, Wickham was able to take his leave. He was thankful that Longbourn was such a short walk, as he did not wish to waste anymore time. Foremost in his mind were the soft green eyes of the gentle Miss Mary.

As he entered Longbourn house, the butler wanted to announce him to the master in his book room when George explained his errand.

"I would like to greet the ladies first, since I have been tasked with a greeting from Mr. and Mrs. North," Wickham said as he handed his hat to Mr. Hill.

"Very well, sir," Hill nodded stiffly, "If you will follow me to the parlour."

"Mr. George Wickham," Hill intoned as they reached the open door.

Bows and curtseys were exchanged before they were all seated again.

"We are surprised to see you again so soon, Mr. Wickham," Mrs. Bennet said before adding, "That is not to say we are displeased. Indeed, it is such a great pleasure to have more young people—especially handsome young men such as yourself—in our home. Is not that right, girls?"

All of the girls nodded, but Mary blushed at her mother's speech. It was certainly true for her that it was a pleasure to see Mr. Wickham again, but the obvious eagerness of her mother embarrassed her. Mary stared at her clasped hands while the curate relayed Mr. and Mrs. North's greetings and his purpose in coming that day.

"Oh, how kind of you to do so," Mrs. Bennet said. "I am sure that our tenants will be most obliged by your visiting them. My Elizabeth and Mary have taken over much of the duties of tending to their needs since my nerves have become such a problem for me. I never complain, but it has become very difficult for me to see to the needs of others when my own health is so indifferent."

Mary was so mortified by her mother's excuses that she stood suddenly. "My father is in his study. I shall show you to him now if you wish."

Taken aback by Miss Mary's abrupt offer, Wickham nevertheless stood and briefly took his leave before following her out of the parlour.

Eyes on the floor as she stood in the corridor, Mary whispered, "Please forgive my mother. She does not always understand how her speech affects others."

"I was not offended," George said just as quietly. "I am certain that she means no harm."

"That is gracious of you to say, sir." Mary allowed a brief smile to cross her face. As much as she would have liked to continue a conversation with Mr. Wickham, she knew he had come to meet Longbourn's tenants. She walked to her father's door and knocked.

Opening the door at her father's bidding, Mary said, "Mr. Wickham is here to see you. He wishes to meet our tenants."

"Do come in, Mr. Wickham," Mr. Bennet welcomed him.

Mary turned to leave, but her father stopped her. "Please wait, Mary. As I am sure that you and Lizzy know the tenants better than I by now, I think that the two of you would be better escorts than I. Go find Lizzy and have her go with you."

It did not take long for Elizabeth and Mary to ready themselves, so that they joined Wickham at the front door within five minutes. After Wickham asked several questions about the tenants they were to visit, Mary began to feel more at ease. What her mother had said about Lizzy and herself was true. They went to the workers' homes. Sometimes they merely visited, other times they brought food, clothing, and even small gifts for the children.

They had visited two of the closer homes before they reached the Taylor residence. Several young children of various ages came running to greet them with shouts of hello. When their mother told them to quiet, they obeyed swiftly.

"Welcome, Miss Elizabeth, Miss Mary," Mrs. Taylor curtseyed while eyeing the gentleman with them.

"I would like to introduce Mr. Wickham to you, Mrs. Taylor. He is the new curate serving with Mr. North," Mary replied before Lizzy could.

"Oh, I had heard there was a new curate." The woman blushed before adding, "My children are just getting over colds. I did not wish to bring them to church when they were ill."

"It is my pleasure to meet you, Mrs. Taylor." Wickham lifted his hat and bowed. "It is wise to keep children from public places when they are ill."

Smiling as the smallest of the four pulled on Mary's hand to get her attention, he said, "It would seem that they are quite well now. I hope to see you and your family at services Sunday."

"You will," she agreed before saying, "Won't you please come in? I have refreshments if you have the time."

Elizabeth answered for them all, "We would be happy to come in for a short visit, but refreshments are not necessary. Besides, Mr. Wickham will need to visit the Henleys and the Beckfords before he goes back to the parsonage."

"I would be happy to take you up on your kind offer at another time in the near future, Mrs. Taylor," Wickham added as he followed the ladies into the cottage.

While the Bennet sisters and Wickham chatted amiably with Mrs. Taylor, the children waited as patiently as they could for their chance to speak. The youngest girl, a perky four year-old named Floral[2], spoke as soon as there was a slight pause in the conversation. "We have new kitties, Miss Mary. Please come see them in the barn."

Glancing quickly at her companions, Mary stood. "If you do not mind, I had promised Floral that I would see the new kittens the next time I came."

---

2   Floral is not a misspelling. It was the first name of my grandmother.

Wickham, who had stood when Mary did, smiled and said, "I would love to join you if Miss Floral would not mind. I have a soft spot in my heart for kittens."

Floral was more than pleased to show the new gentleman her kittens, so she grasped his hand with her free one and led them out to the barn. Elizabeth and two of the other children followed behind.

Once inside the barn, Mary could hear the faint mewing of the kittens. Floral dropped the hands she had been holding and rushed to a far corner of the building that was partially hidden by a stack of hay.

"We mustn't scare the mama cat," Floral cautioned as she peered over the hay. "She is gentle, but she don't like loud noises."

Mary, Wickham, and Elizabeth gazed upon a litter of six kittens of various colours, most of whom where tumbling over each other in feline play. Floral kneeled down close to the bed and lifted two of them, one black and white, and one orange.

Mary took the tiny black and white ball of fluff in her hands while Wickham cradled the orange one. Neither of the little cats seemed to mind the attention they were getting.

"My Mama says we will have to find homes for most of them," Floral sighed sadly.

"The little one reminds me of my first cat, Rosebud," Wickham commented absently while rubbing the kitten between the ears.

"Why did you name it Rosebud?" Mary asked, smiling at the gentle way the man treated the kitten.

"He had a spot on his side that looked like the bud of a rose." He laughed softly and added, "When I found out he was a boy, I just called him Bud. I did not wish him to be embarrassed with a girl's name."

The group laughed at his statement. After one more stroke of the kitten's fur, Wickham and Mary put the little ones back with their mother.

"I am going to ask Mr. and Mrs. North if I could have a cat. I know they do not have one of their own. Please save that little fellow for me until I find time to ask them."

Mrs. Taylor, who had joined the group at the last, agreed. "We will do that. They are not ready to leave their mama just yet, so there is no hurry."

* * *

The rest of the time passed too quickly for two of the party. Elizabeth did enjoy watching the curate in his obvious quest to win the favour of her heretofore overlooked sister. His attention brought a glow to Mary's countenance and a nearly constant smile to her face.

When they arrived back at Longbourn, they found only Mr. Bennet, who peeked his head out of the book room door when he heard them enter.

"Ah, Lizzy, Mary, and Mr. Wickham," he said as he rubbed his chin. "I am afraid that Mrs. Bennet and your other sisters have gone to Meryton to visit your aunt Phillips. You may enjoy the peace and quiet of the parlour if you wish."

Mr. Wickham sighed inwardly as he regretfully declined. "I am gratified at the invitation, but I still have some work to do on my sermon for Sunday. I hope to see all of your family at services if not before." His address was obviously to the whole of the Bennet family, however he never took his eyes off of Mary as he spoke.

Even though Mr. Bennet was not the most observant of men at times, he smiled to see how things were developing. His impish love of a good tease was given full flight. "I am certain that Lydia and Kitty will be most pleased when they hear of this. I am not sure that Mary will attend. She can be most stubborn about Sunday services."

"Papa!" the girls exclaimed at once, their faces red with embarrassment.

Chuckling, Mr. Bennet winked at Wickham before he said, "I am certain that Mr. Wickham has heard of my rather different sense of humour. Sir, I hope you know that I was jesting. Mary is the most devout of my girls, and illness or inclement weather are the only things that have ever kept her from church."

"I have heard many speak of your humour, sir. Also, Miss Mary's moral and religious character is widely known. Mr. North was the first to tell me so, and about how much assistance she gives Mrs. North." He bowed to Mary before taking his leave.

Mr. Bennet smiled and wondered to himself how soon this middle daughter would be leaving the nest.

* * *

The next morning, Lydia awoke far earlier than she could ever remember doing. This was the day when her whole family would learn of her courtship with Colonel Forster. As she lay in the grey light before dawn, she felt the nearly irresistible urge to jump on her bed as she had as a child. Happiness seemed to scream for some sort of release, but if she were to continue on her quest to be ladylike enough to marry her handsome colonel, she was certain she must learn to control these kinds of urges.

Slipping out of bed as quietly as possible so as not to awaken Kitty, Lydia pulled on her robe. Hoping to find Lizzy awake since she was often up before the rest of the girls, she tiptoed down to her elder sister's room and knocked softly.

When Lydia heard the soft reply to enter, she opened the door swiftly. After she entered, she shut the door behind her. Seeing Elizabeth stirring the coals since it was rather chilly in the room, she waited for her elder sister to sit on the bed. Lydia hastened to join her and hugged her tightly, while whispering excitedly, "Oh I am so glad that you are awake. With all of the excitement inside, I feel like it might burst out of my skin if I do not share it."

Although Elizabeth was not used to her youngest sister's affection, she smiled. "You are up so early. I suppose I should not be surprised. It is a very special day for you."

Lydia sighed blissfully. "I am so glad that you understand."

She giggled before she covered her mouth. Lydia added a self-admonishment, "I must be more ladylike. I am sure that gentlewomen do not giggle."

Elizabeth shook her head. "I am certain that even highly born ladies giggle, especially when they are in the company of a sister."

Lydia's face brightened with a big smile. She asked, "I will tell you why I laughed if you promise not to scold me too much, especially since I only thought about doing it but stopped myself."

Receiving Elizabeth's nod, Lydia related, "I awoke so happy and excited that my first thought was how fun it would be to jump on my bed like I did when I was little. But I remembered that I am a young lady now, and as such I would not give into the whim."

At Elizabeth's grin, Lydia continued, nearly choking on her laughter, "Just now, I thought of how shocked Kitty would have been, especially if I had bounced her off the bed."

Grabbing a pillow, Elizabeth stifled her laughter in it. Lydia followed suit with the other pillow. It seemed to take forever for their humour to subside, but when it finally did Lydia hugged her sister again.

"Thank you, Lizzy," Lydia said as she kissed her sister's cheek. "I feel better now. I am not surprised that you would know of some outlet for all of my happy energy."

"But, Lyddie, you were the one who thought of it," Elizabeth corrected. "You showed a great deal of restraint in not jumping Kitty off the bed."

"Oh, Lizzy, do stop. I do not know if I shall be able to see Kitty without laughing. I do not think that she would understand, and I would not wish to insult her."

"Of course, you are right."

Lydia noticed the small clock next to Lizzy's bed. "It is too early for me to get dressed, and breakfast will not be ready for over an hour. What shall I do to keep from going distracted and doing something foolish?"

"I could help you with your hair," Elizabeth suggested. "And we could discuss how you will react to our mother's effusions, for you know that they will be loud and long."

The contented smile slipped from Lydia's face. "I had forgotten about Mama. Do you think she will frighten the colonel away? What if he thinks that I am not worth it with such an excitable mother?"

"My dear, you must recall that Colonel Forster has been in the company of Mama twice, once when he was here in our home. I am certain that if he were upset at our mother, he would not have asked to court you."

Heaving a sigh of relief, Lydia said, "How could I have forgotten? Thank you for reminding me."

Lydia untied the ribbon that held her hair and began to undo the plait. "How do you manage to keep so calm when Mama is so . . ." She stopped talking since she was at a loss as to what word to use that did not insult her mother. She loved her mama deeply, though she was finally seeing her in a different light.

"I try to keep from responding if I am able. You have likely noticed that I leave the room on a suddenly remembered chore quite frequently."

"Yes, and Mama seems vexed when you do," Lydia said, before adding, "I could not leave the colonel that way. It would be rude."

"Of course, you are correct." Elizabeth motioned for her sister to sit at the dressing table.

As Lizzy brushed her youngest sister's hair, a thought came to her. "If the weather cooperates, I shall suggest that we all go for a walk. You know that Mama will not want to join us, and the rest of us girls will be your chaperones."

"What a wonderful idea!" Lydia cried a little too loudly. She clapped her hand over her mouth. She looked at the door as if someone would enter at any moment to ask what the fuss was about.

When no one came, Lydia moved her hand and whispered, "I think Papa is right. You are the most sensible of us all."

* * *

When Lydia and Elizabeth arrived at breakfast, her mother's mouth dropped open.

"Why, Lydia dear, you are in very good looks today," Mrs. Bennet complimented. "Although, I do not see why you should dress so nicely when we are not expecting company."

"I wanted to show everyone how well Lizzy's gift of a new ribbon goes with this dress."

"As it does. You remind me of your mother when we were courting," Mr. Bennet said before sipping his coffee.

Mrs. Bennet blushed at the comment, too moved to speak.

Lydia opened her mouth to protest Mr. Bennet's mention of court-ship, but she caught his sly wink and smile. Settling back to finish her breakfast, she could not but return his expression.

Although the time until morning calls was finally upon them, Lydia felt it had been ages since breakfast. She sat next to Elizabeth while trying to work on a piece of embroidery, but she could not concentrate and finally let it fall to her lap.

Leaning close to her elder sister, Lydia whispered, "What if he does not come?"

Elizabeth took her hand and squeezed it, answering, "He will come, and soon."

Her words were prophetic because but five minutes later, Hill came into the room and announced, "Colonel Forster."

The ladies rose and curtseyed in response to his bow.

Mrs. Bennet exclaimed loudly, to the embarrassment of her girls, "You are very welcome, though we did not expect visitors today."

She looked around the room so that she could offer him a seat. When she saw that the closest one next to Lydia was taken by Elizabeth, she called out, "Lizzy, come sit here, so that the colonel can have that comfortable place to sit. And Hill, bring us some tea and refreshments right away."

Her husband interrupted her. "I have already ordered the refreshments, my dear."

The colonel smiled at Lydia but did not move to take the chair that Elizabeth had obediently vacated.

Confused by her husband and the colonel, who both continued to stand, Mrs. Bennet opened her mouth but closed it again when Mr. Bennet beckoned Lydia to his side.

"Colonel Forster is not here on an ordinary social call." Bennet paused when Hill came in with a tray which, instead of tea and cakes, contained glasses of wine, some larger than others. The butler served the smaller glasses to the ladies first before serving the men.

"Mr. Bennet, I demand you explain yourself," his wife demanded.

"Patience, Mrs. Bennet," he said firmly before he glanced around the room. "I have the pleasure of announcing the courtship of the colonel and Lydia."

Mr. Bennet lifted his glass and said, "To a successful courtship."

Automatically draining her glass, Mrs. Bennet seemed stupefied by the news. She opened her mouth several times, but no words came.

At a nod from his master, Hill poured another glass for his mistress before bowing and leaving the room.

The room suddenly went from nearly complete silence to a babble of female voices as Lydia's sisters rushed to her to express their happiness. It was these sounds and actions that finally brought back Mrs. Bennet's ability to speak.

"Oh my dearest Lydia, to be courting at barely sixteen and to such a handsome officer!" She threw her arms around her youngest daughter and kissed her. She may well have done the same to the colonel, but her husband took her arm and escorted back to the sofa.

Elizabeth heard his whispered admonishment. "Do no let your excitement carry you away."

Not long after the colonel and Lydia sat down, refreshments were brought in. Mrs. Bennet was kept too busy serving the tea and cakes to say much, but once everyone had food and drink, she began to question the colonel about his background and family.

Knowing her mother as she did, Elizabeth knew that very soon Mrs. Bennet would be asking about the officer's income and prospects for promotion. Lizzy looked out the window to see that the weather had cooperated. It was definitely time to suggest a walk.

The next time her mother took a breath, Elizabeth said, "Why do we not take advantage of the weather and give the colonel a tour of our gardens? Mama, Jane and I will be glad to be chaperones for Lydia. Mary and Kitty may come as well."

The colonel stood at Mr. Bennet's nod before Mrs. Bennet could comment and offered his arm to Lydia. "I would love to see Longbourn's grounds."

However, plans quickly changed when the Bingleys and Mr. Darcy were let into the house by the butler. Miss Bingley was secretly pleased that most of the Bennet daughters seemed to be on their way out.

Bingley frowned as he saw his angel donning her cloak and hat. "I see that we have come at a bad time. Perhaps we should call another day."

Mrs. Bennet had leapt to her feet at the sound of Bingley's voice and rushed into the vestibule. "They were only planning a walk in Longbourn's gardens. I am certain that you all would be welcome too, as Mary is to stay to keep me company."

"I would be happy to join everyone on their stroll, if I will not be intruding." Bingley spoke before his sister could object. They had come only to extend a personal invitation to their ball, but Charles wished to spend as much time with Miss Bennet as he could. With that in mind, he offered Jane his arm and guided her, following Lydia and the Colonel Forster, out of the door.

As Caroline stood, sputtering in an unladylike manner, a certain perverseness arose in Darcy. Smiling, he offered his arm to Elizabeth. He would have extended the same courtesy to Kitty, but she had already linked arms with Miss Bingley, while praising her walking partner's hat.

As the couples ambled through the gardens, Lydia and the colonel, and Jane and Bingley walked closely together. Darcy and Lizzy stayed some distance from the others.

"I was wondering," Elizabeth said so quietly that Darcy had to lean his head down to hear her, "how is the investigation going?"

"I have not heard from my man of business, but it has not been very long since I sent the message."

"Will you be attending services tomorrow?" she asked tentatively.

"As I make it a habit to do so, I wonder at your question."

"Mr. Wickham is to preach this Sunday. The Norths are taking a short trip to visit an old family friend. I believe they had planned to leave early this morning."

"I now have even more of a reason to go to church tomorrow. I want to see and hear Wickham for myself. One can tell quite a bit about a cleric by his sermons." He returned her pleased smile. *How easy it is to make her happy. I could get very fond of doing so.*

Though the others were enjoying their stroll, Caroline Bingley was livid. She should be the one strolling with Mr. Darcy, and not some inconsequential country chit. When he leaned his head toward that of Eliza's, he actually smiled at her.

Pulling on the arm that held her fast, Caroline tried to free herself, or at the very least hurry to catch up with them. She had been so focused upon one couple, that she had not been listening carefully to Kitty's compliments or gossipy chatter until Kitty spoke a trifle louder than before.

"Miss Bingley, I do not think you heard what I just said," Kitty commented gently. Quite used to being ignored at times by her own sisters, she was not upset.

"I beg your pardon, Miss Kitty. I was distracted," Caroline apologised insincerely. "What was it you were saying?"

Kitty nodded toward her younger sister and her beau. "I merely commented on what a lovely courting couple they make."

Gasping, Caroline's face lost all colour, and she would have lost her footing had Kitty not been holding onto her arm so tightly. Her own eyes had been on Mr. Darcy and Eliza so that she did not observe the direction in which Kitty had indicated. *It is not possible,* she told herself, but the woman's own sister would not lie to her.

"My dear, Miss Bingley, you do not look well. Let us return to the house. I am certain that one of my mother's restorative teas will help you." Kitty did not wait for an answer, but returned them to the house as quickly as she was able.

The housekeeper opened the door to see a very distressed Miss Bingley leaning heavily on Miss Kitty's arm. She hastened to remove the stunned woman's outerwear before she and Kitty assisted Caroline into the smaller of the two parlours.

"I would summon the mistress," Hill said, deeply concerned, "but she took Miss Mary with her to Meryton to spread the happy news of the courtship."

At the words of the housekeeper, Miss Bingley swooned. Fortunately for her, she had already been seated upon the sofa before she fainted.

Being used to her mother's fainting spells, Kitty ordered Hill to retrieve her mother's smelling salts and a cup of her soothing tea. "Just do not put a sedative in it, for we do not wish to explain why she is asleep."

Hill hurried to do as she was told. Soon she returned with the salts and a hot cup of tea laced liberally with brandy and sugar. Kitty held the vinaigrette filled with hartshorn to Miss Bingley's nose, which soon brought her back to consciousness.

Miss Bingley seemed confused at first, until she remembered why she had been so upset as to faint. Tears filled her eyes, and she would have begun to wail if Kitty had not spoken.

"Please, Miss Bingley, drink this tea slowly. It is a soothing blend that should calm your emotions."

Without as much as a thank you, Caroline sipped the concoction. At first, she nearly spit it out, however she soon began to relax. The warmth of the brandy filled the empty space that the awful news had caused. Leaning more fully against the back of the sofa, she drained the cup and asked for more.

Hill whispered to Kitty, "I am not certain it would be a good idea."

"Miss Bingley is our guest, and we do not refuse the request of one of our guests. What would Mama say?" Kitty asked firmly.

"Very well, Miss Kitty, I shall return directly." As she went into the kitchen. Hill decided not to put as much brandy in this cup of tea.

Chapter 8

A s the walking party arrived back at the house, Caroline finished
the last of her second cup of tea and begun giggling. Charles and
Jane were the first to enter the parlour, having been informed by Hill of
Miss Bingley's fainting spell.

Both Charles and Jane rushed to where Caroline half reclined on the
sofa. "Oh, Brother, Miss Kitty has been most kind to me."

Surprised by the statement, which was so unlike his sister, Charles
wondered if she had hit her head when she fainted. "Mrs. Hill told us
that you lost consciousness."

"I did, but dear Miss Kitty knew just what to do." Caroline smiled
cordially at Kitty before she hiccupped.

By this time the rest of the party had joined them. Caroline refused to
even glance in Darcy's direction. After answering a few more questions
about her health, she implored her brother to return her to Netherfield.
Her head was beginning to spin, and her stomach would not settle.

"What about the invitations we were going to deliver elsewhere?"
Charles asked quickly.

"We can give the Bennets theirs and have a servant deliver the rest
if I do not recover soon." `

The Netherfield party hastened to return to their home. Darcy,
though mystified by Miss Bingley's refusal to even look at him, was
glad that he had decided to ride Apollo to Longbourn instead of riding
inside the carriage.

Charles had chosen to accompany his sister, so he climbed in after
helping her inside. When he closed the door, he was amazed to see his
sister put her feet upon the seat. Caroline rested her head on her arm
and murmured something about taking a nap before she fell asleep.
When he leaned over to see if she had a fever, she belched.

Shocked to hear such an unladylike sound come from his sleeping sister, Charles almost missed the distinct odour of alcohol on her breath. There was no doubt in his mind that his sister was drunk. He wondered how that could have happened in such a short time. Certain that none of the Bennet ladies had the time or the inclination to ply her with spirits, he was stymied as to the cause. Deciding to wait until she was sober, he leaned back against the seat and pondered how he could get her to her chambers without the servants or the Hursts knowing of her condition.

Just as they reached Netherfield, Bingley thought of one servant he could trust to help him. His valet, Simkins, had always been trustworthy.

The carriage stopped at the front of the house. A footman quickly lowered the step and was astonished to see his mistress in a prone position.

"Fetch Simkins right away. My sister is ill, and I will need his assistance," Charles ordered without leaving the coach.

"I'd be more than happy to help you, sir," the footman answered eagerly.

"Thank you, but no, it must be Simkins," Bingley snapped.

Darcy watched the exchange from a short distance. Unable to discern the problem, he came closer as the footman went to summon Bingley's valet.

"Bingley," Darcy called as he reached the door of the carriage, "What is so important that only your man Simkins can help?"

Bingley sighed in frustration, running his fingers through his already unruly curls. "Caroline appears to be drunk. I do not know how it happened, but she is. I can trust only two people in this house to keep this quiet: Simkins and you. And I am certain that you do not wish to be seen carrying Caroline to her room."

The look of pure dismay on Darcy's face almost caused Bingley to laugh. Instead, he nodded and said, "I thought as much. I will have to tell Louisa and Hurst something, anything but the truth."

"Just tell them that she became ill suddenly and, until we know whether she is contagious or not, she should be left to the care of the apothecary. After his treatment of Miss Bennet, we know that he is competent and will keep this to himself."

Just then, the footman returned with Simkins. Charles ordered the footman to fetch the apothecary right away. Once the young man was out of sight, Bingley explained to his valet what must be done and the need for secrecy.

Simkins did not care for Miss Bingley due to her airs and arrogant attitude toward others. However, his loyalty to his master knew no bounds. He was also a fairly large man who could easily carry two Miss Bingleys. With Bingley's help to keep her modesty intact, Simkins was soon carrying the woman into the house, up to her room, and onto her bed.

Unsure of Caroline's lady's maid's ability to keep quiet, Charles instructed his valet to summon the girl to Caroline's small sitting room. When she arrived, she was shocked to see her mistress's brother standing in front of the fireplace.

"Harris, how long have you worked for my sister?"

"A year come June, sir," she answered meekly.

"Do you wish to stay in her employment?"

"I do, sir. I do try my best to do as she wishes, though I do make mistakes." Her honesty pleased Charles.

"My sister is in her room, rather indisposed."

The maid's eyes widened with concern. "I should go to her right away,"

"No." He stopped her. "I shall allow you to go to her in a few minutes, but I must ask for your silence at what you find there. Somehow, while we were delivering invitations, my sister became inebriated. I was not present when it happened. As you know, Caroline does not handle alcohol well. At the moment she is asleep."

Harris nodded and he continued, "If a single word about the true reason for her illness is bandied about, you will be let go and without a reference. Do I make myself clear?"

"Yes sir, I will keep mum about this," she agreed, wringing her hands. "May I go to my mistress now? I know how she would hate for her dress to become wrinkled because she slept in it."

"Go," Charles ordered and walked out of the room. In other circumstances, he would have gone to his study for a drink. However, for the time being, he would drink some strong coffee."

* * *

That Sunday the church in Meryton filled quickly, and with more people than was usual. It seemed that nearly everyone in the market town was eager to hear the young curate preach his first sermon. Very few were absent, with the notable exception of Miss Bingley and the Hursts.

Waking with a blinding headache, Caroline did not leave her room for the evening meal. Harris brought her some broth and a draught, ordered by the apothecary, which helped her to eventually fall asleep. Unfortunately, her imbibing of Mrs. Bennet's soothing tea would keep her from attending church. She felt wretched, she not only a headache, but her stomach complained when she tried to eat much more than toast and broth for the rest of the day.

The Hursts were never avid church attendees, so when they found that Miss Bingley was not well, they volunteered to stay back to tend her, which meant that Mrs. Hurst would send her maid to inquire after the state of her health every hour or so.

Darcy very much wished to hear Wickham preach. One could tell a great deal about a clergyman by observing him in the pulpit. His aunt Catherine's parsons were insipid, toadying men that Darcy avoided as much as possible on his short and uncomfortable visits to her home at Rosings. Since he had arrived late Saturday evening before Easter the previous year, he had no choice but to attend services at the church in Hunsford. The vicar's sermon spent a great deal of time cataloguing the greatness and condescension of his patroness with little mention of the Lord or the Bible.

Darcy knew that his aunt had been forced to replace that parson when he died suddenly. Knowing Lady Catherine as he did, she would likely have found a man even more foolish and ridiculous than the last.

Using Darcy's smaller carriage, the two men arrived earlier than they would have had the Bingley sisters been in attendance. Charles was eager to see the eldest Miss Bennet, not knowing that his friend was just as eager as he to see Miss Elizabeth. They managed to find empty seats in the row behind the Bennets.

While Bingley heard hardly one word in ten because of his admiring of the lovely Jane in front of him, Darcy was able to concentrate on the service with only a few glances toward Elizabeth. As Wickham read from the Bible and began to preach, Darcy's full attention was captured. The master of Pemberley had heard many sermons in his lifetime, but none were so well thought out and delivered as this one.

Not once in the hour Wickham spoke did he slip into the droning of those vicars who merely read their sermons. His words were plain and easily understood, helping his listeners comprehend the scriptures. Even the children were much quieter than usual.

Darcy could not believe that a man who could articulate the truths of the Bible in such a profound manner could be false. In a flash, he knew that it was time to talk to Wickham and hear his side of the story.

He glanced back at the Bennets for a moment and was surprised to see all but the youngest one deeply engrossed in the sermon. Mary seemed the most absorbed by what she heard, but there was something more than the good sermon that held her interest. From her profile, Darcy could see her deep admiration for the man. It was just one more reason to clear the air between himself and Wickham.

Darcy knew that Miss Elizabeth loved her sisters and did not wish for harm to come to any of them, be it emotional or physical. It seemed that more than his own peace of mind was at stake in finding out the complete truth about Mr. Wickham.

By the end of the sermon, Darcy knew what he needed to do. He stayed back as the rest of the congregation stood in a queue to speak to Wickham. He observed many young ladies openly flirting with the curate, but never once did Wickham respond in any way but with politeness and courtesy. However his countenance changed to one of warmth and welcome when he was greeted by the Bennets, Miss Mary in particular. It was plain that his childhood friend was smitten as well.

"Come, Darcy," Bingley said as he nudged his friend discreetly.

"I wish to get home before dark," Bingley whispered his tease.

"I would like to greet Mr. Wickham. He did a fine job today." Darcy's statement was quiet but firm.

Bingley preceded his friend and shook hands with the curate once they were able to take their place in front of him. Once he felt his duty had been accomplished, he searched the church-yard for Jane Bennet. Viewing the lovely young lady patiently waiting for her mother to finish her discussion with several of her neighbours, he strode to her side and engaged her in conversation.

It was a relief to have Bingley leave so quickly. Darcy took a deep, calming breath before he offered his hand to Wickham and said, "Mr. Wickham, that was an inspiring and thoughtful message. I commend you for it."

Wickham's surprised smile brightened his face. "Thank you, Mr. Darcy."

Lowering his voice, Darcy asked, "Does your offer to talk still stand?"

"Of course!"

"When would you be available to speak to me?" This time Darcy's voice showed some nervousness.

"Would tomorrow at nine be too early for you? The Norths are gone until Saturday. We shall have all the privacy that we should require."

Darcy told him that it was not too early and that he was glad that Wickham was free so soon. With a nod, the two men parted in anticipation of what the morrow would bring.

* * *

Monday morning, Darcy awoke early. He was surprised to have slept so well since he had so much to think about, and plan, for his meeting with Wickham. However, sleep had come swiftly and had been sound. As he rang for his valet, he looked forward to his questions being answered. Somehow he knew that he would receive only truthful answers from Wickham.

Once he was dressed, Darcy ordered his horse to be readied before going to the breakfast room in search of something to drink. He had little appetite at the moment. Happily, he found a pot of hot tea from which he enjoyed a bracing cup.

Setting down his empty cup, Darcy rose from the table and headed for the front door. Fossett met him there with a letter in his hand. "Sir, this arrived express. Also, there is another express rider who says he will only give his message to Fitzwilliam Darcy."

"Quickly man, show him to the study," Darcy demanded and strode determinedly to that room, carrying the first express in his hand.

"Mr. Darcy, this is Mr. Toby," Fossett announced formally before bowing out of the room.

"Do you be Mr. Fitzwilliam Darcy?" the young man nervously asked.

"Yes, I am. I suspect that you have a letter for me from Mr. Jarvis."

"Yes, sir," Toby answered with obvious relief and reached into his satchel for the packet he had carried from London.

"Thank you for your diligence," Darcy said as he gave the young man a few extra coins. "If you would like, you might go to the kitchen for some refreshment before you leave. You must have left quite early to be here so soon."

"I'd be much obliged, sir." Toby smiled as he spoke. "Mr. Jarvis told me it was urgent when he give it to me last night. I didn't want to be late, so I left without breakfast."

Darcy rang for a footman and ordered him to make certain that the young man was properly fed before he left.

Since he recognized the handwriting, Darcy hurried to the desk and broke the seal on the first express he had received. He opened it as he sat and read.

Dear Brother,

Please do not worry that I sent this by express. I am well, as is everyone at Pemberley. I did not wish to waste any time in answering your curious letter. Indeed, I was surprised that you had yet to receive any of my three previous letters.

I admit that I believed that you did not answer because you were still angry with me over what happened at R. If only we could have spoken of it before you left. You know that I am always intimidated by conflict, especially with you.

I love you very much and am sad that I have been a disappointment to you, even though what you think happened did not, in fact, happen. I hope that you might return, or that I might meet you in London in the near future, so that I can explain in detail all of those events. I shall not write about it, for I do not have the words at this time, nor do I wish that it should come to the notice of anyone who would not be discreet.

I look forward to hearing from you again.

Your loving sister,

Georgie

Anger raced through his mind as Darcy finished the brief missive. Now he was certain that he knew what had happened to the other letters, though he could not prove it as yet.

Glancing at the mantel clock, Darcy saw that he had a few more minutes before he needed to leave for his meeting with Wickham. Hastening, he opened the packet. It contained a cover letter and several pages of documentation.

Hoping that his man had summarized the contents, Darcy lifted the letter and began to read.

Dear Sir,

Your express came at an opportune time. I had been sorting through old papers left with me by your late respected father. I have included copies of all of those that pertain to the subject of your enquiry.

The old documents are ones concerning your cousin, the then Honourable Richard Fitzwilliam. During his second year of university, he began to run up debts in your name. Your father was contacted by one to whom Mr. Fitzwilliam owed money. Your father paid all of your cousin's debts and made his sign a statement that he would not use the Darcy name in such a way again and would stay out of debt. Mr. Fitzwilliam was told that if he did not agree, your father would go to the earl with the information. Your father also insisted that your cousin go with him when he paid each debt to explain that he had used your name instead of his own.

Since your father kept track of him the next year when you, yourself, first went to university, he thought that your cousin had turned over a new leaf. I believe that is why he kept the provisions in his will pertaining to your cousin.

It was not long after that time that Mr. Darcy became ill. He kept the truth from you until you finished your studies. He told me several time both in person and by letter how proud he was of his son. He was also very happy with the way that his godson, George Wickham, had applied himself to his studies.

At the moment, this is all the information I have, but I will continue to investigate. You shall hear from me as soon as I have more to tell you.

Sincerely, etc,

Miles Jarvis

Folding the two letters, Darcy placed them in his waistcoat pocket. He pulled the bell cord and, when the servant arrived, asked him to fetch his valet. "After you have seen to this, ask that my horse be brought around."

In just a few moments, his man entered the study. "What may I do for you sir?"

Darcy held out the documents that his attorney had sent with his letter. "Put these with my important papers. Make certain that they are secured."

"Yes sir," Peter answered before he took the papers and left the room.

Chapter 9

The ride to Meryton gave Darcy time to ponder what he had learned. Could his closest cousin have behaved in such a devious way? What other lies had Richard told him? Without sufficient answers, he could not be certain. This kind of betrayal was beyond Darcy's imagination. Trying to sort it all out only succeeded in giving him the beginnings of a headache.

Darcy decided that he would wait until he had spoken to Wickham to make a decision. Realising that he had failed to listen to two people—Wickham and Georgiana—he chastised himself. How could he have been so blind that he believed Mrs. Younge, a virtual stranger, over his beloved sister?

When he turned into the short lane that led to the vicarage, Darcy reined in his horse and surveyed the charming building. It was slightly larger than the one at Kympton and well maintained. He could tell that, in the spring and summer, it would be lovely, with an abundance of flowers and blossoming fruit trees.

Finally Darcy urged his horse toward a small paddock where a young man stood. "May I leave my horse in your care?"

"Yes, sir," the young man answered, "Mr. Wickham told me to expect you, Mr. Darcy."

Darcy handed over his reins and turned toward the house in time to see Wickham standing at the door. Walking toward his old friend, Darcy could not help but return the smile Wickham gave him in greeting.

"Come in, Mr. Darcy," Wickham invited with a sweep of his arm. "Mrs. Tyson has refreshments for us in the study. She makes the best scones I have had since Pemberley."

Once inside the study, with tea poured and refreshments served, Wickham was the first to speak. "I am very happy that you have agreed to speak with me. I had despaired that you would ever do so, although I prayed for it continually."

Darcy took a drink of tea to wet his suddenly dry mouth. He had not expected his old friend to be so gracious. Wickham seemed to hold no animosity toward him.

"I am sorry that it took me so long," Darcy said humbly.

"May I ask what changed your mind?"

"I suppose it began when Miss Elizabeth Bennet challenged me to investigate the situation further before I believed only one side of the story. I did ask my man in London to begin enquiries." Darcy looked up and met Wickham gaze. "However, it was not until I heard your sermon that I understood that I could not give credence to everything I had been told and thought I knew."

Wickham did not smile, but he did answer modestly, "I praise the Lord then."

"I do not know where to start now that I am here," Darcy said honestly.

"Perhaps you will allow me to ask a question."

"Of course," Darcy agreed.

Looking into his teacup, Wickham asked, "Why did you insist that I not come back to Pemberley for the reading of the will? You knew that I was only going to be gone for two days. My father's passing in the weeks before your father died left me with several small items that he wished to be given to his two cousins. I was so surprised to have an express rider arrive with a letter instructing me not to come back to Pemberley, but to await further information at the Blue Goose."

The shock on Darcy's face was obvious. "What express? I did not send you an express."

Wickham sighed and pulled a folded piece of paper from his pocket. "I know not why I kept this all of this time, but please read it and see if it is not in your hand."

Taking the letter from Wickham, Darcy unfolded in gently. He read:

Mr. Wickham,

*Please do not return to Pemberley, but await further informa-
tion at*

The Blue Goose. I shall send my cousin to speak to you as soon as possible.

Now that I am master of my father's estate, I find I no longer wish to be seen with the son of his steward. You were an entertaining companion when there was no other to be had. However, I wish to spend my time with those of higher society.

Fitzwilliam Darcy

Darcy sat in complete stupefaction. He knew that he did not write this letter, but the handwriting looked very much like his except for the flourish at the end of his name.

Noting the complete bewilderment on Darcy's face, Wickham spoke first. "You did not write this." It was a statement not a question.

"No, I did not. I have never had such thoughts about you, much less written them down."

"I have often wondered about that bit of embellishment at the end," Wickham said wryly.

It looks like something that Richard would do, Darcy thought but did not say aloud. When he did speak, he said, "I suppose I should ask you a question."

At Wickham's nod, Darcy asked, "Why did you ask for the value of the living my father left you, if you wanted to be a clergyman?"

It was Wickham's turn to be flummoxed. "I did no such thing. When your cousin came to me, he gave me one thousand pounds and had me sign a receipt for it. He told me that was all to which I was entitled. When I asked about the living, he merely said that Mr. Stokes was still very much alive and he left."

The two gentlemen sat in silence for several moments, each contemplating what they had just found out.

"I believe we have been played, well and truly played," Darcy finally commented.

"Indeed," Wickham responded, and then he asked, "So you believe me?"

"Yes, my friend, I do, just as you believe me."

"Is there more you wish to know?" Wickham asked, thinking about Ramsgate.

"I think you wish to speak of Ramsgate as much as I wish to hear it."

Wickham opened his mouth to speak when Darcy held up his hand.

"First, I must ask your pardon for the way I reacted there. I should have listened to you both. Please forgive me."

Wickham smiled and said, "I have already done so, and now I understand why you acted the way you did. I shall tell you everything if you will be patient, because I had a special reason for being there that had nothing to do with Georgiana."

He began his story with something that happened at the mission in Town.

"Three months before Mr. Wickham met Mr. James North, he attended a young man who was dying. He had been brought to the mission house after being found in an alley. He had been so badly beaten that nothing could be done for him but to make him as comfortable as possible.

As Wickham read the scriptures to him, the lad of about seventeen opened his eyes.

"Me mum read the Bible to me every night when I was little." He *began to cough with the effort of speaking.*

"Do not talk. Save your strength, my friend," Wickham told him as he offered him some water.

"No, I have ta tell you who I am, so's you can get a message to me mum."

"Then rest while I get paper and a pencil." Wickham hurried to the small table in the next room where he kept his writing supplies.

Returning and sitting down once more, George asked, "What is your name?"

"Fred Gilbert," the lad whispered.

"Your mother is Mrs. Gilbert?"

"Aye, Mrs. Molly Gilbert of Ramsgate. She be a dipper there. At least that was her job last I knew."

Fred signalled for more water before he continued. "You see, I didn't have the blunt to pay postage for her last letter. Then I had to move on. So she don't know where to send them now."

With eyes filled with pain, Fred gazed at George. "I'm gonna die, ain't I?"

"Without a miracle, yes." George laid a comforting hand on the boy's.

"Would you tell me mum that I'm sorry I couldn't make me fortune? I so wanted to be able to take her away from the drudgery of being a dipper. Tell her I love her."

Wickham asked for and recorded Mrs. Gilbert's direction, promising to do his best to find her and give her Fred's message.

Closing his eyes in relief, Fred asked Wickham to pray for him, as he was afraid that he would not reach heaven.

Wickham administered the last rites of the Church of England, admonishing Fred to confess his sins and to receive forgiveness in Christ's name. Fred did this and received communion before Wickham prayed, committing the boy into God's care.

At the end, Fred whispered, *"Amen."* He squeezed George's hand, and breathed his last.

After receiving permission, Wickham travelled to Ramsgate to fulfil Fred's request. He left by post coach from Cheapside at eight in the evening, riding on the top of the coach to save money. He arrived dusty and chilled, and at the recommendation of one of the porters at the Ramsgate post stop, he found an inexpensive inn over a half mile from the sea. After washing off the dust of the road, he slept several hours.

The breakfast in the public room was basic but filling. As he ate he planned how he would go about finding Mrs. Gilbert. She would likely be working for most of the day. For that reason, he thought he would look for her house, and afterwards do some exploring before he met with her.

As he drew closer to the water, the sounds and smells of the sea beckoned him. Arriving at the sea wall, George watched fashionable people strut proudly along the wooden walkway. At opposite ends of a wide expanse of beach, he could just make out the bathing machines that took bathers for a dip into the sea. Some children ran up and down the shore while others collected shells or built castles of sand.

George continued his perusal of the crowd and was surprised to recognize one of them. He saw Colonel Richard Fitzwilliam walking arm in arm with two ladies. The older one said something to the others before dropping the colonel's arm and moving to a vendor's stall. The colonel and his young companion did not stop, but strolled closer to his position.

George thought the pretty young girl looked familiar. As he searched his mind for several moments, he finally remembered.

The girl, who could not have been more than fifteen, was the very image of Anne Darcy. She must be Georgiana Darcy since she had the same golden hair. As young as she was, she had grown into a lovely woman just like her mother, but she did not seem to have the same confident air of the late Lady Anne.

Although Wickham wished to greet Georgiana, he held back, even hiding himself behind a post. He had been fond of her as a child, enjoying her girlish laughter when he played games with her. However, George was uncertain as to his reception by the colonel, so he considered it best not to speak to them at that time. Just as he moved from behind the post, George saw the older woman follow after the couple without trying to catch up with them.

He felt great unease and could not account for it. The colonel was one of Georgiana's cousins, after all. Still, there was something in Fitzwilliam's look and posture that seemed menacing.

Seeing the older woman rejoin the pair, and without making a conscious decision, Wickham walked on in their direction while maintaining his distance to keep from being noticed. He had travelled some distance when the threesome stopped.

Georgiana appeared distressed and shook her head. The colonel smiled patronizingly down at her while patting her hand as it lay on his arm. It looked as if he awaited her response. When she finally raised her head, she nodded once and smiled wanly. Beaming, the colonel bowed to the ladies and left them, striding down the street and away from the seaside.

George hoped to hear what the woman was saying to Georgiana so he crept closer and kept his head down. As he drew nearer, the woman paused and glanced around her as if she thought she was being followed. George turned to examine a table full of trinkets on display under a large umbrella.

"Can I help you, sir?" The man's eager question startled him.

"No, I was just admiring your wares." George admitted to himself that the wooden carvings of fish, shells, and the like were quite good.

"How much for the shell?" George lifted it before returning it to its place. He hoped it was not too dear, for it would make a good gift for the mission's old cook.

"Thruppence."

"I have tuppence," George countered as he withdrew the heavy copper coin from his pocket.

"I don't know," the man said hesitantly while he watched George toss the coin from one hand to the other.

"Alas, it is all I can spare." George slipped the coin back into his pocket.

Panicking, as he could see the sale slipping away, the man cried, "Wait, sir, you can have it for tuppence."

As George retrieved the coin, he glanced up at the sound of a woman's voice, and he saw the Georgiana and her companion were moving in his direction.

"The colonel will return from London in three days, Miss Darcy, and everything will be as it should be," the woman insisted.

"But what about my brother?" Georgiana protested. "It does not seem right to do this without him."

"My dear Miss Darcy, I am certain that the colonel will speak to your brother while he is in Town. Colonel Fitzwilliam would never do anything against your brother's wishes. Her tone was placid, but George thought he noticed a hint of frustration under it.

"After all, the colonel is one of your guardians," she added quickly.

Miss Darcy did not answer. She walked slowly beside the older woman as they passed by Wickham.

As quickly as he could, without calling attention to himself, George paid for the shell and followed the pair. He heard Miss Darcy ask to return to their lodgings, complaining of a headache. Her companion agreed and told her she would prepare a draught for her. George was even more determined to find out where they were staying. He was quite worried for his young friend.

As it turned out, George did not have to travel far because the lodgings in which Miss Darcy was staying overlooked the sea and was only a few streets from the main thoroughfare. He stood across the lane from the lovely cottage, watching as Georgiana was ushered inside.

George pondered what he could, and should, do until his stomach grumbled. The exercise, sun, and sea air had combined to create a great appetite.

Chuckling to himself, George began to make his way back to his inn when, after a few minutes, he spotted a pub called the Gull and Parrot in a small side street. An idea struck him that caused him to enter the place.

As his eyes adjusted to the dim interior, Wickham noticed only a handful of men, mostly rough workers, hunched over their food and drink. At the bar stood a husky man of undetermined age who wiped the counter with a ragged grey cloth.

The pub keeper eyed him with suspicion before he said, "What can I do for ye?

"I would like something to eat and a pint of ale, if you please," George answered with a pleasant smile. He was used to this kind of distrust of strangers, having encountered it soon after he arrived at the mission in the baser streets of London.

"You have to pay up front. I don't give no credit to strangers."

"And I never ask for any, sir,"

A reluctant smile lifted the corners of the man's mouth. "Sit where you want. I'll send Daisy to take your order." He pointed to a cracked sheet of slate that hung crookedly behind the bar. "Them's the choices."

Four items were listed, all poorly spelled but understandable. He decided upon the bread and cheese as it cost the least. George only hoped the bread was fresh.

George sat at a table near the bar. A young girl in a dirty brown dress and an even dirtier apron soon arrived in front of him.

"What'll it be?" she asked in a bored voice.

"A pint of ale and the bread and cheese, if you please, Miss Daisy."

She started at the polite statement. "Now ain't you a gentleman?" She held out her hand after she told him the total. Once the coins were in her hand, she curtseyed awkwardly before scurrying to the bar. The man at the bar took the money, poured out the pint, and handed it to the girl to take to George. As soon as she put the tankard on his table, she went into the back.

George sipped the surprisingly decent ale and watched two patrons wave at the man behind the bar before leaving.

Daisy came back soon with his meal. She smiled and winked at his thank you.

"She ain't used to gents like ye in 'ere. Oh, we might get a couple officers in here, but it be mostly local, cuz it ain't fancy enough for some."

The man glared at Wickham before he said, "Don't get no idea about tryin' to charm her. My girl's a good'un, and I plan to keep her that way. She does have a beau, but they's too young to marry yet."

"Have no worries, Mr . . ." George paused.

"Name's Hobbes, Gull Hobbes."

"You need not worry, Mr. Hobbes. I was polite as I was taught to be."

"Where you from?"

"My home is in London at the moment," Wickham answered after a swallow of obviously fresh bread.

"But you ain't from there," Hobbes insisted. "You don't talk like a London swell. You talk more like that colonel whose come round here. What was his name?" Hobbes scratched his head as if to dislodge the name from his memory.

"Daisy!" he shouted and, when she hurried out, asked, "What was that colonel dandy's name what came in here a while back?

"Ye mean the one with the grabby hands? His name's Fitzwilliam," she spit out the name with contempt.

"Aye, he thought he were a charmer. Finally, I told him he weren't welcome no more when he wouldn't leave Daisy alone. This ain't no bawdy house."

"Don't worry Da, you showed me how to handle me self." Daisy grinned. "I accidentally spilt stew on his lap when his hands got too personal, didn't I?"

The father and his daughter laughed, George could not help but join in.

Once the laughter quieted, Hobbes asked, "You know this colonel?"

George wanted to deny it, but he would not lie. "I am acquainted with him, but we have not seen each other for several years. I do not consider him to be a friend."

"I'm happy to hear it," Hobbes replied, as he wiped at the counter. "I'll leave you to your meal. Daisy, go back and see what your mum has for you to do."

Unsurprised at what he heard, George was even more concerned for Georgiana than before. He determined to pray for wisdom and guidance about what he should do.

Back at his inn, Wickham prepared to visit with Mrs. Gilbert. He changed from the clothes he usually wore for travel and manual labour into his clerical garments. It only seemed proper, since he was going to perform a spiritual duty. Besides, his travelling clothing needed cleaning and brushing.

The innkeeper's wife promised she could have everything cleaned and pressed by the next morning. So it was that George left the inn, after changing and eating a bite of supper, looking very much the parson.

He found Mrs. Gilbert's address easily. The building housed several of the female dippers. George lifted the brass knocker and tapped the door twice. He could hear the shuffling of feet through the thin wooden door before it opened to reveal a tall, thin woman who stared at him with concern in her eyes.

"Yes?" Worry and caution were heavy in her tone.

"My name is George Wickham. Might I speak to Mrs. Molly Gilbert?"

"You're speaking to her," she answered curtly.

"May I come in and talk to you?" He kept his voice level.

"You're here about my Freddie, aren't ye?" Her eyes filled with tears.

He knew there was no way to soften the blow that she would receive with his news. He sent a silent prayer for wisdom heavenward before he nodded.

The woman surprised him by gesturing him into a small parlour just inside the entrance. "We can talk in here."

"Please sit, Mr. Wickham, and tell me what happened to my boy," she said as she wiped tears from her eyes.

Mrs. Gilbert did not take her eyes off him all of the time he was telling her about finding and caring for her son. When George told him he had given Fred last rites, she smiled.

"My Freddie was a good boy," she said with a far away look on her face. "When his father was lost at sea, as he was a fisherman, and Freddie was only seven. He never caused me any trouble, but when he was old enough, he wanted to make more money so I wouldn't have to work so much. Freddie saved enough to go north to look for better pay. I prayed for him everyday."

Wickham listened as the woman shared memories of her son and late husband. The tales seemed to flow as if they had been collecting in a bottle, and his visit had uncorked it. After about three quarters of an hour, she finished and gripped her hands together.

"It is my fault that he's gone," she stated plaintively.

"I do not believe that. The vicious person, or persons, who beat him are at fault. He was honouring you by trying to better himself. He told me how much he loved his mum, and he wanted you to have this." George lifted a small book of Psalms from his pocket. *"He kept it with him at all times. Fred told me that it gave him comfort when he was parted from you and hoped it would give you the same."*

"Thank you, sir, and God bless you."

George returned to his inn with a heavy heart. Mrs. Gilbert had been so grateful to him for travelling so far to bring word of her son. She had also told him that she would help him if there was ever anything she could do. It was hard to even conceive of that happening, but as he made it back to his room, he pondered the other person in Ramsgate that had been on his mind. It was then that he realised he could not leave Ramsgate without seeing if he could aid Miss Darcy.

Early the next morning, George broke his fast and pondered his options. He decided to walk back to the cottage with the idea of possibly meeting Miss Darcy at the sea and re-introducing himself to her.

A lovely breeze moved the grass and bushes growing next to the lane as George strolled along toward the tidy cottage. When he drew closer, he heard what sounded like weeping. The nearer he came, the more distinct the weeping became. Without thinking, he opened the front gate and followed the sound to a small side garden. There, on a bench, sat Georgiana Darcy, sobbing into her hands.

"Miss Darcy, may I be of assistance?" he asked soothingly.

The girl jumped and gazed up at him forlornly. Her face expressed confusion at first, before recognition dawned upon her. *"Mr. Wickham?"*

"Yes, Miss Darcy," George smiled. *"I am your old friend, George Wickham.*

"I am astonished to see you here." She tried to wipe away her tears. *"I did not know you lived in Ramsgate."*

"I do not live here," he explained. *"I had business in town, and I saw you yesterday with your cousin and, I believe, your companion."*

Georgiana swallowed back another sob, and turned her face away in embarrassment.

"May I sit?" He did not move until she gave him a quick nod.

"Where is your companion?" he inquired in a near whisper.

"I know not," she admitted. *"I awoke alone in the house."*

"*Is there not a maid?*"

Shaking her vigorously, she said, "*Mrs. Younge and Peg have left me again.*"

"*What do you mean, again?*" he asked incredulous that those paid to care for this young girl would abandon her.

"*Oh,*" she sighed, "*I am certain that they will return by the time they think I will awaken.*"

"*I still do not understand your meaning.*" George was confused.

"*It is quite a fantastic tale, one that I would not have believed had I not lived it,*" she began. "*I now know that they have, on several occasions, given me a sedative. Usually I am an early riser, but in the time we have been here, I have often times slept until past mid day.*"

"*Could it be the sea air that helps you sleep longer?*"

"*That is what I thought at first, but I began to be suspicious when I found the chamomile tea Mrs. Younge would give me at bed time tasted different the nights before I would sleep so long. Last night, I thought to test my theory. I took a very small sip of the tea. It had a strong, bitter taste that even a large amount of honey could not mask.*"

She watched intently as a butterfly flitted from flower to flower, as if envying its ability to fly so freely. Georgiana returned to her narration. "*I pretended to drink the tea, speaking about our outings planned for the next few days. Then I asked Mrs. Younge to fetch a book I purposely left in the front parlour. While she was gone, I poured the tea in a potted plant. Soon after she returned I pretended to read a few pages before I declared that I was getting sleepy, and I made my way to bed.*

"*I awoke to someone opening my door. I suppose they wanted to be sure that I was sleeping. Soon after, I heard the front door open and close. I walked softly to the front window and peered out only to see both Mrs. Younge and Peg walking toward the main thoroughfare. I dressed myself as quickly I could without help and came out here. I have been trying to figure out what to do. My cousin is due to return in two days, and I do not wish to be here.*"

"*Why do you not write to your brother?*" George asked, knowing that Fitzwilliam Darcy would want to assist his sister in any way possible.

"*I have written,*" she said dejectedly, "*But he does not answer or come.*"

"Could it be that your companion is responsible? Could she be destroying your letters?"

"She is the one who insists upon taking all of the mail to the post."

"Why is it that you do not wish to see your cousin?" George could not help but ask.

"You will think me a simpleton," Georgiana declared sadly.

"I know I will not."

She took a deep breath and said, "He wishes to elope with me. He told me he loves me too much to wait. He said such pretty words that sometimes I thought I felt the same, but I cannot think of marrying without my brother's consent."

"What did the colonel say when you told him that?"

"He said that he was certain his brother was too busy to concern himself with his young sister and that William would be happy to hand over the full responsibility of caring for me to him. He shares guardianship with my brother. He told me I only need one guardian's permission to wed, and he would give it."

Tears were rolling down her face. "Do you think that William wants to be rid of me? He did send me here without him, after all."

"William would never think of you as a burden. He is fierce in his loyalty to his family. You are his closest family," George assured her. "In fact, I think that he will have a difficult time finding anyone he is willing to give you to in marriage."

A pleased smile brightened Georgiana's face, but after a second, it faded. "I still do not know what I am to do."

"I do have a suggestion." Wickham had been thinking on the subject.

When he had her attention, he continued. "You could send him a brief message by express, telling him that you will arrive in London with a companion some time this evening."

"You mean that I should travel to London with Mrs. Younge?"

"No, I shall go with you." Before Georgiana could protest, he added, "And I know of a decent woman who would be happy to be your companion for the trip."

"Could this be arranged so soon?" The girl was doubtful.

"I believe that it can, but we shall need to make haste." George stood and offered his hand to help the girl rise. "You write the letter as simply as possible. I do not think it would be wise to mention the

colonel at this time because, if he meets Darcy, we would not wish him to know that his plot is foiled just yet."

Georgiana knew that her old friend was correct, so she hurried back to the house and ran up to her room after watching Wickham walk through the gate and up the lane. As she wrote the brief message, relief from the worry of the past weeks replaced the fear and anxiety that had plagued her.

After adding the direction to the folded missive and sealing it, she made her way to the cottage's cosy little sitting room. Georgiana could easily view to the lane through the window. It was not long until she saw Mr. Wickham and a young man leading a horse striding rapidly in her direction. Hurrying to the door, she threw it open.

Wickham spoke as he met her in front of the door. "This is Rob Timmons. He will ride to London to deliver your letter."

Georgiana handed the missive to the young man. "How much do I owe you, Mr. Timmons?"

"It's already paid, miss," Timmons replied with a short bow. "I'll be on may way."

As the young man mounted his horse and was off, Georgiana looked to Wickham. "What do we do now?"

"Are your bags packed?"

"Nearly, I just have a few more things to put in the trunk," she answered.

"Good, Mrs. Gilbert should be here soon. I have hired a carriage. I gave the driver a note for her. He will take her to her lodgings to retrieve a bag before coming to us. We should be off within the hour." George was nervous, though he kept it to himself. There was no need to worry the girl.

"Perhaps I should finish my packing and see to some food for our travels," Georgiana offered shyly.

"That is an excellent idea, Miss Darcy," he commended her. "I shall wait here for the carriage, since I have already packed and stowed my things on the carriage when I hired it."

Within thirty minutes, Georgiana had completed her tasks and brought a basket of food and drink to the gate. Wickham had carried out her trunk and bag, so they merely had to wait for the carriage, which arrived sooner than expected.

The driver and Wickham had begun to load the trunks and baskets when another larger carriage approached the cottage.

Wickham paused at that point in the story.

"That was when I showed up all fury and no sense," Darcy said in self-derision. "Again, I apologise for my arrogant assumptions."

"Darcy, please, no more apologies. I might have acted much the same way if I were in your shoes. No one is perfect, especially not myself. I know that full well. I will not cast any stones."

Humbled once more, Darcy nodded and thanked him.

The two gentlemen sat in silence, contemplating what they had just learned. Darcy remembered the letters in his pocket and withdrew them. After finding the one from his attorney, he held it out toward Wickham.

"What is this?" Wickham asked.

"I told you that I had my man in Town investigate you, but this is the letter he sent me. There is corroborating evidence with it, which I have safely secured in case it is needed. Please read it."

Wickham read the brief missive quickly before looking up. "Did he truly manage to stay out of debt after your father's involvement?"

Darcy's frustration and embarrassment showed on his face. "No, I believe he did not. He came to me with tales of your debts and intrigues. Also, he said that he had paid the ones of which he knew with his own pocket money. I foolishly believed him, repaid him, and gave him enough to see him through until his next allowance from his father. Richard told me that he wished to save my father the grief of knowing how you turned out."

Rising suddenly, George angrily paced the room. After several moments, he seemed to regain his composure and took his seat again. "What a great deal of time has been wasted believing his lies! You know now that I did not, and will not, live such a life?"

"Yes, I do. I not only lost years with a good friend, but the one I thought I could trust with my life wishes to betray me even more. I must make certain that Georgiana is safe from him."

With that thought, Darcy was the one who began to pace, mumbling about the possibility of his cousin getting leave and abducting his sister from Pemberley.

"Darcy, please sit down. I have an idea to help keep her safe," Wickham bade him gently.

Chapter 10

In the days before the ball at Netherfield, Lydia enjoyed her courtship with the colonel. He was not always available to squire her
around Meryton, but she understood that his first duty was always to
his command. On the days when he was too busy to visit, he would
send her flowers or small gifts of sweets along with short notes.

Kitty was not jealous of Lydia's actual beau because she thought
he was too old and boring, but she was envious of her younger sister
being in a courtship. Her thoughts centred on the fact that she herself
was two years older and felt that she should have a courtship before her
little sister. It did not occur to Kitty that she had no more right because
of age than Lydia, since she had three sisters who were older still than
she, all of whom were without courtships.

So it was beyond logic that Kitty became vocally opposed to the
relationship between Lydia and the colonel. To her chagrin, she found
no one in her family who would agree with her. In fact, only a few of
her friends, including Maria Lucas and Sandra Goulding, would even
listen to her complaints.

Kitty spent so much time arguing with Lydia and complaining to her
mother about her younger sister getting a new gown that, one morning
at breakfast, Mrs. Bennet finally put a stop to it.

"Kitty, if you cannot be quiet, you shall stay home from the ball,"
her mother threatened. "You will have your turn. Stop complaining and
find a nice young man for yourself."

Throwing down her serviette, Kitty stormed from the room,
announcing that she would visit Maria Lucas.

Silence descended upon the room, and surprise overtook the family
as they heard the front door slam. Finally, Lydia spoke softly. "Perhaps

I should not have a new gown for the ball. I have a perfectly good one that I have only worn twice."

Mrs. Bennet opened her mouth to object, but was stopped by Mr. Bennet.

"No, Lydia," her father answered. "I appreciate your sense of fairness, but Kitty must not be rewarded and you punished."

"I have an idea that might help to soothe Kitty's feelings," Jane offered.

The rest turned their attention to Jane, waiting to hear her suggestion.

"Why do we not make over one of her dresses? I am certain that amongst the five of us, we can refashion a gown."

The idea was met with enthusiasm, and soon many proposals flew around the table. Offers of ribbons, lace, and bits of fabric were canvassed. Breakfast lasted longer than usual after Elizabeth produced a pencil and paper, so that she could record everything.

Mr. Bennet smiled as his ladies planned how to regain Kitty's good humour. He usually did not like talk of feminine things such as this, but at the moment, the camaraderie he was witnessing warmed his heart—especially what he was seeing in Lydia. He never would have thought that the attention of a good man could help his flightiest daughter change so. Instead of decrying Kitty's anger and jealousy, he heard her offer the best of her ribbons to the cause.

Once the Bennet ladies had finished their meal, they traversed the stairs to Kitty and Lydia's room. Lydia went immediately to the closet and pulled out a light blue gown. She laid it on the bed and smoothed it. A medium sized stain could be seen on the lower half of the skirt.

"How can this be refreshed?" Mrs. Bennet exclaimed as she stared down at the garment. "I remember when Kitty received that stain. John Lucas tripped and spilled some of his wine. The liquid splashed up from the floor. Hill tried everything to remove the stain, but to no avail."

"I rescued the gown from the rag bin," Lydia explained. "The colour is the most flattering on Kitty. I knew not how to fix it until just now."

Turning to face her mother, Lydia asked, "Do you remember the length of blue silk you had left over from the gown you had made for last Christmas?"

Her mother nodded, so that Lydia continued, "We can remove the stitching in the front, cut out the stain, and fold the skirt back. If we attach the blue fabric on the underside, there should be enough left after hemming to trim the sleeves. It would only take a few rosettes and matching ribbons to finish it perfectly."

Everyone else in the room was pleased with Lydia's idea. Mrs. Bennet hurried to find the blue silk, while the others gathered everything they had that might do. Within a quarter hour they were ensconced in their mother's chambers and had begun the task of the gown's makeover.

* * *

Darcy left Wickham's abode, feeling relief that he had finally discovered the truth. However, guilt overshadowed that relief. He chastised himself for believing his cousin without talking to George. How could he have abandoned his childhood friend? His own father had always trusted his godson. Why had he been so eager to even consider what Richard had told him? At least, Wickham seemed to hold no grudge. He resolved to do better in the future and not to judge people before he knew all of the facts.

Wickham's idea of how to keep Georgiana safe was sound. Impatient to put the plan into action, he made his way to the post. He wished for the missive George had written to be on its way as soon as possible. Paying for an express rider seemed to be the best way to achieve that goal.

Once he had finished that task, Darcy rode swiftly to Netherfield so that he could write a letter to his sister to inform her that he now understood the truth of what had happened, and wished for her to prepare to go to a safe place for a period of time. He hoped that everything would be in place within the week. Georgiana needed to be away from Pemberley since he did not dare try to keep guard over her there. It would cause talk, and his cousin could charm his way past nearly anyone on the staff.

When he arrived back at Netherfield, Miss Bingley tried to question him about where he had been that morning. Citing urgent business correspondence, Darcy paid her little heed as he mounted the stairs. He closed and locked the door before sitting at the desk. He wrote a brief letter to his steward, who had proven himself worthy of trust during the many years he worked at Pemberley.

His letter to Georgiana was short, but Darcy tried to be as reassuring as possible. He did apologise for not listening to her account while explaining to her that he had reconciled with Mr. Wickham as well. After he had written out the direction on the front and was about to seal his missive, he called for his valet.

Before Darcy could explain to Peters that he wished the letters to be sent express, there was a knock on the door.

"See who it is, Peters."

Unlocking the door and opening it a fraction, Peters peered out. "It is Mr. Bingley, sir."

"Let him in and relock the door," Darcy said while slipping the folded letters into his waistcoat pocket.

Bingley waited until Darcy invited him to be seated before he slumped in the chair. He took several folded letters from his jacket. "These belong to you. I do not know when they arrived, since Louisa just gave them to me."

Darcy glanced at the handwriting and recognized it as Georgiana's. He turned one over to open it and exclaimed, "The seal has been broken!"

Sighing in frustration, Bingley agreed. "It has. Louisa found it among Caroline's correspondence. She knew that Caroline had received a letter from our aunt this morning, and as Aunt Bradley addresses her missives to all of us, Louisa wished to read it for herself. Caroline told her it was on the desk in her chambers, but Louisa had to search for it, as our younger sister is not known for keeping her papers tidy.

"Louisa found some letters and, being familiar with your sister's handwriting, she was curious as to why Caroline had not told her of receiving any correspondence from Georgiana. When she saw the salutation, she abandoned the search for our aunt's letter and immediately brought them all to me."

Angered at the invasion of his privacy, Darcy said, "One of these is dated three weeks ago. Surely it arrived here before this morning. If I had not written her express and she returned her answer the same way, Georgiana would have continued to think I refused to answer her."

"That is what Louisa feared as well." Bingley grew red in embarrassment. "I wonder how many of my letters she has opened. I must apologise for this breach of your privacy. I just wish I knew what to do about this."

"If you wish to hear my advice, I will tell you."

"Indeed, I do!"

"First of all, you must confront her about this. I cannot have her invading my personal business. And since she invaded yours as well, that should be your first priority. I have some very important matters about which I will be receiving mail. I do not want her reading any of it, nor should I have to worry that she will do so. I might have to move to the inn in Meryton to avoid it happening. I am just happy that we recently insisted that Fossett start to give us our personal post."

"You are right, Darcy," Bingley responded. "I will not have my guest driven away by my interfering sister. She will have to leave. Especially since I know that a mere reprimand will do little to no good. I shall ask Louisa if she will be my hostess for the time being."

"I appreciate you doing this for me, Bingley," Darcy said gratefully.

"I must do it, but I do it for myself as well. I have been too lenient with her, as were my parents. It may take a week or so to sort out the details, but she will be leaving as soon as arrangements can be made." Bingley stood with a look of firm determination upon his face. "In the meantime, I shall have Fossett bring all other correspondence directly to me, not just ours. I do not trust my sister to keep from trying to make more trouble."

"In addition I feel I must repeat that I will not marry your sister, no matter the situation," Darcy remarked, feeling he must make himself perfectly clear to his friend.

"Of course," Bingley agreed as he turned to leave, "And I would not ask it of you even if it would mean ruin for Caroline."

Darcy watched Bingley leave the room. Still not trusting his host's resolve, or underestimating Miss Bingley's ability to get what she wanted, he decided upon his own precautions. He reopened the missive he had just folded and added instruction to his sister that any correspondence from her was to be sent express. He would inform the butler of this new order.

* * *

Charles was apprehensive as he mounted the stairs to the family level. He truly hated confrontation, and it was doubly difficult when it came to his sister, Caroline. He had given in to her demands and arguments countless times. However, he knew, for the sake of his friendship, and if he had any hope of marrying the lovely Jane Bennet, he must be a man and stand firm.

Arriving outside his sister's chambers, he drew in a fortifying breath before knocking firmly. Her maid opened the door to him.

"Charles, whatever are you doing here?" Caroline asked testily. "I am afraid I am quite busy at the moment. You will have to come back later."

Turning to the maid, Charles said, "You may go. Return when we ring for you."

"How dare you dismiss my maid like that? She has not finished with my hair. I wish to be presentable at dinner tonight," she said as she looked in her mirror, turning her head one way and then another.

"You will not be joining us for dinner tonight. You and your maid will be too busy packing your things. You will be leaving as soon as it can be arranged to visit Aunt Bradley in Scarborough."

"I certainly will not be going to visit our aunt!" she cried indignantly. "Who would hostess your silly ball? Besides, I am sure that Mr. Darcy would miss me greatly if I were to leave."

The look of scorn and pity Charles gave her made her pause in her objections.

When her brother spoke, his tone was harder and more serious than she had ever heard from him. "You are a fool, Caroline, if you think that of Darcy. You steal his correspondence, and that of your family, and you can still seriously believe that we would merely forget it and move on. Darcy could have you arrested for mail theft if he wished. It is because of the friendship he and I share that he is willing to overlook it, but only if you are gone from this house."

"As I explained to Louisa," Caroline began, "my maid is not the brightest person. I told her to take the letters to Mr. Darcy when I noticed whose correspondence it was. I cannot be blamed if she did not obey me."

"I do not believe a word of it, neither does our sister," Charles scoffed. "I wish to retain the friendship of the Darcys. If you stay, that friendship will be in jeopardy."

Caroline's eyes hardened as she practically screeched, "I am going to be his wife! Why would he want me gone?"

"Keep your voice down, Caroline," he cautioned. "I have told you many times that Darcy is not interested in taking you as his wife. He has only tolerated you because of me. Now I wish I had not subjected him to your company so often."

Caroline stared at her brother, open-mouthed. Charles could not miss the look of cunning that soon covered her face. She took up a handkerchief and dabbed at dry eyes. "That cannot possibly be true. He has given me every indication of his regard for me. You just do not see it."

His eyes now opened to her many manipulations, Charles threw his head back and laughed heartily.

"You go ahead and laugh," Caroline sneered. "I am certain that Mr. Darcy will not agree with you."

"I will not stay and argue," he said as he turned to the door. "I have better things to do."

"Oh, I suppose you wish to call on the lovely Miss Bennet again." She let out a snicker. "She does not love you and is only after your wealth and status."

"I do not agree," he answered, but a seed of doubt was planted.

"Get Mr. Darcy's opinion," she suggested, feeling that she had carried her point. "He will confirm it."

"I will consult Darcy," Charles said. "However, I suggest you begin packing because you are still leaving for Scarborough as soon as possible."

As soon as he left and closed the door, Charles heard her cry of frustration and the crash of something hitting the wall.

* * *

About an hour later, Bingley caught Darcy as he was leaving the house.

"I have something I would like to talk to you about. Might I have a few moments of your time before you go on your ride?"

"Of course, why do you not walk with me to the stables? I have yet to order my horse," Darcy moved through the door with his friend close behind.

"I had a long talk with Caroline. She is not well pleased to be shipped off to our aunt's, but that is not what I wish to ask." Bingley chewed on his lips for a second before he blurted out, "Caroline says that Jane Bennet does not care for me but only for my money. She told me that you would agree with me."

"Bingley, allow me to tell you what I have observed, and what I know as fact."

* * *

Kitty returned to Longbourn, only half satisfied with her visit with Maria. Although her friend had been sympathetic, she had shown Kitty the new gown that Lady Lucas had commissioned for her for the ball. How she wished her favourite sister would revert to her old self, teasing and flirting as she had always done. Now she was nearly as dull as Elizabeth, always sitting in quiet conversation or even reading something beside her usual novels.

Sighing, Kitty walked into the front parlour, finding Lizzy and Lydia working on what looked like ribbon roses. She dropped unladylike into a chair. "I think I shall stay home from the ball," she announced.

"No, Kitty." Mrs. Bennet entered the room behind Hill who brought in the tea things. "I have decided that it will not be said that any of the Bennet family has shunned the Bingleys. We shall all attend and enjoy ourselves. Besides, you do not wish to miss the opportunity to dance with the handsome officers."

Heaving another sigh, Kitty picked up a book and began to read, ignoring the happy chatter around her as her sisters talked of the upcoming ball and some local gossip they had heard. Because of her mood and her interest in her novel, Kitty missed seeing the sly winks and grins that passed between the others in the room.

* * *

Once Darcy explained what he had heard from Miss Elizabeth, and what he had observed of Miss Bennet, Bingley stood still with the widest possible smile on his face.

"You are certain of this?" Bingley asked in a whisper.

"I am," Darcy said as he mounted his horse.

Bingley continued to smile as he stared after his friend. "Jane Bennet does care for me. I can see that Caroline was lying to try to keep me from pursuing Miss Bennet. I must talk to her again. This time I will not be so easily sidetracked. I shall give her the choice of Aunt Bradley or setting up her own establishment. I shall no longer be soft with her."

Thus determined, Charles strode purposefully to the house. Fosset opened the door to him. After thanking the servant, he asked after his older sister and her husband. He was informed that they were in their private sitting room.

Above stairs, Charles went straight to the Hurst's chambers and knocked. When a maid answered the door, he asked to speak with her mistress and master. He was soon shown into the cosy room and was taken aback at the scene of domestic harmony he saw there. Louisa was sitting on a sofa knitting while her husband sat next to her reading a book.

They both looked up at him in surprise. "We were not expecting you to come to see us," Louisa said quietly.

"I hope I am not interrupting." Charles felt some embarrassment at disturbing them.

"No, indeed," said Mr. Hurst, who had stood when Charles entered the room. "We were enjoying the quiet of our chambers."

"I will be brief," Bingley said as he turned to Louisa. "I would like you to hostess for me. Caroline will be leaving Netherfield quite soon."

Louisa nodded and replied, "I thought you might want to send her away. She has gone too far this time. Invading the privacy of a guest and her own siblings is beyond the pale. I am nervous about hosting the ball, but I shall try."

"Aye," Hurst replied with a smile. "We have been wondering how to persuade you to remove your sister. Louisa and I tire of her inter-ference in our lives and others'. She will not be welcome in our town-house any longer. I would give her the cut direct if it would not cause undue scandal."

Charles dropped into a nearby chair in great relief. "Thank you both. I am very close to cutting her off myself but will not, for the same reason."

They discussed what should be done with Caroline for several minutes. Louisa did not wish for their sister to be established in Town.

"She will make herself out to be the victim. She is entirely too good at that."

"And knowing your kindly Aunt Bradley as I do, I do not think that she could control your sister well enough," Hurst added.

Sighing, Charles asked, "Then what shall we do?"

"Unless you can find someone to marry her, I suggest that she travel to Scotland. I have family there. They live some distance from Edinburgh. Being religiously strict, they would not tolerate Caroline's foolishness. Also, it would give you time to search out a match for her. After she has spent a bit of time with my aunt and uncle, she will be more than willing to agree to a marriage that does not include Darcy."

"How long would it take to get word from them?" Charles asked, eager to be rid of his troubling sibling.

"We will not have to contact them first. They are always willing to take in disturbed souls, as they call them. I shall send an express to inform them of her arrival and will arrange for the transport to take her there. I will have to find a few strong men to ensure she does not escape. I have met a few in Meryton that might do." Hurst grinned as he rubbed his hands together in glee.

"I suppose that I should not delay in telling her of her fate." This was not a conversation that Charles wished to have.

Louisa stood and took her husband's hand. "We will all go. A show of unity will help."

The following conversation was not pleasant. At first, Caroline argued and wept. Finding that her weapon did not move her siblings, she screeched and insulted them, calling them unloving and cruel. When they were still unyielding, she threatened to create a scandal.

By this time, Charles had had enough. "Caroline, do be quiet," he ordered in an eerily calm voice. "You have lost all chance of having your way. I control your dowry and your allowance. You will not be welcome in the Hursts' home, and I shall make it my goal to make certain that all of your so-called society friends know you are in disgrace, if you do not go quietly."

"You would not dare," she hissed with less certainty.

"Oh yes he would, as will Mr. Hurst and I," Louisa chimed in. "I have had enough of your interfering actions."

Caroline was by no means willing to give up the fight, but she thought it best to agree for now. Perhaps she could persuade Mr. Darcy to help her. If he was on her side, her brother and sister could do nothing.

"Very well," Caroline replied after along pause. "I will have my maid begin packing for me."

Relieved that she had finally given in, the rest of her family left her chambers to arrange for her travel.

* * *

Three days before the ball at Netherfield, a heavy rainstorm deluged the village and the surrounding area. Lydia was especially disappointed because Colonel Forster was unable to visit. Her downcast mood differed from previous days in that she did not bicker with her sister, but only sat next to the window gazing out at the downpour.

Jane tried her best to be cheerful, but her own emotions were stretched by her mother's moaning and complaints of nerves. Mrs. Bennet constantly lamented that the ball would likely be cancelled, and that Mr. Bingley would leave the country without asking for Jane's hand.

Elizabeth tried to distract her sisters with conversation. It seemed to help some, however not as much as she would have liked.

Kitty seemed almost to enjoy her sisters' melancholy. She acted as if the ball was of no consequence to her as she chatted about the officers she had met at previous gatherings.

That evening after dinner, Mr. Bennet asked his second and third daughters to play some lively tunes for the rest of the family. He would not allow Mrs. Bennet to continue her whinging. "We shall have an impromptu concert tonight. I have asked Cook to bring us some more of her delicious lemon cake to be served afterwards. Let us hear no more about balls or wet weather."

The hour of music lifted everyone's spirits, as did the refreshments, which included a bit of wine for everyone. Mr. Bennet made certain that his wife had enough of the wine to mellow her mood, but not so much that she would have a headache in the morning.

* * *

Unfortunately, the weather had not improved the next day, which was Sunday. Mr. Bennet determined that the roads were too muddy to travel to the church service, so he led his family in reading the Bible and a prayer.

Normally, Mary felt some melancholia when she could not attend church. However, along with a lowered mood because of the weather and missing services, she knew she would be unable to see Mr. Wickham or have even a short visit with him. Try as she might, she could not get the curate out of her mind. His manners toward her gave her hope of a love match, where before she had had no such expectation.

After devotions and breakfast were over, Mr. Bennet looked at his family, noting the still sad faces. Even Kitty was beginning to feel the loss of company and the possibility of the ball being cancelled. He decided to see if he could help.

"My dear Mrs. Bennet," he said in a casual tone. When his wife lifted her head, he continued, "I remember that you might have a certain surprise for one of our daughters. Would not now be a good time to reveal it?"

By the time he had finished asking his question, all of his ladies were smiling except Kitty who had no idea what he was talking about.

"Oh yes, Mr. Bennet, what a splendid Idea!" Mrs. Bennet tried to contain her happiness though her voice was filled with enthusiasm.

Rising from her chair, she said, "Come girls, all of you, to my sitting room."

When Kitty did not obey, Mr. Bennet said, "You too, Kitty. You do not want to miss out."

Reluctantly, Kitty followed her mother and sisters out of the room and up the stairs. She did not wish to see one of them get another treat, but she knew when her father was to be obeyed. As she entered her mother's sitting room, Kitty was astonished to see a lovely dress laid over a chair. It was a familiar shade of blue, but it was like nothing she had ever seen before.

As she stared at it with longing in her eyes, Kitty's sisters all called out "Surprise!"

Still unable to comprehend what was happening, Kitty looked around the room at the smiling faces of her mother and sisters. "I do not understand," she responded in a timid voice.

"This is your gown for the ball, silly," Lydia declared as she reached for Kitty's hand to pull her closer to the garment. "It was Jane's idea, but we all worked on it. I knew it was the perfect dress to do over."

Tears of joy and contrition welled up in Kitty's eyes. "You all did this for me even though I have been so nasty lately?"

"Do you like it?" Mrs. Bennet asked.

"Like it? I love it. It is so beautiful. I was so upset when it was ruined, but it is now better than ever." Kitty used the handkerchief that Jane offered her to wipe her tears. "Thank you, all of you."

"Do you wish to try it on?" her mother asked.

"Yes, but first . . ." Kitty embraced each of them starting with her mother.

The next hour was spent in laughter and joy as Kitty donned the gown. There were a few alterations to be made which were accomplished swiftly with so many hands to work on it. She finally decided that her papa should see the gown as well. The rest followed her to her father's book room. At her knock, Mr. Bennet opened the door and grinned at his smiling family.

"You look lovely, my dear," Mr. Bennet complimented. "Your mother and sisters did a wonderful job on the gown, did they not?"

"Oh yes, Papa." Kitty laughed. "I cannot imagine a new gown would look better."

It was at that moment that Hill entered the corridor. "I thought you would like to know that the rain has stopped. If it does not start again, the roads should be dry enough by Tuesday evening."

Exclamations of delight followed the housekeeper's announcement. When the noise had settled, Mrs. Bennet insisted that Kitty change into another dress, so that the ball gown was not accidentally damaged.

Chapter 11

The first few days of Collins's visit with the Langfords at Wywyn were some of the most comfortable he could remember. Both of his host and hostess listened to his opinions upon every subject as if he were an oracle from heaven. Of course, most of what he said he had heard from the lips of his patroness. He did not think to mention the origin of his statements because he had begun to believe that he had always been in possession of the knowledge. His bedchamber was larger than the guest room at Longbourn and nearly as large as his own at Hunsford. Best of all, Collins was fed often and in ample quantities.

Collins was pleased with the service the footman, who was acting as his valet, provided. He had never had a man-servant. He felt awkward at first, but soon thought he could become accustomed to it.

Feeling as if he were the most fortunate of men, Collins wandered the halls and grounds of the great house with Eleanor. When he had first met her and her father shortly after he first came to the Hunsford parish, he had thought Miss Langford to be quite plain. However, he was rapidly coming to a different conclusion as she smiled and flirted with him in a most flattering manner. It was not long before she was more than attractive to him, especially in her dinner gowns. They displayed her lovely figure to its best advantage.

Collins began to see what a blessing in disguise it was that his cousin had made him leave. He, also, started to see why his cousin Bennet had been so upset at him. For the first time in ages he felt shame for his actions. However, he was not certain he could change his habits.

After ten days in her company, Collins thought he had found the right woman to be Mrs. Collins. With that thought in mind, he approached Mr. Langford for permission to propose to her. That lady's father was more than happy to give his blessing, as his permission was not strictly required.

Collins found Miss Langford in the back parlour going over the menus with the cook. She smiled brightly when she spied him and swiftly asked the servant to bring some tea.

"I hope you are finding your stay here enjoyable, Mr. Collins," she said as she gestured for him to be seated in the chair the cook had just vacated. "I shall miss your enlightening conversation when you leave us in a few days." Her smile was replaced by a melancholy expression.

"I do not recall ever experiencing such gratification and hospitality, excepting of course the condescension of my noble patroness, when she deigns to invite me to Rosings." His face reddened as he wanted very much to compliment the Langfords, but he was not in the habit of insulting Lady Catherine in any way.

"You are most kind to rank our hospitality on the same level as that of Rosings," she reassured him softly.

"I am grateful that you and your father invited me to stay. I am not certain that Lady Catherine would have been happy for me to return when she had been so benevolent as to give me the time away from my duties."

"We are most pleased to be of service to you after your short and unfortunate stay with your relatives. We have been more than compensated by your pleasant company." Eleanor hoped she would be rewarded for the time spent with a proposal.

Although Collins had rehearsed the speech he would have given to one of his cousins, this was a completely different set of circumstances. All the flowery words that usually came so easily to his lips flew out of his mind.

Thinking that he should at least kneel, Collins bent down on one knee and said quickly, "Miss Langford, Eleanor, will you do me the honour of becoming my wife?"

"Yes, William, I would like to marry you, but . . ." She stared down at him.

Grasping her hands in his, Collins covered them with rather wet kisses. "You have made me the happiest of men."

Eleanor pulled her hands away from his clasp and ordered him to return to his seat. "Before our betrothal can be official, I have some questions and stipulations."

* * *

In the evening, two days before the ball, Caroline's maid, Harris, knocked on the study door. She had been told that she would find Mr. Bingley there. When she entered, at his bidding, she found him in the company of his brother-in-law and Mr. Darcy.

Curtseying, she said, "I beg your pardon, sir, for interrupting, but I thought you should know . . . but perhaps, I should wait."

"Do not worry about these gentlemen, they can be trusted," Bingley reassured her.

Swallowing hard, she handed him a folded paper and said, "Miss Bingley has asked me to post this letter and said she wants me to go to Meryton to post it. She does not wish to have it go in the house mail.

"Also, I am embarrassed to say that she wishes for me to take her through the servants' passages to Mr. Darcy's rooms.

"I was uncomfortable going behind your back to mail the letter, and it would be wrong of me to help her to compromise Mr. Darcy. That'd be very wicked. My mama would tan my hide if I ever did such a thing."

During her explanation, Charles's face had turned from red to white. It became obvious that Caroline had not truly conceded to his demands.

With her final words, Charles opened the missive and quickly read it. Sighing heavily, he spoke. "She wanted to send an engagement announcement to the *Times*. Caroline thought that her scheme would succeed and wished for all of London to know her good news."

"She thought that I would agree more readily if it were already in the papers," Darcy voiced sarcastically.

The gentlemen nearly forgot the presence of the young maid until she asked, "What am I to do, sir?"

Silence descended upon the room as the men considered the action. Charles finally smiled hugely and said, "Go to back to my sister. If she asked if you delivered the letter, tell her that you took care of it. Tonight, do as she asked and show her to Darcy's room."

Before Darcy could object, Charles added, "You will spend the night in my room, and I will be waiting for her in yours. I wish to deal with this personally."

Hurst, who had been sitting silently during the exchange, began to laugh heartily. Once he had recovered, he said, "I wish I could be there to see her face."

"I think that is a capital idea. You will be able to witness it. Caroline will not wheedle her way out this time," Charles agreed with conviction.

* * *

It was nearly half past twelve that night before the house had finally quieted. Since Caroline did not join the family for meals, she had to rely upon her maid to keep her abreast of things. Harris had assured her that everyone, including the servants, were in their rooms.

Caroline donned her most transparent of nightgowns and put on a thin robe over it. She shivered because the fire was waning. For a brief moment, she wondered if she might be making a mistake. Surely there was another way to meet her goal of becoming Mrs. Darcy of Pemberley. However, she shook her head to clear it of doubts. *I have no more time. If I am stuck in Scotland, I will likely never see him again. No, this is my last chance.*

"Harris, it is time for us to go," Caroline whispered.

"Yes, Miss Bingley, right this way," the maid answered, before she picked up a candle and moved to the dressing room. Once inside, Harris opened a door in the panelling. Leading the way into the passage, she paused for her mistress to follow.

Caroline was surprised at the warren of passages. She knew that she would have easily gotten lost, but her maid seemed to navigate them as if they were the broad streets of Town. The chill of the unheated route caused gooseflesh to rise on her arms, and she started to shiver in the thin fabric of her nightclothes. She was certain that her teeth would begin to chatter at any moment when Harris stopped and pushed at a panel in front of her.

Warmth and dim light from the room beckoned Caroline inside. So happy was she to be warm again that she did not notice her maid staying in the passage. She stood for a few moments in the man's dressing room, deciding how to proceed. Making her decision, she whispered softly without looking back, "Wait a moment or two before you come and find us. I must have a witness, or else he might try to deny it."

Her slippers made no noise as she approached the cocooned figure in the large bed shown in the faint light from the dying fire. Caroline smiled at the bundle of blankets covering him from head to toe. She would enjoy the surprise and the shock that she would surely provoke when he woke to find her in his bed.

Moving to the other side of the bed, Caroline lifted the covers and slid onto the bed. She leaned in to kiss him when she heard a voice that made her freeze in place.

"Good evening, Caroline," Charles said with eerie calmness.

"What are you doing in Mr. Darcy's bed," she squeaked out.

"I should ask you the same thing, but I already know the answer, do I not, Hurst?"

The answer was a deep throaty chuckle, followed by the lighting of several candles.

When the room became brighter, Caroline squealed and pulled a blanket over herself.

"I wonder why you are so modest now," Charles mocked her as he got out of the bed, fully clothed.

"She might tell us her maid brought her to the wrong room, but why was she in the servants' passages in the first place, and who else would she be looking for in that garb?"

Charles picked up a heavier robe that had been lying over one of the chairs and threw it to her. "Put this on and Harris will take you back to your room."

"But . . . but . . ." Caroline sputtered, "Mr. Darcy sent for me."

"Hmm, is that so?" Charles rubbed in chin, before asking, "Then I wish to see the note."

"I cannot."

"And why is that?" Charles asked with feigned curiosity.

"Because he did not send a note," she said hastily. "He sent the message through my maid."

Her brother nodded to Hurst who walked to the door and opened it to let Harris enter.

"Harris, did Mr. Darcy ask you to bring Miss Bingley to his room?" Charles asked.

Glancing fearfully at Miss Bingley, the maid shook her head. "No, he did not."

"Thank you, Harris," Charles smiled. "You may help Miss Bingley return to her room."

Though she did not like to admit defeat, Caroline stood quickly and pulled on the robe. Glaring at the maid, she spat out, "You are dismissed as soon as you finish packing my clothes, and do not expect a reference."

"Harris is not your employee," Charles informed his sister. "I pay her wages, and she will have a position in this house as long as she wishes it."

"You will be sorry, Charles," she answered defiantly, suddenly remembering the letter she had written. "There will be an announcement in the paper tomorrow of my engagement to Mr. Darcy. It would cause a great scandal if he does not marry me."

"Oh, you mean this letter?" Charles pulled a folded paper from his waistcoat pocket.

"How dare you read my private correspondence?" she exclaimed angrily.

"Is that not the pot calling the kettle black?" Hurst asked laughingly.

Caroline was silenced by this rejoinder. Lifting her nose in the air, she left the room as quickly as she could.

* * *

Finally, the day before the ball, Caroline was ready to travel to Scotland. Hurst had hired Tobias Hill and another large man to ensure that his sister-in-law arrived safely in Scotland and to prevent her from escaping. Besides the two extra men, two footmen, the driver, and a postilion attended the coach. Charles had hired an elderly woman to be his sister's companion. Her maid had not wished to work for Caroline any longer, so another was found to take her place.

Although he wished to be strict with his sister, Bingley did not truly wish her to go without some of her usual comforts, such as a maid. He had heard enough from Hurst about his relatives to know that they would not provide one for her.

Caroline had tried to appeal to Darcy, but she failed completely. He had looked down his nose at her and had shaken his head.

Finally, Darcy remarked flatly, "I would never have married you, even if you had succeeded in your plot and the announcement had gone to the papers. I could have weathered the scandal."

He then turned and walked from the room. His anger was too great and, being a gentleman, he did not wish to stoop to insult a woman, even if she was not a true lady.

The travellers left at first light with no one to see them off, though Charles watched from the window to make certain that Caroline did not pull some last minute trick. He was not completely untouched by her tears, but he knew he must be strong if she were ever to learn her lesson.

Only the thought of the upcoming ball and seeing Miss Jane Bennet kept him from despair. His future seemed brighter than it had before, so he would ponder that instead of the past.

* * *

After finishing her tea that morning, Elizabeth rose and announced that she was going for a walk. She did invite her sisters to accompany her, but they all declined, wishing to finish the tasks they had set before them.

Donning her outer garments, Elizabeth left the house. She had nearly decided to head for her thinking place in the hopes of seeing Mr. Darcy. When she had seen him at church the week before, he seemed tense and single-minded as he waited to speak to Mr. Wickham. Although she truly wished to find out what he had discovered, she knew that it was not her business. If he wished her to know, he would seek her out.

Resolving instead to walk to Meryton, Elizabeth moved down the lane and onto the road to the village. She walked for some distance when she heard the sound of hoof beats coming from the opposite direction. Moving the side of the road in order to let the horseman pass, Lizzy was surprised to see that the rider was Mr. Darcy.

"Miss Bennet!" He stopped and greeted her with a tip of his hat. "I was on my way to Longbourn to see you."

Curtseying, Elizabeth answered with a smile, "I was just taking a walk. I can turn back if you wish."

Dismounting, Darcy came to stand by her. "I would prefer to join you on your walk. We might not be afforded the privacy at Longbourn that we have now. Is there possibly a longer way into Meryton? I wanted to discuss what I have found out about Mr. Wickham."

Elizabeth nodded and entered a path that veered from the road. "This way will take us to Meryton eventually. I admit that I have been especially curious since I saw you speaking to him after services Sunday."

"It is a long tale," Darcy began as he told her everything he had learned from Wickham. He appreciated the fact that Miss Elizabeth did not interrupt, for parts of the tale were difficult, even embarrassing, for him to tell.

When he had finished, Elizabeth touched his arm in compassion. "You must have been very surprised and shocked at your cousin's betrayal, for that is the only word for what he has done. May I ask what you have done to protect your sister from him?"

"Wickham has a married cousin some ten miles east of Pemberley. The colonel has no knowledge of the couple. I have sent an express to Georgiana, explaining that she must be ready to leave home. I have sent another express to my steward to take one of the smaller Pemberley coaches. It is plain and unmarked. I plan on having him take her and her companion directly to Wickham's cousin, even before one of us hears from his relative. If he cannot accommodate my sister, I have instructed my steward to find a place for her to hide until I can deal with my cousin," Darcy explained. "All that the rest of my staff, except my housekeeper Mrs. Reynolds, will know is that Georgiana is visiting a friend for at least a month.

"My housekeeper is very much like a second mother to us, and for some reason she has never been fond of Richard. It shows some great wisdom on her part."

"I wish you success in this, Mr. Darcy," Elizabeth said sympathetically. "I feel so sad for your sister, but I am happy that she has such a caring brother. I am also happy that you have regained your friendship with Mr. Wickham."

The pleasure of Elizabeth's compassion and understanding flowed over him, helping to soothe the sting of his closest cousin's treachery.

Shaking himself out of the comforting haze, Darcy asked, "How is your family faring, Miss Bennet?"

"They are all well and particularly excited about the ball."

Smiling down at her, Darcy said, "I do hope that you remember that you have promised me two sets."

A gay laugh came in response to his tease. "I never forget a promise, sir. I look forward to our dancing together."

"Good," was his simple reply, but his happy countenance spoke more than words could.

"May I ask what your plans are for dealing with Colonel Fitzwilliam?" Elizabeth asked softly.

"I must return to Town the day after the ball. My cousin has always had the run of Darcy House, which I cannot allow to continue. I shall need to confer with my uncle on how to proceed. I do not wish to bring scandal to his family unless they are also involved somehow."

"Do you plan to return to Meryton?"

"Would I be welcome?" Darcy asked hesitantly.

"I am surprised that you would ask me? I am certain that the Bingleys will be happy for you to come back to Netherfield."

"I agree, but it is your opinion that I seek." Darcy stopped and turned to look intently into her eyes. "I have a particular reason for wanting to determine your view on my return."

"I am curious as to what that reason is, sir," Elizabeth said as her eyes flashed with good humour.

"I shall tell you, but first, I do not expect an answer right now." Darcy faltered for a moment before going on, "Would you do me the great honour of entering into a courtship with me upon my return?"

A deep blush of delight covered her face as Elizabeth stood staring up at him, completely speechless. This handsome young man who had once seemed so aloof was asking for a courtship with Mrs. Bennet's least favourite daughter. Elizabeth tried to remember when she disliked him, but none of the old feelings were present, only giddiness and joy danced in her heart.

When Elizabeth did not answer, Darcy's shoulders drooped. *She must not wish to offend me by refusing. I am sure that she must be trying to figure out a way to say no.* He turned and made to start walking again, but her small hand reached for his.

"I do not have to wait to answer you," she said softly. When he restored his gaze to her face, a smile, the radiance of which he had never seen before graced her countenance. "I would be happy to be courted by you, Mr. Darcy. My silence was one of surprise, not disapprobation."

"You have made me happy, indeed." He lifted her hand to his lips and kissed it before placing it upon his arm. Shall we continue our stroll? I have another bit of news that I am sure you will be happy to hear."

"You are full of information, Mr. Darcy. What more can you have to tell me?" Elizabeth teased him with a grin.

"Would you be pleased to hear that Mr. Bingley plans to propose to Miss Bennet at the ball?" He returned her grin with a huge dimpled smile. "He plans to travel back to London with me to procure an engagement gift for her. Bingley does not think that he could find something good enough for her in Meryton. He does not mean to insult your village. It is just that he wishes the very best for your sister."

Raising her free hand to her mouth, Elizabeth stifled a cry of pure delight. More than anything, she wished she could twirl around as she did as a child when she received a lovely surprise. A giggle escaped before she could stop it at the thought of what Mr. Darcy would think if she actually did it.

"I can tell that you are not displeased by my news, but why the giggle?" Darcy asked enjoying the happiness that radiated from her.

"I was just thinking of the joyous news and wished I could twirl around like I did as a little girl. I then thought of your reaction," she confessed as another laugh escaped her.

Pondering what she would look like as she spun in a circle, her ankles slightly exposed and her curves more visible, Darcy could not help but smile. "I do not think my reaction would be what you expect, Miss Elizabeth. I believe I would rather enjoy the sight."

Her cheeks pinked as she lightly slapped his shoulder. "I shall not venture to guess why. I think it would be improper." Though her voice took on a note of reproof, her eyes told him she was not upset.

Soon, Elizabeth began to quiz Darcy about his knowledge of his friend's intentions.

* * *

Once Darcy and Elizabeth arrived again on the road leading to Meryton, he excused himself. He needed to approach Mr. Bennet about the courtship.

"I will to seek your father's permission for our courtship," Darcy explained as he stopped just out of the view of the village. "However, would you mind if we kept it a secret until after the ball? I wish to enjoy the knowledge quietly for a few more days. Besides, I think that Bingley and Miss Bennet should have time to announce their betrothal and not share the attention with us immediately."

Elizabeth gazed up at him with a teasing smile. "I know that you wish to postpone experiencing the raptures of my mother. Since I happen to know that my father would feel the same, I give you leave to ask it of him. He will be glad to have only one source of exultation for my mother."

Bowing over her hand, Darcy said, "Thank you, Miss Elizabeth. I shall see you tomorrow evening. Have a safe walk home." He mounted his horse and rode off toward Netherfield.

Having no particular destination in mind, Elizabeth spent her time looking at the window displays. She had just paused in front of the mercantile when she heard a familiar voice greet her. Turning, she spied Mr. Wickham crossing the street in her direction.

"Good morning, Mr. Wickham," she said as she curtseyed.

"Well met, Miss Elizabeth," he replied. "I was on my way to Longbourn to ask after your family since you all were missed at church. I hope it was the weather and not illness that kept you away."

"Indeed, it was the weather. Papa did not think it wise to use our old carriage in such mud. I am happy that the sun made its appearance late yesterday. As it is, my boots are quite dirty, as you see."

"I did not notice," he said without looking down. "Do you by chance plan on returning home soon?"

"I do, sir. I only came to Meryton for the exercise. Why do you ask?"

"If it would not be too much to ask, I would like to accompany you." As he spoke, his face flushed.

"I would be happy for the company and I know that my family will be happy to see you."

As they walked to Longbourn, Elizabeth asked about the service and the attendance. Wickham told her that not many had attended due to the rain. He continued to give her a short synopsis of the sermon, making her wish she had heard the complete message. As much as she cared for Mr. North, there was something about the way this young man spoke the word of God that made her want to hear more.

"Mary would love to hear about the sermon, too," she said quietly to herself, but Wickham heard her and blushed again with pleasure.

Chapter 12

Upon hearing Eleanor's declarations, Mr. Collins was greatly confused. "Dearest Eleanor, I do not understand what you could mean."

"Might I ask you some questions before we become officially betrothed?"

Still bewildered, Collins nodded his agreement.

"First of all, what does having a wife mean to you?"

"I believe it will add greatly to my enjoyment of life. A wife is a helpmeet, one who obeys and respects her husband."

"What does the Bible say about the relationship?" Her question sounded like a patient teacher who was trying to lead a student to the correct answer.

"A wife should be submissive and respectful to her husband," was his immediately reply.

"That is true, but the Bible also outlines the responsibilities of a husband. He is to love his wife as Christ loved the church and gave up His life for her. Are you willing to love me in the same way?"

Her question silenced Collins as he pondered this as if it were the first time he had heard it. His father had never treated his mother in that way. He had always quoted the verse about wives submitting to their husbands. Collins had only ever thought of the advantage a marriage would be to himself, but never what it should be to his wife.

"I can only promise to try," Collins finally replied. "This is a new idea to me although I know I should have understood it before."

"That is a perfect answer, William," Eleanor commended with a smile.

"Then we are in agreement?"

"I still have a few things to discuss with you. You must be perfectly honest with me. Otherwise I shall know, and you will have to leave this house immediately." Her expression and tone showed that she meant every word.

"Of course, my dear," Collins said eagerly. "Ask anything you like and I will tell you the truth."

Eleanor gazed upon the cleric in front of her for several moments. She was aware of some of his past habits. Also, she knew how much deference he paid to his patroness. Determined not to live with either, she was convinced that living as a poor relative was preferable to having a husband who worshiped another over the Lord and who might stray from their vows.

"I wish to know the full truth of why you left Longbourn so soon. I do not believe the story you have been telling and elaborating upon these past several days." She stared at him until he dropped his gaze.

Collins had no idea how to make the real reason sound anything but ghastly on his part. However, he knew that somehow Eleanor would ferret out the truth. Clasping his hands together, he began to tell her exactly what had happened, and why he was asked to leave.

Once he had finished, the guilt that he should have felt in the beginning laid heavily upon him. Collins was certain that Eleanor would ask him to leave. He would have to return to Hunsford without a wife and with no prospects of ever having one.

"Do you understand how abominably you acted?" Eleanor asked softly.

Sighing and without lifting his eyes to hers for fear of seeing the condemnation he so richly deserved in them, Collins nodded his agreement.

"Would you act in such a way again, should I agree to marry you?

Shocked at the question, and the fact that she did not order him to leave, Collins looked up. "No, I am thoroughly ashamed of my behaviour toward my cousins. I deserve to be defrocked, but my cousin Mr. Bennet did not wish to subject his family to the scrutiny an inquest by the bishop would bring."

"I can see that you are repentant, although I believe that you will need guidance, so that you do not return to such behaviour again."

Instead of believing that she was willing to marry him after his confession, he whispered, "When do you wish me to leave?"

"I have two more questions for you," she said instead of answering him.

"And they are?" he asked just as softly as before.

"Are you willing to stop your worship of your patroness and cleave to me as your wife over her?" She held up her hand to stop his protest. "I understand you must give her the respect and deference that she deserves as your benefactress, and I would be willing to listen to her advice. However, if said advice is not to my liking, I shall reserve the right to proceed with my own inclination. If I do not agree with her, I shall explain my reasons to you. You are welcome to discuss it with me. I may even change my mind sometimes, but the parsonage shall be my domain, not hers. I would never think of telling her how to run her home. I would like for us to have a peaceful home with as little strife as possible. It would not be possible for me to live under her thumb."

Eleanor paused and waited for his response.

"Lady Catherine would be most displeased if she was not obeyed to the letter." There was a hint of fear his voice.

"That might be true, but you would have a happy wife who would show you in many ways how happy she is. It seems to me that the lady is a petty tyrant. She needs to learn that not everyone will bow down to her dictates."

His eyes became huge at her accusations, and Eleanor smiled benevolently. "And if you are worried about her forcing you from your position, she has not the power to do so unless you continue in your past behaviours, and she should find out. You have nothing to lose if you agree to my terms and much to gain."

Collins knew that what she said was true. There were times when he had resented her ladyship's involvement in his affairs. The shelves in the closets were an absurd example of her advice, which he did not like but had heeded anyway. He wondered at the possibility of a life without bowing to the tyranny of his patroness. Eleanor made him believe that he could have such a life with her assistance.

"What you describe sounds very agreeable indeed." Collins paused before stating his apprehension. "I feel that I am too weak to stand up to her. She is very forceful when disagreed with."

"I shall be at your side to give you strength." Eleanor leaned forward and took his hand. "I believe that you will not need to stand against her often. However, I would like to see your sermons reflect the doctrines of the church and not those of her ladyship. I know that she is the one who edits your sermons. You will simply state that you do not wish to bother her ladyship with corrections, and your wife will take up the task of making certain there are no mistakes in them. You must understand that her pleasure or displeasure is not your responsibility."

"You are so strong, my dear," he said simply. "How ever do you manage it?"

"My mother was strong and kind. I learned much from her example, and for years now I have run Wywyn's household. I have had to be strong. I believe I can help you as well."

"You have been most gracious to me, especially after you heard of my indiscretions." Collins bowed his head again in shame. "I shall try to be worthy of your confidence and respect."

"In that case, William," she said kindly as she waited for him to lift his head, "You may consider yourself an engaged man."

* * *

That evening just, before it was time to change for dinner, Fosset opened the drawing room door to announce a visitor. "Colonel Fitzwilliam."

Darcy was the first to stand and address his cousin. "Cousin, I did not expect you. I thought you were in the north."

"I was until my commander ordered me to deliver some papers to the major general in London. He allowed me a week's leave for my trouble. When I found that you were not at Darcy house, I thought I would come to see this Netherfield about which you wrote me earlier," the colonel responded with a cocky grin. "I hope that Bingley does not mind."

Already on his feet, Bingley put out his hand in greeting. "Of course, I do not mind at all. You are most welcome. In fact, you are just in time for dinner."

Turning to the butler, Bingley said, "See to it that an extra place is set at table."

Bowing, Fosset left the room while Bingley offered to show Richard to a room. "We are hosting a ball tomorrow evening, so several of our guest chambers have been made ready for the possibility of visitors from town. None of those guests have arrived because of the recent rains. How were the roads?"

It was obvious by the mud splattered on his uniform that the colonel had encountered bad conditions on at least part of his journey. "The last few miles were dry enough, but closer to Town, they were quite muddy. It made me glad for my steed's sure footedness. As you can see, I could do with a good washing. And could I ask that my uniform be cleaned? I shall change into the clothes I brought with me after I clean up."

* * *

That evening, Darcy felt very uncomfortable. Disguise of any kind was abhorrent to him, but he could not in good conscience make public his personal matters in front of those at Netherfield. Charles and the Hursts were already upset at having to send Caroline away. Darcy did not wish to cause more distress to them. For that reason, he tried to be civil with his cousin.

As difficult as it was, Darcy took part in the conversation at dinner and later at cards. He even allowed himself to be teased by Richard, smiling at the jokes he told. Unwilling to sit still to play whist, he took up a book. Turning the pages so as to look like he was absorbed in the volume, Darcy pondered what he should do.

Darcy finally decided that he would send word to his uncle, explaining briefly what Richard had done, including the near elopement with Georgiana. Since he had already planned to speak to Lord Matlock while in Town, the letter would give Richard's father the information he needed to know before they met. Otherwise, Richard might be able to lie his way out of the trouble he had made.

Closing his book, Darcy moved to the writing desk in the corner and began the note to his uncle. He was careful to keep an eye on the others in the room. It would not do for his cousin to find out to whom he wrote the missive. Once he was finished and had sanded his letter, he put the paper in his waistcoat pocket and took up his book again.

* * *

When the Hursts excused themselves to retire, Darcy rose to follow their example. Richard called to him, asking for a moment of his time before he went to his chambers for the night.

"I am rather tired," Darcy said, hoping to avoid any private conversation with his cousin. "Could it not wait until morning?"

"I will not keep you long from your beauty sleep," Richard quipped as he came to stand beside Darcy. "Let us share a brandy. We will both sleep better after a drink."

Fighting his frustration, Darcy led the way to the study. He had a bad premonition about which topic the colonel wished to speak. He steeled his expression as they entered. Fitzwilliam walked immediately to the liquor bottles that sat on a sideboard and poured a generous amount of Bingley's brandy into snifters. After handing one glass to Darcy, Richard swirled the liquid to warm it before he sipped it in obvious pleasure.

"Bingley may be a bit of a puppy, but he does know his liquor," Richard commented with a grin.

"You have not seen him in two years. He has done a great deal of maturing in the meantime." Darcy felt he needed to defend his best friend.

"Oh get off your high horse, Darcy. I know that he is a good sort of chap, for the son of a tradesman, but you must admit he will never be equal to us in status." Having finished his brandy, the colonel turned to pour himself another.

Insulted for his friend and impatient to leave his cousin's company, Darcy asked, "Why did you wish to speak to me?"

Richard moved to one of the stuffed leather chairs and sat with his feet stretched out in front of him. He wished for a cigar, but he thought that would not go over well with Darcy. Sighing slightly and with a more sober mien, he answered, "I wish to leave the army. I am tired of following the orders of others. I want to settle and get married."

Knowing full well the likely identity of his cousin's intended bride, Darcy showed curiosity and asked, "And who is the bride to be? She must have a good dowry for you to quit the army."

"Oh, she is a lovely young thing with a large dowry, and I am certain that her family would be so happy to secure such a match that they would provide an estate so that we would not need to spend much of the dowry on such things as acquiring a house."

Having finished his second glass of brandy, the colonel was feeling relaxed and had more than his usual level of confidence. He smiled at Darcy as his cousin waited for his answer. Enjoying the suspense, Richard leaned back with his hands behind his head.

"Can you not guess the name of the young lady of whom I am speaking?"

Upon seeing Darcy's face harden, Richard finally said, "You must be tired if you cannot, or will not, play along with me. I wish to marry Georgiana. I have fallen under her spell. What do you say to that, Cousin? We shall be brothers."

Darcy, who had neither sat nor finished his brandy, set his glass on a small table, lest he crush it in his bare hands. He stared at the colonel without speaking for several moments.

His glare caused his cousin to laugh. "You did not expect it, did you? Well, it is true, and Georgiana loves me as well. All you will have to do is ask her."

"You have spoken to her before coming to me?" Darcy asked while barely containing his rage.

"About that, Darcy . . ." Richard hesitated as he conjured up an explanation. "I was sent to Ramsgate on a mission for my commander. I knew from your letters and hers that she would be there, so I decided to visit her. We went to the boardwalk, fully chaperoned by Mrs. Younge. It was then that we understood our love for one another. Georgiana was so overcome with her affection for me that she begged to elope, so that we would not have to part, but I would not hear of it. You would have been wounded to not be a part of our nuptials, would you not?"

Feeling very satisfied with his tale, Richard relaxed, waiting for his cousin to commend his actions, but what Darcy said next shocked him.

"No, I do not give my permission for you to marry my sister."

Taken aback, Richard replied, "Why, may I ask, with so little explanation are you willing to destroy our happiness?"

Darcy bit back a sardonic laugh as he answered, "She is not of age, nor has she come out. I forbid it."

"Oh, but I am her guardian as well as you. I believe I have equal say. I can petition the court for permission to marry her. I think that the son of an earl will have more sway than a mere gentleman such as yourself."

"That may be," Darcy calmly stated, "However, I believe that your father has more power than a younger son such as yourself."

"What?" Richard shouted, "My father has nothing to do with this."

"Ah, but he does. If you had stayed for the complete reading of the will, you would have known that my father put in a provision for such a time as this. If we could not agree upon whom Georgiana should marry, Uncle Matlock would decide."

Richard relaxed as he heard his cousin's explanation. His father would most certainly decide in his favour. He had made sure that none of his previous misdeeds had come to his father's notice. The colonel knew he had never used his own name when he seduced a young woman. He had narrowly escaped a few angry fathers and brothers— and the occasional husband—, but he had not been caught out. While he was on the continent, he had had several pleasant encounters with French women, especially those who had nearly no food and would do most anything for a loaf of bread or a chunk of cheese.

"I will go to my father tomorrow morning. I am sure that I can make him see the rightness of the match."

Darcy wanted nothing more than to wipe the smirk off his cousin's face, but he knew that it would be more satisfying to wait until they met with Lord Matlock. "I had planned to return to London with Bingley the day after the ball on business for a few days. I am certain Bingley would be amenable to you joining us in his carriage, unless you wish to make the trip again on horseback."

Smiling, Richard agreed, "It will be most pleasant to travel with the two of you. The luxury of a well-sprung carriage is not often to be had. I do not wish to miss the opportunity of dancing with the lovely ladies of Hertfordshire, especially the lovely Miss Bennet that Bingley spoke so highly of this evening at dinner, and her sisters."

Darcy did not wish to spend another moment with his reprobate cousin. He bowed quickly and left for his chambers, leaving Richard to scheme some kind of revenge on Darcy for forbidding his union with Georgiana.

* * *

The next evening at his abode on the outskirts of Meryton, Colonel Forster impatiently submitted to his batman's ministrations. He wished to look his best for the Netherfield ball, but mostly he wanted to see Miss Lydia. It had been a tiring week, what with the rain and his command duties which kept him from Longbourn. Without a doubt, he knew he loved her. If only he had not agreed to wait for a betrothal! He was more than ready to have a home of his own, and he was certain that the youngest Miss Bennet was the perfect wife for him.

"Do you wish to use the looking glass to see if I have performed my work properly, sir?" The young soldier's voice broke into his thoughts.

"No, Patrick, I do not need to do so. I trust your work and always have." The colonel pulled at his sleeves before turning to the door of his chambers. "I heard that there is to be a gathering of some of the servants at the Crown and Bell. Do you plan to attend?"

The young Patrick blushed as he met the colonel's eye. "I would like it very much if you give me leave to do so, sir."

Smiling, Forster clapped his batman on the shoulder. "Of course, you have my permission. See that my curricle is ready, then, go make yourself ready."

Patrick saluted as he fought back a smile. "Yes sir."

As he watched his man leave, he chuckled to himself. *I wonder if he is sweet on someone in the village.*

Forster lifted his shako from its stand. *It will not be as difficult as I thought to give up this uniform. Although, I shall keep it because my sweet Lydia loves me in red,* he thought as he made his way to the door.

"Lovesick old fool," Forster told himself.

* * *

While Colonel Forster made his way to Netherfield, the Bennet household was strangely unruffled. That is, aside from Mrs. Bennet. She fussed over the girls, especially Jane and Lydia, since she thought they had the best chance of catching husbands. However, it did not take her long to see that all of her girls were in good looks. Even Mary looked quite lovely. The sight of her daughters—splendid in their finery—caused her to ponder how they had grown, and that they would likely be soon gone from her home.

Mr. Bennet found her sitting on the wooden bench near the front door, dabbing at tears.

"What is the matter, my dear?" Bennet asked in a concerned tone. "Are you ill?"

Mrs. Bennet sniffed and shook her head. "I am so very happy. All of our girls look so lovely tonight. I dare say that even Mary will have many partners this evening. I did not know I could be so proud of them all. It is disconcerting."

Taking a seat next to his wife, Mr. Bennet wrapped his arm around her waist and kissed her cheek. "How could you not be proud of them? I have been astounded myself at the maturity they have shown lately. We must have done something right for this to happen."

Disregarding her newly coiffed hair, Mrs. Bennet leaned her head upon her husband's shoulder and sighed, "When did we lose this closeness, Thomas?"

"I am not certain," he admitted softly.

"I think that I am to blame. I have not listened to you, thinking that I knew better how to get husbands for our girls." Fanny Bennet paused to decide how to put into words how she felt without injuring this intimacy.

"At the first assembly in which you asked me to dance, I was stunned. You, a gentleman, would ask the daughter of a country attorney. You were so witty and smart although I did not always understand what you were saying.

"By the time you asked my father to court me, I already loved you so much. However, when I could not give you a son, I began to think that I was being punished for my unworthiness. Lizzy is so much like you, and most of the others take after me. I could never hope to teach Lizzy what you could, but I could relate to Lydia and to a lesser degree, Kitty."

By the time, Fanny had finished her speech, she was weeping openly.

"Fanny Bennet," Mr. Bennet's voice was kind but firm. Once he had her attention, he continued. "I have been an indolent man for most of our marriage. It was easy for me to teach Lizzy since we are indeed similar. However, I failed my younger girls, and I failed to help you. I am wholly ashamed of myself for my neglect and laziness. However, it would seem that despite our failings, our girls are becoming women of whom we can be proud.

"Will you forgive me for not showing you my love as I should have?" he asked as he put his handkerchief into her hand.

"I do forgive you, Thomas, and I ask yours as well." She wiped her eyes and blew her nose rather noisily. The look in her eyes as she gazed up at him was one of deep affection.

"Let us put this in the past and begin again, shall we?"

Smiling, she leaned in to kiss him on the mouth, which was something she had not initiated in many years. The spark of renewed desire for her husband surprised her.

Mr. Bennet pulled back and smiled down at his wife. "My dear, I believe you still have time to repair your appearance and to put cool water on your eyes. I would not wish anyone to think I have an unhappy wife."

"Husband!" she admonished with a giggle before she stood. "I shall not take long since Hill and Sarah have finished with the girls."

Watching his wife move to the stairs, Mr. Bennet grinned before he followed her to fetch another handkerchief.

* * *

The Bennets were among the first of the guests to arrive at Netherfield. Once their carriage stopped at the bottom of the front steps, they could see the lights shining from nearly every window. The footman let down the steps, and Mr. Bennet emerged to help his ladies alight from the vehicle.

As she followed her parents and older sister, Elizabeth was surprised to find Mr. Darcy at her side, offering his arm.

"I did not expect to see you until we gained entrance into the house," she whispered.

Also in a quiet voice, Darcy answered, "I wanted to be the first to greet you and to inform you that my cousin the colonel arrived unexpectedly last night. He asked my permission to marry Georgiana."

Elizabeth stifled her anger at Darcy's cousin's temerity. "I find it hard to believe that he would have the audacity to do so after his attempt . . ."

Interrupting her, Darcy leaned closer and said, "I do not wish him to be aware that anyone knows about that incident. I will explain more when we have a bit more privacy."

Elizabeth nodded as they reached the door and entered the foyer. Hoping that she could keep her countenance during the introduction that was sure to come, she gave her wrap to a servant before taking Darcy's arm once more.

As the Bennets were announced into the ballroom, Elizabeth spied Mr. Bingley, and a stranger dressed in regular army regimentals. Both men walked toward them with smiles on their faces.

Bingley was the first to bow in welcome before he introduced the other man to the Bennets.

Colonel Fitzwilliam greeted each of them with compliments and warmth. Beginning with Jane, he asked each of the ladies for a dance. After each of them accepted his offer, he turned to Elizabeth and asked for the supper dance as well.

"I am sorry, Colonel, but that dance is already taken," she answered with a smile that did not reach her eyes.

"That is a pity." He frowned but quickly smiled again. "I should not be surprised if all of these fair ladies have partners for that particular dance. I must say that I have never seen so many lovely women in one family."

His eyes travelled to Elizabeth again, but he quickly turned them away when another group of gentlemen came to claim a dance with the other Bennet sisters.

Elizabeth had felt great discomfort under the colonel's gaze. He was jovial enough, but it seemed more a role he played, instead of his true character. She noticed that he was not as tall as Mr. Darcy or nearly as handsome. Knowing what she did about Colonel Fitzwilliam, she wished that she did not have to dance with him.

"Mr. Darcy," Elizabeth commented, "I see Charlotte Lucas over by the window. Would you kindly escort me there? I believe that I might not make it in this crush."

"I would be happy to," Darcy said and excused them from the group.

"I believe your cousin is planning something. Would you please see to it that my sisters are watched over, especially Mary?"

"You do not have to ask," he answered. "I have already taken some precautions."

"What will happen when Mr. Wickham arrives?"

"He has already arrived. I advised him of my cousin's presence as soon as he entered the house. We decided that he would wait until just before the first set to show himself. I do not believe that Fitzwilliam will cause a scene in front of so many people."

Once they had made their way to Charlotte's side, Elizabeth chatted with her dear friend, complimenting her upon her new gown. Talking to Charlotte helped to keep her mind from wandering to the possibility of drama at the ball.

After several minutes, the first dance was called, and the couples began to line up in the middle of the ballroom floor. Darcy and Elizabeth stood next to Jane and Bingley, on their left, and Mary and Wickham on their right. Colonel Fitzwilliam stood down the line with Kitty as his partner.

It was not until the first few steps in the dance that the colonel looked around and saw Wickham. He stumbled once and righted himself, laughingly apologizing to Kitty.

"How long has Mr. Wickham been in Meryton?" Fitzwilliam asked, as if offhandedly.

"Oh, he has been our curate for just over two months, I believe," Kitty said as she skipped around him in the dance.

"I am surprised."

"You know Mr. Wickham?"

"I do," he said with a sneer. "He was the son of my uncle's steward."

"Of course, I had forgotten that he lived at Pemberley."

Meanwhile, Darcy forgot all about his cousin as he danced with the lovely Miss Elizabeth. She was light on her feet and smiled as if she was happy to be with him. They talked of several subjects of little matter for the first part of the set.

However, Elizabeth finally asked the question that had been gnawing at her since Darcy first told her about his cousin being there.

"What did you say to your cousin when he asked his question?" she asked softly as they passed each other.

Waiting to answer until they were once more close enough not to be overheard, Darcy said, "I said we would have to speak to his father because of a provision in my father's will."

The dance parted them again which frustrated Elizabeth. If she had her way they would be walking in the garden instead of dancing.

This thought led to more intimate feelings. Her face reddened as she pondered walking arm in arm through the evening with Mr. Darcy. Only, she would not wish to speak of his reprobate cousin.

"Miss Elizabeth." Darcy's voice took on concern. "Are you well? You look as if you were becoming overheated."

Her colour heightened even more at being caught blushing. "No sir, I am well. Perhaps I am a bit overheated, but I shall be fine."

"I shall fetch you something to drink once the set is finished, Darcy promised.

Chapter 13

Mary Bennet could barely believe her good fortune. She was dancing the first set, and with the only man she would have wanted for herself. Mr. Wickham had invited her to partner with him immediately after receiving an invitation to the ball. How was it that such a handsome man would wish to be with her? She could not credit it; however here she was, standing up with the smiling curate.

"How are you this fine evening, Miss Mary?" Wickham asked as they passed in the dance.

"I am well, sir," she responded demurely.

"Have you a partner for the supper dance?" His question seemed rather timid.

"No, I have not been asked as yet."

"I would like to have the honour, if you will grant it," he said softly as they walked down the line.

Blushing, Mary agreed with a shy smile. Her heart fluttered with the thrill of being asked for two sets by the young man who had already captured her heart. *If only*, she thought wistfully. Inwardly she shook herself. She would not allow herself such thoughts. They would likely lead her to heartbreak.

Mary would have been comforted if she had known that Mr. Wickham's thoughts mirrored her own. He had come to the ball with the intention of asking for a courtship after he spoke with her father, but with the presence of Colonel Fitzwilliam, he wondered if it might be prudent to wait until another day. He was pleased that Darcy had given him warning of the colonel's presence at Netherfield, yet he worried that there would be a scene that night. He did not wish for such a scene to overshadow the beginning of their relationship, if his suit was accepted.

Briefly glancing in the direction of the colonel, who was dancing with Miss Kitty, Wickham worried what Darcy's cousin might say to Miss Mary's younger sister. He tried to keep his mind on the pleasure of dancing with the young lady who had taken residence in his heart and, for the most part, he was successful.

* * *

Later, after Colonel Fitzwilliam had danced with Jane Bennet, he came to claim the hand of Miss Elizabeth who stood with her mother. He was surprised to see his cousin talking pleasantly with the two women. Never before had he seen Darcy spend more time than was necessary with any dance partner. He seemed different somehow, more at ease tonight.

It was not until the colonel arrived and bowed to the ladies that he noticed a change in his cousin's expression. Suddenly, Darcy wore was the stiff and stoic visage that he usually did at gatherings such this. This caused Colonel Fitzwilliam to wonder if his younger relative could be jealous of his attention to Miss Elizabeth.

Suppressing a smile of satisfaction, the colonel offered his hand to Miss Elizabeth. "This is our set, Miss Elizabeth."

"It is, sir," she answered placing her hand lightly on his. "Excuse us, Mama, Mr. Darcy."

Colonel Fitzwilliam heard her mother comment to Darcy about how handsome the colonel looked in his uniform. He smiled as he looked down at Miss Elizabeth and said, "You look lovely this evening, Miss Elizabeth."

"Thank you," was her short reply.

As they lined up for the dance, he noticed a few officers lined up close to them. Miss Kitty had explained that the _____shire militia was stationed in Meryton for the winter. She had surprised him by informing him that her younger sister was in a courtship with the militia's commanding officer.

"I see that the militia is most welcome in Hertfordshire."

"Yes, they have been a pleasant addition to our society," she replied with a half smile.

"Has no officer caught your eye, Miss Elizabeth?" His tone was light and teasing.

"No, sir," her tone seemed to match his, "My eye is not so easily turned by a red coat as some might be."

The colonel felt the sting of her words. He watched as she looked away from him to give Darcy a smile. His cousin, who was dancing with a rather plain young woman, smiled back briefly. Deciding it was time to act, Fitzwilliam asked as nonchalantly as possible, "How does Darcy comport himself in Meryton?"

"He is a complete gentleman," Elizabeth answered, curious to find out what the officer would say next.

"I am glad that he has been able to keep himself under good regulation." His inflection seemed to reflect relief.

"What makes you say that, sir?" she asked indifferently.

"I would hate to cause a lady any discomfort by speaking of indelicate matters, but I wish to put you on your guard." His lowered voice sounded reluctant to continue.

"If it is a matter about which I should be warned, please do not think me so weak that you cannot be specific, Colonel."

Lowering his voice even more, he said, "I am afraid I must inform you that my cousin Darcy is not to be trusted. He is a habitual gambler and womaniser. I have paid off many of his debts over the years. Please pardon my plain speech, for I know not any other way to explain."

Elizabeth fought her anger at the web of lies this despicable man was weaving. Pale-faced, she whispered, "I admit to great astonishment at what you have told me. There has been no hint of impropriety relating to Mr. Darcy in Meryton."

The colonel sighed as if reluctant to say more. Nevertheless he said, "I have heard rumours that there have been unwelcome consequences due to his frequent liaisons with young ladies."

Gasping at the audacity of the falsehoods Colonel Fitzwilliam would spread about his own cousin, Elizabeth flushed with anger but controlled her tongue. Once she felt she could speak, she said in a trembling voice, "This is grave indeed. It is hard to comprehend."

"Well, he will soon be married to our cousin, Anne de Bourgh. It is an engagement of long standing; the family hopes it will bring an end to some of his . . . activities."

Still keeping her voice soft, Elizabeth spoke the next time they were close in the dance, "I wonder that Mr. Bingley is not aware of Mr. Darcy's behaviour."

In a near whisper, the colonel replied, "I am sorry to speak thus about the host of this grand ball, but Bingley is a rather dull pup. He believes only what he wishes to believe, and he is usually too involved in falling in love with his latest angel to notice my cousin's doings."

"Are you saying that Mr. Bingley is a rake as well?" Again, Elizabeth fought back rage.

"No, I would not say that about him. He is a shallow-minded man who loves being in love, but once he is out of sight of his current *amour*, he forgets her and is on to another."

As the couple glided around each other, Fitzwilliam asked, "Did you know that Bingley and Darcy planned to leave Netherfield tomorrow for Town?"

"Yes, and I had heard that they would return in a day or two," she replied quickly.

Shaking his head as if in pity, Fitzwilliam said, "They often leave a place, promising to return, without the slightest idea of actually doing so."

Elizabeth pondered all that he had told her in silence for several moments, but knowing that the set would be over soon, she knew she had to do something to keep these falsehoods from circulating. Hoping she could play to his sympathy, she put on a pleading expression and said, "I pray that you will grant me a favour after telling me such ghastly things about those men."

"I only told you for your protection," he insisted.

"Of course you did, sir," she said while keeping her eyes lowered. "I would like to ask you not to tell anyone else of these things. Those men will be gone tomorrow, and I do not wish to destroy the enjoyment of all the guests with such facts. I shall inform my father and the others tomorrow. It will be soon enough for the rest to know. I especially wish for my sister to enjoy the rest of the evening, for she will be heart-broken when she finds out Mr. Bingley will not return."

As the music ended, Colonel Fitzwilliam bowed and agreed with a satisfied look on his face, "I shall not say a word for your sake and your sisters'."

* * *

Colonel Fitzwilliam stood and watched Elizabeth join her sister with a sense of contentment and triumph. He had no doubt that the young lady had believed him. Her shocked expression and her words of surprise were obvious. He had no intention of speaking to anyone else about his cousin. Poisoning the mind of the one lady who had caught the fancy of his cousin was more than enough. It mattered not that Darcy might return, for he would find his reception in the neighbourhood quite different from the one he now enjoyed.

Early on in his conversation with Miss Elizabeth, the colonel had decided that it would not do for his cousin to hear his tales. Darcy would not take lightly the stain on his reputation and would likely challenge him. Being that his cousin was an excellent shot, and a champion at swords, he would most definitely defeat the colonel in a duel. Fitzwilliam was actually quite the coward, which was why he had nearly begged for a homeland assignment. His father, the earl, had helped him obtain many of the postings he had enjoyed. However, if he was not successful in his quest to marry Georgiana or another heiress soon, he would very likely be sent to the continent or Lower Canada.

He sought out his partner for the next dance. Miss Lydia Bennet was quite young to be out and in a courtship with Colonel Forster, which told the colonel that she would likely fall for his flattery quite easily. Fitzwilliam did not know the militia commander personally, but he knew Colonel Forster had an unimpeachable reputation, even among the regulars. If the younger Bennet sister was the type to be attracted to a uniform, and if he had more time to spare, Fitzwilliam was certain that he could have a bit of sport with her.

As he reached her, he bowed before offering his hand. "Miss Lydia, I believe this is our set."

Lydia gave him a curtsey and allowed him to lead her to the dance floor.

"I am stunned at the beauty of the sisters Bennet," Fitzwilliam stated as the dance began. "I was surprised to hear from your sister Miss Katherine that none of you have had a season in London. You all would have made a grand impression upon the Town."

Lydia thanked him for the compliment. However, it was her only response.

It was Colonel Fitzwilliam's turn to be surprised. Most often his practiced flatteries were received with far more enthusiasm. Most of the Bennet sisters were certainly of a different ilk than those he met in the *ton*.

Deciding to use a different tack, the colonel asked her about her friends. She told of her closeness to her sisters, especially Elizabeth and Kitty. Maria Lucas was her dearest friend outside of her family. The colonel listened with half an ear as she spoke of the Lucas family and their welcoming home.

"I observed you talking to Colonel Forster. He seems a gentlemanly sort of man," he stated when she had finished.

"Oh, he is!" Lydia smiled broadly at his mention of the other officer.

"So he is well liked in the neighbourhood, is he?" he asked with a hint of mocking.

Lydia looked at the colonel with scepticism at the man's tone. "He is greatly respected here in Meryton. His officers all give him a good name."

"I am gratified that he is a good officer." His voice trailed off as if he would wish to say more.

Fitzwilliam was frustrated when Lydia did not take his bait. In fact, for the rest of the set, she gave only brief replies to his attempt at further conversation. Further irritated by her lack of response, he glanced around the room. He saw Darcy and Miss Elizabeth in an intense conversation, and she seemed upset at his cousin.

Fuming inwardly, Lydia did not even take Colonel Fitzwilliam's arm when he escorted her back to her family. After thanking him perfunctorily, she turned to her sister Kitty and asked about her dance partners.

* * *

Lydia was thankful to see the colonel walk away. After her recent quick conversation with Elizabeth, she understood that he had been trying to glean information and to plant some sort of doubt or falsehood with his veiled hints.

Happy that the next set was the supper set, Lydia wished to find out what her colonel would have to say about the other. Knowing full well that Colonel Forster was not a gossip, he still might be able to explain why the other officer was trying to disseminate misinformation.

"Miss Lydia." Colonel Forster's voice alerted her to his presence.

"Colonel," Lydia acknowledged him with a curtsey. "I am happy that you arrived early for our dance."

"I am glad to hear it, but you seem a trifle perturbed," he said as he offered his arm and moved some distance from her family.

Giving a trill of laughter, Lydia agreed. "That I was, until you came. That other colonel was rather unpleasant."

Leaning in to speak softly, Colonel Forster asked, "How so, my dear?"

Smiling at the appellation, Lydia answered, "He seemed to want to suggest that you are not the gentleman I know you to be. I would have informed him of our courtship, but I did not wish to give him the satisfaction of thinking I needed to defend you, because I know that I do not."

"Thank you for your confidence," he replied. "I know little of his character other than that he is Mr. Darcy's cousin and the younger son of an earl. He does not serve in the militia, so there is little interaction between us.

"Do you wish for me to investigate him further?"

Sighing, Lydia said, "No, I do not wish to hear anymore of him. I wish to enjoy our dance, and supper afterwards."

Colonel Forster nodded his approval and led her to the floor.

* * *

Darcy observed Miss Elizabeth as she stood up with his cousin. Although not everyone would have been able to tell, he noticed that she was uncomfortable. Normally, her countenance was open and cheerful. However, even when she did smile, it did not reach her eyes. He wondered if the information he had imparted to her about Fitzwilliam had coloured her response, or if it was something his cousin was saying.

As the set came to an end, Darcy moved closer to where Mrs. Bennet stood. He was surprised to see Elizabeth quickly whisper something to her sister Lydia as Elizabeth left the dance floor, not waiting for Colonel Fitzwilliam to escort her to her mother.

Once he saw his cousin bow to Miss Lydia, Darcy came to stand next to Miss Elizabeth, whose rigid stance indicated her disquiet.

"Do you not have a partner for this set, Miss Elizabeth?" Darcy asked.

"I do not, for which I am grateful," she stated bluntly.

"Might I ask what has caused your obvious unrest?"

"Your cousin," she fairly spit out in disgust, "is a liar of the first rank."

Scanning the crowd around them, Darcy could tell that no one was listening to their conversation. Nevertheless, he lowered his voice. "What falsehoods did he tell you?"

"He tried to lower my opinion of you and Mr. Bingley." Her expression softened when she continued, "I am so glad that you and I have discussed my first impressions, and you have enlightened me as to the colonel's actions. If you had not, I might have fallen for his smooth lies and flattering words."

"I have confidence that you would have understood him, Miss Elizabeth," Darcy told her.

"I thank you, sir, for that confidence," she whispered as she gazed at her shoes.

"I asked him not to tell anyone else about you for the sake of the others' enjoyment and for my sisters' sake. He agreed not to say anything, but I do not know if I trust his word," she explained rather timidly.

"Normally I would not trust it either, but he knows that, if I heard him speak such tales, I would inform the earl, and he would not look favourably on Richard's suit of Georgiana. Also, I am certain that my cousin knows I would likely challenge him on the field of honour." Darcy wanted to do just that as he watched Fitzwilliam dancing with Miss Lydia. However, he now had even more proof of his cousin's perfidy.

"What shall be done now, Mr. Darcy?" Elizabeth asked as she met his eyes.

"I am afraid that we must not be seen in much conversation. It would be wise if my cousin thinks that you believe him at least in part. Since you have already told him that you have a partner for the supper set, we will need to dance it with each other."

"However, you believe we should not attend supper together," Elizabeth finished his thought.

"I hope you will not be offended," he said as he gave her a quick glance. "He will think that you believed him, and I shall be able to keep him occupied so that he is not tempted to spread more of his lies."

"I admit to being disappointed, but I understand, therefore I am not offended," she replied, glancing at the dancers.

"I believe I shall join my mother and father, for your cousin has been looking at us with some curiosity." Elizabeth gave a small curtsey and drew closer to her parents.

* * *

Bingley excitedly awaited the supper set. His heart beat wildly as he contemplated his proposal. He knew that he would have to wait until after the set for a private moment to ask for Miss Bennet's hand, but he also anticipated their dance very much.

As soon as Jane's partner returned her to her family, he moved to join them. Bowing, he asked the group in general how they were enjoying the ball.

"Oh Mr. Bingley, your home is so elegant, and the decorations are so fine," Mrs. Bennet gushed. However, when Mr. Bennet gently laid his hand on the small of her back, her tone calmed, "I am sure that Mr. Bennet and I have never enjoyed a ball so much as this."

"You are correct, my dear." Mr. Bennet smiled down at his wife. "I am enjoying it enough to wish to dance again with my wife for the supper set."

Mrs. Bennet glowed with pleasure at her husband's statement.

Watching her parents, Jane was astonished by the accord between them. It gladdened her heart and brought a big smile to her lips.

Finally answering Bingley, Jane said, "I am certain that this ball will stay in my memory as one of the loveliest I have ever attended. Thank you for inviting us."

"It has been my pleasure," Bingley said with another bow.

Just then the signal for the next set sounded, and the two gentlemen offered an arm to their chosen partners.

Mindful of the people around him, Bingley leaned in slightly and spoke quietly. "Would you allow me a few words after the dance and before we join the others at supper?"

Jane blushed, but agreed before laying her hand on his as he led her to the dance floor.

* * *

Colonel Fitzwilliam frowned as he saw Elizabeth Bennet join the dance with his cousin. Did she not believe him? Quickly, his expression changed when his partner asked him if something were amiss.

"I beg your pardon, Miss Lucas," he answered with a practiced smile. "I allowed a stray thought to pass through my mind. It shall not happen again.

"Now please tell me about yourself," he said, charm oozing from every pore.

As Charlotte Lucas told him a little of her history, he listened with only half an ear. He tried to puzzle out why Miss Elizabeth would not avoid Darcy. It was then that Fitzwilliam realised that she must have agreed to the set before he had an opportunity to speak to her. Since she did not wish for anyone else to be aware of his cousin's bad reputation until after the three men left for London, there was nothing she could do but dance as promised.

Relaxing in the sure knowledge, that his plot to ruin Darcy in the eyes of Meryton—and of Miss Elizabeth's in particular—had succeeded, the colonel continued to be his amiable self. He answered Charlotte's enquiries about his service to the king with a few embellishments, which had the express purpose of making him seem braver and nobler than he truly was.

Fitzwilliam found that Miss Lucas was neither a flirt nor unintelligent. If she had had money, he might have chosen to pursue her. Alas, besides being nearly on the shelf, her face and figure did not inspire him, especially since she was obviously poor. No, he would wait for his father's approval—which he was certain would come—to wed both money and beauty in the form of his lovely cousin Georgiana.

* * *

Jane Bennet's heart raced as the dance ended. She hoped that Mr. Bingley would ask her for a courtship, but she tried not to allow her wishes to overwhelm her good sense. They had not known each other for a great deal of time. Perhaps he only wished to express a private farewell, since he was to go to Town on the morrow.

Mr. Bingley offered his arm and led her to chairs at the side of the room. They both sat watching the crowd move to the supper room. Once the majority had left, he turned to her and cleared his voice.

"Miss Bennet, I have greatly enjoyed getting acquainted with you. From the moment I met you, I have been grateful that I decided to take the lease at Netherfield."

Jane shyly met his eyes and smiled, "I am also happy that you chose to move here. Your party has been a wonderful addition to our neighbourhood society."

"I had hoped that you would have welcomed my particular society," he replied with wistfulness.

Jane blushed and looked down at her clasped hands. "Indeed, sir, I did."

Covering her hands with his, Bingley sighed. "I am so pleased to hear it, for I have come to love you very much and would be honoured if you would agree to be my wife."

Jane beamed at him with a radiant smile and tears glistening in her eyes. "I would be most happy to accept."

Glancing around him to see if anyone was watching and finding none, he lifted one of her hands to his lips and kissed it. "You have made me very happy. Shall I find your father?"

"Please let us wait until you return," Jane whispered. "It would be too obvious if you were to do so now. I do not wish to experience my mother's enthusiasm in such a public place as this."

"Very well, my dear, it shall be as you wish. I shall be perfectly content in the knowledge that you have said yes. I shall not be gone more than a couple of days. That will be soon enough to petition your father."

Standing he offered his arm. "Shall we join the others?"

L eading Miss Lucas to the supper room and to a table, Colonel Fitzwilliam quickly went to the buffet and prepared a plate for himself and his supper partner. Once seated, he allowed his gaze to wander over the other diners. He noticed that Miss Elizabeth was sitting across from Bingley and Miss Bennet. His observation told him that not only was she not happy, but Darcy was nowhere to be seen. Miss Elizabeth had taken his information as truth and would not dine with him. This knowledge caused him to smile with satisfaction.

"Cousin." Startled from his reverie by Darcy's greeting, Colonel Fitzwilliam glanced up at him. "May I join you?"

"Ah, Darcy, I had wished to speak to you," the colonel replied as he stood. "May I have a moment of your time?"

Before Darcy had time to reply, Fitzwilliam bowed to Charlotte, saying, "I hope you will excuse me for a few minutes. I promise I shall return to your delightful company shortly."

Charlotte nodded her consent with a faint smile. "I shall await you here, Colonel Fitzwilliam."

Darcy and Fitzwilliam left the room and walked through to the corridor outside the ballroom. Darcy stopped and turned to his cousin. "You wished to speak to me?"

"Yes, I do," the colonel answered while keeping a sober countenance. "I was concerned that you were not sitting with your dance partner. Did you and Miss Elizabeth have an argument?"

Fitzwilliam saw Darcy's nostrils flare in obvious annoyance. "Miss Elizabeth wished to dine with her sister, and said it would be better if I found another supper partner."

"Did she give you any indication as to why?"

"She seemed unusually grave during our set. I decided that she must have something weighing heavily on her mind and that she would tell me if and when she wished. I did not press her." Darcy's face showed great irritation and frustration.

The glee that Fitzwilliam felt at this admission made it difficult for him not to smirk, but he managed to keep a sympathetic look on his face. "I am greatly sorry for you. You seemed to like her a great deal. It must be quite a blow to find her cross with you for no reason. Perhaps it is something Wickham might have said about you. I know that he has maligned you in the past."

Darcy appeared to ponder this before he shrugged. "I suppose that might explain it. Perhaps I should confront him about it. I cannot have anyone spreading lies about me."

Panic seized the colonel since he did not want his cousin finding out about his duplicity. Trying to keep his voice calm, he said, "No, Darcy, from what I have heard, from those I danced with and conversations I have overheard, no one would believe you. Wickham is well liked here, and you know that you appear austere and cold with strangers. No, I do not believe it should be attempted at this time. Give Miss Elizabeth some time. I believe she is intelligent enough to see him for what he is."

"I will return in a few days. I will be certain to find time to speak to her then," Darcy said thoughtfully.

Fitzwilliam was pleased that he had convinced Darcy to wait. He would not find welcome in Meryton once Miss Elizabeth spread the tale the colonel had spun.

At last, he would have his due. His cousin had always had more than he. Darcy was his father's pride and joy—his only son and heir—while Fitzwilliam was a second son, an afterthought. The earl had never had time for him, but showered his older brother with attention. By order of birth, he was nothing. And, worse yet, neither his father nor uncle gave him his due share of their wealth. He had had to become a soldier as his appetites foreswore the church. School was a challenge, so a profession in the law was out of the question, and life on the sea did not agree with him. However, he was certain that his father would agree that he was a good match for Georgiana. The earl had familial pride, and another marriage between the Fitzwilliams and the Darcys would strengthen that pride.

Having decided what he would do with her dowry, Fitzwilliam planned to ask Darcy for a small estate. That was where he would leave Georgiana while he enjoyed his newly-earned life of leisure in Town. Of course, he would enjoy his marital rights, for little Georgie was a lovely creature. She was not as beautiful and lively as Miss Elizabeth. However, the pretty Bennet girl might be perfect for a proper mistress as he was tired of going to brothels where he had to share the ladies with other men. At the present time, he could not afford to set up house for a mistress, but that would change once he had married his young cousin. Being convinced that Miss Elizabeth would in no way turn away the money and status he could offer her after his marriage, he smiled at the pain of loss Darcy would feel once it happened.

* * *

As she sat across from her sister, Elizabeth silently raged against Colonel Fitzwilliam. She had sincerely wished to show him her true feelings, but she wished to give Mr. Darcy a chance to confront him first. She had watched Mr. Darcy and the colonel leave the table at the far end of the room, leaving Charlotte alone. Despite her desire to join her friend, she was aware that it would not be wise. Charlotte was able to discern her moods and would tenaciously demand an explanation. It was better that she stay away from her for the rest of the night.

Turning her attention back to Jane, Elizabeth finally noticed a subtle difference in her sister. Jane fairly beamed with happiness. She smiled at the answering look on Mr. Bingley's face. *I believe that Mr. Darcy was correct. I shall be obtaining a brother soon. Jane shall be very happy with such an amiable man.*

Sighing inwardly, Elizabeth wished that Mr. Darcy had proposed to her instead of merely asking for a courtship. She knew that the purpose of courting was to come to know a person in order to discern whether or not they were the right one to marry. She was already certain that in every way Mr. Darcy fulfilled all of her dreams of a marriage partner. However, understanding that it was only proper that her elder sister marry first, she would not repine but would enjoy her courtship.

* * *

Before the ball had actually ended, Colonel Fitzwilliam excused himself to go to his room. His stated reason had been his need for rest before the planned trip later that morning. However, he wished to have stronger drink than the punch or wine served during the evening. He kept a supply of good brandy in his possession at all times.

Darcy was glad to see his cousin leave when he did. It gave him the opportunity to bid his farewell to Miss Elizabeth away from the watchful eye of the colonel. As the Bennets were among the last to leave, he found the time to speak to her in relative privacy.

"I am very sorry that I was unable to spend supper with you." The sincere tone of his voice relayed the truth of his statement.

"As am I, sir," she said with a quick wink. "However, if you will recall, you had no other choice."

"Alas, what you say is true, but it does not mean I do not regret having to do so."

Glancing to see Mrs. Bennet looking on them with speculation, he bowed over her hand and whispered, "I shall return as soon as I am able and shall speak with your father about our courtship."

Darcy bit back a smile as he watched a blush steal over her countenance.

"Safe trip, Mr. Darcy," she answered more formally, while a hint of a smile graced her lips

* * *

During the last days of his visit to Wywyn, William Collins found himself very busy at the behest of his betrothed. First, she insisted that he sign the marriage settlement she had had prepared by the local solicitor. He was not pleased to find that her dowry was to be saved for his wife in case he died before her. He was to receive only the interest on the funds during his lifetime. Her pin money was nearly the same amount as the interest. Eleanor informed him that this would keep him from having to provide the extra from his own income. Knowing what she did about the parsonage and the interference of Lady Catherine, she insisted upon a certain amount of household funds. This was not much more than he spent already, so this did not cause him any further discontent.

Once the settlement was signed and a copy given into the safe keeping of the solicitor, Eleanor tasked him with writing an apology to his cousin Bennet. This proved to be more difficult for him than the settlement. His ire still rose at the thought of the indignities he suffered at the hand of Mr. Bennet.

"I will certainly not apologise to my cousin. He should have been pleased that I would condescend to wish to marry one of his daughters," Collins stated emphatically when Eleanor first firmly suggested it.

"Mr. Collins," Eleanor said, her tone was cold and severe. "You will if you wish to marry me. You know, that in the settlement you signed, there is a provision for me to rescind the contract for any moral failure on your part. I will do so immediately, for your lack of repentance shows me that you may not keep your word during our marriage. I suppose it is your choice. What shall it be?"

Collins suddenly wondered if he could weather Lady Catherine's wrath and return without a promised bride to be. It only took him seconds to realised that he needed Eleanor more than she did him. His patroness would not take kindly to his lack of a wife, and there would be no one to console him at home. As the short time of their engagement passed, he had come to care for this woman. She was able to challenge him without belittling him, and her lovely female figure promised many delights in the marriage bed.

He straightened in his chair and said, "I shall write the letter, but I have a request of my own."

"Which is?"

"I wish for us to marry as soon as is possible. When I return to Hunsford in two days, I will inform my curate that he shall publish the banns on Sunday. We may marry in less than three weeks."

Eleanor smiled inwardly because that had been her next item to discuss with him. It was likely a good thing for his self-pride that he thought it was his idea. She acted as if she were pondering his proposition before she nodded. "I agree, William."

"Excellent," he exclaimed. "I shall retire to the study to write to my cousin immediately."

"I would like to read the letter before you send it, if I may."

Too pleased by the prospect of a quick marriage to argue, Collins assented without a protest. He stood and bowed out of the room.

* * *

Even though the ball had finished in the earlier hours of the morning, Darcy, Bingley, and the colonel left a couple hours before noon. Colonel Fitzwilliam groused a bit at the need to leave so early, but Darcy ignored his complaint, saying that he wished to have the subject addressed as quickly as possible. Bingley was his usual cheerful self during the ride to Town.

Bingley wished to speak of nothing but his betrothal to the lovely Miss Bennet, but Darcy had reminded him that he did not as yet have the blessing of her father, and it would be presumptuous to say anything until he did.

Instead, Bingley spent nearly the whole of the trip rhapsodizing about the ball and those who attended. Soon after they began, the colonel closed his eyes and slept until their first change of horses. He would have liked to take the time to try to convince his cousin of the positive benefits of his marrying Georgiana instead of listening to Bingley. However, he did not mind the comfort of riding in a well-sprung carriage rather than the weariness of riding a horse the entire distance.

They arrived in London by late afternoon and, after taking Bingley to his club, Darcy gave orders to the driver to take them to the home of the earl.

"I thought that we would refresh ourselves at your house first," Fitzwilliam said when he heard Darcy's instructions to the coachman.

"No, I do not wish to bother my servants for just two nights," Darcy replied. "I am certain that your father will allow me his hospitality for such a short time."

When they arrived at Dunstan House, the earl's home, the butler led them to rooms where they could refresh themselves before meeting with Lord Matlock. Darcy was the first to return downstairs and greet his uncle.

Lord Matlock stood and bowed before shaking Darcy's hand. "I am sorry that it has come to this, nephew. I wish I could have prevented it."

"I do not blame you," Darcy interrupted him. "I had no idea, and even my father did not know the full extent of his depravity."

"That may be true, but he did make provision for the possibility." He sighed, before he offered Darcy a glass of port.

The earl sipped his drink before he spoke again. "I received a packet of letters from your attorney fairly soon after your letter arrived. I now have a clearer view of my son's activities and have begun the process of revising my own will accordingly."

"Do you have a plan for dealing with Fitzwilliam?"

"Yes. I do," his uncle replied with a weary smile. "However, I will not explain because I can hear Richard's footsteps."

"Hello Father, you are looking well." The colonel greeted the earl a moment later before making his way to the liquor and pouring a generous glass of brandy.

Swirling the liquid to warm it, he grinned. "Has Darcy explained why we are here?"

"He has not mentioned the reason. Perhaps you will enlighten me," his father answered.

"Gladly," Fitzwilliam answered after he had taken a large swallow of his brandy. "I wish to resign from the army and marry Georgiana."

"What is Darcy's view?"

A frown crossed Fitzwilliam's face before he replied, "He did not consent. And as I am co-guardian, I told him I did not need his consent."

"I see," his father said as he rubbed his chin. "Did you not know that I have final say in such matter?"

"I was ignorant of that fact, which is why we are here now. I am asking for your approval, so that we can marry without delay."

The earl stood and paced the floor for a few moments, as if he needed to consider his answer. Finally he sat again and said, "I cannot in good conscience give my approval to a match that would ultimately end in misery for my beloved niece."

The colonel leapt to his feet and shouted, "How can you say that? I love her and would care for her with all my ability."

"And where would you live?" Lord Matlock asked in a deceptively calm voice.

"I was certain that you or Darcy would give me one of your smaller estates and, with that and Georgiana's dowry, we could live very comfortably together."

"That is very interesting, considering I have no plans to part with any portion of your brother's inheritance to finance your scheme."

"You have always favoured my brother in everything," the colonel angrily replied. "Just as my uncle favoured his son. Even Wickham was given more than I."

"You would have been given more if you had not been so dishonest in your dealings with your uncle Darcy and your cousin." His father motioned for Fitzwilliam to be seated again. "Now I will tell you what is to happen."

Glaring at his father and Darcy, Fitzwilliam sat on the edge of the chair.

"I do not wish for scandal, so you will resign and sell your commission. The proceeds will be given to George Wickham to repay him for your swindling him out of the value of the living he was promised."

When the colonel opened his mouth to protest, the earl raised his hand. "I am not finished."

Lord Matlock emptied his glass before he continued. "I have an old friend who owns and operates a plantation in India. He is always looking for workers since his business is in a remote location and it is difficult for him to keep local workers for long."

Unable to keep silent any longer, Fitzwilliam protested, "There is no reason for me to leave the country. Allow me to continue in the Army, and I will stay away from Darcy and his sister." Suddenly the alternative to permanent exile seemed very appealing.

"No, my son, your other choice is transportation to Van Diemen's Land," the earl said firmly. "Between us, Darcy and I have more than enough evidence that could send you to debtor's prison for most of your life. I suppose you could choose that instead."

"Will you give me until tomorrow to decide?" Fitzwilliam growled.

Turning to Darcy, who had remained silent throughout the discussion, the earl raised a brow in question.

"I will agree to that, but you will not leave this house," Darcy demanded.

"Of course not, you have my word as an officer and a gentleman that I will stay, so if you will excuse me, I shall go to my room."

* * *

Since the family returned home in an early morning hours after the ball, Elizabeth slept late. However, she arose at her usual time the following morning. It had become her habit to invite Lydia to walk with her, but knowing her youngest sister's love of sleep, she decided not to wake her. As it was, she wished to spend some time alone to sort through all of the events of the past few days.

As she donned her favourite walking dress and boots, her thoughts centred upon Mr. Darcy as they had ever since she awoke after the ball. She no longer had a doubt about her feelings for him. Love throbbed in her heart for him. As happy as she was for his offer for courtship, she could not help but envy Jane's engagement. *How long would it be before she would also be betrothed?* This question seemed to race around in her mind since there was no way for her to know the answer as yet.

Forcing the frustrating dilemma from her mind, Elizabeth trod lightly down the stairs and put on her outerwear. Grateful for the weak sun so late in the autumn, she smiled as she walked across the grass toward one of her favourite footpaths. Enjoying the sounds of nature, she entered the woods, lost in memories of the night before. Her only negative thought was of Colonel Fitzwilliam's presence. If he had not attended, she would have been able to take more pleasure in the evening.

Shaking her head as if to clear the depressing thoughts, Elizabeth rehearsed the dances she had had with Mr. Darcy. She was also pleased the he had trusted her enough to listen to her suggestions about how to proceed with his knowledge about his cousin. She could not help but wonder how things had gone in the meeting with the earl.

So lost was she in her ponderings, Elizabeth entered the clearing without Realising it. She smiled when she finally noticed her surroundings. However, she was startled to hear someone speak.

"Well, Miss Elizabeth, I am glad you could finally make it. I had wondered if you would arise so soon. I have become a bit chilled while waiting for you."

"Colonel Fitzwilliam, What are you doing here?" Elizabeth gasped.

He stood from the log upon which he had been sitting and gave her a courtly bow. "I was not able to give you a proper farewell from the ball. I enjoyed our conversation and hoped we could come to know each other better."

"How it is that you came to be in the woods instead of calling at the house during the usual hours for social visits?"

"That would not have served my purpose." Fitzwilliam chuckled softly. "I received a great deal of information about your habits from your sister and your friend Miss Lucas. I was especially charmed by the knowledge of your ramblings about Longbourn's grounds. Miss Kitty gave very good directions, so it was easy for me to find your favourite private place in the woods."

"You told me that you would be in Town for several days," Elizabeth stated nervously. She could not understand why he was here and not in London.

Taking a step closer to Elizabeth, the colonel said with a smirk, "Oh, I have been to Town and back. I need very little sleep as it is, so it was no difficulty for me to leave while it was still dark this morning. Can you not discern my reason for returning?"

Retreating a couple steps away from the colonel, Elizabeth shook her head. "I cannot account for it, sir."

He leered at her as he stepped closer and closer to her. "I had noticed my cousin's admiration for you. I shall take pleasure in ruining you. It will break his heart that you are no longer pure, and that I have taken what he hoped would be his someday."

Elizabeth backed into a tree in her effort to escape his advances. "Please, Colonel, do not hurt me. What have I done to you?"

Grasping her arms in a tight grip, he laughed. "Nothing! You are only a tool I plan to use to avenge myself on my lofty cousin. Darcy has always been blessed with good looks, money, land, and a father who loved him. I was always the spare, of no value except to keep the line going if something should happen to my brother. Now that Anthony is married and has two sons, I have even less value in my father's eyes."

He lifted one hand and caressed her cheek. "You are a lovely chit. I shall enjoy tasting your delights."

Elizabeth slapped his hand away and struggled to get loose from his grip. When he tightened his hold on her with both hands and shook her, she let out a scream.

"Go ahead and scream, no one will hear you." He leaned in to kiss her and whispered, "In fact, I rather like my women to protest. It makes my triumph more satisfying."

* * *

At Dunstan house, Darcy woke early. Predawn was just lighting the sky outside the chamber he occupied. His sleep had been disturbed by worrying dreams and thoughts. Unwilling to try to return to slumber, he arose and rang for a man to help him dress. He wished he had brought Peters with him, but he would make do with one of the earl's servants.

Darcy soon exited his room, wishing to take an early ride before breakfast. The evening before had not been relaxing due to his cousin's refusal to even speak to him or the earl after their argument that afternoon. Richard had taken a tray in his room, so Darcy had no idea of his cousin's current frame of mind or what decision he had made about his future.

Rather than send for his horse, Darcy made his way to the stables behind the house. As he walked to the stall where his mount was usually kept, he noticed that his cousin's horse was not in its regular place.

He addressed the groom who was mucking out the stable, "Where is the General? Is this not his usual stall?"

"Aye, sir, that be where Colonel Fitzwilliam's 'orse is kept," he replied as he removed his cap. "The colonel took it out real early-like, two hours or so ago. It was still dark, but the moon was bright. I offered to 'elp 'im, but 'e told me to go back to sleep."

"Did he say where he was going?"

"No, sir, 'e didn't"

Darcy tossed the young man a few coins and asked for his horse to be saddled immediately. He was uncertain as to the direction his cousin may have taken, but since Darcy knew that Georgiana was safely hidden, he decided to go back to Hertfordshire. Was it possible that his cousin had seen his interest in Elizabeth Bennet? His heart raced at the thought of Richard hurting her.

As soon as his horse was ready, he leapt into the saddle and hastened out of the mews and out of Town. Fortunately, there were few on the road at that time in the morning. He knew he must keep his pace steady, although he wanted to gallop as quickly as possible to see his love. He was even more aware of his affection for Elizabeth now that he thought she was in danger. If his cousin had harmed her, he would make him pay for his actions.

After he had ridden about half the distance and his horse was tiring, Darcy stopped at an inn and asked about hiring another horse. He asked the innkeeper about any riders who might have arrived early that morning, and was told that a gentleman had stopped for breakfast. Darcy thanked the man, and he went to look over the horses that were available for hire. He spied the General among the others in the paddock.

"Is that horse for hire?" Darcy asked pointing to his cousin's mount.

"No, he be resting like you wish for yours to do," the man replied. "His owner says he'll be back for him later today. He paid well for the privilege."

"Very well, my good man," Darcy said as he pointed to the horse he wished to hire. "I will pay you well too. Please cool him down before you feed and water him. I will send my man Peters back for him sometimes today. Make certain that you give him a good rub down as well."

"Yes sir, he is a fine animal, and I'll take good care of 'im."

Now Darcy was sure he was going in the right direction. However, knowing this did not relieve his agitation. He was a few hours behind Richard. He could only pray that Elizabeth had not gone out for a walk alone or early. With her name on his lips, he urged the animal to a quicker pace toward Hertfordshire.

Chapter 15

L ydia Bennet was just getting dressed when she heard the closing of the front door. Hastening to the window, she saw Lizzy slowly ambling toward one of her favourite paths.

Sighing in frustration, Lydia hurried to finish dressing in her usual clothing for walking. Lizzy had shown her the gown that was easiest for her to don for a walk so as not to bother the servants in the morning. Her older sister had explained that she must, as a lady, learn to be concerned for the welfare of her servants. A compassionate mistress could earn loyalty in that way.

As she leaned down to pull on her half boots, Lydia hoped that she would be able to swiftly join her sister since they had not been able to talk over the ball in private due to their sleeping in the day before. She smiled as she remembered her sets with her dear Colonel Forster. He was so gallant and handsome in his uniform.

Lydia rushed down the stairs, careful to be as quiet as possible. After wrapping herself in her cloak and putting on her bonnet, she slipped from the house and hurried across the lawn toward the path Elizabeth had taken. As she entered the edge of the woods, Lydia heard a scream.

"Lizzy!" Lydia whispered in panic. *Should I return to the house and summon help?* It was another cry that helped her decide. *Lizzy needs me now.* As she ran along the path, she spied a fallen branch. When she stooped to lift it up, Lydia happily found that it was not too heavy for her to carry, but it felt sufficiently strong enough to use as a weapon.

As she finally reached the clearing, Lydia watched with horror as a man threw Elizabeth to the ground. As he proceeded to hold her down and try to unbutton his fall, Lizzy fought, bit, and kicked in her struggle to keep him from ruining her.

Lydia stepped closer with stealth, but when she saw him raise his fist to strike Lizzy, she lifted the limb above her head and shouted, "Do not hit my sister!" For a brief second, the man turned his head to see who was there. At that moment, two things happened; Lydia recognized Colonel Fitzwilliam, and she brought the branch down on his head.

To Lydia, it seemed like an eternity before the colonel dropped to the ground, unconscious.

She hurried to her sister. "Lizzy, are you hurt?"

"I am bruised, but quite well considering what he had in mind," Elizabeth replied, blinking tears of relief from her eyes. "Help me get him off my legs."

Fitzwilliam's body lay over Lizzy's feet, and it took several minutes to get him rolled over.

"Let us hurry before he awakens," Lizzy began to tremble at the very thought the colonel returning to consciousness.

"No, we must secure him, so that he cannot come after you again," Lydia insisted, looking around for something with which to tie him. She grinned as she saw that since he had not worn his uniform, he wore a cravat. She quickly removed it from his neck.

"We need to get him against the tree so that we can tie his hands behind it," she said as she took on of his arms. "Are you able to help me move him?"

Elizabeth cringed at the idea of touching the man who attacked her, but she did not wish her sister to have to try to move him on her own. Summoning her strength and courage, she grabbed his other arm and helped Lydia position the colonel with his back against the tree. The trunk of the maple was small enough for his arms to go round it, but it was sturdy so as to not break if he struggled.

Once his hands were securely tied, Lydia searched his pockets for a handkerchief, which she used to gag him.

"I do not wish for him to call for help. There may be someone who does not know his crime who would let him loose," Lydia explained as she stood and brushed her hands together.

Assisting Elizabeth to her feet, Lydia wrapped her arm around her sister's waist to steady her as they made their way back to Longbourn.

* * *

The last mile before reaching Meryton seemed to stretch on forever. Darcy let out a sigh of relief when the village buildings came into sight. As he entered the high street, Darcy scanned the few people going about their business. He noticed George Wickham making his way in his direction.

"Wickham," Darcy called out as he jumped down from his horse.

George greeted him with a smile before he saw the stern expression on Darcy's face. "What is wrong? I am surprised to see you here so early in the morning."

As quickly as he could, Darcy explained the situation. Once he was finished with his tale, he said, "I believe that he is headed for Longbourn. I am afraid that Miss Elizabeth may be in danger."

"What might I do to help?"

"I was hoping you would ask," Darcy said. "I will need help in bringing my cousin back to Town. Would you be willing to go to Colonel Forster and summon his aid? I shall head for Longbourn immediately."

"Of course, I shall go at once, and Darcy," George said as he laid a hand on Darcy's shoulder, "I will be praying that no harm come to Miss Elizabeth or any of the Bennets."

The two men parted ways, and Darcy pressed his mount to a gallop as he left Meryton. All he could do as he rode along the road was hope and pray that he would not be too late. His Elizabeth was too vital to his life. *Please God, keep her from harm,* was his repeated silent petition.

Finally arriving at the lane to Longbourn, Darcy had to slow his horse so that they did not miss it. Out of the corner of his eye he caught a glimpse of another rough-looking horse tied near some bushes. *It seems that my cousin did come here.* Facing ahead once more, he saw two young women walking across the expanse of grass toward the house. He recognized Miss Elizabeth, who was leaning heavily on her sister, Miss Lydia. Not waiting for his horse to come to a full stop, Darcy leapt from the saddle and ran toward the pair.

"Elizabeth!" he called, unaware of his use of her Christian name. "Are you well?"

The fear in her eyes gave way to relief when Elizabeth saw who he was. As Darcy came toward her, she let go of her sister and threw herself into his arms and sobbed.

Darcy's arms came around her so naturally that he did not even think about how it might look to anyone else. His heart ached for her sorrow as he whispered soothing words to her as she cried.

"Mr. Darcy I do not think it is proper for you to hold my sister like that," Lydia protested, sounding more like the protective sibling than ever.

Darcy could not disagree, but he was not going to reject his love in her time of need. Wanting to know what happened he turned to Lydia. "What has befallen your sister?"

"Your cousin," Lydia spit out in disgust, "He attacked my sister. I heard her cry out and went to help. I hit him with a stick. We tied him to a tree."

"Did he . . .?" Darcy could not form the words.

"No, I am certain that was his intent, but I stopped him before he could do any more than bruise her a bit. I think Lizzy is in shock. We should get her into the house and cleaned up before my mother sees her."

It was then that Darcy noticed that Elizabeth was without a bonnet and that her dress was dirty and torn in places. "Yes, let us go into the house."

Elizabeth pulled away from the comfort of Darcy's arms and apologised, "Forgive me, Mr, Darcy. I did not mean to become so hysterical."

Offering his arm, Darcy said gently, "You have nothing for which to be sorry. I am so very unhappy that I did not reach you in time to keep my cousin from even trying to harm you."

Elizabeth placed one hand in the crook of Darcy's arm and gripped her sister's with the other. "I want to change immediately. It shall be easier to keep my mother calm if she does not see me in such disarray."

By the time they entered the house, a groom had taken Darcy's mount to the stable with orders to tend to the other animal that was tied near the road. Mrs. Hill opened the door as they reached it and gathered Elizabeth into her arms. "Oh Miss Lizzy, what has happened?"

"Hill, we will explain later, but for now, please take my sister to her room and help her clean up and change into something suitable," Lydia ordered gently.

"Of course, Miss Lydia," the housekeeper said as she guided Elizabeth to the stairs. "My poor little lamb, we will have you set to rights in good time."

Lydia invited Mr. Darcy into the front parlour before going to the kitchen to order some tea. A few minutes later, she returned with a maid carrying a tray. She poured a cup for Mr. Darcy before she headed for her father's book room.

Receiving a call to enter at her knock, Lydia opened the door and walked inside.

Her father looked up, taken aback by the sight of his youngest daughter, when he had been expecting Elizabeth. "What is it you need, Lydia?"

"Papa, please come to the front parlour," she responded in a serious tone. "I will explain once Lizzy comes down from her room."

With sudden dread arising in his heart, Mr. Bennet threw down his book and left his desk. "Has something happened to Lizzy?" he asked as he hurried out the door.

Lydia was only able to repeat her previous statement when Lizzy spoke from the stairs. She was leaning on Mrs. Hill's arm. "I am fine, Papa. Let us go into the parlour where we can talk."

Her pale face and obvious weakness belied her words. Mr. Bennet ran up the remaining steps and aided his Lizzy down the rest of the stairs and into the parlour. "My eyes tell me differently, my dear. However, I can tell you need to sit down, so I shall wait to question you until then."

He guided her to a sofa and sat beside her, holding her hand. He noticed that Elizabeth's hands were ice cold and trembling. "Hill, bring Lizzy some sherry."

Hill, who had anticipated the order, immediately brought the liquor and gave it to Elizabeth. Her father helped Lizzy to hold the glass since her hands were shaking. Once the sherry was gone, her face regained some colour, and her trembling ceased.

"Now, will someone please tell me what has happened?" It was only now, looking around the room, that Bennet noticed Mr. Darcy. "Do you have something to do with my daughter's discomfort?"

"Oh no, Papa," Elizabeth exclaimed quickly. "He only just arrived a few minutes ago."

Lydia came to sit in a chair next to the sofa on which her father and Elizabeth sat. "I shall explain all. I must be brief because I have reason to believe the rest of the family will be down soon. I am not certain Mama should hear the details."

Her father impatiently gestured for her to continue.

"Elizabeth left the house for her usual walk, but she likely thought I was asleep. I think she did not wish to wake me so early, and thus did not take me with her," Lydia began her tale and went on to tell all that she knew and had done. She finished with, "After I bashed him on the head with a big stick I found, we tied him to a tree with his own cravat. Then we came back home."

With eyes filling with his tears, Mr. Bennet reached for Lydia's hand. "You are a heroine, my little Lyddie. I am glad you were so brave."

He pulled Elizabeth into a fierce embrace before releasing her to reach for his handkerchief in order to wipe his face.

"What has been done to deal with the scoundrel?" he asked as he rose. Without waiting for an answer, he stated, "We need to call for the authorities. We cannot allow him to get away."

Darcy moved closer to the seated group and said, "I found Mr. Wickham in Meryton, and he is alerting Colonel Forster of the need for soldiers to come and help." Pausing for a moment when he heard the sound of horses and wagon on the lane, he continued, "I believe that they are arriving now."

Mr. Bennet rose to greet them, but Lydia stopped them with her hand. "Let me go and I shall show them where the villain is." Preventing him from voicing a protest, she added, "I shall take a groom along. Besides, I am positive that Colonel Forster would never allow any harm to come to me."

The older man sighed and returned to his seat. He took Elizabeth's hand and asked, "What would you have me do?"

Without hesitation, she answered, "Please stay with me and Mr. Darcy. I would feel safer if the two of you were here."

Patting her hand, Mr. Bennet said, "I shall greet the men and give them my permission to allow Lydia to accompany them. Do not worry, Lizzy, I shall return shortly."

Once Mr. Bennet left the room, Darcy was swift to sit next to Elizabeth. "Please forgive this breach of etiquette, but we will not likely have another moment of privacy for some time."

Elizabeth blushed but did not object. "Have you decided not to ask my father about a courtship after all that has happened?"

"What happened does not change my feelings for you. I wanted to ask you something else before he returns."

Pleasure flooded Elizabeth's countenance at the understanding that the colonel's attack did not change his regard for her. "What is it that you want to ask?"

"I was so frightened when I pondered what my cousin might attempt. I was so far behind him, and I worried what he would do to you or one of your family members. I do not wish to be separated from you again. Will you do me the honour of agreeing to become my wife? I love you beyond description."

Happy tears filled her eyes as she choked out a yes.

"Oh Elizabeth, you have made me the happiest of men." He took her hand and quickly kissed it before abruptly standing when he heard footsteps in the corridor.

* * *

Wrapping her cloak around herself and tying on her bonnet, Lydia opened the front door as Mr. Hill joined her. Her father had summoned the butler to go with his youngest to ensure her safety. Mr. Bennet knew that Colonel Forster would keep watch over her too, but he was going to err on the side of caution.

The soldiers were grouped behind Forster and Mr. Wickham as the two men stood at the door ready to knock. The gentlemen bowed and greeted Lydia.

"Is Mr. Darcy here?" the colonel asked.

"He is here but he is busy," Lydia answered quickly. "Hill and I will show you where to find Colonel Fitzwilliam."

"How is it that you know where he is?" Wickham said, incredulously.

Lydia forced a gay laugh and said, "Let us go. I do not wish for him to get away. I will explain as we go."

By the time they reached the clearing, the men were astounded by Lydia's tale. "Is Miss Elizabeth well?"

"A bit bruised and shaken, but not injured. I came upon them before he could truly harm her," she told them proudly.

Fitzwilliam was still tied securely to the tree, but they could tell, by his muffled moans, that he was regaining consciousness.

Forster's men surrounded the tree and looked to their colonel for orders.

"Carter, make sure that his feet are in shackles before you untie him. There should be no way for him to escape."

"Yes, sir," Carter replied with a satisfied expression, for he had not trusted the man when they were introduced at the ball, and this proved his intuition correct.

By the time Fitzwilliam's feet were locked in the irons, he was fully aware of his surroundings, and he began to struggle against the cloth that bound his hands and his mouth. When one of the soldiers released the gag, Fitzwilliam screamed. "That little bitch hit me when I was trying to help her sister from the ground where she had fallen. I demand that you arrest her."

Forster scowled fiercely and shouted, "You will keep a civil tongue in your mouth, or I will personally cut it out. We know the truth and you are the one who is under arrest."

Being the coward that Fitzwilliam was, he closed his mouth. He began to think of a way out of the situation. Surely his father would still allow him his choice of places to go. Suddenly, the earl's offer of work in India looked much better than it had the day before.

Soon, Fitzwilliam's hands were also in shackles, and he was forced to his feet. He found that it was hard to travel with the heavy chains that bound him. This, combined with the nearly blinding headache he was suffering, made for a miserable march out of the woods. Arriving back at Longbourn, he spied a wagon with a cage in the back nearly covered with a dirty piece of canvas. He had seen a few of these vehicles in his career, but he had never ridden in one. Soon, a few of Forster's men lifted him and tossed him in before slamming the door shut and locking it.

When Fitzwilliam opened his mouth to protest, Forster glared at him as if daring him to say a word. The disgraced colonel set his lips in a frown before he curled up on the thin layer of straw inside the cage.

"Carter, escort the prisoner back to the lockup. Take the back way there. Make certain that he is not recognized. Once his chains are secured to the wall in the cell, make sure to station a guard inside and two outside. No one else is to enter the cell or visit the prisoner without my consent. Is that clear?"

"Also, there is to be no talk of what has happened here. Do you understand? If one word gets out, I shall find the culprit and have him flogged." Forster looked into the eyes of each of his men as they each agreed. "Good, now off with you. I shall join you later."

* * *

Just as they arrived inside Longbourn, Forster, Wickham, and Lydia watched as the three remaining Bennet sisters came down the stairs. After a brief greeting, Lydia asked them all to come with her to the parlour. Forster offered his arm to Lydia while Wickham offered his to Mary, who flushed prettily at the gesture.

"Where is Mama?" Lydia asked when she saw only her father with Mr. Darcy and Lizzy.

Jane answered that she would be down in a moment. Apparently there had been a tear in the gown she had planned to wear, so another had to be found.

Mr. Bennet, who had stood at the arrival of the others, looked directly at Forster and asked, "Has your business been successfully accomplished?"

"Yes sir, there shall be no more trouble on that score," Forster answered obliquely.

"Being that my wife has not yet been informed that we have company, I have taken the liberty of informing my housekeeper that we shall have guests at breakfast."

There were no objections, since no one had had time for a meal except for Wickham. He would not miss the opportunity to spend time with the Bennets, especially Miss Mary, no matter what the circumstance.

"Excellent." Bennet resumed his chair while inviting the others to be seated. "As there are those present who do not know what has taken place, I would rather wait for my wife before explaining."

As if on cue, Mrs. Bennet fluttered into the room just a moment later. She had just been told that there were several guests who would be partaking of breakfast with them. A slight frown graced her face as she spied everyone. "I beg your pardon for my tardiness. My husband did not tell me that we were expecting company this morning."

Patting the seat beside him, Mr. Bennet smiled kindly at his wife and said, "Please come sit here, my dear. I had no inkling we would have such a full house this morning, but it is a good thing that they are all here."

Mrs. Bennet opened her mouth and squeaked out, "Then why?

"Patience, Mrs. Bennet, patience," he scolded mildly. "I must ask you to speak of this to no one outside of this room. Our family's reputation may be damaged if the information gets out. It might cause a great deal of injurious gossip. Promise me that, for the love of your daughters, you will not say anything of what you hear."

His wife examined his face for seriousness and saw that he was indeed not teasing. And the love and trust in his eyes gave her no other alternative than to agree. She knew that she was a gossip, but she wished to protect her girls from any taint of scandal. "I shall say nothing," she simply replied.

Bennet smiled down at his wife before he looked up at those assembled. "I do not believe I need to exact a promise from the rest of you, but I believe you all see the wisdom in this matter."

Seeing nods of agreement, he looked to Elizabeth. "Do you wish to tell the story?"

Lizzy looked down at her hands as she twisted them in her lap. Her skin went from red to pasty white as she shook her head. Normally her courage always arose in time of need, but this time her embarrassment overrode it.

"May I do the telling, Papa," Lydia asked in a quiet voice. "I was there for most of the time."

After his nod of approval, Lydia began the tale without embellishment. By the time she was finished with the story of how they tied Fitzwilliam to the tree, there was complete silence, except for their mother's quiet weeping.

The colonel took up the tale and explained in detail how the prisoner would be kept locked up, so that the Bennets would be safe.

Once the explanation was finished, Mrs. Bennet hurried to Elizabeth and knelt before her, grasping her hands tightly. "My poor Lizzy, I am so sorry that this happened to you, but I am so grateful that our brave little Lydia came to help. I could not be prouder of the pair of you if you were sons."

Elizabeth was so overcome by her mother's outburst of affection that she threw her arms around her shoulders, and they wept for a few moments before gathering themselves.

Darcy handed Elizabeth his handkerchief, and Bennet helped his wife to her feet while offering his own handkerchief to her.

"Forgive me, gentlemen." Mrs. Bennet's voice was thick with emotion.

She was given assurance of their complete understanding. Mrs. Bennet's smile was a bit watery, but she seemed to recover quickly. "I shall go see how much longer our breakfast will be. If you will excuse me . . ."

A few minutes after Mrs. Bennet left the room, Hill announced another guest. "Mr. Charles Bingley."

Chuckling, Mr. Bennet stood to greet him. "You find us with a large gathering, but you are most welcome, I assure you, if you can find a seat. And all of these folks will be joining us for breakfast, so you must join us as well."

Bennet turned to Kitty and said, "Please go inform your mother that we shall have need of another place at the table."

Chapter 16

It had taken Mr. Collins most of two days to write his letter of apology to his cousin Bennet. Eleanor had sent him back to the desk four times with many corrections and additions. He admitted to himself that it was terribly humbling for a man of his status and education to be treated as if he was in the schoolroom. However, he could not complain of her methods. Never had anyone pointed out his faults with such loving kindness and grace. It seemed as if, the more she showed him his sins and failures, the more his self-blindness fell away.

The final missive he handed her that day was one of the most honest he had ever written. The burden of pleasing everyone in every way had disappeared somewhere between, "My dear cousin Bennet" and "I beg your forgiveness for my abominable acts in your home."

William watched with far less nervousness than before as Eleanor read the latest version of his letter. He knew he had succeeded when she looked up at him and smiled. The love and pride in her expression filled him with great peace and joy.

"So you approve, my dear?" Collins asked eagerly.

"There is nothing of which I would disapprove."

She folded the missive again and said, "Now I must write a cover letter, for we wish for your cousin to read it and not consign it to the fire immediately, do we not?"

Collins sighed. "No, we do not, and if he saw my hand first, he might do just that. And I have come too far in my understanding of myself. I want him to at least read it. It might take him some time to believe me, but I cannot make him change his mind."

"Very good, dearest William," Eleanor commended him before continuing, "I wish to discuss what I plan to say. We are to be wed and there should be no secrets between us unless it has to do with a gift or some such."

Collins nodded his agreement.

"First of all, I shall introduce myself and explain why I have written to a complete stranger, though we are soon to be related. I will vouch for your sincerity and good intentions. I will even invite the family to our wedding and to stay at Wywyn House while they are here. I shall then ask if we might visit during an afternoon once we are married to discuss matters related to the estate. As you know, Mr. Bennet may live a long time."

Curiosity raced through Collins's mind. *What could they discuss before the passing of his cousin? I am to inherit, and there is no more to be said.*

As if reading his thoughts, Eleanor touched his arm and gestured to the settee not too far from where they had been seated. "Let us sit together, and I will explain of what I am speaking."

After they had sat down once more, Eleanor placed her hand in his. "Do you trust me to protect our interests?"

"Of course, I do," he answered without hesitation.

"Very well," she said as she gave him that smile that always gave him such pleasure. "I have been thinking about what the Bible says about loving my neighbour. Your Bennet family will be mine as well, will they not?"

"Yes."

"I have given much thought and prayer as to what it must be like for Mrs. Bennet to live with the thought that the home in which she has lived, raised a family, and loved all these years will be taken from her at the same time as her beloved spouse. If her daughters are not all well married, they shall be forced to live in genteel poverty, at the mercy of the rest of her family. The same kind of poverty I would have been forced into had you not offered for me."

Collins rubbed his chin while contemplating, not the benefits to himself, but the horrors of his beloved Eleanor living as a poor spinster or widow, beholden to her family for everything. He had been at Wywyn long enough to meet his future brother- and sister-in-law and to understand how they treated Eleanor with even less respect than they gave the housekeeper. They had seemed overjoyed at the prospect of not having to support her in the future. In general, her father was more affectionate. However, he paid her little attention once his son arrived home.

"I had not looked at things in that way."

"I am not surprised. Most men are able choose their life's work and do not understand the plight of women."

"So what is it that you wish to speak of to my cousin concerning his estate?"

Eleanor collected her thoughts before she spoke again. "Since you have such a good living at Hunsford, there would be no reason to leave in a great hurry. I have no idea if there is a dower house or a cottage at Longbourn that would accommodate the Bennet ladies. If there is not, I do not wish to rush our family from their home." She put strong emphasis on the word *our*.

Staring into space, Mr. Collins pondered what she had said. He knew nothing about running an estate and enjoyed being a parson. What if it were possible for him to stay on as the rector and hire a steward while his relatives continued to live at Longbourn for some time?

His thoughts were interrupted by his betrothed's soft voice. "What are you thinking, William?"

His thoughts came tumbling out, and Eleanor was not only delighted with his ideas, they were more than she had pondered herself.

"Oh William, what a marvellous idea! The potential for blessing to both families is beyond what I had envisioned. May I write and hint at this?"

"Please do," he agreed with a happy and sincere expression on his face.

* * *

The general mood in the large Bennet parlour was one of relief and joyfulness, though Darcy could see that Elizabeth was still rather shaken after her ordeal. He did not wish to leave her side, but he knew he needed to ask for an audience with Mr. Bennet as soon as breakfast was over. He had many other responsibilities to take care of, which included informing his uncle of Colonel Fitzwilliam's most recent crime. He also knew he needed some rest before riding back to London, unless he could borrow Bingley's carriage.

Excusing himself to Elizabeth, Darcy moved beside Mr. Bennet and spoke softly. At the older man's nod, Darcy returned to stand sentinel behind his Elizabeth. And, only five minutes later, breakfast was announced.

Inside their large dining room, the seating was informal, much to the pleasure of all. The chatter around the table was perhaps a trifle gay after what had happened, but everyone felt such great relief that nothing more had occurred. Knowing that the man who had done such a thing was in chains strengthened the feeling of safety and respite. Even Elizabeth began to relax, especially with Darcy sitting at her right side and Jane at her left.

Once the meal was finished, Lydia suggested a short walk in the garden. She would have enjoyed some time alone with her beau. However, it turned out that her proposal was met with great enthusiasm. The only ones who stayed indoors were Darcy, Elizabeth, and the elder Bennets.

The two men retired to Mr. Bennet's book room while Elizabeth waited in the small parlour. She was surprised when her mother joined her on the settee.

"Is there something you need, Mama?"

Fanny Bennet smiled lovingly at her second daughter. "No, I just thought I would join you while you wait for your young man."

Elizabeth opened her mouth to deny the fact, but her mother shook her head. "Do not say it, Lizzy. Anyone with eyes can see how he feels about you. A man such as Mr. Darcy does not ride so far after leaving the day before for a mere friend. You already have said yes to him, but he is doing what he must to secure your father's permission. I do hope that Mr. Bennet does not tease him too much."

"We will not announce anything until the business with his cousin is sorted. And there are other reasons to wait as well," Lizzy tried to explain without giving away Jane's secret.

Giving a tiny giggle, her mother answered, "If you mean Jane and Mr. Bingley's understanding, that will be resolved very soon, I am certain."

Elizabeth stared at her mother in stunned incredulity. She could not seem to find the words that would not insult her. How was it possible that Mrs. Bennet knew and was not in spasms of delight and near hysteria?

It turned out that Elizabeth did not have to ask. Mrs. Bennet frowned slightly before she said in all sincerity, "I owe you an apology for the mother I have been, to all you girls but to you especially. I want to explain what happened. I am not trying to make excuses. I would like you to know the reasons behind some of my actions. I hope you find it in your heart to forgive this foolish old woman."

Seeing her mother's face and the nearly palpable fear in her eyes, Elizabeth took her hand and squeezed it. "I will listen, but I do not have to hear anything more to forgive you."

Mrs. Bennet returned the pressure, a smile gracing her face. With her other hand, she caressed the locket pinned to the lace at her throat. She took a deep breath and began, "As you know, my Gardiner family were not gentlefolk. My mother had plans for my sister and me. We would marry gentlemen so, with that in mind, she read anything she could find about how gentlewomen were to behave, all of the kinds of accomplishments that they had. Of course, at the time, my father's business did not make enough for us to have tutors or masters, although I did make friends with some of the local gentry's daughters.

"Both my mother and grandmother had very good sewing skills and had hosted some of the best social gatherings Meryton had ever seen. Soon, his business and our income rose. Papa was so proud when he was able to tell Harriet and me that we would have five thousand each for our dowries.

"I do not say that I had a difficult childhood, but I did not learn much beside the domestic arts. Your grandmother told me that no man wanted a smart wife. He wished to be the one with the knowledge. I was rarely even allowed into the garden without her or my father to make certain I was always the little lady. It was hard because I loved to run and even play in the mud."

Her mother paused for a few seconds to collect her thoughts. "When I was but fifteen, my parents allowed me to attend my first assembly. That was where I first saw your papa. He was the most handsome man I had ever seen. He finally asked me to dance the supper set after William Lucas introduced us.

"He was so witty, intelligent, and a very good dancer as well. I fell in love that evening. I believe at first he thought I was too young to even consider courting, but about five months before my sixteenth birthday, he sought permission and it was granted. We married three days after my birthday that year.

"We were so happy, especially when I began to increase with Jane. Just as she is now, in the womb she caused me not a moment of discomfort. Her birth was easy, and she never gave her nurse any trouble."

Lifting the locket, she explained, "This was a gift from your father on that occasion."

"I can remember you wearing that locket quite often and showing us the pictures inside. You always said, 'see how handsome your papa is.'" Elizabeth had to smile at the childhood memory.

"But you would always answer back, 'Yes, and you are mostest pretty of all Mamas.'"

Clearing the thickness in her throat, Mrs. Bennet continued, "When I became pregnant with you it was completely different. I was ill most of the time. You seemed to move all of the time."

Thinking that was the beginning of her mother's discontent with her, Elizabeth opened her mouth to protest.

However, her mother smiled. "Do not misunderstand me. I was thrilled. I felt certain that I was going to give birth to the heir to Longbourn. I admit to having wished for less discomfort, but I embraced it, impatient to meet my little boy. I admit I was disappointed when another daughter was announced, but that only lasted until I saw you. You looked so much like your father. How could I be unhappy with such a handsome child?

"You started to speak full sentences before you were even a year old, and were smart like your father, so curious about everything." Fanny Bennet chuckled lightly. "You thought I was smart as well. Do you remember the walks that we used to take with Jane?"

"We used to find wild flowers and press them." Elizabeth's memories flooded over her. "You and I slipped and fell into some water. What were we doing?"

"You wanted a tadpole to bring home. Jane, who sat primly on a rock watching us, wanted nothing to do with something that turned into a frog. I had always wanted to catch one when I was young, so I saw no reason why we should not at least try. You fell in first, and I was so afraid that something would happen to you. I overreacted and found myself sitting in the stream, while you climbed onto my lap laughingly saying, 'Let's do it again, Mama.'"

Elizabeth finished the story. "You said, 'We need to get dry. Since the water is so cold, we do not wish to become ill.' Once we changed, we had tea and cake in the parlour, even though it was where only guests were usually allowed."

Embracing Lizzy, her mother exclaimed, "I am so glad you remember that. I loved being with my two different girls." She lowered her voice to a whisper. "I loved Jane, but she never enjoyed our excursions as much as we did."

Answering with a giggle, Elizabeth said, "I always thought your frowns were for me. I did try to be more like Jane, but when I was about six, you stopped taking me outside with you. You didn't answer my questions anymore either, telling me to ask my father. At first, I thought it was because of the other babies. Then I was to spend my time learning from Papa. What did I do wrong?"

Mrs. Bennet's eyes filled with tears. "I began to feel that my lack of knowledge might be hurting your education, so I asked your father to hire a governess for you girls. I had hoped to sit in on some of the lessons to learn more myself. However, Mr. Bennet only laughed and said that he would take over your education. After all, he had gone to university."

Taking out her handkerchief, Mrs. Bennet quickly wiped her eyes. "Soon after your father started to tutor you, I became ill while carrying Lydia. You did come to visit me at first, but it was obvious that you enjoyed your father's company, and the midwife ordered that you have only restricted time with me.

"Once Lydia was born, and the doctor said I could have no more children, you seemed to have transferred your affections to your father. I am afraid that in my jealousy, I did not treat you as I should have."

Elizabeth wrapped her mother in her arms and hugged her tightly. "I forgive you, and please forgive a selfish child who never understood what happened."

After few moments of embrace, Elizabeth pulled back and asked, "What has happened to bring about this recent change?

"The night of the ball at Netherfield, your father found me in a melancholy mood. I saw very clearly how blessed we are to have such lovely and unique daughters, and how wrongly I had treated you. As your father comforted me, it was as if I had been given another chance to show my love for him and for you. He and I talked nearly the whole evening at Netherfield and well into the next day after we returned home.

"I am not afraid of hedgerows or the like anymore. Of course, as Mr. Bennet pointed out, he thought there shall be several weddings in the near future. However, the most important point is that we still love each other. We will work together to ensure that there is enough for me to live on, even if I do not live with any of you. I am certain that I will fail to remember, but this locket has already helped to remind me of my responsibility."

"Thank you for telling me about this, Mama," Elizabeth leaned over to kiss her mother's cheek. "I love you."

"It seems that our ladies are doing well while waiting for us to return," Mr. Bennet said as he smiled."

"Indeed," Darcy agreed.

"My dears," Mr. Bennet announced solemnly, "There shall be a wedding as soon as Mr. Darcy is able to settle things involving his wayward cousin."

Mrs. Bennet stood and curtsied. "I hope that my husband did not give you much grief."

"No, I believe that he wished to tease me at first, but I was not intimidated." Darcy's dimpled smile dazzled both of the ladies.

"Too true, too true," Bennet pretended to lament. "I have promised Darcy here that he might have a brief private chat with you, Lizzy. He is merely waiting for Mr. Bingley's return to see if he might be able to borrow his carriage to return to Town."

"Come dearest," Mr. Bennet said as he offered his arm to his wife. "Let us give the couple a few moments."

Mrs. Bennet's smile was radiant as she stood and winked at Lizzy. She linked her arm with her husband's and leaned her head against his shoulder as they walked out of the room.

* * *

Once outside, the party paired up for more private discourse, but remained close enough to the others for propriety's sake. Walking on one side of Lydia, with the colonel on other, Kitty looked so forlorn that Lydia squeezed her arm.

"What is troubling you, sister dear"?" Lydia enquired.

Sighing, Kitty blushed. "I had hoped you would not notice." Glancing first at the colonel, she added, "I promise to tell you later."

Taking out his pocket watch, the colonel was surprised at how long they had been walking, and understood that the two sisters needed some time alone. "Miss Lydia and Miss Kitty, I must return to Meryton to see to the prisoner. I believe it would be wise to keep what happened quiet for a while for the sake of your sister's reputation. My prisoner may try to use his attack to his advantage by saying more went on than actually did. I have instructed the same to my men. Hopefully, Mr, Darcy and the earl will be able to come to a conclusion about his punishment that will cause the least amount of gossip."

Lydia was disappointed that her beau had to leave, but she dutifully summoned one of the grooms to fetch the colonel's horse. Mary joined her in disappointment as Mr. Wickham decided to ride to Meryton with the soldiers.

With her arm still in Kitty's, Lydia held back slightly before following Mary back into the house. She said softly, "I think now would be a good time for you to tell me what is troubling you. Let us go to our room."

Inside their shared room, the sisters sat together on their bed. Now that the moment had come, Kitty was reluctant to tell Lydia what was on her mind.

Seeing that Kitty was hesitant, Lydia started the conversation with a question. "Are you feeling abandoned because the rest of us have beaus?"

Tears stung Kitty's eyes. Sniffing, she replied, "I am sorry that I have been so petty lately, but I am finding it difficult to think of losing my best friend, and there is no one who seems interested in me. What if I never find happiness like the rest of you?"

"Oh Kitty," Lydia sympathized, "You will find happiness. You know that, logically, I should not even be in a courtship before you. I can promise you that the colonel and I will help find you a worthy man. You will just have to be patient."

"Thank you, Lydia," Kitty exclaimed and hugged her sister. "I will certainly try to have patience."

* * *

Darcy took Elizabeth's hand and kissed it before he sat down next to her. "I must leave for London as soon as possible. I regret that I cannot stay with you longer. I hope that you are truly well."

Still holding his hand, she tried to reassure him. "Indeed, I am perfectly well with only a few bruises. I am grateful that Lydia followed me as she did because I do not know what I would have done if she had not."

"I shall be ever grateful to her as well." Silence hung over them as they fought not to imagine the unthinkable.

Darcy shook his head to clear it of the picture, and of his wish to strangle his relative and one-time closest friend.

"Will you take your cousin back to London with you?" she asked as she noticed his grim expression.

"No," he answered, "I am afraid that I might not have the strength to keep from challenging him. I must allow the army and my uncle to make the decisions about his punishment."

"Thank you for that." She kissed his hand. "Since I do not think we have much more time together, should we not discuss a more pleasant topic?"

"Yes, my dearest Lizzy," he smiled widely as he agreed. "I wish I could obtain a special license. However, even if this um . . . episode is kept quiet, I do not wish for any scandal to be attached to us. I shall send an express to my parish rector, so that the banns can be read as soon as possible. I shall have to make certain that Georgiana is informed and brought to Netherfield as well, with Bingley's permission."

She laughed. "I understand and I do not foresee any objection from this quarter. It will give my mother a chance to plan with me."

A swell of love came over Darcy as he listened to her laughter. "I would kiss you right this moment, but I do not wish to be interrupted. I fear that I can hear the others at the front door already."

It was only a minute later that the group, minus those who returned to Meryton came into the parlour. Soon Mrs. Bennet entered, following a maid carrying a tray of tea and sweets, which Mrs. Bennet served to everyone while announcing, "Mr. Bingley and Mr. Bennet will join us shortly, I am sure. They are currently in the library."

The room took on an air of celebration as the youngest two sisters chatted with their mother about weddings, while Darcy winked at Elizabeth as Jane sat in red-faced silence.

"It would seem that the party has started without us, Bingley," Mr. Bennet declared jovially from the doorway.

"So it would seem." Bingley grinned.

"Still, I will make the announcement," Mr. Bennet said. "There shall be two weddings from Longbourn. I have given both Mr. Darcy and Mr. Bingley permission to marry my daughters, Elizabeth and Jane."

Congratulations and good wishes flowed around the room. Mrs. Bennet sat contently next to Lydia while she watched her two future sons-in-law speaking with one another. Bingley nodded his head vigorously in agreement to what Darcy asked.

Soon after receiving Bingley's approval to use his carriage and his welcome for Georgiana to stay at Netherfield, Darcy left, bidding everyone goodbye.

Elizabeth walked him to the horses so that they had a private moment in which to say farewell. She stood and watched Darcy ride away until he turned onto the main road. She felt bereft of his company and the feeling of safety she had experienced. Shivering, Lizzy wrapped her shawl tightly around her and turned to enter the house.

Once inside, Elizabeth sought out her mother who was still in the parlour, speaking with Jane about her wedding.

"Come join us, Lizzy," Mrs. Bennet invited. "We have an idea we would like to discuss with you."

After she was seated and was given a cup of tea, Elizabeth asked, "What is this idea?"

"You know how we always spoke of sharing our wedding day?" Jane began cautiously.

"Yes, I remember, but if you do not wish to do so, I understand."

"Oh no, dearest," Jane protested, "I told Mama about our wish. She wisely advised me to ask you before planning further. You might have changed your mind."

"Oh, I was afraid that you had changed your mind," Elizabeth said quickly. "I am happy that you still wish it."

"Wonderful!" Jane exclaimed happily. "It will be less work for Mama as well."

When Elizabeth nodded her agreement, Mrs. Bennet said, "Do not worry about me. I shall be happy either way." Then, with a twinkle in her eye, she said, "I suppose I might change my mind if Colonel Forster and Mr. Wickham propose soon."

The sisters laughed and began explaining to their mother what they had considered ever since they had discussed having a double wedding several years ago. Mrs. Bennet had many ideas of her own, some of which Elizabeth and Jane loved. Although their mother brought forward some that they did not like, she handled their objections with unusual grace and little argument.

While Jane and Lizzy planned their wedding with their mother, Mary played the pianoforte, and Lydia and Kitty worked on their embroidery in the smaller parlour, there was a knock on the door which Mr. Hill answered. There was an express for Mr. Bennet, and the butler brought the missive to Bennet's book room immediately.

The puzzled master of Longbourn did not recognize the postmark or the handwriting, which looked rather feminine. Finally, after futilely searching for a clue as to its author or origin, Bennet broke the seal. Folded around another letter was a brief note that explained who the author was and why she was writing to a complete stranger.

Shock and surprise fed his curiosity, so that Mr. Bennet opened the other letter. Disbelief was his first response since it seemed impossible that the humble and contrite missive could have been written by his cousin, Collins. After reading the letter three times, he was closer to giving credence to its contents. The idea that his Fanny would not have to leave Longbourn when he died gave him hope and comfort. Could this woman be strong enough to control Collins's bad habits and withstand the interference of Lady Catherine? He supposed the only way to find out was to meet her and see how much Collins had truly changed.

He rang for a servant and asked her to invite Mrs. Bennet to come to his book room. He realised that he would have to explain the circumstances that led to Mr Collins's sudden expulsion from Longbourn. Considering their recent resumption of closeness, he was worried she would be hurt. Hoping he would find the right words to convey his reasoning, he poured a glass of port and drank it quickly.

Within a few minutes, a smiling Mrs. Bennet entered the room. "You sent for me, Mr. Bennet?"

"I did," he said as he motioned toward a chair near the window, "Please be seated, my dear. I have a tale to tell, but first there is something I wish for you to read."

Once they sat down, Mr. Bennet handed his wife the two missives and watched her face carefully as she read. At first, her face showed confusion and then downright bewilderment once she finished.

"I do not understand what Mr. Collins is apologising for. He was a bit of a bore and did not propose to one of the girls, but all has ended well for them. And could it be true that I will not have to leave Longbourn upon your passing?"

"I told you that I have a tale to tell, and then I will explain why I did not say anything to you at the time," he said softly as he took her hand.

"Very well."

By the time he had finished telling his wife what had occurred during Mr. Collins's visit, she was stunned into silence and blinking back tears.

Quickly handing her his handkerchief, Mr. Bennet spoke. "Forgive me for causing you grief. At the time, we had not yet come to our present understanding. I was afraid that you would be so offended by his actions that you would tell your sister and your friends, which could have embroiled us, at best, in much gossip and, at the worst, in scandal and ruination of the girls' reputations. I thought it best to keep it to myself. I would have carried out my threat to expose him if he ever came back or said anything negative about the Bennet family. I hope you understand."

Mrs. Bennet gave him a weak smile. "I do understand that I was a terrible gossip. I do not comprehend why it took me so long to see how harmful my loose tongue could be to our family. I wondered why you had always kept things from me, but I see now that you were wise to do so. I forgive you if you will forgive me."

"Of course, Fanny," he said as he leaned over to kiss her. "We have both made a mess of things, but we have begun a new chapter of our lives, and I believe it will be a much better one."

"Do we allow them to visit and, if so, when?" Mrs. Bennet asked and quickly added, "I am not certain we should make the decision without consulting Elizabeth. This Miss Langford wrote about me staying at Longbourn. I would like to hear more about that."

There was a soft knock at the door. Mr. Bennet called out, "Enter."

Elizabeth peered through the slightly opened door. "Hill told me you had received an express. You and Mama have been so long in here that I feared something must be wrong."

"Come sit, Lizzy," her father invited. "We have something to discuss with you."

Leaning back against the squabs of Bingley's carriage, Darcy tried to relax. Once he reached London, he foresaw a difficult and arduous discussion with his uncle, but he hoped that the earl would see that his son should not escape punishment for his crimes. Not usually a violent sort of man, Darcy wished for blood. His cousin had nearly ruined his sweet Elizabeth out of pure jealousy, after years of lies. His trust and affection for Richard was completely broken. The memory of how frail his beloved looked when she ran to him caused him to wish to rain his anger down upon his cousin.

The coach was nearing Meryton when there was a shout. Darcy did not believe it could be highwaymen so close to the village, but he lifted the pistol he always carried with him from the satchel at his feet. He replaced it when he heard a voice he recognized.

When the carriage came to a stop, Darcy climbed down. "Captain Carter, I did not expect to see you until I returned."

"Colonel Forster wished for me to deliver a letter to you to give to the earl. It explains the full charges against Colonel Fitzwilliam, and what the military will do if his lordship wishes to pursue that course." Carter handed a thick packet to Darcy. "The colonel thought it best that you deliver it."

"Thank you, Captain, and please thank the colonel for me." Darcy hesitated before continuing, "Although I am reluctant to ask, I know that my uncle will wish to know. How is Colonel Fitzwilliam faring?"

"He is complaining loudly about the chains and demands that the earl be fetched immediately. He tried to lie about Miss Elizabeth, but one of the guards quieted him with a well-placed punch to the mouth." The captain grinned slyly and added, "I do not think he will be biting into apples anytime soon."

"I suppose it is inappropriate for me to say that I wish to shake that guard's hand when I return."

"Given the circumstances, I would not say so, sir," Carter answered.

After bidding the officer goodbye, Darcy re-entered the carriage, which resumed its journey to Town.

* * *

Darcy woke abruptly as the carriage entered the cobbled streets of London. With a jaw-cracking yawn, he stretched as much as he could in the close quarters of the vehicle. Disorientated by his short nap, he was pleased that earlier, he had instructed the driver to take him to Darcy House first. He was in great need of a bath, a change of clothes, and some strong coffee.

In a little over half an hour, Darcy stepped down from the carriage and up the stairs to the front of his home. His butler, Carson, quickly opened the door, welcoming him home.

"I wish for a bath, and since Peters is not here, I shall need a footman to assist me in dressing," Darcy said as the butler helped him out of his coat. "And I need some toast and strong coffee sent up as soon as can be arranged."

"Yes, sir," the butler replied, "Your bath shall be ready within a quarter hour and the coffee even sooner."

Pausing on his way to the stairs, Darcy remembered that his sister had mentioned writing to him from Ramsgate. "Carson, please think back to when I made the trip to visit my sister in Ramsgate. Did an express come for me while I was gone?"

The butler took a moment to think before he answered, "Yes, sir, I recall that one came just after Colonel Fitzwilliam arrived. He took it, saying he would see you soon and would give it to you."

Sighing inwardly, Darcy knew that his cousin must have destroyed the letter. Surely Fitzwilliam did not wish for the truth to be known. *I wonder how many of my letters he has opened in my absence.*

Before he wearily climbed to the family level and into his room, Darcy sent a note to his uncle informing him of his arrival and that he would be visiting shortly. A waiting footman helped him to remove his clothing and don a robe while he waited for the hot water. When the food and drink arrived, Darcy consumed it gratefully

Soon, Darcy was relaxing in a tub of hot water. All he wished to do was finish his bath and to crawl into bed, but he knew that he needed to speak to his uncle as soon as possible. His love for Elizabeth demanded that he deal with everything pertaining to his cousin before returning to her. He wanted to be able to tell her that the man had been dealt with and that he would never bother her again.

Less than an hour later, Darcy was dressed. He ordered his cousin's horse to be saddled. He struggled as to the best way to explain to the earl what had happened. Deciding to allow things to take their course, he arrived a short time later and handed to reins to a footman.

The butler announced him to his uncle who was pacing his study. The earl stopped and asked abruptly, "Did you find Richard? Is he with you?"

"I found him, Uncle," Darcy replied as he as shook his head, "But he is still in Hertfordshire at the moment."

"Why did you not bring him back with you?"

"If I may?" Darcy gestured to a chair. "This could be a long conversation."

* * *

In Mr. Bennet's book room, Elizabeth carefully pondered what her parents told her. Stunned that they would consider allowing Mr. Collins to visit, she shook her head. "I could not possibly attend his wedding. Is it possible that he could change in so short a time?"

"Your mother and I must discuss whether or not to attend their wedding," Mr. Bennet said quietly. "If the date is too close to yours, of course, we will send our regrets. However if we do go, we will not insist that you do so."

"Considering his past behaviour," her mother added, "I am reluctant to go as well. If we visit, it shall be for the purpose of determining his sincerity."

After a moment of silence, Mr. Bennet said, "I hope you understand if he seems sincere, and we can keep in his good graces and him in ours, your mother may not have to leave Longbourn when I am gone."

"But Mr. Darcy and I would never allow Mama to be homeless."

"Of course, I understand," Mrs. Bennet answered. "But I would rather live in the home that has been mine for over twenty years. I would be in the way if I came to live with you."

"You would not, Mama, but I do see why you wish to remain at Longbourn," Elizabeth conceded. "I understand you must do this."

"I believe it for the best to explain that, with a wedding to plan for and with Christmastide so close, we are unable to attend their wedding which, by the sound of things, is to be soon. We would welcome them in the spring, or we could visit them at Easter." Her father walked to her and patted her shoulder. "His response will show us more."

"Do not forget a date has not been set for Jane's and Lizzy's weddings, nor likely is to be until Mr. Darcy returns," Mrs. Bennet added with a smile. "I am sure that, once this nasty business is concluded, he will be back wanting to fix a date as soon as may be."

Elizabeth stood and asked to be excused. "I am certain that you need time and privacy in which to compose your response to Mr. Collins."

Nodding, her father smiled. "I am sure you are right, Lizzy."

Mrs. Bennet asked, "Do you wish for my help, Mr. Bennet?"

"I wish for you to read what I have written. I would not want to be too harsh or sarcastic, though I would like to be."

Grinning happily to see her parents working together on a task, Lizzy left and went to the parlour.

* * *

As he finished his story, Darcy watched his uncle read the letter he had given him from Colonel Forster before the earl slumped back in his chair. He decided to wait for the earl to digest what he had heard and read before he spoke of what was to be done. Surely transportation was the best option considering the circumstances and the possible scandal if he were to be court martialed.

Darcy was surprised when suddenly his uncle rose from his chair and went to his desk. The earl picked up a piece of paper and gave it to Darcy. "So it is far worse than I thought."

The missive was on official military letterhead from the office of Major General _____. It asked after the earl's health and begged pardon for calling his son away if he were still ill. He ordered Colonel Fitzwilliam to report to him by the next day, or he would be considered a deserter.

"Do I understand this correctly? Richard claimed that you were ill so as to get leave?" Darcy sounded incredulous.

"That is what I comprehended from the letter," the earl agreed. "Seeing that he lied to his commander, I now completely agree with what Colonel Forster wrote in his letter. There are only two alternative punishments: court martial, with likely death by firing squad, or he should be transported. Because of my position in society and in the House of Lords, a court martial would mean great scandal, especially if Richard speaks of your Miss Elizabeth. Transport from any of the regular ports could generate gossip as well. This Colonel Forster informs me of a port in southern England where the transport ships dock for a short time to pick up prisoners whose families do not wish for the publicity."

"How are you to arrange it?"

"This letter indicates who to contact and how to travel so as not to be recognized."

The earl scratched his chin before he continued. "It will take a few days to accomplish everything in preparation for travel to Meryton to see Richard off to this southern port. I hope you will be able to come with me to Hertfordshire. I will need introductions to Colonel Forster, Miss Elizabeth Bennet, and her family."

"I would be honoured to do so, but I must first await Georgiana's arrival. I sent an express to have her brought to London. Will you be able to wait until she arrives?"

"I am sure I could," the earl agreed. "There are a few ships that are scheduled later. I shall see what can be arranged and get back to you."

"Thank you, Uncle," Darcy said as he stood. "I have things to do before I return. Would be so kind as to order a carriage for me? I rode Richard's horse here so that you could decide what to do with it."

"Of course," the earl answered and rose to ring for a servant. "Will you return for dinner?"

"I shall send word if I am able."

* * *

Having decided not to leave as planned, and with only one final day before he had to return to Hunsford, Collins paced the library nervously. He had written his Sunday sermon without any input from Lady Catherine, which was something he had never done before. His beloved Eleanor had read it and approved, but he felt certain that her ladyship would not. She always wanted him to stress the law in his sermons. However, Eleanor had gently reminded him that preaching only the law would leave his parishioners in despair. They also needed to hear the good news of Jesus' death and resurrection to bring forgiveness for all.

When he heard a soft knock at the door, Collins stopped his frantic movement. "Come," he called.

Eleanor entered with tea tray. "Oh good, I am not interrupting. I thought you could use some refreshments."

As she set the tray on a small table, Collins found his favourite shortbread beside the teapot. "You will have me growing so fat that I shall need new garments."

"Nonsense, William," Eleanor said as she served him a cup of tea and shortbread, "You are on vacation. Besides, sweets will be a treat for Sundays and holidays in our home. We will both be too busy to grow fat."

"How have I been so blessed as to win your heart, and why did I not see you for the jewel that you are before this?" he asked with a wistful sigh.

"It was just a matter of Providence's timing. It is always perfect."

Collins smiled at her while he lifted the cup to his lips. "I agree, but will need repeated reminders."

Sitting down and taking up her own cup, Eleanor remarked, "I suppose that Lady Catherine will not be happy that you did not consult her before you preach on Sunday."

"I believe she will be very upset, and I was just worrying about that very thing before you knocked." Pausing first to sip his tea, Collins added, "However, I know that this sermon is better than any I have written before, thanks to you. Therefore, I shall trust God to help deal with her chiding. As you have often reminded me, she will not be able to force me out just because I do not allow her to write my sermons."

When Eleanor nodded in agreement, Collins took a generous bite of shortbread and savoured it before he spoke again. "She will likely punish me by not inviting me to dine with her for some time."

"I shall see to it that you have sufficient meals so that you do not starve." Eleanor's smile was evident in her voice.

"Worry not, my dear, my larder is well stocked, and the cook I hire part time is a decent one."

"We shall not be in need of a cook often after we are married. I enjoy cooking and baking, especially for an appreciative person such as yourself," she said sincerely.

"I do appreciate your domestic talents, but I do not wish you to work so hard that you wear yourself out. I will wish to have my cook make our meals at least once a week, so you can have a day of rest." Collins reached for her hand and squeezed it.

"That is very generous of you, William," Eleanor responded. "I will agree on one condition, and that is that you have one day that you relax as well. I know there will be times when a parishioner will need your guidance, but neither do I wish for you to be worn into an earlier grave."

"I suppose that we shall help each other in this and many other things in life," he declared happily.

* * *

Darcy dined with his uncle, but left soon after. His heart ached for his beloved, so that he was not good company. Once he was in his room and dressed for bed, he sat in front of the fireplace in a comfortable chair. Staring at the flames, he was reminded of his Elizabeth's flashing eyes and wondered how soon he would see her again.

Feeling melancholy without her company, Darcy pulled out his drawing pad and gazed lovingly at the image he had drawn of Elizabeth. He hoped to see her within the week and to marry her within the month. It was then that he conjured up a picture of how she might look on their wedding day.

Darcy hastened to find a pencil and began to draw. As he moved the implement across the paper, a portrait of Elizabeth crowned with a circlet of roses took shape. She wore a half-smile as if she had a secret delight. Around her neck, she wore his mother's pearls. He only sketched her head and shoulders. It seemed a trifle presumptuous to decide what she might wear to their wedding. Once he finished, he sighed with longing. If only he could hold her close again.

At that moment, a realization dawned on him. He could and should have already written her a letter. Darcy had spent a great deal of time that day penning missives to various people, including his solicitor regarding the marriage settlement, but he had not remembered to compose one to his betrothed.

Hastening to his desk, Darcy sat and pulled out pen and paper. Words of love and longing flowed onto the page. Although he would have preferred to tell her in person, the act of writing helped to soothe the pain of loneliness. At the end he added a postscript, which read, "Please wear white roses in your hair for our wedding." Next to it, he drew a rose.

After sealing the missive and extinguishing his candles, Darcy crawled into bed, promising himself he would have it posted first thing in the morning. He smiled as he lay his head on his pillow and fell into a deep sleep, dreaming of his Elizabeth.

* * *

The days since Mr. Darcy had gone to London seemed to be the longest Elizabeth had ever lived through. Her sisters tried to cheer her, but nothing filled the void left behind by his absence. After the first banns were read at church that Sunday, she was inundated with good wishes on her engagement. Her attempt at appearing sanguine was generally successful, but her good friend, Charlotte Lucas, pulled her to one side in the churchyard.

"What is troubling you, Eliza?" Charlotte asked in a soft, concerned tone.

"Nothing," Elizabeth replied shortly.

This caused Charlotte to smile. "I have known you all of your life, and we have been friends for most of it. I believe I know when you are upset, and can even guess why."

She paused and pressed Elizabeth's hand. "You are missing Mr. Darcy, are you not?"

Lowering her gaze to the ground, Elizabeth nodded. "I have never missed anyone so much, and he has only been gone a few days. I feel like I am being ridiculous."

"I personally know nothing about romantic feelings," Charlotte soothed. "However, I think that it must be perfectly natural for you to miss your beloved."

"Thank you, Charlotte, for being so understanding," Elizabeth said before giving her a light kiss on the cheek. "Oh, I see that my family is ready to leave. I hope to see you soon at Longbourn."

"Of course," Charlotte replied happily.

* * *

William Collins awoke early in the morning, having arrived at Hunsford the night before. He had gotten home only a few hours before his usual Saturday bedtime. After practicing his sermon a few times and eating a light repast prepared for him by the Langford's cook, he retired to his chamber.

As he saw to his morning ablutions, Collins felt quite nervous. He had not informed his patroness of his return and was planning to preach a message that she had not personally reviewed and approved. It was a good sermon that he was sure of, but he was certain Lady Catherine would not view it as such.

Straightening his collar and checking his appearance in a mirror, Collins took a deep breath. Deciding that his beloved was more important than anyone but the Lord to him, he would brave her lady-ship's disapproval. There was no way he wanted to disappoint Eleanor. A genuine smile graced his face as he descended the stairs and went to his study. Picking up the sermon pages from where he had left them the night before, he put them in a folio and walked out the door toward the church.

Despite his resolve to face the likely censure of his patroness, Collins's stomach felt knotted. Also, he must have his curate read the first of the banns. That was not apt to please Lady Catherine either. She had always insisted upon being the first to be informed as to any and all affairs of the church.

Collins shook his head at the foolishness to which he had submitted since he had become the vicar of the parish. Eleanor had been instrumental in helping him to see his folly and his own guilt. Lifting up a prayer for help and courage, he trudged on his way.

Once he arrived at the church, he found the curate, Mr. Andrews, just opening the doors.

"Good morning, sir," the curate greeted him, handing him some sheets of paper. "I was not certain that you would be back. Lady Catherine gave this to me yesterday, telling me to use it for today's sermon if you did not return."

Taking the sheets from the curate, Collins slipped them behind his own sermon, not intending to use them. "Forgive me, Mr. Andrews, I should have sent word as soon as I knew when I would arrive. Let us go inside, for I have something I wish for you to do for me today."

Mr. Andrews was not shocked at Mr. Collins's request for him to read the banns, but he was surprised at the bride-to-be. He had been told that the parson would be returning engaged to one of his cousins. Shaking off the disbelief, he readily agreed to do the honours.

As the congregation began to arrive and take their regular places, Mr. Collins tried to calm his nerves. He felt a jolt of panic when just a few moments before the service was to begin, Lady Catherine came down the aisle to her pew with her daughter and companion following her just a few moments before the service was to begin. He could feel her displeasure, even though he did not meet her eye. Instead, he searched the congregation before he found his Eleanor's softly smiling visage. His heart responded by calming. He could not help but briefly return her smile before his face took on a more serious mien.

Nodding to the curate, Collins remained in his seat. He thrilled to the reading of his name and hers. His breath came out in a sigh when no one stated an objection, although he thought he heard a "humph" from her ladyship's pew.

The curate sat down as Collins began the service with a prayer. After the singing of hymns and reading of Scriptures, he ascended the steps to the pulpit and started to preach. The sermon was so different from any other that he had given that the people were pleasantly surprised. Most of them listened in rapt attention to the message. They heard the familiar tale of the great fall of Adam and how that fall affected the whole human race. However, they had rarely heard of the mercy of

God who sent His son to die for the sins of the world. By the time their pastor had finished, many had hope in their hearts instead of despair.

After dismissing the congregation with a final benediction, Collins walked to the back of the church to await the people who would wish to greet him. Usually, Lady Catherine would force her way to the front, give him a few words, and leave before the rest. However, this time she sat in her pew, staring forward with a deep frown on her face.

His parishioners praised his sermon and congratulated him on his engagement as they shook his hand. Never before in his tenure had Collins received such a positive response to one of his messages. While he stood there greeting his people, he felt a gentle hand on his arm and found his Eleanor standing next to him. Her warm look made him straighten his back even more.

As what he thought was the last of the congregation left the building, Collins turned to Eleanor. "I am glad you are here, dearest," he whispered as he bowed over hand.

Eleanor opened her mouth to speak, but was interrupted by Lady Catherine.

"What do you think you were doing, Mr. Collins?" she boomed out as she confronted him. "That was not the right sermon, and you were to marry one of your cousins."

"My cousins and I found that we would not suit, lovely as they are." Collins refused to explain further.

"But that sermon! I gave a sermon to Mr. Andrews, which he says he gave to you. I am displeased that you took it upon yourself to write a sermon entirely without my input."

"I have taken up far too much of your valuable time bringing my messages to you. Since I am fully capable of writing my own, I decided to begin this week. I am grateful for your assistance in the past, but it will no longer be needed." His statement was firm although he trembled inwardly.

Her ladyship was stunned into silence for a few moments; her face stained a bright red. Finally, eyes wild with temper, Lady Catherine turned on Eleanor.

"You contrived your way into an engagement, turning my parson into a Methodist," Lady Catherine hissed as she lifted her cane as if to strike Eleanor.

Mr. Collins put himself between his beloved and her ladyship while grabbing hold of her cane. "You will not harm my betrothed. Miss Langford is virtue itself. And I am certainly nothing but a rector of the Church of England."

"I will have you defrocked," she threatened as she pulled on her cane. "I demand that you pack your things and leave the parsonage as soon as possible."

"I beg your pardon, Lady Catherine," Collins spoke calmly while not releasing his hold. "I have not done anything here to warrant dismissal, let alone defrocking. Besides, only my bishop is able to remove me from my duties here."

The lady's mouth shut with a sharp click. Lady Catherine looked from Collins to Miss Langford and back again before she let go of the cane. Stepping back, she turned to her daughter's companion and said, "Jenkinson, retrieve my stick," before moving through the doorway.

After she was a few feet outside, her ladyship glanced back over her shoulder and said, "This matter is not settled. I will know how to act."

"Do you think she will be able to remove me from the parish?" Collins whispered in anxiety.

"No, but I am certain that she will try," Eleanor answered back. When she saw Collins shoulders slump at her statement, she took his hand and said, "She will not succeed and will possibly cause some scandal for a while. However after this morning, I predict that she will find few to back her. The congregation was inspired by your sermon."

"I hope you are correct because my past conduct has not been exemplary," Collins murmured softly. "What if she finds someone to speak against me?"

"I do not foresee that happening," she tried to reassure him. "Her ladyship is not well liked in Hunsford. Not everyone will say so, but she is generally considered an overbearing and interfering tyrant."

"I hope what you say is true. I would not wish to enter into marriage and not be able to provide for you."

"I do not believe in such worrisome speculations," Eleanor said as she tugged on his arm toward the door. "Together we will deal with what trials may come."

Chapter 18

Monday morning, Elizabeth had to drag herself out of bed. Although she would have liked to sleep all day to hide from the loneliness and a bit of anxiety that covered her heart and mind, she managed to arise only a half hour after her normal time. Unlike her usual wont, Elizabeth felt apprehensive about walking out alone so soon after what had happened to her. Even the thought of Colonel Fitzwilliam being in jail was not enough to quell her unease.

Once she had dressed and pulled her hair into a simple bun at the back of her head, Elizabeth moved slowly down the staircase to the breakfast parlour. The rest of the family was sitting around the table as she arrived.

"We had thought you to be on one of your rambles this morning," Jane said as she passed the teapot to Elizabeth.

"No, I merely overslept," Elizabeth replied, adding a touch of milk to her teacup before pouring the hot liquid into it.

Elizabeth ate and spoke little as her family chatted around her. It was not until Jane, Mary, and Kitty excused themselves from the table that Lydia sympathised, "Your Mr. Darcy will not be long in returning, I am sure."

"Ah yes, being in love is sometimes a painful thing," Mr. Bennet quipped.

"Do not tease Lizzy, Mr. Bennet," Mrs. Bennet chided.

"Forgive me, my Lizzy," he said with contrition as he stood. "I was just trying to lighten the mood." After a few more minutes, he excused himself to go back to his book room.

Mrs. Bennet moved to the chair next to Elizabeth that Jane had recently vacated. "I have something that will likely cheer you, my dear."

Pulling a folded paper out of her pocket, her mother handed it to Lizzy. "I did not give it to you sooner because I thought you might wish to read it in privacy."

Seeing the large "D" in the sealing wax, Elizabeth swiftly opened the letter, certain it was from Mr. Darcy. As she read through the missive, much of her loneliness and anxiety fled in the wake of his words of love and of his own desire for her company. She finally realised that part of her melancholy was due to thinking he might, even now, have changed his mind about her.

Tears filled her eyes as Elizabeth finished the letter and saw the lovely drawing of a rose after the postscript. Sniffing, she searched her pocket for a handkerchief.

"Is something the matter, Lizzy," Mrs. Bennet asked.

"Oh no, Mama," she smiled after wiping her eyes. "I am merely happy and touched. Mr. Darcy wishes for me to wear white roses in my hair for our wedding."

"What a lovely idea!" Lydia cried out as her mother nodded in agreement.

Elizabeth folded the letter so that only the rose was visible. "See he even drew a rose in the post script."

While Mrs. Bennet examined the sketch, Lydia hurried around the table to see for herself.

"I did not know Mr. Darcy was an artist," he mother said while handing the paper back to Elizabeth.

"Nor did I," Lizzy said, putting the refolded letter in her pocket.

Smiling, Elizabeth asked to be excused so that she could respond to Mr. Darcy's correspondence.

"Of course, my dear, you must write immediately."

* * *

Wednesday, Darcy received two letters, both of which gave him joy. The first was from his steward, who was escorting Georgiana and her companion to Town. He stated that he would arrive some time the next day. That meant he and his sister could make their way to Hertfordshire as soon as Friday.

The second was from his Elizabeth. She told him how much his missive meant to her, and how she looked forward to seeing him again. While loving his drawing and the idea of wearing roses for their wedding, she was not certain how it was to be accomplished in the winter in Hertfordshire.

Darcy smiled as he had already planned to order roses sent from London once the date for their nuptials was fixed. He would keep that detail a secret for now, but he wanted to respond to her letter as soon as he wrote a note to his uncle to be ready to travel to Meryton in two days. He prayed that nothing would delay his sister's journey.

Once he finished his note to his uncle, Darcy rang for a footman. When the man arrived, he ordered, "Take this to Lord Matlock's house."

As the servant left to do what he was commanded, Darcy himself sat down to write to his beloved Elizabeth. He knew that the letter might arrive the same day he did, but he wanted the pleasure of sending her another missive.

There was a knock on the door just as Darcy sanded the letter. "Come."

The footman entered and handed Darcy a folded piece of paper.

"Thank you," Darcy replied and dismissed the servant.

Opening the missive, he read:

Nephew,

I am glad to know that we will not have to wait much longer to conclude this business. I made arrangements for a physician to travel with Richard in a special carriage I have hired. I will not use one of my own, as I do not wish my crest to be recognized during the trip. I believe that Richard will not go quietly, so the best solution will be to keep him sedated and chained during the journey.

It will be good to see my dear niece again. I look forward to meeting your betrothed as well. Since I do not want my relationship with Richard to be widely known in Meryton, I plan to stay quiet while I am there.

I rejoice that my dear wife did not live to see what kind of man Richard has become. It would have broken her heart.

I will wait for word from you that Georgiana has arrived, and then will come to Darcy House to begin our travel.

Your uncle,

Frederick Fitzwilliam

Appreciating the wisdom of his uncle in deciding not to make the trip south himself, Darcy again wished his sister and her companions a quick journey.

* * *

As the weak winter sun came through her window, Elizabeth rose and dressed quickly. Being too anxious for the return of her beloved William to stay abed, she pondered a walk. Peering out of the window, she saw that frost covered the ground and thought better of going outdoors so early. She did not wish to read or sew to keep herself busy. She knew full well that she was too distracted to give either the correct attention.

Picking up her shawl, which lay over a chair, Elizabeth wrapped herself in it to ward off the chill and made for the breakfast room. No doubt there would be hot tea and muffins waiting.

Upon entering the room, Elizabeth saw that Mary had preceded her there.

"Good morning, Mary," she said as she sat and poured a cup of tea. Reaching for a muffin, she continued, "I am surprised to see you up so early."

"It is early for me, but I could not sleep any longer," Mary answered as she sipped her tea. "I am not certain why, but I thought I would not waste time trying to sleep. I am glad you are awake now too.

"Papa has taken his breakfast in his library. It seems he has a new book he wishes to finish reading."

"There have been many a time in which I have eaten alone because Papa could not wait to read the ending of a book. I shall have to ask him what volume he is so interested in this time."

The two sisters continued to chat for about a half hour before the rest of the family began to join them. The talk turned to weddings with Mrs. Bennet exulting in the fact, once again, that two of her girls were to be married, and one was officially courting.

Once their meal was over, the ladies retired to the front parlour to continue their conversation. Their mother enjoyed discussing the many ideas for the upcoming wedding. It gratified Elizabeth that her mother no longer argued with her about what she wanted for her nuptials. She was happy to be in such accord with her mother.

At ten there came a knock at the door. Soon, Hill announced Mr. Wickham.

"Good morning, ladies," he greeted them. "I hope you are all well."

"Good morning, Mr. Wickham. We are well, sir," Mrs. Bennet responded as they all stood. "It is a pleasant surprise to see you this morning."

"I hope I am not imposing, but I wanted to visit the Taylors to see if their kittens have been weaned and are ready for new homes. Mr. and Mrs. North have no objection to having a cat in their home," he said before adding, "I was wondering if Miss Mary and any of her sisters who wish to would like to join me."

Turning as red as beetroot, Mary nevertheless assented as did Kitty and Lydia. Elizabeth smiled inwardly as she noticed Mary's blush. Mrs. Bennet asked Jane and Elizabeth to stay behind to keep her company.

Some time later, the group arrived back at Longbourn with smiling faces and reddened cheeks.

Lydia was the first to speak. "It was awfully cold, but the kittens made it quite worth the walk. Oh, Mama, the little black and white one was so adorable. I do wish we could have a house cat." Her voice took on a bit of pleading.

Mrs. Bennet smiled in response. "I would have to speak to your father before I consented. It would have to be your responsibility if we did have a cat."

"Of course, Mama, I would be happy to take care of the kitten."

"We shall see," Mrs. Bennet answered without committing. She turned to Mr. Wickham and asked, "Would you care for some refreshments? I was just going to ring for tea."

"Actually, I would like to speak to Mr. Bennet before I sit with you ladies."

"You are welcome to go to his book room. I do not believe he is very busy at the moment," she said.

Once the curate left the room, Mrs. Bennet turned to Mary and said, "Is there any special reason Mr. Wickham wants to speak to your father?"

Mary turned bright red, but she did not speak.

Lydia was not so reluctant. "I am certain he wishes to court Mary. They were in such close conversation all of the way home." She winked at Mary before she said, "I am certain they were not still speaking of kittens."

Kitty giggled. "No, they were not saying anything about cats."

"Do not tease Mary so," Elizabeth scolded, "It is unkind."

"I am sorry," Lydia said and was quickly echoed by Kitty. "I just think it is a wonderful thing that someone has seen the worth of our sister."

"Lydia is correct," Mr. Bennet replied from the doorway before he preceded Mr. Wickham into the room. "I am pleased to announce that I have agreed that Mr. Wickham might enter into a courtship with our Mary."

Hurrying to Mary, Lydia and Kitty embraced her in their excitement while Mrs. Bennet sat with tears of joy in her eyes.

Jane and Elizabeth shook hands with Mr. Wickham and congratulated him before they joined the rest encircling Mary to express their best wishes.

Mr. Bennet sat next to his wife and took her hand. He whispered in her ear, "Are you not pleased, my dear?"

"I am overjoyed, but I do not wish to be as vocal about it as I used to do."

Smiling, Mr. Bennet answered, "I am certain that no one would mind, but I appreciate your self-control."

"It would seem that we shall be on our own sooner than we ever expected, and I, with all my worrying and fussing, had nothing to do with it. In fact, I may have lengthened the process," Mrs. Bennet said softly.

"We shall be fine, now that we have found each other again. I look forward to the upcoming years," he said as he squeezed her hand. "Do not forget that we still have Kitty. Who knows how long it will be before she finds her match."

Playfully slapping his arm with her free hand, she responded with a grin, "You do delight in teasing me."

* * *

After finishing a light supper, Darcy was surprised by the arrival of his sister's party. He welcomed her heartily before greeting his steward Mr. Fraser and Georgiana's companion, Mrs. Annesley.

"I am happy you have arrived so early. I did not expect you until tomorrow morning at the earliest," Darcy said as he shook Mr. Fraser's hand.

"We had very good roads and we started out quite early this morning from the inn in which we stayed," Mr. Fraser answered.

"I am certain that you all would like to refresh yourselves. Mrs. Glendale will show you where you can do just that."

Turning to his sister, Darcy said, "Georgiana, would you stay with me for a few more minutes?"

"Of course, Brother," she agreed before asking, "Is something amiss?"

He did not answer, but took her hand and led her into a small parlour. Gesturing to a settee, he sat next to her, retaining his hold on her hand.

"What I have to tell you will likely distress you, but I do believe it is best that you know the truth."

Looking into his sister's anxious eyes, Darcy began to explain the events of the last few weeks and what he had found out about his cousin. He did not give many details, but enough for Georgiana to understand.

Watching her face grow pale before the tears started to fall, Darcy tightened his grip on Georgiana with one hand while reaching for his handkerchief with the other. He gently wiped her eyes and murmured soothingly to her.

Georgiana took the handkerchief and blew her nose, looking into his eyes. "Richard is far more wicked than I could have ever imagined. How could he do such horrid things, especially trying to ruin a young lady merely to take jealous revenge on you? It is entirely my fault. I should have been more insistent in telling you what he was about in Ramsgate." She hid her face in her hands and wept bitterly.

Wrapping his arms around his sister, Darcy rocked her and said, "It is just as much my fault because I would not listen when you tried to explain. For years I have heard and believed the lies he told me. I never once stopped to think he might not be telling the truth."

Once she had quieted and wiped her tears, she looked up and asked, "Is Miss Elizabeth truly well?"

"Yes, and we are to be married as soon as a date can be arranged."

"Oh brother, I am so happy for you!" Georgiana exclaimed joyfully. "When will I get to meet her?"

"We are for Meryton first thing in the morning. I would like to go now, but I know that you need to rest after your days of travel from Derbyshire."

"I should go to my room," she said quickly, "I must clean off the road dust and decide what to pack and what to leave here." Georgiana kissed her brother's cheek and wished him a good night before she left the room.

Darcy sat down and quickly penned a note to his uncle, explaining when he wished to leave in the morning, and sending a footman to deliver it as soon as possible.

The party left London at first light. Little was said during the journey apart from the earl explaining that a second more secure hired carriage would follow them in two hours for the escort of his wayward son to the transport ship since he did not wish to make the journey himself.

The earl, Georgiana, and her companion dozed during the final two hours of the trip, but Darcy was too eager and excited to see his Elizabeth that he could not keep his eyes closed. He hoped she would be at home for his arrival.

Sighing, he turned to the window to watch the scenery pass by. His heart longed to hold his beloved in his arms. However, it was not likely to happen that day. Perhaps he could invite himself on one of her rambles. He, then, wondered if she was comfortable with her regular walks after she had been attacked. After that thought, he vowed with everything in his power to keep her safe from anything like that happening again.

* * *

Recognizing some of the passing scenery, Darcy gently woke his sister.

"We are nearing Meryton," he announced.

He smiled as his uncle and sister came fully awake and straightened in theirs seats.

"You will take me to the militia headquarters first," the earl stated.

"Yes, that was my plan," Darcy answered. "Do you wish for me to send the carriage back for you?"

"I shall hire a horse if you will give me the directions to this Netherfield."

"It is not difficult to find," Darcy said with a smile. "The lane is the first one on the right off the main road out of Meryton, and if you do not find it, all you need do is ask Colonel Forster. He knows the way."

"Very good," Matlock said as he tried to smooth his waistcoat before re-buttoning his jacket.

Mr. Darcy had given his driver instructions to make their way via a back street to Colonel Forster's headquarters. Soon they pulled to a stop in front of the building. He asked his sister and her companion to stay in the carriage while he escorted the earl to meet the colonel. A soldier who stood at the door opened it for them to enter and signalled for another soldier to take them to Colonel Forster who was expecting them.

Once inside the colonel's office, introductions were made. Forster dismissed his aide and closed the door. "I do not believe you wish to discuss this business publicly."

"You are correct, Colonel," Matlock said, before turning to his nephew. "I think you should go now. I will tell you what happened when I see you next."

Bowing to both men, Darcy left. He was pleased that he did not have to see his cousin again. He was not certain if he could maintain control in his presence.

* * *

After both men were seated, Colonel Forster offered the earl a brandy, which he gratefully accepted. The two men sipped their drinks in thoughtful silence before Matlock spoke. "I want to thank you for your letter and the helpful suggestions. I did not know how to avoid the scandal of a court martial, even though he deserves to be shot."

"I admit that I had a personal motive which prompted my advice."

Intrigued, the earl leaned forward in his chair. "And what could that motive have been?"

"In this case, any scandal involving your family would also involve the Bennets." The colonel paused to swallow the last of his brandy. "I will do all I can to prevent that because I am courting the youngest of the Bennet daughters."

"I take it you mean to marry her, eventually," the earl said with a slight lifting of the corners of his mouth.

"Yes, and sooner rather than later," replied the colonel without hesitation.

"You will then be brother to my nephew."

"As things stand now, yes," Forster said as he smiled.

"Congratulations, Colonel," Matlock exclaimed. "From what Darcy tells me, the Bennet daughters are rare beauties."

"Indeed, sir, with no exception, they are the jewels of the county."

Setting his glass on to the side, Matlock's demeanour changed. "As pleasant as it is to speak of pretty women, we must tend to the business at hand. How is my son?"

"Aside from the bruise and the lump on his head that my lovely Miss Lydia gave him, he is well, but not at all resigned to his incarceration. Also I should mention that one of my men could not keep from darkening his daylights once. My men tell me the only time he is not complaining is when he is sleeping."

"I suppose it is time that I see him," the earl said as he stood. "I have hired a carriage and the doctor as you suggested. He should arrive in less than two hours."

Chapter 19

Mr. Bingley welcomed the Darcy party to Netherfield, meeting them on the front steps. "Come in, warm yourselves. Your rooms are prepared and there shall be hot beverages in the parlour once you are refreshed from your journey."

While waiting for his friend and Miss Darcy to rejoin him, Bingley paced in front of the fireplace. After receiving a short note from Darcy the day before telling him when they would travel, Bingley had foregone his usual morning visit to his beloved in order to be at home when the Darcy party arrived. He hoped that they would wish to call upon the Bennets this afternoon.

A few minutes later, Darcy entered the room with his sister on his arm. "Thank you for allowing us to come on such short notice."

"Think nothing of it. You know that you are always welcome in my home," Charles replied as he rang for tea.

The housekeeper and a maid came in with trays of tea and refreshments. They were dismissed once they had deposited the things on the table.

"Will you pour, Miss Darcy?" Charles asked as they sat down. "My sister Louisa was not well this morning. She and her husband are staying in their chambers and asked me to give you their apologies for their absence."

Georgiana blushed slightly, but nodded and began to serve the tea.

After everyone had their refreshments, Charles said, "I thought that your uncle would be joining you on this trip."

"Yes, he did travel with us, but I left him at the militia headquarters," Darcy answered. "He had business to take care of there."

"I am sorry if I sound rude, but will his business take long?" Charles asked sheepishly. "I only ask because I had hoped we would be able to call upon the Bennets today."

"As do I," said Darcy as he gave his friend a sympathetic smile. "My uncle wishes to meet Miss Elizabeth and her family as soon as possible."

"Good, good," Charles proclaimed eagerly. "We shall make a merry party while we wait for his arrival."

* * *

Lord Matlock followed Colonel Forster through several spartan corridors until they came to a large barred iron door guarded by two soldiers, both of whom stood at stiff attention when they saw their commanding officer.

"How is the prisoner?" asked Forster.

"Well, but complaining as usual," was the quick answer.

"Unbar the door and close it after us," the colonel ordered. "Leave it unbarred, for I do not think we will be long."

"Yes, sir!"

The first thing the earl noticed upon entering was a small corner fireplace with a pleasant blaze warming the room. Close by the fire was a plain wooden chair occupied by a soldier who immediately stood when they came in.

Turning his gaze to the right, Matlock saw the cell. Inside on a cot lay his son. Richard seemed to be napping, so the earl examined him for a moment. It was evident that he had not shaved or bathed in several days. The clothes he wore were stained with grass and dirt. One side of his face was still swollen from a punch. His unkempt, matted hair stuck out like dirty feathers around the bandage wrapped around his head. He looked more like a vagabond than a soldier.

"Fitzwilliam," Colonel Forster called out, "you have a visitor."

Richard threw back his thin blanket and sat up. Staring at the earl, a sly smirk crossed his face. "Father, it is about time you came. Get me out of here. I need some decent food and drink. And a bath and clean clothes," he demanded in rush.

The earl stared at his unrepentant son without answering. He could not help but wonder where he had gone wrong in Richard's upbringing. He remembered the joy both he and his wife experienced at his birth. Never had he loved his second son less than his first, but it had always been difficult for him to express his affection to either child. He supposed that it was possible that he spent more time with Anthony since he wanted to train him in the ways of a landowner. Sighing, he knew he could not change the past.

"I might be able to convince Colonel Forster to bring you a drink, but we need to talk first about your reprehensible actions." He moved closer to the cell.

"I do not know what you have been told, but I was attacked by a young chit when I was only trying to assist her sister," Richard answered with bravado. "I am willing to overlook her offence if I am allowed to leave."

Matlock laughed without humour at his blatant falsehood. "I have heard enough of your lies over the years, and I know the truth of what happened. You will not escape the consequences this time."

"You would leave me to face court martial? If you do, I will testify that I ruined that whore, Elizabeth Bennet and that she invited me to meet her while trying to get me to marry her," Richard threatened with a sneer.

"That is exactly what Darcy said you might do." The earl frowned and shook his head. "No, you are not to face court martial."

Richard relaxed a bit and said, "Then, I am to go to India as you suggested last week?"

"No, you will be transported. I have hired men to escort you to a more discreet port. This is the last time you shall ever see me. You are no longer my son."

The spate of foul language that exploded from his son's mouth could have made the most hardened sailor blush. Richard tried to throw himself against the bars, but his chains prevented him. He could only reach the iron rods with his hands. Roaring with frustration, he pushed away and sat heavily on the cot.

In an eerily calm voice, Matlock spoke. "If you are quite finished with your tantrum, I will ask the colonel if you may have a drink."

"Fine," Richard grunted.

"Goodbye, Richard," Matlock said before he turned to Colonel Forster and nodded toward the door. The two men moved through the door, which was closed after them.

"I have something that Dr. Wallace suggested be put into his food or drink." The earl explained the dosage to be added. "I was told that whiskey would be the best to hide the taste. Wallace's carriage should be here before the drug wears off.

"Now, I would appreciate it if you would tell me where I could hire a horse. I could walk, but I am suddenly quite weary," Matlock admitted.

"If you will wait until I retrieve the liquor, I will take you myself to Netherfield in my curricle," Forster offered.

"I accept gratefully."

* * *

At Longbourn that morning, joyous excitement seemed to permeate the house. Elizabeth and Lydia had invited their sisters to join them for their usual stroll, to which they all agreed. Much giggling and chatter accompanied the girls as they returned a half hour later.

During the outing, Jane noticed that Elizabeth did not smile or tease in her normal way. So, when the ladies were seated and involved in various activities, Jane approached her closest sister and sat next to her.

"Lizzy, are you well?"

Looking around the room to be assured they were not overheard, Elizabeth responded in a near whisper, "I am well in body, but I feel the loss of the company of a certain gentleman quite keenly."

"Poor Lizzy," Jane said as she hid her smile of understanding. "I knew when you fell in love you would do so in a grand way. Nothing is ever half-hearted with you. Take heart, I am sure that he will return soon."

"I do hope so," Lizzy sighed. "I did not know love could be like this, and to think I did not like the man at first."

Pausing, she rolled her eyes at her own statement. "That is not quite true. I thought him quite handsome until he insulted me. I did not realise it at the time, but when I heard his speech to Mr. Bingley my pride was injured. Without knowing it, I chose to feel insulted and to retaliate by making it a joke. Fortunately, I was able to learn his true character sooner rather than later. In doing so, I saved us both from a great deal of misunderstanding."

Jane patted her sister's hand and said, "That is why I try to think of the best in people, until they are proven otherwise. Colonel Fitzwilliam was one such person. I am glad, however, that we found out the truth right away. I just wish you had not been hurt in the process."

"I rarely think about that man. I know that he is safely locked away, and I shall not walk alone until I know he is no longer in the region." Elizabeth squeezed her sister's hand and said, "Here I am talking about missing Mr. Darcy, while I am certain you are missing Mr. Bingley just as much."

"I admit to missing Mr. Bingley, but you must not feel that you are causing me harm by speaking of your feelings. I believe that we can help each other while they are gone."

"Leave it to my Jane to say just the right thing," Elizabeth said as she stood and pulled Jane up with her. "Let us find Mama. She shall have much to say, which will help as well."

* * *

Colonel Forster left Lord Matlock in the small reception area of the headquarters while he went to his office to retrieve his bottle of whiskey. On his way from the cell, he had picked up the tin water cup that Fitzwilliam had used. At his desk, he removed the small bottle of the sedative the earl had given him and put the prescribed amount of the liquid in the empty cup, followed by a generous portion of whiskey.

Although he usually would trust his men to perform their duties to the letter, the colonel did not wish for any of the guards to be tempted to drink the altered liquor. Once he reached the barred door and ordered it reopened, Forster entered the room.

"Fitzwilliam, here is the drink your father asked me to bring to you." The colonel pushed the full cup through the small opening in the bars.

Stepping back, Forster watched as the prisoner lifted the cup to his lips and took a swallow.

"It is not the best whiskey I have ever had, but it is better than most," Fitzwilliam commented before gulping down one swallow after another until he emptied the cup. He pushed it back through the bars and said in a slightly slurred voice, "Could you see fit to bring me another?"

Colonel Forster nodded for the guard to pick up the cup. He took it and turned toward the door. Glancing over his shoulder, he saw the prisoner sit down on the cot, yawn and, seconds later, pull up his feet as he lay back.

Satisfied that the drug was doing its work, Colonel Forster left the room. On his way out, he informed his aide that if a Dr. Wallace came while he was away, he was to be made comfortable in the office.

Forster found the earl pacing the small reception space. "I hope I did not keep you too long, my Lord."

"No, it is merely my own nervous energy," The earl admitted truthfully. "I am eager to be away."

"My curricle is awaiting us. Shall we go?" the Colonel swept his arm toward the door in invitation.

"I believe that we should decide what to tell others about your visit here today," the colonel remarked once they were on their way.

"I thought that I could say that I knew your father years ago, and that I planned to visit with my nephew and niece at Netherfield when I heard that you were stationed in nearby Meryton."

"I believe that is as near to the truth as possible since I know my father met you years ago before you become an earl." Forster manoeuvred his curricle along High Street in Meryton while nodding to those he knew as he passed them.

"I vaguely remember a Forster, Stephen I believe his name was. He was a few years ahead of me at Cambridge," Matlock said, smiling.

"Yes, my father was Stephen Forster. My brother, also Stephen, has taken over the estate since our father's death." Forster's voice took on a note of sorrow.

"I am sorry to hear of his passing. He was a brilliant scholar. I had hoped that he would decide to run for the House of Commons once he was finished with school. My party would have been the better for it," Matlock said thoughtfully.

"My father was a homebody. I doubt if he came to Town more than every other year and only upon my mother's insistence. He enjoyed being a country gentleman, as does my brother."

"Do you plan to continue in the militia?" Matlock asked as the colonel turned his horse onto a country lane.

"No, if I am fortunate enough to marry Miss Lydia Bennet, I will resign. My father purchased a small estate for me several years ago. I only wanted a wife before I took full charge of it," Forster said with a hint of anticipation in his voice.

"I wish I had done so for Richard," the earl sighed. "Perhaps he would have turned out differently."

A moment later, Netherfield came into view, successfully ending the conversation.

Lord Matlock was happy to see his niece, nephew, and Mr. Bingley standing on the front steps, waiting for his arrival. He wanted nothing more than to be in the bosom of his family and friends. Pride and love for Darcy and Georgiana welled up. In his heart, he purposefully put aside thoughts of his younger son to dwell on the positives of the times to come.

As the two men stepped down from the curricle, they were greeted and invited to come inside. Forster asked to be excused to return to his headquarters. The earl thanked the colonel once more and bid him farewell before following the others into the house.

After being introduced to Mr. Bingley, Matlock stated wearily, "I would like to refresh myself before relating what took place in Meryton."

"Of course, your lordship, a footman will show you to your chambers." Bingley nodded to a man standing next to the butler.

As the others watched, the earl ascended the stairs after the footman.

"Let us go into the green room to await your uncle's return," Bingley suggested.

Once inside the ornate green-walled room, Mr. Darcy found that—as was usual when he was impatient—he could not sit. He strode to the window and stared out of it without seeing. More than anything, he wished to see his Elizabeth again. It seemed ages since he last saw her. The corners of his mouth lifted slightly when he remembered her delighted agreement to his proposal. He really wished to pace in his eagerness to see her, but he held himself back for appearance's sake.

A maid arrived with refreshments, and Charles had just asked Georgiana to pour out when the earl returned from above stairs.

"Capital!" Matlock declared, "I could use a cup of tea right now."

Once everyone had been served, the rest of those gathered waited for the servants to leave before turning to Matlock. He took several sips of his tea prior to lifting his eyes to the others.

"I am very sorry to say that my youngest son was not in the least repentant. He blamed everyone else for what he has done. Colonel Forster was prudent indeed to keep him away from the rest of the soldiers. He was especially crude and disgusting in what he tried to say about Miss Elizabeth. I was told, and saw the evidence, that one of the guards quieted him with a swift blow to his face.

"When I did not give him a choice in the matter of his punishment, he unleashed a vulgar tirade against my person. I do wish that I could have known how far he would go. I might have been able to stop him."

"Uncle, please do not blame yourself," Darcy corrected. "He had many opportunities in his life, ones that many others would envy. Richard chose his path, no one else."

Georgiana listened quietly with tears running down her face. She moved to sit next to her uncle and wrapped her arms around him.

"You have Anthony and his sons who are decent, moral young men," she soothed. "And you have William and me."

"Thank you, my dear Georgie," he said as he patted her back. "I am blessed with a son to whom I can pass on my legacy. That is the main reason I did not wish to have scandal stain my name. Anthony does not deserve that fate."

* * *

The morning light brightened William Collins's book room as he read the text for the following Sunday morning. He had already written his sermon, but he wished to make certain that it properly followed the advent verses. Relieved at not having to walk to Rosings to consult her ladyship, he wished that he was already married to Eleanor. He valued her input far more than he had ever imagined he could.

He looked up at the calendar on his wall and smiled as his eyes fell on Sunday's date. The final reading of the banns would be that day, and his wedding the following morning. His joy at the prospect could hardly be contained. It had become more difficult each day to concentrate on his parish work for thinking of his beloved and their upcoming nuptials.

A knock on his door interrupted his thoughts.

"Enter," he called.

His part-time housekeeper opened the door and handed him a letter.

"It just came, Mr. Collins, and I thought you might wish to read it right away, seeing as it is from Longbourn," she told him and, curtseying, she left the room.

With suddenly clammy hands, Collins nervously broke the seal and opened the missive.

It read:

Greetings Mr. Collins,

You must be aware that your letter came as quite a surprise to my wife and me. Considering your behaviour during your last visit, I did not expect to hear from you again. Although I admit to being sceptical of your change of heart toward me and my family, I am not so intractable as to not at least give you a chance to prove yourself.

My wife and I will not be able to attend your wedding as we are preparing for the marriage of two of our daughters before long. Instead, we would like to visit you during Eastertide if that is acceptable to you. This would give your new bride time to settle into her role as your wife, and we would have more time to get acquainted.

If this is agreeable to you, you have only to write when it would be most convenient for you both.

Miss Langford sounds like a generous sort of woman. Please express our best wishes for your future felicity and our gratitude for her thoughtfulness in regards to Mrs. Bennet's staying at Longbourn once I pass from this life.

Thomas Bennet

Collins released a sigh of contentment. Of course, he would have liked for his cousin to witness his nuptials, but he was elated that Bennet had not refused to see him again. It would be a pleasure to relay his answer to Eleanor when he saw her on Sunday.

As he reread the letter, Collins stopped to wonder just which of his cousins were to be wed and to whom they were betrothed. He decided to wait to ask for that information in his next missive to Mr. Bennet.

Chapter 20

About fifteen minutes after Colonel Forster returned to his head-quarters, a plain carriage pulled up to the building. Dr. Wallace disembarked and strode purposefully to the door. He was shown to the colonel's office immediately.

After greetings were exchanged, and a brief discussion was had about how the doctor wished to retrieve the prisoner, Forster led the man to the cell and ordered the door unbarred. Inside, Fitzwilliam lay snoring loudly on the cot.

"Please ask my men to come and assist me," Dr. Wallace stated as he moved to the cell door. "As soon as they get here, I will need access to the cell. We have restraints and a stretcher to carry him from the building. I have no objections to your guards accompanying us to the carriage."

The task was accomplished with little trouble. They kept a blanket over Fitzwilliam's face so that no one would recognize him. It turned out that particular disguise was not necessary since there was no audi-ence to witness his leaving. Once the prisoner was secured inside the vehicle, the doctor and his men entered and they were off moments later.

Colonel Forster was pleased and relieved that the transaction had gone off so easily. Now his thoughts went to Lydia. He felt compelled to see her. Lydia's bright and welcoming smile would help to dispel the gloom of the morning's activities.

He ordered his horse to be saddled. While he waited, he repeated his strict orders to the men who had been involved. No one was to speak of the prisoner or his misdeeds. Once he was certain they understood, he mounted his horse and was off to Longbourn.

Once he reached Longbourn, Colonel Forster was greeted by Hill, who escorted him to the parlour. The hum of voices quieted when he was announced, but rose again after Mr. Bennet welcomed him and bid him be seated.

After he searched the room and found a vacant chair near Lydia, Forster moved quickly to occupy it. His heart leapt with joy when she smiled and whispered, "I am happy you came. I have missed you."

"And I you," he murmured back.

At Mrs. Bennet's offer of refreshments, Forster brought his attention to the gathering and accepted the tea and cake she gave him. He found that the whole Netherfield party was there, as was Mr. Wickham. *This will be my family, if she will have me,* he thought cheerfully. *Soon there will be no more lonely barracks for me.* It was then that he wished he had not agreed to wait to propose. He wondered if it would be possible to change her father's mind about that. Resigning from the militia would take some time, but the sooner it was attempted, the sooner it would be achieved. Glancing down at Lydia, he could not help but return the look of love and longing he saw in her eyes.

* * *

Thomas Bennet looked over the group seated in Longbourn's largest parlour. His wife was at her best, as she loved to host people in their home. However, she wore a rare look of contentment. Gone were her loud and often absurd remarks for the purpose of pushing forth one or another of her daughters. She sat calmly next to him, occasionally meeting his glance with a loving one in return.

It seemed like it had been ages since Bennet wished to stay in his wife's company for more than a few minutes. However, since the night of the Netherfield ball he felt as if their love had somehow been revitalised. In fact, he was even deeper in love with her than when they were first married. Finally, after their long and sometimes difficult talk, he understood his spouse's point of view after so many years.

Mr. Bennet reached over to pat his wife's hand before turning his attention to his oldest daughter who sat demurely, hands clasped in her lap, while smiling softly at something Mr. Bingley said. Jane was such a sweet-natured girl. It made his heart glad that she had found love with another of a similar personality. If Bingley had not stood up to his sister, Bennet may not have been so ready to give his eldest to him.

Hearing a tinkle of delighted laughter, Bennet glanced toward his next eldest. Elizabeth was responding to something that Lord Matlock had said, while Darcy's face flushed. No doubt, the earl had just relayed a story of the younger man's childhood. Mr. Bennet could not help but be pleased that his favourite daughter had found a man who appreciated her wit and intelligence. Mr. Darcy had proven himself a faithful and honourable man in his dealings with the former colonel.

A few feet away from the cheerful threesome, his middle child sat quietly, listening carefully to her beau. Mr. Bennet knew that this couple would be engaged soon, although he was certain they would not be in a great hurry. How he wished to laugh at the fact that he would have a clergyman for a son, especially after his cousin's visit! This young curate would be a welcome addition to the family and perfect for his Mary.

Realising the task he had begun, Mr. Bennet smiled and looked over at Kitty who was chatting earnestly with Miss Darcy. The two had gravitated toward each other, being the only unattached young ladies in the room. It did not take them long before they were conversing as if they were old chums. Currently, his daughter was discussing the latest in millinery with Miss Darcy. He could not help but wonder how long it would be before Kitty was claimed by a young swain.

Lastly, Bennet's eyes sought his youngest. She sat calmly next to Colonel Forster. Their conversation must have been a pleasant one because they each were smiling. It still surprised him that a courtship with a man like Colonel Forster could bring about such changes in Lydia. He still could see her vitality and youthful eagerness, but it now was tempered with a new purposefulness and poise. He would always be thankful this young man had looked beyond his daughter's silliness and that, as her father, he had finally done the right thing by her in agreeing to the courtship. Having witnessed the loving glance the couple exchanged, he began to wonder if he should speak to the young colonel about an earlier engagement.

Bringing his attention back to his wife, Bennet heard her invite their visitors to share a family meal with them that evening. As he had no objections to the company, he smiled and added his voice to the invitation. As everyone was eager to accept, he felt a sigh of satisfaction from his wife. He took her hand and lifted it to his lips and whispered, "I love you, Fanny."

Pleasure and some embarrassment painted her face a lovely shade of pink. Quickly looking around the room before she responded, Mrs. Bennet said, "I love you too, but I believe this is not the place for such sentiments."

Laughing heartily at the comment, he answered, "I do not agree, my love. I believe this is a perfect place for such sentiments."

Mrs. Bennet blushed again, but she smiled and did not disagree.

Their little tête-à-tête was interrupted when Mr. Wickham stood and announced that he needed to go home before returning for dinner. Similar intentions were expressed by the others before the earl spoke.

"Mr. Wickham, I would like a moment of your time before you go." Lord Matlock turned to Mr. Bennet and asked, "Could you please allow us the use of a room for privacy?"

"Of course, your lordship," Bennet answered. "You may use my book room."

Being a trifle confused by the earl's request, Mr. Wickham followed the older men as Mr. Bennet led them to his book room. He hoped the conference would not take long because he wished to hasten to the parsonage to change before dining at Longbourn.

Once Mr. Bennet left and closed the door behind him, the earl sat first and gestured for Wickham to do the same.

Lord Matlock's countenance was pale as he seemed to search for words. After a few moments of silence, he spoke. "I must apologise for my son's theft of what should have been yours years ago. From all I have heard from my nephew, you are a man of integrity who serves the church well."

"Thank you, my lord," Wickham replied earnestly. "I am honoured that Mr. Darcy would give me such a compliment. However, there is no need to ask, as I have already forgiven your son and I have never held anything against you for what he has done,"

"Be that as it may, I intend to make amends for what Fitzwilliam has stolen from you." Matlock lifted his hand to stop Wickham from speaking, and continued. "Before I left London, I spoke with my son's commanding officer, explaining how I wished to keep scandal from the rest of my family. He approved of the scheme I have undertaken, including selling his commission back. The major-general was pleased since he had a young officer in mind who he knew was looking to buy one.

"I have a bank draft for the amount of four thousand pounds made out to you. You only have to go to the bank to receive the money. I understand that you wish to purchase the living in Meryton. I am certain you will be able to do so now. I plan on using the remainder from the sale to help any of my son's offspring, if they can be found." Lord Matlock pulled a piece of paper from his waistcoat pocket and handed it to the curate.

George Wickham did not speak for several moments as he stared at the information written on the parchment. He fought an inner battle about whether or not to accept such a liberal gift. His first thought was that he could ask Miss Mary to marry him much sooner than he had ever imagined, but he did not think that it was fair for the earl to have to pay for his son's offences.

"Your lordship is very generous, but I have suffered no true harm," Wickham said humbly. "On the contrary, I have likely learned far more than I would have had I become vicar at Kympton. Also, I would have never met the Bennets or Miss Mary. No, I do not think I should accept." He held out the draft to the earl.

Matlock refused to take it back. Instead he stood and smiled kindly down at the younger man. "I will not take it back. It is yours to do with as you please. For one thing, I believe that you will be able to not only become Meryton's rector, but Miss Mary's husband much sooner. Think of her happiness and future, if not your own. Perhaps you should consult Miss Mary on the subject. She might give you a different perspective," the earl added with a smirk.

"Would you give me time to think upon it? I must return to the parsonage to change for dinner. I shall speak to Miss Mary about it after we dine."

"I do not wish to have the money back, so you may take as long as you wish to think about it." With a sly grin, Matlock gestured to the paper in Wickham's hand and said, "Put that into a safe pocket. You wouldn't want to lose it."

The earl rose and offered Wickham a ride into Meryton.

Wickham declined, stating that he had ridden Mr. North's horse and must return it.

Countering, Lord Matlock offered a carriage ride back to Longbourn that evening which Wickham reluctantly accepted.

Still stunned, Wickham followed the earl from the room. He stood to the side as the farewells were made, barely aware of what was being said.

It wasn't until Mary softly touched his arm and spoke that he became attentive to those around him.

"I beg your pardon, Miss Mary," he said as his face reddened. "I was wool gathering. What did you say?"

"I merely asked if something was amiss," she replied in a low voice. "You looked quite lost."

"Nothing is amiss, but I find myself in quite a dilemma." Wickham kept his voice hushed. "His lordship has offered me a large sum of money as recompense for what his son did. When I tried to refuse, he suggested that I seek your opinion. I know that we have only just begun courting, but I believe you understand that I asked with every intention of marrying you. This money would make that possible much sooner than I have ever dreamed."

He glanced around the room and when he found that no one was taking notice of their conversation, he continued, "I will not presume to ask for your hand at this moment, but I do wish for your thoughts on whether I should keep the money. Will you think on it and give me your opinion after dinner this evening?"

With a shy smile and pink cheeks, Mary nodded. "I shall think and pray about it."

Wickham was about to say something more when a servant announced that his horse was ready for him. He quickly bowed over Mary's hand and left the house.

* * *

After reviewing his sermon one last time, Collins took up his pen to answer his cousin's letter. He would wait to send it until after Eleanor had read it, but he wished to put his thoughts on paper. He expressed his disappointment and also his understanding. He included his good wishes to whichever of his cousins were to be wed. Deciding to go against his own curiosity, he did not ask which of his fair cousins were marrying. Instead, he agreed that any of the Bennets who wished to visit during Eastertide would be welcome at Hunsford. Contrary to his usual correspondence, the missive was short and to the point, without flowery words or phrases. After sanding and folding it, he tucked the paper into his desk drawer.

Collins rose and took a tour of the parsonage. He wanted to be certain that everything was in order for his bride's arrival two days hence. He did not think he had ever been so happy and content in his life. His beloved and his Lord had wrought a wonderful change in his life, and he prayed he would not disappoint them.

* * *

As the Bennets awaited the gentlemen's return, Lydia sought her mother. She found her in the kitchen, going over last minute details with Hill and Cook.

Mrs. Bennet looked up and smiled. "What brings you here Lydia?"

"I wanted to ask you a question when you are finished," Lydia said as she returned her mother's smile.

"I was going to my chambers to dress for dinner in a moment. Since I see that you have already changed, you may come with me and help me chose a gown."

Soon, Mrs. Bennet and Lydia climbed the stairs to the mistress's chambers. Once inside, Fanny opened her closet and gestured for Lydia to choose a gown.

In the not too distant past, Lydia would have chosen the dress with the most lace and flounce. However, this time, armed with what she had learned from Elizabeth about true elegance, she found one of the gowns that her aunt Gardiner had given her mother. It was a soft coral with a simple rust-coloured trim. The frock was flattering both to Mrs. Bennet's complexion, but also to her figure.

"Are you certain, Lydia?" her mother asked reluctantly as she examined herself in the mirror. "It has no lace and is very plain."

"Mama, you are beautiful, and the colour compliments you," Lydia explained patiently. "Besides, someone as lovely as you are does not need lace or flounces. They only distract from you beauty. Papa will agree. I am sure."

Mrs. Bennet blushed at the praise from her youngest. She went to her jewellery box and searched through the contents until she found a string of amber beads.

Holding them up to her neck, she turned and asked, "Do you think these look well with the gown?"

"They are perfect, Mama. I have never seen you wear them before."

"They were a gift from your father for my birthday several years ago. I did not think they would look well on me, so I never wore them. I think your Papa will like seeing me wear them now."

"Oh yes, he will fall more in love with you than ever." Lydia bounced a little in her enthusiasm. "Let us go down to show him."

"I thought you wanted to ask me a question," her mother reminded her.

"Oh, I completely forgot about that." Lydia giggled. "I want to know if you would begin to teach me about managing a home. If the colonel should propose and we marry, I will need to know how to do so, will I not?"

Mrs. Bennet's face glowed with love as she beamed at Lydia. "Of course, you will, and I apologise for neglecting your training. I believe that I should give lessons to your sisters as well. We shall begin on Monday."

"Thank you, Mama." Lydia impulsively embraced her mother before joining arms with her to leave her chambers.

Bennet was just leaving his book room when his wife and daughter reached the bottom of the stairs. His mouth dropped open at the vision that was his wife. Always aware of her beauty, there was something different this evening. The gown she had on was far simpler than any she usually wore, but the simplicity and colour only enhanced her loveliness. He continued to stare, speechless, as he spied the necklace he had gifted her years ago. A strong desire to sweep his wife into his arms and carry her to his chamber nearly overwhelmed him.

A quiet giggle from Lydia brought him back to himself. Bennet shook his head and smiled hugely. "You, my dear, are a true vision of beauty. I am very glad that the young men who we will be entertaining tonight have fallen for our daughters. I would not wish to fight them." He scratched his chin and hummed, "I shall have to keep an eye on the earl though."

Mrs. Bennet's face pinked with pleasure. She laughed softly before she kissed his cheek. "No one shall turn my eye from my own dear husband. Shall we go to the parlour to await our guests?"

Offering an arm to each of the ladies, Mr. Bennet escorted them into the front parlour where his other daughters sat in quiet conversation. The girls looked up and greeted the new arrivals before standing and surrounding them. Many heartfelt compliments flowed forth. Each daughter was surprised and pleased with their mother's new look and told her so.

Mrs. Bennet was not used to such positive notice from her girls. Finally, she interrupted them, "Enough, girls. While I appreciate your kind words, I am uncomfortable with all of the attention. Let us sit down and speak of other things."

Chuckling, Mr. Bennet replied, "My dear, I am afraid you must become accustomed to such attention, for I am positive you shall receive more before the night is over."

The family sat and conversed until the gentlemen began to arrive. Colonel Forster had just been announced when the carriage carrying the earl, Miss Darcy, Mr. Darcy, Bingley, and Wickham pulled up in front of Longbourn. Each of the four men joined their chosen lady while Lord Matlock complimented all of the women.

His lordship could not help but grin as he watched Mr. Bennet move closer to his wife. He laid his hand on Bennet's shoulder and whispered in his ear, "Your wife is in no danger from me. I admit that she is quite lovely, but I am not my younger son, and still hold my own departed wife in my heart."

Mr. Bennet returned the earl's smile sheepishly and relaxed. The three sat down and watched the rest of the young people as they conversed. Kitty seemed quite happy to spend time with an amiable person such as Miss Darcy. Gone was any hint of the envy that had plagued her earlier.

A short time later, dinner was announced. The earl offered his arm to Mrs. Bennet while her husband escorted Miss Darcy. The seating was formal only in that Lord Matlock sat to Mrs. Bennet's right and Miss Darcy was given the place to Mr. Bennet's left. The rest of the party moved so as to be seated exactly where they wished.

As usual, Mrs. Bennet set a fine table and served a delicious meal. She was pleased when the earl complimented her on the food.

Conversation was studded with laughter and camaraderie as the delectable fare was consumed.

Mr. Wickham leaned closer to Mary and asked softly, "Have you considered what I should do about the gift the earl has given me?"

"I have, sir," Mary said as she glanced around the table to make certain no one was listening. "I believe you should accept it. He is trying to make amends for what he sees as his failure. As long as you make it clear that you do not blame him in the least, I think both of you need this closure."

Wickham was silent for several moments while he pondered her words. Finally, a hopeful smile graced his face. "Will you allow me to speak to your father?"

With an impertinent glint in her eyes reminiscent of her next elder sister, Mary asked, "And why would you wish to do so?"

"I believe you understand my reasoning, but I will ask you outright." He paused, as he too looked about him. Wishing that he had more privacy, Wickham, nonetheless, continued with a soft, "Will you marry me?"

As pleased colour rose to her cheeks, Mary answered, "Yes, to both questions."

"You have made me very happy, Miss Mary," Wickham responded. "I will seek him out as soon as possible."

The men did not spend a great deal of time over their port and cigars. The younger of the gentlemen were obviously eager to rejoin the ladies. Mr. Bennet nearly extended the occasion just to see them squirm in their seats, but the earl leaned toward him and said, "You shall have a revolt soon if you do not allow them to leave."

Bennet chuckled as he stood. "I believe that we should go to the parlour. No doubt my wife has tea and coffee waiting."

The two elder gentlemen laughed to see the others nearly race to get through the doorway. "I am barely less eager to join my lovely wife tonight."

"I fully understand, for she is a beautiful woman," the earl added as he followed his host out of the room.

Before the night was out, Mr. Wickham had spoken to Lord Matlock and Mr. Bennet. The latter was not truly surprised to hear the petition from the curate for his middle daughter's hand. He was a bit taken aback that Mr. Wickham had asked so soon. The cleric explained that he was now able to secure the rectory of Meryton from Mr. North, which would give him the means to support a family.

With a smile on his face, Mr. Bennet made the announcement of the newest engagement. As expected, the ladies exclaimed happily over the news, while the gentlemen quietly congratulated Mr. Wickham.

The evening ended after toasts had been made, and the subject of possible wedding dates was canvassed. It was decided that Jane and Elizabeth would share their nuptials as soon as the banns could be read. They were to be married on the seventh day of January.

Mary and Mr. Wickham deferred setting a date until Wickham could speak with Mr. North. Neither of the couple wished to rush into the marriage state so soon after becoming engaged. Mrs. Bennet's pleasure at having three weddings to plan was enhanced by the fact that Mary would wait to decide.

As the carriages were readied for departure, many cheerful farewells and best wishes were shared. Lydia sighed softly knowing that she was still not engaged. Colonel Forster took her hand, kissed it, and whispered his love with a fervour which was enough to ease her mind that he felt the same as she.

Mrs. Bennet stood, arm in arm with her husband, smiling broadly as the guests took their leave. "I feel as though I am in the midst of a delightful dream," she said as she leaned her head upon Mr. Bennet's shoulder. "I wonder that I ever worried about my girls finding husbands. I am quite ashamed of my nerves."

"Do not fret over the past, dearest," Mr. Bennet said as he turned them forward the house. "I have not had your nerves, but I did not take the care to ensure that you and our daughters would be looked after as I should. I am glad that my neglect has not hindered their happiness."

Chapter 21

Monday morning had come at last to Hunsford, and Mr. Collins greeted it with great enthusiasm. His dearest Eleanor would become his wife this day. They had decided to be wed at the church closest to her home. After speaking to the vicar there, Collins had been able to convince him that showing forgiveness to the Langfords would be to the benefit of his congregation. He may have also mentioned that her ladyship might possibly attend the ceremony without promising that she would.

The wedding breakfast was to be held at the Wywyn estate. In an unusual gesture of beneficence, Eleanor's brother and sister had offered to host it, and they spared no expense in doing so. Collins agreed with his betrothed that they were trying to show their approval in the show-iest way possible, but the couple did not have cause to complain, for it gave an opportunity for both parishes to share in their joy.

Lady Catherine had not spoken more than a stiff word of greeting at services the day before. She failed to respond to the wedding invitation as well. Collins was not certain he wished for her attendance, so he did not feel put out at the slight.

Mr. Langford had sent one of his footmen to assist Collins in getting ready for his big day. His father-in-law-to-be also sent one of his smaller carriages to bring him to the church. Being unused to any clothing other than his clerical garb, Collins felt uncomfortable in the type of cravat he was to wear. However, he wished to look his best for Eleanor, so he allowed himself to be dressed as a gentleman for this one day.

As nervous and excited as he was, Collins tried not to show it as he rode in the pleasant carriage the five miles to the Dinsbury church. He forced himself to enjoy the scenery as they journeyed. The closer he came to his destination, the more he was thankful for his present situation at Hunsford. It seemed that of the forests and meadows he passed, none compared to those closer to his home.

Once he arrived at the church, Collins was met by the curate of the parish. Mr. Clark led him to a room where he could brush off any travel dust and wait for the time when he was to take his place in the front of the church.

Since the driver had made good time, Collins was left to himself for ten minutes before the vicar, Peter Whitley, arrived to speak to him about the service and give him the speech Collins himself had given several young men in his time at Hunsford. He smiled inwardly at the words of admonition from scripture that were familiar, but of deeper meaning than he had ever noticed in the past. The solemn and sacred vows he was about to take made him sober but eager.

Once Mr. Whitley left the room, Collins prayed that he would be a husband worthy of Eleanor. His heart was heavy with guilt from his past attentions toward women. While he had never gone so far as to lay with a woman, he had certainly lusted after them. He begged for God's forgiveness and asked for help to keep from straying from his wife. Never in his life had he been more repentant. Knowing himself not to be the cleverest of men, he had enough knowledge of the Scriptures to understand that he was absolved of his sins, based not on his own worth, but upon the work of Christ. Armed with this awareness, Collins straightened quickly when a knock sounded at the door.

The curate opened the door and gestured for Collins to follow him. Soon he was standing in front of the altar, awaiting the entrance of his beloved. A moment later, the organ began to play. Eleanor, on the arm of her father, walked down the aisle, pausing when she came to Collins's side.

Although he had performed the rite several times before, Collins had not felt the beauty and solemnity of the words prior to this time. He listened carefully to every word and was happy to pledge his troth to Eleanor. When the vicar pronounced them man and wife, Collins thought he had never been happier.

As the newlywed couple walked to sign the register, Collins was surprised to see that Lady Catherine had come. He nodded his acknowledgement as he passed her, but soon forgot her as he wrote his name next to his wife's. Eleanor was now his helpmeet until death should part them.

The couple did not speak until they reached the carriage. Once seated next to each other, Collins took Eleanor's hand and kissed it.

"I love you, Mrs. Collins," he whispered huskily.

"And I love you, Mr. Collins," Eleanor answered with a laugh. "I do hope you will not be so formal in your address in the future."

Collins blushed, but said with a smile, "It is just that I am so proud that you are indeed Mrs. Collins that I may continue to address you thus for a while longer."

"In that case, I shall not be concerned for the time being." She tucked her arm into his and leaned against his shoulder. "I find I like the appellation quite well."

When the couple reached Wywyn, they were hurriedly ushered into the ballroom, which had been lavishly decorated for the wedding breakfast. They were soon joined by Eleanor's family before the guests arrived. Mr. and Mrs. Collins stood close to each other as they were greeted by everyone who came through the door.

It was a pleasant experience, until Lady Catherine stopped in front of them. "I suppose I am to congratulate you," her ladyship said imperiously. "I shall only add that I will be watching you. Make one mistake, and you will be gone." She lifted her nose in the air and walked away without saying another word.

Those around them who heard Lady Catherine's words were not surprised by her cutting threat. In fact, most of those from Mr. Collins's parish smiled to themselves because they were pleased both to have Mrs. Collins as their parson's wife and that the fact irritated her ladyship. Many a conversation that morning centred on their willingness to do everything possible to support their rector and his wife.

* * *

At Longbourn, as Christmastide drew closer, plans for the holiday and the following weddings began in earnest. At times, Mrs. Bennet forgot herself and fretted as much as she had in the past. However, these moments were few and far between, especially after her husband took her aside. A small glass of sherry and a bit of loving conversation was enough to calm the lady.

After the invitations had been sent, and the trousseaux purchased, the family joyfully anticipated celebrating Christmas with friends and family. The Gardiners arrived a few days before the holiday and planned to stay until after the wedding.

One morning, two days before Christmas, an express rider came to the door of Longbourn. Hill immediately took the missive to Mr. Bennet who sat with his family in the breakfast room.

Everyone watched in anticipation as Bennet opened the letter. The frown that creased his brow soon smoothed into a slight smile. Turning to Hill, who waited near the table, he said, "Please send a messenger to Mr. Darcy and ask him to bring Lord Matlock with him to Longbourn at their earliest convenience."

The earl planned to leave the next morning to be with his elder son and family for Christmas, but he had wished to stay with his niece and nephew as long as possible.

As Hill bobbed a curtsey and left to do his bidding, Mr. Bennet spoke to his anxious family. "Do not fear. The express is from Mr. Collins, warning us that, after his patroness received her invitation to Lizzy's and Jane's wedding, she became irate. Apparently, she is coming to try to stop our Lizzy's marriage to Mr. Darcy. Since she is sister to the earl and aunt to Mr. Darcy, I had thought it only right she should be invited."

"But why would she try to stop the wedding?" Mrs. Bennet asked in a trembling voice.

"If you will recall when Collins stayed with us, he claimed that Mr. Darcy was engaged to his cousin, Miss de Bourgh. Mr. Wickham was quick to disabuse him of the notion. However, it seems that her ladyship is still of that opinion," Mr. Bennet explained.

"Mr. Darcy would never have engaged himself to Lizzy if he was otherwise intended," Jane added.

"You are correct, Jane," Elizabeth answered with a grin. "He explained the situation to me a long time ago. It is true only in her ladyship's imagination."

After swallowing the last of his tea, Mr. Bennet stood. "Gardiner, please join me in my book room until either the gentlemen or her ladyship arrives."

All of the ladies retired to the front parlour and took up various activities to help pass the time. The Gardiner children had taken their breakfast in the old nursery and were enjoying playtime away from their studies.

When Mr. Darcy, Lord Matlock, and Mr Bingley arrived an hour later, they were announced to the ladies before Hill knocked on the book room door.

Hill was bid to enter.

"Have the gentlemen from Netherfield arrived?" Bennet asked as he set down his empty port glass.

"Yes, sir, and they await you in the front parlour."

Standing, Mr. Bennet said to his brother-in-law, "Let us join them."

They found Mr. Darcy and his lordship in earnest conversation with Elizabeth and her mother.

"I see that I do not need to give the details of Mr. Collins's letter," Mr. Bennet jovially announced as he and his brother entered the parlour.

The earl answered, "I cannot say that I am surprised that she would make an appearance. I am happy that I was still here to help in dissuading her. I warn you all that it will not be pleasant. I would advise the younger ladies go to their rooms. She is never so verbose and stubborn as when she has a large audience. Also, I know for a fact that the Bennet girls do rise to the defence of their elder sisters with a vehemence that, at this time might not be in everyone's best interest."

With a nod from both their parents and Elizabeth, the three youngest sisters reluctantly left the room. Kitty and Lydia decided to visit their cousins in the nursery while Mary went to her room to pray.

The earl and Darcy spent some time answering questions, which helped the others understand Lady Catherine a little better. The information did not explain why she felt she would be entitled to order the lives of others, but they felt they had a better grasp of what to expect when she arrived.

And arrive she did, less than an hour after the gentlemen. Hill tried to announce her before she entered the room, but Lady Catherine was more determined and pushed her way past the servant so roughly that the poor woman had to lean up against the wall to stop from falling.

However, her ladyship stopped with mouth open ready to spew her insults when she spied, not only her nephew, but her brother. "Darcy, Brother, what in the world are you two doing here? I came to make my case to the upstart, whichever of these two young women she may be. You may leave her with me, and I shall make known to her all of the reasons this supposed engagement cannot be."

Lord Matlock put a steadying hand on his nephew's shoulder so that he could be the one to take charge. "Before you go any further, you should be introduced to the people whose home you have invaded unannounced."

He took the time to introduce each one in the proper order and with evident pleasure. His sister gave only grunts and slight nods in answer as greetings.

"Catherine, you have no reason or authority to be here. You have wasted your time and energy in coming."

"No authority? You know my sister and I agreed that Anne and Darcy were meant for each other when they were in their cradles! And since they are engaged, this supposed betrothal cannot be," her ladyship protested.

"Listen to me, Cathy." His lordship interrupted her tirade, using the nickname he knew his sister detested. "Darcy is in no way obligated to fulfil your wishes, as mere wishes they are. I know for a fact that neither Anne nor Darcy have ever wished for this union."

He took a fortifying breath before he continued. "Normally, I would not speak of this in front of relative strangers, but you have done so first. I have been the silent trustee of your daughter's inheritance since Lewis died. It is one of the reasons that Darcy and Richard have spent Eastertide with you. They have kept me informed as to the financial status of Rosings. You have personally overspent while neglecting the upkeep of much of your lands and tenants' cottages.

"Since Anne has reached her majority in the terms of the will, she is now the mistress of Rosings. I shall be hiring a competent steward to help her in the transition. He will take his orders from Anne and myself alone. You will have three months to move into the dower house. I will personally interview each of the servants to make certain that they fully understand who shall be in charge.

"Anne will come to visit Matlock House in Town where my own physician will determine the condition of her health. I have long felt that Mr. Ellison is a quack, or at least incompetent to treat her."

Lady Catherine had been stunned into silence and, as her brother finished his dictates, her face paled. She had known of the will but thought she had kept it safely hidden. When she had first read it she had been irate that she had not been put in charge of Rosings even for her lifetime, and she had taken many steps to keep it in her control. Now, all of her plans fell broken at her feet. Knowing she could not fight her powerful brother, she still spoke firmly, "Anne is in my carriage with her companion. She will stay here with you if you are so determined to take her from me."

Without another word, Lady Catherine left the room with the earl following in her wake.

He paused in the doorway and asked, "Mr. and Mrs. Bennet, would you object to having more guests for tonight? I am quite certain that my poor niece is fatigued after such a long journey. If you are unable to accommodate her overnight, I am sure a place to rest would restore her until we could return with my carriage to take her to Netherfield."

Before Mr. Bennet could even open his mouth, Mrs. Bennet announced happily, "We would be more than honoured to welcome Miss de Bourgh to stay as long as she might need to. My housekeeper will see to the guest room as quickly as possible, and we will have hot water readied for her as well.

"We shall have some tea brought in while the rooms are refreshed," added Mrs. Bennet.

Hill arrived and scurried to do her mistress's bidding.

"Very good," the earl boomed cheerfully, "I shall soon have the pleasure of making Anne known to her future family."

Within minutes, Lord Matlock returned to the house with a frail looking young lady leaning heavily on his arm. After quick introductions were made, the refreshments were served.

Once Lady Catherine's carriage left Longbourn, the younger girls rejoined those in the parlour. All of the Bennet ladies tried their best to make Miss de Bourgh comfortable, but it was obvious she was timid and unused to the kind attentions she was receiving. Mrs. Bennet was the first to notice how wan their guest was becoming and took the matter in hand.

"As delighted as we are to have your company, Miss de Bourgh, your journey was an early and long one. My housekeeper tells me that rooms are ready for you and your companion. Please feel free to rest as long as you need. We keep country hours for dinner. If you are unable to join us for dinner, ring for a tray. It would be no inconvenience at all."

Although Anne's voice was strained by her weariness, she smiled as her cheek took on pleased colour. "I thank you all for your kindness to a stranger. I look forward to knowing you all better after I rest."

Turning to the earl, Anne asked, "Uncle, might I have your assistance to the room? I find that my legs are quite weak at the moment."

"Anne, would you wish for me to carry you?" Darcy offered.

"Oh no, that will not be necessary," she answered with a slight laugh.

His lordship offered her his arm, and the three, including Mrs. Jenkinson, followed Hill from the room.

* * *

It was the custom when the Gardiners visited that the children came to the parlour before their dinner was served above stairs. The two six year olds, Timothy and Theodore, chatted happily about the toy horses they had found in a box in the corner of the nursery. Jenny, who felt all the maturity of her ten years, smiled and spoke gratefully of the various books her cousins had laid out for her, while cradling a small china doll in her arms.

Into this happy domestic scene, Miss de Bourgh and her companion entered. They were not noticed at first, but Timothy spied them and bowed as neatly as he could and said, "I am Timothy Amos Gardiner. Might I show you two ladies to a seat?" He offered an arm to each.

A soft titter of laughter sounded about the room, but Timothy was not discouraged, especially when the rest of the company stood.

His uncle Bennet was the first to speak, a wide smile gracing his face. "I see that I have been remiss in my hosting duties. Timothy, as you have already introduced yourself, may I present Miss Anne de Bourgh and her companion, Mrs. Jenkinson. Miss de Bourgh is cousin to Mr. Darcy."

Bennet turned to the other children and introduced them as well.

The party were all seated, with Timothy and his brother seated as closely as possible to the small, frail lady. He studied Anne's face for a few moments, before he said, "We shall be cousins after Lizzy marries Mr. Darcy."

"You are correct," Anne replied with a smile. "I believe I will like having more cousins, will you?"

"Oh, ever so much," the three children chimed in together.

Theodore gazed up at Miss de Bourgh for a moment before stating, "You remind me of a fairy princess. Are you able to cast spells or do magic?"

Anne's tinkling laugh was as surprising as it was lovely. "I suppose if I were a fairy I could, but alas, I am only a lowly human like you, but I do have a special talent that you might enjoy."

This rest of the room waited quietly as Anne asked the young ones if they had handkerchiefs she could borrow. The children each quickly produced one. Miss de Bourgh took one from Theodore and folded, twisted, and knotted it, producing a tiny white horse. With the cloth belonging to Timothy, she fashioned a bear, and finally a tiny baby doll out of Jenny's lacy square.

"Take care of your horse, Master Theodore, that Master Timothy's bear does not frighten it," Anne said with a wink as they thanked her profusely before showing their treasures to the members of the family.

After thanking her, Jenny did not leave Anne's side until she asked, "How did you learn to do this?"

"You see, I was not well as a young girl," Anne explained, "And I was easily bored, lying in bed as I had to do. My nurse, Miss Lily Gray, taught me how to make various animals like these."

Smiling, Jenny asked, "When we have more time together, would you teach me?"

"Of course, but you must promise me something." Anne's voice reflected the twinkle in her eyes.

"What must I promise?'

"I shall tell you a short story about these little pets." Anne blushed when she realised that she once again had the attention of the room, but she was committed to her tale. "One day, I had folded all of the handkerchiefs available to me, but I wished to make more. What do you suppose I did?"

Jenny's eyes were big with curiosity, and she merely shook her head.

"I folded and knotted many, many animals and dollies using my sheet. The poor maid had a great deal of extra work, undoing my labours. So do not use your sheets."

The two laughed together and the others joined in. It was to this joyous sound that the gentlemen and Miss Darcy from Netherfield were announced into the parlour. Soon, more invited guests arrived including the Lucases and the Philipses.

"I see that the party has begun without us," Lord Matlock declared, joking. "I knew we should have come back earlier."

The Gardiner children were soon called to their supper by their nanny. The courting adults moved together after introductions were made. The earl took a seat next to his niece, pleased to see that she looked much revived.

Since dinner had yet to be announced, the room soon was abuzz with jovial conversation. Elizabeth had not been able to speak more than a hello to Darcy because Charlotte wished to hear of the plans for the double wedding. Lizzy noticed her beloved moving quietly toward one of the windows. Once he reached it, he seemed be staring out into the darkness.

Concern for his well-being spurred Elizabeth to excuse herself from her conversation with Charlotte. When she arrived at his side, she asked, "Is something amiss, Mr. Darcy?"

He turned slightly and caught her eye. The look of pure love and bliss she saw across his face nearly stole her breath.

"I had to look away from the scene behind me," he sighed. "My heart is so full that I was afraid of being overwhelmed by it. Because of you and your encouragement, I found out the truth about my cousin. Although it was painful, I also gained much more than I ever imagined. Within less than a fortnight, you will be my own dear wife. These people will be a happy part of our life together.

"Somehow I knew that you would come to me, and with you at my side, I am under better regulation." He smiled and offered his arm to her.

The couple made their way to join Jane and Bingley who were visiting with Lydia and Colonel Forster. As Darcy and Elizabeth stopped, the youngest Bennet girl giggled and pointed toward the ceiling. There hung a kissing ball.

"Kitty put it there, and we have been caught as you are now," she gloated cheerfully.

Darcy reached up to pick a berry before leaning in to kiss Elizabeth. The dreamy expression on her face tempted him to kiss her again, but he stopped himself in time as dinner was announced.

Waiting their turn to follow the others, Darcy leaned in and whispered, "I must find a way to thank your sister."

Elizabeth's pink face and happy laughter brought smiles to all those around them. She answered, "I most heartily agree with you, my love."

Epilogue

Jane and Elizabeth shared their nuptials on a cold but sunny day in January. After a short stay in London, the Bingleys returned to Netherfield while the Darcys, including Georgiana, took up residence at Darcy House in Mayfair.

Mr. and Mrs. Darcy preferred to stay at Pemberley for most of the year, following Georgiana's come out and marriage. They happily raised five children, two boys and three girls, and welcomed many nieces and nephews to their home each summer.

Jane and Bingley eventually settled in Derbyshire as Netherfield became too crowded for their family of eight children, of which only two were girls. Charles wished to have a bigger income, so that his boys would have more opportunity for occupations that did not necessitate their joining the military, unless they truly wished it. With Darcy's help, he managed to save and invest in various new industries, such as locomotives. Because he did so, he was able to amass a great fortune that would have surpassed Darcy's if he had not also made the same sound investments.

A second double wedding took place in late April of the same year. Mary and Lydia were lovely spring brides. Mrs. Bennet ably assisted her daughters in learning household management, so that even with the smaller incomes of their husbands, they were able to save for future children.

Mary and George Wickham stayed in the Meryton parish, ministering to the spiritual, as well as the many physical needs, of the villagers. They had three children, one of which died of a childhood disease, at the age of ten. Dorcas was much missed by her family, but their faith brought them comfort in their bereavement. Early on in their marriage they housed many an orphan, educating them and helping them to find work. Their home seldom had an empty table, even after their children were grown with homes of their own.

After Colonel and Lydia Forster married, they moved with the regiment to Brighton. Their presence there was of short duration due to the couple's wish to take up residence at Colonel Forster's estate. Once a replacement was found to take the command of the Colonel's troops, they left for Essex. Lydia proved to be an excellent household manager. She had learned to economize during their stay in Brighton. With her help, Forster was able to expand and increase his holdings so as to provide well for their three daughters and one son.

After two years, Kitty Bennet married the former Captain Carter after his promotion to major. He rose in the ranks rather quickly after that. When he finally retired, he was a major general. Their only child, Amy Elizabeth, made a match with one of the Bingley boys who had become a soldier.

Nearly a year after his youngest son's transportation, Lord Matlock received a short, concise missive from the authorities in Van Diemen's Land. The former colonel had wandered into the night while the others were sleeping. It was not known if he was seeking to escape, but in his ramblings, he apparently lost his footing and fell to his death in a ravine.

His body was found two days later. The earl mourned the wasted life of his second son, but his family rallied around him and saw him through the worst of his grief.

Caroline Bingley's life was not so happy as her brother's. She lived lonely, bitter years with Hurst's relatives until she met a Scottish laird. He first caught her eye when they were introduced in Edinburgh during a rare journey there. Laird Ceiteach was large and ruggedly handsome and, even better from Caroline's point of view, he was unattached and looking for a wife with a dowry.

During her three week stay in Edinburgh, they spent a great deal of time together. By the end of the third week, they were betrothed. They married at his home chapel. Caroline had dreams of finally spending a great deal of time in society, possibly even in London. However, she found, to her dismay, that her husband preferred his estate, and rarely visited Edinburgh and never London. To her further consternation, Ceiteach was a deeply pious man. His chaplain held services each day, which she was required to attend. Their home was sparsely furnished, and their meals plain. She was given a fairly generous allowance, but since there was no place to spend it, Lady Ceiteach was forced to save it for the rare times they visited a market town or went to Edinburgh. For many a year, she repined her decisions but always seemed to find someone else to blame for her foolishness. Her husband was attentive to the Scriptures and wished their union to be fruitful. As a result, their family grew by a least one child every two years for the first twelve of their marriage, including several pairs of twins, until there were nine in all.

Charles did not receive much correspondence from Lady Ceiteach. However, letters did come from her, announcing every birth until the last child was born. Her husband wrote at the time, because she was so ill after the birth. Fearing for her life, Caroline wished to confess to her husband about the letters she stole while she was at Netherfield, and the reason she did it. She wished to find private information about Mr. Darcy and her brother, thinking it might help her in her quest to marry Darcy. Laird Ceiteach forgave her. She did survive and was humbled by the experience.

Continuing to grow closer, Mr. and Mrs. Bennet were extremely pleased with the good matches that their daughters had made. They visited them all frequently, especially once the grandchildren began to arrive. They lived to even hold a few great-grandchildren in their arms before they passed.

They had visited Hunsford at Eastertide as planned and were pleasantly surprised to see not only the changes wrought in Collins, but to find such a kind and compassionate woman in his wife. Because of the upcoming double wedding, they did not stay as long as they eventually wished to do, but it was the beginning of much closer family ties between them.

William and Eleanor Collins raised three children in the parsonage. Eleanor's guidance continued to help Collins to overcome his worst faults, and to become a better shepherd to his flock. While Lady Catherine continued to advise the couple on all aspects of life, even though she was no longer truly their patroness, they learned together how to please her sensibilities without forfeiting their harmony at home. When Collins died at the relatively young age of fifty, from pneumonia he contracted after helping a stranded family during a violent storm, his widow wished to move with her youngest child and only son, William

Junior, to a small cottage in Meryton which she had planned to lease. By this time both of her daughters had homes of their own, married to local squires.

After being informed of the death of his cousin, Mr. Bennet invited Mrs. Collins to visit Longbourn. Mr. Bennet was eager to see his heir again. The lanky fifteen year old had planned to enter Oxford with the intention of entering the clergy, but the death of his father and the period of mourning had prevented it. Bennet quizzed the boy and found him to be intelligent and well read. Collins senior had trained his son well to be polite and respectful, with none of his father's former obsequiousness.

After a few days in his company, Mr. Bennet spoke to Mrs. Bennet and they were agreed that the young man should be taught to run an estate. Tutors would to be hired to see to his education. In addition, William would spend several hours a day with Mr. Bennet learning about Longbourn. Mr. Bennet was astonished at William's bright mind and quickness in learning.

Her husband was not surprised when Mrs. Bennet insisted that both the Collinses live permanently at Longbourn. Her whole outlook on life had changed with her husband's renewed attentions and the Collins's kindness toward her. She and Eleanor Collins were already fast friends despite their age difference. Because of her years of experience handling Lady Catherine, Eleanor had no trouble understanding Mrs. Bennet. She always deferred to Mrs. Bennet in matters of the household. Grateful for the Bennet's generosity, Eleanor could overlook the few quirks of the elderly mistress of Longbourn.

By the time Mr. Bennet died, William Collins Junior was well able to take over the running of his inherited estate. Mrs. Bennet deeply mourned her husband. She wore only black for the rest of the two years she survived him before she succumbed to influenza just after Christmas.

After being treated by her uncle Matlock's physician, Anne de Bourgh regained some of her strength. With the help of the steward he hired, she learned a great deal about the running of her estate. Although she enjoyed her trips to London, she was quite content to live in Kent. Her home was frequently filled with her family and neighbours, which was how she met her husband. Sidney Roth was a colleague of Mr.

Gardiner whom she met on a visit with the children at the Cheapside house.

The two were very fond of the Gardiner children, and their time spent with them helped to fix their regard for each other. After they were wed, they lived quietly at Rosings. After four years of marriage, Anne was delivered of a son. Lewis Roth was to be the only child, but his disposition was such that he was never spoiled by the love and attention of his parents.

Although his grandmother de Bourgh clearly disapproved of her daughter's union, she doted on her grandson. Had she lived long enough, she would have been delighted to see the heir to Rosings married to one of the Darcy girls.

Two years after Jane and Elizabeth were married from Longbourn, Mrs. Phillips died suddenly. Her sister had written to share the news of the arrival of her first two grandchildren born within days of each other. Henrietta Philips hurried to spread the news before anyone else had heard. The weather that day was unseasonably hot, but she persevered in hastening from home to home before she dropped dead of apoplexy in front of the mercantile near her house.

Many of the single ladies—both spinster and widow—brought food and sweets to the grieving widower in the hopes of catching the eye of the successful solicitor. However, throughout his mourning period, the lady who was of the most comfort was Charlotte Lucas. Once said period ended, Mr. John Philips married Charlotte in a private, family-only service. They had one son who took over for his father when he retired. Charlotte never was the gossip that her predecessor had been. Instead, she had a knack for inspiring trust in others. Many a lady sought her advice and trusted her to keep their confidence as much as they did her husband.

The five former Bennet ladies mourned the loss of their parents, but every time they gathered together, they spent happy times recalling their beloved family and the blessings of the time they had had with them. Their own unions were blessed with long life and great happiness.

The End

Jadie Brooks has lived in the Northwest for most of her life, forty-four years of them with her husband, Stan. She has two grown children and eight grandchildren. The internet has provided the wonderful opportunity for the author to make friends from all over the world. Travelling, reading, quilting, bit of gardening, and, of course, writing are among her hobbies.

Jadie would love to hear from you at:
author.jadiebrooks@gmail.com

or like her Facebook page at:
https://www.facebook.com/Jadie-Brooks
1405087469715558/notifications/

Made in the USA
Monee, IL
22 January 2021